BLOOD
AND
FIRE

BLOOD
AND
FIRE

SHANNON
MCKENNA

𝐵
BRAVA

KENSINGTON BOOKS
http://www.kensingtonbooks.com

Acknowledgments

A lot of people helped me with the writing of this book, but first, I must mention my invaluable critique partners, Elizabeth Jennings and Lisa Marie Rice, without whom I cannot even dare to imagine the agony, the solitude and the mess. Thanks for always being there for me!

And a heartfelt thanks to Adam Firestone, for his generosity with arcane lore about weapons and strategy, and also to George Young, who was so patient and forthcoming with my questions about detective work in the Portland Police Bureau. You helped immeasurably. Any mistakes and absurdities are unquestionably mine—the result of asking the wrong questions! You have all my gratitude.

PROLOGUE

Upper West Side, Manhattan
Seventeen years ago

*T*he summons came at three A.M. *Three short hits on the in-*
tercom.

Dr. Howard Parr leaped up, knocking over his drink. His
cigarette flipped, sparks scattering. He made his way slowly
down the steps to the door of his town house, swaying, clutching
the banister. He peeked out the spy hole. The big envelope lay on
the stoop. He opened the door, not even bothering to touch the en-
velope with care to avoid obscuring possible fingerprints. They
all knew that he wasn't going to the police.

Two objects inside. One was in pieces; the smashed remains
of the closed-circuit camera he'd put up in an ill-conceived at-
tempt to monitor his front door. Someone had ripped it out days
after it had been installed. He'd been braced for a slap-down
ever since, wishing he hadn't done it. That he could roll onto his
back, showing his throat, saying, "I'm sorry." But they didn't
care. The other object was a videotape. His guts lurched.

His eyes swept the darkened, car-lined street. No one was

there, but he felt malevolence oozing from the darkness like poison gas.

Howard trudged up the stairs, slid the tape into the VCR, docile as a beaten dog. A burning smell tickled his nose. He looked down. His cigarette was smoldering in the carpet. He crushed it as footage began.

He realized, with a sickening rush, that the camera's jolting progress showed the interior of his own house. It turned a corner, zoomed in on Howard himself, passed out on the kitchen floor. He could not have said what day it was. His nights often finished there. He found the hard, cold floor tiles vaguely comforting, pressed against his hot face.

The camera moved up the stairs, past Howard's bedroom. A featureless hand in a rubber glove turned a knob and walked into his eleven-year-old daughter's room. Howard's guts began to spasm.

The camera moved toward Lily's bed. Light from the hallway spilled in. The camera focused on her half-open mouth. The hand held up a spray bottle with a "ta-da" flourish and sprayed Lily's face. She murmured but subsided without waking. The camera sank as the man sat on the bed, bouncing. He slapped Lily's face. She did not stir.

The hand pulled the sheet and coverlet down with taunting slowness. The camera surveyed the girl's body, curled into a huddled comma. She wore a T-shirt and panties. The rubber hand shoved the garment up over her ribcage, petted her budding breasts. The hand arranged her body, bent up her knee, splayed out her thigh. It zoomed in close onto the crotch of her chaste cotton panties, staring directly at that featureless field of white for many long, horrible seconds.

Howard clutched his mouth, struggling not to vomit.

A knife appeared in the hand. A short, dark blade. Howard's breathing hitched. Lily was fine. Asleep upstairs. She'd scolded him before she went to bed, for being drunk, like always. She'd been OK, apart from angry. She hadn't been . . . hurt.

Howard gnawed his fist as the blade moved intimately over her body, pressing here and there.

It paused over her femoral artery, then the disembodied hand replaced the coverlet, tucking it tenderly under her chin. Fingers wrapped around her throat for a moment. Then the hand thrust a finger into her mouth and slowly withdrew it, petting her soft lips as he did so.

Howard lunged for the bathroom, but did not make it. Spewed the alcoholic contents of his stomach in the hall. Fell to his knees, belly heaving. He crouched there for the better part of an hour before he dared to rise to his feet. Before he found the nerve to do what he had to do next.

He shook two pills from the special bottle, hesitated for a moment, and shook out a third.

It was for love, he told himself, over and over. He did this for her. His precious girl. The only way to protect Lily was to shut up, swallow the poison. Roll a rock over what he knew. His awful secret. He needed help for that. Stronger help than booze. If it killed him, so be it.

Lily would be better off.

1

*J*ust *a dream, man. Just a dumb dream.*

Right, and so? Knowing it was a dream didn't help. When he was in it, he was in it. Stuck in a white nowhere, that booming voice in his head saying words that made him want to scream, though they were just bland numeric sequences. "... *DeepWeave four point two, combat level eight, sequence five commencing ... four, three, two, one ...*"

Then Rudy came at him, stinking of drink and sweat. Slashing at Bruno, switchblade in one hand, broken beer bottle in the other.

Mamma lay on the floor behind Rudy, beaten and bleeding, eyes pleading over the gag. All because her useless, pussy son hadn't had the balls to steal Rudy's Beretta and shoot the scumbag dead. Kitchen shears would do fine, too, slashed across the jugular. A bread knife right between the ribs. A machete. *Take that, dickhead.* Or a chainsaw, even better. Swoosh, swing. Splatter that rabid bastard every which way. *That's what you get for hitting my mamma, fucking shit-for-brains.*

But he never killed Rudy in the dream, even if he landed a perfect blow. The bastard just winked out of existence, and a fresh, unharmed Rudy popped out from another direction.

The video game from hell, but somebody with a forked tongue was plugging in the quarters.

He fought grimly on, ducking, lunging, slashing, punching, and kicking, then Rudy cloned himself into six Rudys, and they slammed him all at once, knocking him to the ground—

The images broke apart, fighting to maintain their space in his head, but waking reality rushed in through the cracks.

Ouch. It should have been a relief, but God, his head. It throbbed, like he'd been clobbered with a bat. His heart banged against his ribs.

He'd hit the floor. That was what had wakened him. He was on the floor, next to his bed. He was Bruno Ranieri, and he was thirty-two, not twelve, and this was his own king-sized bed, in his own condo, not Mamma's tenement apartment in Newark. The sweat-soaked sheet wound like a noose around one ankle was custom-made high-thread-count Egyptian cotton. His picture window framed the pink-tinted Portland skyline and a view of Mount Hood, not a sooty brick wall over a cluster of garbage cans. No drunken Rudy bellowing through thin walls as he beat up Mamma. He stared around at his own space, his own life.

Tried to believe it. To own it.

He gasped for breath. Hoarse rasps. Drenched with sweat, muscles twitching like he'd been electrocuted. He pried the twisted sheet off his ankle and sprawled flat against the cool wooden floor.

It was all behind him now. Rudy was dead, decades ago. Uncle Tony had seen to it. Mamma was dead, too, eighteen years ago. Nothing could hurt her anymore.

Just . . . a . . . fucking . . . *dream.* Long past. Dead and gone.

He'd moved on, gotten his shit together. He was not that helpless boy anymore. He deepened his breathing, got up on wobbly legs. He'd use the tricks Kev had taught him. *When you can't stand what's happening in your head, float back from it,* Kev always said. *Three steps. Turn down the volume. Then look at it. Idly curious. It's just a bunch of monkeys fighting in a cage. Stupid. Irrelevant. Can't hurt you.*

He stumbled into the living room, air cooling his naked skin. The city lights reflected off the broad swath of planked flooring. He sank down into horse stance and began the kung fu forms Kev had taught him. His legs shook, and monkeys screeched and flailed in their cage for a while, but eventually, he got where he needed to be. One with the night, crouching, leaping, punching. *Black panther climbs the tree. Crane guards his nest. Crane flies into the sky. Wild tiger raises his head. Golden dragon stretches his left claw.* Time flowed, smoothing.

Buzzzz. Buzzzz. Who the hell would call at this ungodly hour?

Oh, man. Maybe it was Kev. The blaze of hope broke his mellow Zen trance, had him leaping for the phone like a fish for a bug. "Yeah?"

"It's Julio." The cigarette-roughened voice of the fry cook at Zia Rosa's restaurant rasped uncomfortably over Bruno's nerve endings.

Bruno's stomach thudded down a couple notches. Not Kev.

Of course not. Why would Kev call? He was traveling the globe with his true love, Edie. Tied up in erotic knots on some sugar sand beach under the moonlight. Which was fine. Bruno was thrilled for that. He'd hoped and schemed to get Kev happy, smiling, sexually fulfilled. He loved that scenario, *loved* it. Kev deserved blithering happiness and non-stop screaming orgasms after the horrific shit he'd been through.

But those dreams, man. Kev was the only person Bruno could talk to about that stuff. Kev had saved him, back when he was thirteen. He'd been wild-eyed and desperate with the grinding, constant Rudy nightmares. At the time, the idea of throwing himself under a bus had been looking kind of rest-ful. Kev had understood that. The way he understood everything. He'd saved Bruno's ass, so many times, on so many levels.

But then, Kev was a freaking genius. Nobody argued with that.

". . . is the matter with you, man? Do you even hear me?"

Bruno shook himself out of his daze and tried to zero in on Julio's grating monologue. "Sorry. Still half asleep. What did you say?"

"I was saying that Otis didn't come in tonight at all, and Jillian called, said she can't make it in at six, either, and I am so done, man. I've been here for twelve and a half hours."

"Not coming in? What's the matter with those guys?"

Julio grunted. "I don't know or care, buddy. Call 'em yourself if you're curious. But I'm outta here, at six sharp. Closing the place up and locking the door. Just lettin' ya know."

Bruno glanced at the clock again, calculating dressing time, driving time. "Make it six thirty?"

Julio paused, considering it. "On the nose, dude," he growled.

Click. Julio was gone. Bruno let the phone drop, slid down the wall until his naked butt hit the floor. Great. An extra shift at the diner. This negated the mellow kung fu vibe in one crushing blow.

There was no logical reason to be so uptight about closing Tony's Diner while he scoured the city for some decent waitstaff. But the place had been a fixture in his life since Mamma sent him there at age twelve, right before all the bad stuff happened. Bruno had worked there throughout his adolescence, bussing plates, waiting tables.

Thirty years ago, after Vietnam, Uncle Tony decided that he wanted to run a food joint in his adopted West Coast city of Portland, Oregon. A no bullshit place that slung great hash twenty-four-seven, like the diners of his youth in New Jersey and New York. Where a guy working swing shift could get great fries or chops anytime, day or night. He'd persuaded his unmarried sister, Bruno's Zia Rosa, to move out and help. Zia had added her own heroic efforts to the production of food that made your taste buds burst into six-part harmony while simultaneously clogging your arteries with deadly plaque.

But Uncle Tony was dead. He'd died a hero, almost a year ago, now, saving Bruno's life among many others. He could hear his uncle's gruff, Marines drill sergeant voice in his head. *What's this? Ya wanna close Tony's Diner because of, what? Nightmares? Fuckin' stress? You tired, boy? Fuck tired! Tired's for pussies! You can rest when you're dead!*

Tony was resting. It was Bruno that couldn't seem to manage it. Not with the Rudy dreams and Zia Rosa missing in action. Zia had gone haring off a few weeks ago to attend the birth of yet another of the McCloud crowd's innumerable spawn, expecting Bruno to pick up the slack. Kev was off the hook, because Rosa wanted so badly for him to procreate, and all that sweaty humping took time and effort, right? But Bruno, man. Anything goes. Put that boy to work, day and night. Never mind lost sleep. Never a thought for his own kite and toy business.

Fortunately, his own outfit was a smoothly functioning perpetual-motion machine. One of Bruno's talents was to pick good staff and motivate them well. Too bad Zia Rosa couldn't do the same.

But the restaurant was his most visceral link to Tony. God, how he missed the old bastard. Tony had loved the place. Bruno owed Tony his life, several times over. Tony had never closed the joint but for a couple of very notable days; one being the day eighteen years ago that Rudy and his goons had come to the diner to kidnap and murder Bruno. They had not succeeded, thanks to Kev, aka white-hot ninja maniac, and Tony. His uncle had carted the goons away in his pickup to an unknown fate. Or, well. Unknown, maybe, but certainly not un-guessed. It had been a day of blood, terror, and broken glass.

The other day the diner had closed had been the day Tony died. Another day of blood, terror, and broken glass. Bombs and bullets, too.

Jesus, Mary, and Joseph. Thought about in those terms, closing down Tony's Diner was starting to look like the knell of fucking doom.

Aw, hell with it. He'd cover at the diner, for as long as it took. He wasn't sleeping worth a damn anyhow, with Rudy coming at him full bore every night. His sex life was decimated. A guy couldn't invite lady friends over for erotic frolics when he had an early-morning date with monsters from the depths of his damaged psyche. Real mood-killer, that. Hadn't seen any between-the-sheets action in months now.

Or missed it much, to be honest. Too tired.

He headed into the bathroom, stared at his face over the sink. He looked bad, he noted critically. Reddened eyes, cheeks starting to cave. He'd lost about twenty pounds since the dreams started up again. His head still throbbed, now that the calming spell of the kung fu forms was broken. He yanked open the medicine cabinet, rummaged 'til he found a cluster of prescription bottles, rubber banded together.

He'd gone to a shrink with his problem a few weeks ago. This eerie cocktail of antidepressants, antianxiety meds, and antipsychotics had been the guy's recommendation. Bruno checked it out on the Internet, discovered that his dose of the antipsychotic was higher than the max recommended dose for schizophrenia patients. Similar to what they were giving Iraq veterans suffering from PTSD after multiple combat tours. He'd made a real impression on that shrink. Possible side effects included, but were by no means limited to: diabetes, weight gain, muscle spasms, slurred speech, disorientation, tremors. And to top it off, some of the vets who took it were dying in their sleep.

Yet here he was, getting out the bottles. Rereading those labels.

No. Aside from possible side effects—like, say, death—he had a creeping sense that if he drove Rudy underground, the guy would really be able to fuck with him. At least when Rudy was in his face, he could see what he was dealing with. Who knew? He was feeling his way. He wasn't great at introspection. He liked action. Constant, restless motion.

Don't think about it. Shine it on. The hole in his belly was deep enough as it was. Just stay shallow, that was the trick. Babbling- brook shallow. He was great at that. Ask any of his ex-girlfriends.

He batted the bottles aside with the back of his hand and kept digging. Found some aspirin, swallowed it dry, and turned on the water to wash that fried look off his face. Maybe he could sneakily do for himself what Kev had done for him years ago. Kev had researched lucid dreaming, speed reading hundreds of books and medical journals. Every night, Kev made him practice kung fu forms in the wide part of the alley out back, behind the diner, practicing stepping back from the cage of monkey. And after, Kev sat next to Bruno's bed as he went to sleep, helping him visualize Rudy putting down his weapons and fading away. Imagining that booming voice getting softer, until it disappeared.

Then Kev stretched out with a blanket and slept on the floor. And when Bruno had the nightmare, Kev woke him and did it again. Every night, for months. And bit by bit, it started to work. A night would go by, no dream. Then another. Bruno stopped freaking out in school, for the most part. He'd stopped getting straight D's and F's. He'd never gotten particularly good at sleep, being hyper by nature, but it was better. And finally, the dreams stopped altogether. He was cured.

Or so he thought, until a couple of months ago.

He could make a recording similar to Kev's mesmerizing monologue, and hypnotize himself, as Kev had hypnotized him. Problem was, he suspected it was the force of Kev's will that made the technique work. Kev had been a bulwark by his bed. No one messed with Kev.

But Rudy knew damn well he could mess with Bruno. No lame guided visualization with waves crashing and birds chirping was going to change that. But what could he do? Call Kev, bleating for him to come home, tuck Bruno into bed? Whining to be rescued, like the zinged-out twelve-year-old dingbat he'd been when Kev met him?

No. Grow up. Get a spine transplant. Get the fuck over it.

He muscled himself into the shower and slumped against the tiles for support. Let the water beat down against his closed eyelids.

Move your pansy ass, Ranieri. They ain't payin' you by the hour. He almost laughed. Tony, again. Made him nostalgic to channel the old guy's brusque rudeness. Aw, hell with sleep. Kev would be back soon, for the wedding that Edie's terrifying aunt was planning for Kev and Edie in a few weeks. He could talk to Kev between tux fittings, wedding rehearsals, dinners, showers and all that standard nuptial fluff.

In the meantime, he'd face his monsters like a man.

Brave words, dude. Brave words, an inner voice commented.

So? he shot back. *Shut the fuck up, or say something useful.*

He listened in the silence for more as he got ready, but surprise, surprise . . . the little voice said nothing further.

2

Lily Parr stared into her laptop. The taxi's swerving on the bends in the highway was making her queasy, but she powered on. Nausea was nasty, but if she shut the laptop and closed her eyes, she'd have to think about what she was about to do. And the way it made her feel.

She'd rather cram psych texts into her brain until there was no room for so much as a fleeting thought. After all, she had six years worth of studying to do in four short days for the grad thesis she was writing. A steep learning curve, but the guy who'd hired her to write it for him had forked over the 50 percent in cash she asked for up front this very morning, thank God, so she was committed. With that, plus the other fees she'd scraped together, letting utility bills slide and paying the minimum on her maxed-out credit cards, she'd covered the monthly fee for Aingle Cliff House, Howard's private clinic. Assuming she didn't need to buy anything frivolous, like subway fare or groceries, until some fresh fees trickled in. But once they did, she'd already be budgeting for next month's check. She wasn't sure what was left in the dark corners of the pantry, but she was going to get friendly with it this week. And who needed subway fare? She lived in Manhattan. She could walk. Her thighs could use the workout.

She muscled her mind back to the screen. The trick was to keep her mind constantly applied, like a pen that did not dare leave the paper. If only she could forget she had a body. Just be a vaporous cloud. Things would be simpler. Talk about saving on the grocery bill. Her inconvenient body was the medium through which feelings made themselves known. She hadn't been able to afford feelings since she was ten, but they never figured out that they weren't welcome. Clueless.

Ironic, to be writing a thesis in psychology. A crash course in the inner workings of the human brain, yay. That stuff belonged to the category of things that she could not afford to personally worry about. Like, for instance, the fact that a guy who'd paid another person to study for him, take his exams for him, and write his papers and his graduate thesis for him was about to graduate with a PhD, probably cum laude, thanks to Lily, and then go out to find work in the field of psychology, perhaps diagnosing or even treating people.

Yep. She, Lily Parr, had made that scenario possible.

Too bad. She pushed it away. She hadn't chosen to do this. It just happened, and then it snowballed, and now she had no way out, not with Howard to take care of. The world was a shitty place, and she was sorry, but an ethical dilemma was another luxury she could not afford.

It was better than robbing banks, or dealing drugs. It really was.

The last paper she'd been paid to write had been on ethics. Hah. But at least a false ethicist wasn't likely to hurt anybody once he was unleashed upon the world. There had been some small comfort in that.

Every month, she pulled together the eleven thousand bucks, plus her own cruelly pared-down living expenses on top of it, and forked the dough over to the professionals who'd promised to watch her father like a hawk twenty-four hours a day to make sure he didn't kill himself.

She'd put Howard in less expensive facilities before Aingle Cliff, and every time he'd managed to get his hands on some pills and swallow them. God knew how. But he'd been at Aingle Cliff for four years now. They'd kept him under control. So far, so good.

Not that one could really describe the situation as "good." Good in the sense of "not dead." Everything was relative.

So here she was for the monthly torture. Checkbook at

the ready. Stomach in knots. Locking Howard up was all she could do. She couldn't help him any other way. She'd almost killed herself trying when she was young and dumb. She knew about addiction, codependency, blah, blah, blah. She'd written papers about it, taken online exams. On behalf of others, of course. She knew the material. She got it already.

Her presence was not a comfort to Howard. He never asked her to come. In fact, he begged her to stay away. Real ego-pumper, that one. Her own father, pleading for her not to visit him.

So why did she feel compelled to visit every month?

Her best friend, Nina, a social worker who worked in a battered women's shelter and knew self-destructive behaviors up and down, told her it was guilt that spurred her, but Lily didn't buy it. Who had time for guilt? She was a floating cloud, a disembodied entity. Detached and cold, except when it came to Nina and a select handful of other friends, but Nina was the main one. Nina kept her marginally human. Not that she had time for a social life. No more than she had time for feelings.

Bullshit, Nina said. *Your feelings would roll over you like a tank if you let yourself feel them. You've driven them underground.*

Lily contemplated that grimly. And so? Denial was the way to go. Climb on the hamster wheel to pay off Aingle Cliff. Not a thought for irony or ethics. Swallow the bitter taste in her mouth. Do the jobs, pay the bills, write the checks. Get the tiger by the tail.

Scramble to keep it from tearing her to pieces.

Almost there. Lily snapped the laptop shut and stared at the imposing façade of Aingle Cliff House as they wended up the drive.

Dumb name for the place. No cliffs to be seen. In fact, the place seemed to be situated in a bowl. Hardly a reassuring name for a facility where one stashed people with suicidal tendencies. The first thing Lily thought of when she heard the word "cliff" was a running jump, a long fall, and a *splat* at the bottom. But then, she was twisted.

The cab stopped. She sat there, like a lump.

"Uh . . . miss?" the cabbie prodded. "Are you, uh . . ."

Lily dug out her wallet. "Can you come pick me up in an hour?"

The cabbie agreed. Lily paid him, uncomfortably aware of how little money was left. She'd put it all into the check she was about to write and had barely enough to get back to the train station. Nothing left over for a tip on the outward-bound cab ride. Ouch.

The cabbie pulled away. Lily's sneakers crunched on the gravel of the path as she walked up to the imposing building. Patients were out on the grounds, taking in the afternoon sunshine. Not Howard. Patients considered a danger to themselves were kept in a special ward. Howard was special, in that sense. He'd tried to kill himself eight times, maybe more. The episodes had started to blend together after a while.

She'd been fifteen the first time she'd gotten home from school and found him blue-faced, barely breathing. If she'd gone to her after-school tutoring job that day as she'd planned, she'd have found him thoroughly dead. Which had, of course, been his intent.

That day, she stopped calling him Dad. She was the adult, not him. Had been for years. Her mother had died the day she was born, so there had been no one to miss in the mom slot. It had always been her and Howard. Or Dad, as she'd called him in the old days. Before.

But before . . . what? It still tormented her. It hadn't always been like this. Dad had been a research physician, a sought-after expert in emerging IVF technologies, back in the good old days. He'd been a crappy cook and a worse housekeeper, but so much fun. Smart, funny.

They'd been close. They'd had their own special schtick.

Lily and Dad, comedy duo. The two of them against the world. Watching classic horror movies on Saturday afternoons, playing cards, choffing Chinese food. Sunday picnics in the park, with deli sandwiches, Mint Milano cookies, and Snapple.

And then it all went to hell, when she was about ten. Abruptly, Dad had stopped working and started sitting around the house in his bathrobe in a bourbon-soaked stupor. It got worse. Progressed to harder drugs. Sometimes she'd wake at night and find him on his knees by her bed, tears streaming down his face. Freaked her out, big-time.

Lily signed the guest book and headed to the administrative office, where she wrote out her monthly blackmail payment to her deepest fears. She exchanged bland chitchat with the staff, and when she could think of no other earthly reasons to procrastinate, she headed into the elevator and went up to the fourth floor. Howard's ward.

The fourth-floor ward was guarded. She exchanged smiles with the security guy. He unlocked the door and waved her in.

She jerked back as Howard's door opened. Miriam came out, one of Howard's nurses. Not Lily's favorite, though the thought was unworthy. Miriam Vargas was a light-skinned black woman, supermodel gorgeous, with bee-stung lips and a body that was sexy even in baggy scrubs. Though that wasn't what bugged Lily. Miriam was just too bouncy for Lily's mood. It grated on her. Made her feel like a stone-cold bitch, being annoyed by mere friendliness, but there it was.

Miriam flashed spectacular teeth. "Lily! How are you?"

"OK." Lily tried to return the smile, but it was a purely muscular effort. "How is he doing?"

Miriam's smile faded. "He's been a little agitated for the last couple days. I planned to talk to Dr. Stark about it when he comes in today. He may need to have his meds reevaluated. I'm sure he'll be glad to see you, though! You'll perk him right up!"

Hah. Lily was not about to argue with that supposition today. She let out a sharp sigh and went on in. The room was pleasant, with a nice view of the wooded grounds, but Howard wasn't looking at the view. He was hunched up on the bed, hugging his knees. Rocking.

Alarm bells jangled inside her. That obsessive rocking had often preceded his suicide attempts. "Howard?" she asked gently.

He looked up. His pale, wasted face was wet, eyes streaming.

"How can you forgive me, Lil?" he asked.

Lily suppressed an urge to roll her eyes. Howard didn't need any snotty attitude from her to compound his misery. She sank down near his bed. "I already have forgiven you," she said, wondering if it was true. How could she know, if her real emotions were in hiding?

Aw, hell with it. It was true enough, she decided. Howard was forgiven. By executive decision from on high, and feelings had no part in the decision. This was not a democracy. This was fricking martial law.

But in any case, Howard was shaking his head. "No," he said hoarsely. "You couldn't. Ever. If you knew."

She let out a silent sigh. "Knew what? Try me."

Howard's lank gray hair had gotten long, and it flapped against his sunken face as he waved his head back and forth. "Please," he begged. "Please, don't ask me that, Lil."

Around and around, like always. She knew this song by heart. There was the plea for forgiveness, the heebie-jeebie-inducing hints, then the coy retreat. "OK," she soothed. "Whatever. It's all good."

"No. That's just it. It's not good. It'll never be OK." His bloodshot eyes were wide and desperate. "I can't stand it anymore. It's like my chest's caving in. It's breaking my bones. I can't breathe anymore."

Lily gazed at him, helpless. She'd written papers on ab-normal psych, on Jungian symbolism, on Freud. She'd studied the esoteric knowledge of all the world's great religions. One might think she'd know how to unravel Howard's ravings, or have a clue as to how to comfort him with a little lofty wisdom. But her brain wasn't really wired for that slippery, subjective stuff, though she invariably got good grades in it. Or rather, her clients did. She took a tiny bit of secret pride in all those A's.

In her heart of hearts, she was practical, nut-and-bolts Lil. No funny stuff, no woo-woo, no rabbit tricks, no fluff. No excuses, either.

But oh, Christ, how she hated to see him suffer.

She reached out to touch his hand. It was ice cold. "So lay it down, Howard," she suggested. "Tell me what's bugging you."

Howard's clammy hand twitched in hers. "It'll put you in danger." His voice was a thread of a whisper. She had to lean down to catch it. "They're listening, Lil. They're always listening. If I tell you, they'll know. They'll come for you." His scratchy voice broke off into a hacking cough, eyes rolling to the right, the left. "They'll kill me. They'll kill both of us."

She patted his hand. "No, they won't. Not here," she assured him. "You're safe here." God knows, she paid enough for him to be.

Howard's hair flopped again. "No. Nowhere is safe," he insisted. "You're my little girl, Lil. I can't do that to you. My first responsibility was to you. Always to you. That was the reason for . . . for all of it."

Lily winced. Responsibility, her ass. His drug binges had made her feel orphaned ever since she was ten. *Let it go, Lil.* "I'm not little anymore, Howard," she said. "I can look out for myself."

"Don't think that. Ever. We're all still in danger. Magda warned me. She said they're listening. Even now, after all these years."

"Magda?" That was a name she'd never heard. In fact, she'd had no idea Howard had visitors at all, other than herself. He'd isolated himself from the rest of the world decades ago. "Who's Magda?"

"Magda Ranieri. They killed her," Howie whispered.

A chill started around the small of her back, fluttering nastily upward. Visits from dead people. Not a good sign.

"Howard?" she said. "What the hell are you talking about?"

His hand tightened, grinding her fingers together. "Magda tried to stop them," he burst out. "She wanted me to help, but I was so scared, Lil. For you. We were trying to get proof. But they found out."

"Proof of what, Howie?"

"Of what I'd done, for him. I swear, Lil, I didn't know what he was planning. I didn't know he was a . . . a demon. And by the time I understood, it was too late. I had you to think about, and he—"

"He? Who is *he?*" she demanded, her voice getting sharper. "And who the hell is this Magda Ranieri?"

"Don't say the name so loudly!" he hissed, with unexpected force. Then his mouth started shaking again. "They killed her, Lil. In front of me. They beat her to death. They told me you'd be next if I . . . if I . . ." His voice choked off. "I still see it. Whether my eyes are open or closed. All that blood. I can't stand it anymore. I tried to kill myself so you'd be safe. No reason to punish me if I'm dead, right? But I was never man enough to finish the job." His voice choked off. His hand shook.

Lily squeezed his fingers, trying not to shiver. The torment in Howard's eyes was very real. Whether the events that caused it were also real was unlikely, but that did not make his pain any the less.

And this did not feel like rambling. This felt . . . genuine.

She stared down at him. She'd written papers for future health professionals about PTSD in combat stress, or victims of rape or other attacks. And Howard was so terrified of blood. He had been ever since she could remember. Could this be . . . ?

No. It couldn't be. This was mental illness. Years of systematic drug abuse that had worn holes in his brain. She would not fall for this. She was a grown-up. She knew better.

But even so. Howard was detailing the contents of his delusions, which he'd never done before. Dr. Stark, Howard's psychiatrist, always complained about the fact that Howard refused to do talk therapy. Maybe Dr. Stark could use this information to treat him. Lily couldn't waste this opportunity, no matter how much it was creeping her out.

"Who is this Magda to you?" she repeated. "Tell me more."

Howard shook his head, but he kept talking, as if some desperate part of him was breaking loose of the cage of his fear. "Magda keeps coming to me," he moaned. "She says, find her son, and tell him. But I can't. You could find him, Lil."

"Who? Me? Who's Magda's son? Tell him what?"

"Shhh!" he hissed, dragging her hand closer so that her butt slid from the hard chair. She perched on his bed instead, bending to hear his croaking whisper. "You could tell him. He has to lock it. With the key. It's the key to everything. Her son will know when he sees it."

His eyes rolled. He was losing steam, getting spooked. She hurried to keep him talking. "When he sees what, Howard?" she prompted.

"He'll know," Howard muttered. "Magda told me he'd understand as soon as he saw it, and he can—"

"What on earth is going on in here?"

Lily and Howard practically levitated, they were so startled.

Miriam stood in the open door, her large eyes flashing in outrage. "What is the meaning of this?" she demanded, her voice razor sharp.

Lily's mouth worked, struggling for something, anything to say in the face of the woman's inexplicable anger. "Ah, we were just talking—"

"Talking?" Miriam's voice slashed over hers. "Just look at him! You're deliberately upsetting him!"

Lily looked. Howard had jerked his hand away and wrapped his arms around his knees, eyes squeezed shut, streaming with tears.

Shit. That brief, rare moment of opening up was closing down again, all because of that stupid nurse's wretched crap timing. *Shit!*

"No," Lily said, through clenched teeth. "He was perfectly fine! You were the one who agitated him when you burst in on us like that! Howard, just finish what you were telling me about Magda and her—"

"No!" He jerked away as if she'd struck him. "I never said anything! It's just stupid, bullshit raving! I'm a crazy old man, a paranoid junkie! Get away from me, before I bring you down, too! You shouldn't come to see me at all! I've told you that! Please, go!"

True. But he never told her to stop writing the checks. Though, to be fair, it may never have occurred to him that she poured out her heart's blood to pay for this place. She'd never rubbed his nose in it.

"Just go. Don't come back. Forget all this. Forget about me. Please." Howard began to rock again, shoulders shaking with sobs.

"Well?" Miriam prodded. "You heard the man! Go! Right now!"

Lily shot to her feet, shocked and affronted. "No, I will not! I am here to talk to my father, and I demand privacy."

"Demand all you want," Miriam retorted. "This is my shift, and he is my responsibility, and I'm standing by it! You need to go! Right now!"

Lily turned to Howard, put her hand on his shoulder. "Howard—"

"No! Don't!" He shook her hand off, moaning and twitching.

Miriam marched over, her steps full of grim purpose. Before Lily quite knew what was happening, the needle was in Howard's arm, the plunger going in. Howard went rigid . . . and sagged, suddenly limp.

"There," Miriam said, in obvious triumph. "Now he can rest."

Lily was appalled. "How dare you?" Her voice shook. "I open my veins every month to pay for this place!"

"That is not my concern," Miriam said. "You can complain to my boss if you want, but I'm going to be filing a statement today, too, about how I witnessed you abusing him! Deliberately agitating him!"

Lily's jaw dropped. "Abusing him? I was just talking to—"

"Leave! Now!" Miriam's voice rang with command. "Or I'll have you forcibly escorted out! And don't think for one second that I'm bluffing!"

Lily stared at the woman, her cheeks hot. She looked at Howard, slumped on his side. Air wheezed into his half-open mouth. Eyes half closed, blurred with drugs, like they'd been most of her life. He'd run off to his safe place and left her out in the cold, alone. Just like old times.

She could have strangled that bitch for killing what amounted to the only real moment she'd had with Howard in years. But it would serve no purpose. Howard had retreated. He wouldn't be back today. What was the point? She might as well go through official channels to make her complaint. It would be more dignified. She'd move Howard to some other facility if she didn't get an appropriate outcome.

Miriam frog-marched her to the door of the ward and shut the door in Lily's face, hard, once she was outside it.

Lily just stood there, at a loss. The guard was giving her a strange look. To the elevator. One foot in front of the other. She wanted to lodge her complaint immediately, but she was so angry and rattled, she'd flub it and come across as a hysterical idiot. Better to wait. Keep it together.

So she powered through the lobby and out onto the grounds without speaking to anyone. The late summer sunshine felt incongruous. All those bugs and birds tweeting and chirring, wind rustling, boughs waving. The cheerfulness was unseemly. Her body felt as tight as piano wire.

As if having her father be a suicidal drug addict weren't enough for her nerves to handle. Now ghosts, eerie warnings, cryptic requests. Buckets of blood. Murderous bad guys out to get him, and Lily, too. Brrr.

She hadn't thought things could get any worse for Howard, but he'd never scared her like this. She needed distance, or she'd go crazy herself. She, unlike Howard, had no family members left who would sling themselves up into a strangling financial noose in order to lock her up someplace attractive and safe to be crazy. Nope, she'd be muttering-to-herself, eating-out-of-Dumpsters crazy. The image did not appeal.

She was shivering. She wanted to crawl under a bush, huddle like a hurt animal. The sky seemed so empty. Weirdly threatening.

She hadn't gotten the number of the cabbie. She should have gotten his card. She could go back inside, ask for a car service, but that would require mental organization, social skills, and a certain measure of calm that she simply did not possess. The other option was to sit down on an ornamental rock and wait for forty minutes.

She glanced up at the fourth floor. Miriam stood in the window of one of the rooms, staring down. Talking into a cell phone.

About Lily, no doubt. Probably telling her supervisor about the incident, painting Lily as the hysterical hag of the situation. Lily quashed the thought. It sounded grandiose, paranoid. *The whole world is looking at me, plotting against me, out to destroy me.*

She was not giving in to that. Not even if it were true.

Miriam stared down, still talking. The reflection on the double-paned glass window obscured her expression, but Lily fancied she could feel the hostility radiating out of the woman, even at this distance. She got up, strolled along the grounds. She felt so exposed, under that blank sky. Like a raptor might swoop down, claws out to grab and rend.

They killed her, Lil. In front of me. They beat her to death. They told me you'd be next . . .

A wave of faintness came over her. She had to grab a tree branch to keep steady at the remote possibility that Howard actually . . . no.

She couldn't go down that road, even in the privacy of her own head. That way lay madness. There weren't enough funds for both of them to be bonkers. But damn it, she'd wondered for years what the hell had broken Howard. Why would a normal, successful, relatively happy person suddenly fall to pieces? From one day to the next?

One wouldn't, she thought. Not without a precipitating cause. And witnessing this Magda's brutal murder . . . that would do it.

But her longing for a logical explanation was a trap, too. She was wise to all traps now. Suspicious of everything. Even her own mental processes.

The grounds merged into forest at the end of the neatly mowed lawn. Shivery prickles on the back of her neck urged her to run, hide. Go to ground. Stupid impulse. She didn't do nature, and besides, nobody was after her. The world didn't pay much attention to her, and she liked it that way. She flew under the radar. Almost no one knew what she did for a living, and by necessity, her referrals were extremely discreet. She worked too many hours to know many people, other than Nina. And a few disgruntled men from her occasional forays into dating.

She glanced up. Miriam was still there, still talking on the phone.

It embarrassed her to stand out here, like a dog put out for piddling on the rug, while that awful woman glared down. She was out of this place. Right now. On foot. How far off base could she go? She had on sneakers. She couldn't get lost if she stayed parallel to the road and kept the sound of traffic in her ears. A walk in the woods to clear her mind, just the thing. Unless some fanged predator ate her, of course, but she didn't think bears or cougars or wild boars lurked in the woods of New York. Plus, she'd save ten bucks of cab fare and avoid the embarrassment of not being able to tip the cab driver. And the money could then be put toward tonight's dinner. A happy bonus.

Lily pushed through the hedge and plunged into the forest.

3

"Come get her, Cal. Come *fast*." The nurse Miriam, who was not, in fact, a nurse, nor was her name Miriam, whispered fiercely into her cell as she slipped into an unused patient room.

"Did King say what to do with her?" Cal asked, sounding bored.

"I haven't spoken to him yet, but when I do, I certainly don't want to have to tell him that we've lost track of her!" she hissed. "That would suck for you, too, Cal. I'll give you more instructions in a few minutes! For now, just step on it! Get your ass back here!"

Click. Cal hung up on her. Bastard. She'd never liked him much.

Calm down, Zoe. Focus, Zoe. She used her name, like King did in her personalized programming sequences, trying to recreate his voice in her head repeating the commands. It helped the message go deeper.

The situation was still containable—barely. Howard had surprised her, finally blurting out his piece. The processing delay had been longer than she'd anticipated. The gulper had bleeped the data to her laptop, run it through the word-recognition bot, and subsequently beeped her, but a dangerously long time had passed between when Howard pronounced the key words, "Magda Ranieri," and when Zoe had gotten the signal. Almost four fucking minutes. Zoe could tell by the time she'd gotten to the room that Howard had spilled his guts completely.

That bad, bad boy. They would have to scramble to clean this up.

She didn't understand why King had not simply ordered her to kill Howard years ago, but he had his reasons. And, of course, he'd wanted to maintain his power over Howard to the end. Howard had to understand who was boss. It was appropriate that he submit, that he behave and obey, to the moment of his death. And that he be punished for transgression. That was something she could well understand.

In fact, she understood it so well, her guts churned with apprehension. King would be so angry. She needed for this assignment to go well. Her last assignment had been compromised by her lack of emotional self-control. She'd been working on that problem, putting in the hard time with DeepWeave XIII, the latest of King's brilliant programming sequences. Four hours a day; two before work, two before bed. The same amount of time she spent working out.

Please, let him not be angry. It wasn't her fault. It was the time delay in the word-rec bot, not her. But King did not accept excuses.

Zoe stared out the window as she touched a speed dial on her cell. Howard's daughter stood outside by the entrance to the rose garden, her long, curly red hair flying in the breeze. As Zoe watched, she looked straight up at Zoe, with disconcerting directness.

Zoe suppressed the urge to step back, away from the window. She had this situation under control. No one could intimidate her.

So the Parr woman had opted not to make an immediate complaint about Miriam the nurse's shocking rudeness. A stroke of luck in terms of timing, since after today, this place would never see Zoe's face again. She was grateful this hadn't happened when she was off shift. But that was due to her own careful planning and scheduling. Howard's daughter was regular in her visits. The first Tuesday of the month, never weekends, no other visitors. After taking into account this dull regularity, King had decided that Zoe could handle the long-term surveillance job without backup. And until this moment, Zoe had been convinced that this job was make-work, inflicted to punish her with boredom. But she never complained. Not even when forced to do the disgusting, mind-numbing personal services nurses performed for their patients. Cheerfully, with professional perfection. For fucking *years*.

Anything to make him forgive her. Approve of her again.

The phone rang and rang. Ten times, fifteen. Zoe waited patiently, watching Lily wandering aimlessly in the flowerbeds. King was a busy, important man, with many things to attend to. She must wait her turn.

Lily glanced up again, and Zoe stared down, composing herself. She began to mentally recite a DeepWeave emergency intervention in her mind to calm herself before—

Click. "Zoe, my dear," that beloved voice said. "Tell me everything."

Oh. Zoe sucked in air, nostrils flaring. That voice. So deep, so rich, so sparkling. It just undid her. She fought the jolt of excitement, clenched her body, ruthlessly pulled herself together.

"Howard's been bad," she announced. Her voice barely quavered.

A considering pause from the other end. "He told the girl?"

"Yes." She braced herself and confessed. "He named names."

"Ah." That agonizing silence ticking by, again. "And how is it that you allowed him to do this, my dear?" King asked, his voice terrifyingly gentle. "What was the scope of this assignment? Had you *forgotten?*"

"No!" She gulped. "They were alone together in the room, like always, and, ah, he took me by surprise! I've studied every transcript of their monthly visits over the last four years, and he never said a word about anything so far, so I—"

"Zoe." He cut her off, softly. "Calm yourself. You are babbling."

Zoe clenched her jaw. "I set the word-rec bot to beep me if he said Magda Ranieri's name, but there were a few minutes of lag time that I didn't anticipate. So I . . . it was a technical glitch. He, ah, talked for a while. I haven't had time to listen to the data yet. I wanted to get your orders first. Do you want me to send you the raw data now? I could—"

"No. First things first. Where is the girl now?"

"Waiting outside for the cab," Miriam replied. "I'm at the window, looking at her right now. Cal picked her up at the train station and brought her here. I've already told him to come back as soon as possible to pick her up. He'll take care of her for you. Though I very much doubt that she believes what he told her. Nobody would, at this point."

"It doesn't matter." King's voice sounded almost fretful. "I'm done wasting time and money on this. The last thing I need is that stupid business to inconvenience me now, when things are finally taking off."

"Of course," Zoe agreed hastily. "Of course, you're right."

"I should have cleaned this mess up years ago," King went on. "I want it done today. And then I never want to hear about it again."

"Certainly," she said. "Shall I tell Cal to—"

"I'll contact Cal. Concentrate on Howard. Is everything prepared?"

Her heart leaped at the starting gates. "Of course."

Zoe pocketed her phone, tingling with excitement. At last! After years of tedium, the punishment was over. Finally, she got to do what she was trained for. She'd do it just right. He'd be so proud of her.

The endorphin-pumping fantasy that thought provoked derailed her concentration for eight seconds. She yanked herself together and retrieved the prepared gym bag from her locker in the staff area. She went to Howard Parr's room, glancing up the quiet corridor before she went in. The sedative she'd given him had put him in a dreamy doze. He was unlikely to notice her preparations. Or have the wit to interpret them.

Even so, she was quick. Fresh latex gloves went on, then a lightweight plastic poncho over her uniform. She'd have to take care not to get her white sneakers stained. Upon reflection, she pulled out a couple of plastic bags, encased her feet to the ankles. Details, details.

She reached under the bed, plucked the small, supersensitive sound gulper she'd attached to the bed frame with gummy adhesive. She activated its power source only on the days that Howard's daughter came to visit, when it would transmit its signal to the laptop humming away in the duffel bag in her staff locker. Its job was now done.

She pulled out the stretchy Ace bandage. Howard began to stir as she wrapped it quickly and firmly around his arms at the elbow, trapping them together. Still, he didn't cry out.

He did try to yelp when she popped the plastic ball into his mouth, but by then, it was too late. *Pop*, the gag was in place. She pulled out the long, sharp shard of broken glass that she'd stowed under his mattress long ago, and sat on him. She grabbed one of his hands, pressing his fingers randomly over the surface of the glass. He struggled hard, mewling and flopping, but she was five foot nine, a hundred and fifty-five pounds of rock-solid, gym-toned muscle, though she appeared quite slender. Far heavier than frail, wasted Howard.

She smiled into his terrified eyes. "Poor Howard," she crooned. "This is your lucky day, you know that? I'm going to help you finish what you've been trying to accomplish for years. Aren't you happy?"

His eyes rolled frantically. He shook his head.

"Aw," she murmured. "Well, I'm sorry you feel that way. If only you'd kept your mouth shut, hmm?"

His struggles were so weak. It was so easy. She was up to more challenge than this. The shard bit deep into his flesh, a long, vertical gash into his pallid, clammy skin, and she'd angled his arm so that the hot black-red arterial gout aimed toward the floor. He fought, as best he could, but his blood pressure dropped fast, and his strength with it.

Blood pooled under the bed. She watched it spread. So fast. Wow. This was by no means her first time, but somehow, it was always like the first time for her. Something about the combat programming, maybe, that revved her for the kill. It made something dark inside her swell, breathless with delirious excitement. Her heart boomed heavily against the cage of her ribs. Her thighs clenched, released.

She kept her finger on his pulse as it slowed, reminding herself constantly not to squeeze too hard. She mustn't leave bruises.

When it was over, she slid off, careful not to step in the puddle. Pleased with her own frosty poise. White coat, pristine. Sneakers as pure as an alpine ski slope. Only the latex gloves were slippery and red.

Except that she was sweating, profusely. A glance through

the open bathroom door at the mirror over the sink confirmed that she was red, hot, her face shiny. She'd have to wait a few moments before she was presentable. Very bad. Maybe she needed to have her programming sequences tweaked, or her meds. She'd have to tell King. The thought made her wince, but keeping secrets would be a far worse infraction.

In her training period, overexcitement had always been her downfall. She'd risked being culled for it on every single cull day. King always concluded that her other gifts compensated for that glitch.

God, how she hoped he'd continue to think so.

Zoe peeled off the gloves, tucked them in the bag she'd prepared for them. Took off the rest of the plastic, folding it carefully. Put on fresh latex to peel off Howie's gag, fish out the ball, the Ace bandage.

She closed his hand carefully around the bloody shard, pressing his fingerprints over it again. Dropped it gently into the dark pool.

She peered out the window one more time, seized with sudden tension when she did not see Lily Parr in the garden, or Cal's cab.

Could Cal have possibly already come and gone away with her, while Zoe was busy with Howard? She certainly hoped so. She peered down the road, wondering if she should call . . . No. She had to concentrate on her part. No distractions. Distraction would be her downfall.

She pulled the door shut, quietly stowed her bag, and poked her head into the nurses' station. "I'm running down to grab coffee and a muffin from the bakery cart," she said to her colleague, marveling at her own perfectly casual tone. "Want one?"

"No, I'm good," the woman said. "See you in a few."

Zoe unlocked the ward, exchanged some flirtatious comments with the guard, and called the elevator. God, she was good. Now, a shot of simple carbs to calm the jitters, slow down her heartbeat, and it would be time for the fun part. The discovery, the trauma, the blood.

Too bad she couldn't tape the show somehow, for King's benefit.

She had to fight not to giggle, imagining it.

Lily was foul-tempered and footsore by the time she got on the uptown West Side express train. Her stupid impulse du jour had reminded her, in itchy, crawling detail, why she didn't do nature. She'd misjudged the time it would take to walk to the Shaversham Point train station by two endless, plodding hours, and arrived at the train station stumbling with exhaustion, chilled to the bone, shoes slimed with mud, and creeping, itchy sensations under her clothes. Ticks? Spiders? Ick.

By some pathetic crumb of luck, she'd burst out of a thicket next to the train tracks just as the last NYC-bound train was about to leave. She practically decapitated herself diving for the open door and spent the trip taking notes about Howard's revelations, jotting them on the laptop to fix the details in her mind. She left three messages on Stark's voice mail during the trip, and two more during the exhausting cross-town walk through underground tunnels to the uptown West Side trains. Too busy to call her back? Damn doctors.

The only thing that made it all bearable was the fact that Nina had promised her Indian food, a soothing cool mango lassi to wash it down, and sympathy. Lily was desperately in need of all three. She was mustering the oomph to climb the stairs to street level when the phone finally buzzed. Howard's doctor. Finally. She snatched it out of her purse, covering her other ear in a vain attempt to block out the rattling screech of the train as it pulled out. She yelled into it. "Dr. Stark? I'm so glad you called! I wanted to talk to you about Howard."

"Lily. I have bad news." His voice was unusually stiff.

Bad news? What strength she had drained promptly out of her legs and left her wobbling on the stairs. What could be worse about Howard's condition other than . . .

Her belly lurched with dread. "What bad news?"

"I'm so sorry to tell you this," the doctor said. "But after you left this afternoon, I'm afraid Howard, ah . . . well, he took his own life."

"Took his own . . ." Her voice trailed off. "He *what?*"

"I'm afraid so."

Afraid so? Afraid of what? What the fuck did this guy have to be afraid of? She was the one who'd lived in fear for eighteen goddamn years.

Her mind picked at the guy's stupid word choice so she didn't have to process what he'd actually said. What it meant for her.

Ah, God. For so long now, the whole purpose of her existence had been to stop Howard from doing this. And he'd done it anyway. After all these years. All the nets she'd held out. They hadn't been enough to catch him. All pointless. All her frantic effort. Flailing like an idiot. Oh, God.

Stark's voice droned on. She couldn't make out his words. She was seeing all the times she'd found Howard on the floor and sat with him there for hours, waiting for him to wake up. Feeling his pulse, holding a mirror in front of his nose, trying to judge if this was a normal opiate binge that he would sleep off, or one of the deadly biggies, before she called the ambulance, again, and wasted the EMTs' valuable time, to say nothing of her meager household budget.

The man's whole fucking life, one long goddamn suicide attempt.

And he'd pulled it off. That selfish *bastard*. She wanted to scream, explode, shoot things, smash things. Her chest burned, her throat was imploding. She felt stupid. Made a fool of once again. Just another little joke of Fate at Lily Parr's expense. Hah, hah.

Dr. Stark's voice came back into focus. ". . . what arrangements need to be made, so you should contact our administrative—"

"How?" she cut in.

"Uh . . . uh, what? You mean, how should you contact our administrative—"

"No, I mean, how did he do it? Was it pills? Where the fuck did he get pills in that place? What the fuck was I paying you guys for? Wasn't he locked up? Wasn't he guarded, watched all the time? Wasn't that the deal we made? I pay, you guys watch? Exactly what part of that arrangement was unclear to you?"

Stark hesitated, clearing his throat nervously for several seconds. "Ah, well, no. It wasn't pills. Believe me, Lily, I'm mortified about this. We're all so shocked . . . We just can't imagine how he found it. He got a piece of broken glass someplace, evidently. I can't imagine where, or from what. He never went out, and you were his only visitor. He was constantly supervised. I'm so sorry, Lily, but he opened the artery in his wrist with the glass shard. It was probably over in a couple of minutes."

"Bullshit," she said.

That cut off Stark's monologue, startling him into a nervous stammer. "Ah . . . ah, ex-excuse me?"

"I said, that's bullshit," she repeated. "Howard would never cut himself. Not in a million years. He was terrified of blood. Blood made him pass out. Howard liked pills. He would never slit his wrist."

"Ah." Dr. Stark's voice strengthened. "Well, I'm sorry to say it, Lily, but he did. He most unquestionably did. I saw him myself."

Then someone else killed him. She almost blurted it out, but stopped herself. Howard's words echoed in her head.

They're listening, Lil. They're always listening.

The world retreated. She felt the jostle of people forcing their way past her on the stairs, but they seemed very far away, and the real Lily was deep within, locked in a place of breathless, gelid stillness.

If I tell you, they'll know. They'll come for you. They'll kill both of us.

She clawed her way back. Forced lungs to breathe, legs to climb. She tried to tune in to what Stark was saying, but there was so much noise. Her ears buzzed. So loud. She stumbled out onto the sidewalk. Autopilot guided her toward Nina's apartment.

"Who was the last one to see him?" she blurted, cutting off the senseless babble from the phone.

Stark made a huffy sound. He did not like to be interrupted. "As I said, the nurse on duty, Miriam Vargas, was the one who found him."

The cold inside her deepened, spread. "I want to talk to her," Lily said. "Now. I'll come right back up. I'll take the next train."

"No," Stark snapped. "You can't speak to her now. She was shocked. She couldn't stop crying. She's been sedated."

"Oh, really? That poor, sweet baby. You're breaking my heart."

Stark sucked in air audibly. "Ms. Parr," he said, his voice tight and prissy with disapproval. "I know this is shocking news for you, and very painful. It's impossible to accept all at once. You might need help processing it, and no one could blame you, believe me. If you like, I can give you the number of someone you can call—"

"She'll have stopped crying by tomorrow, right?" She couldn't keep the edge out of her voice. "Will the drugs have worn off by then?"

"Leave the interviews to the professionals." Stark's voice was crisp. "There will be a police investigation. The last thing Miriam needs is for distraught family members to descend upon her and—"

"To be honest, Dr. Stark, I really don't care what Miriam needs."

"It doesn't sound like you cared what Howard needed, either!"

Lily stopped dead, jaw sagging. "Excuse me?" she said. "What the hell is that supposed to mean?"

"Ms. Vargas gave me a full report of what transpired between you and she and Howard this afternoon, Ms. Parr—"

"Well, then, she lied!" This conversation was a lost cause, but so was her self-control. "She was the one who agitated him, not me! And Howard would never have cut himself!"

"Ms. Parr?"

The new voice called to her, from outside the babble of the doctor's scolding voice coming through her cell. Lily looked around to see where it was coming from.

A man in a gray hoodie, standing above her on Nina's stoop. Young, dark-haired, good-looking. Smiling a blank sort of smile. He was familiar. The kind of familiar when you don't really know a person, but you see him regularly, like the guy who sold her bananas from the fruit cart on the corner. She knew him, but from *where . . . ?*

It exploded in her mind, jolting alarm through her rattled system. The cab driver from the Shaversham Point train station. What in the hell was he . . . oh. Oh, God. Oh, *shit.*

And this was Nina's apartment. Not even her own place. So how did they . . . how could they . . . her mind couldn't even embrace it.

How had he known where she was?

She looked at the cell phone in her hand, heard the tinny warbling still coming from it. Dr. Stark was continuing his rant, but she no longer heard him. She had bigger problems now. Much bigger.

Her heart thudded. Her eyes locked with his and stuck there.

He took a step toward her. "Can I have a word with you, please?"

The scrape of a door sliding open behind her. It was a big SUV, humming on the curb. It all came together. The prickles on her neck, Howard's garbled confession, his impossible suicide.

And now, this guy with the blank, empty smile advancing on her from above, and the open SUV yawning behind—

Fuck this. She flashed the guy her most blinding bimbo bombshell smile. "Oh, my God! You're the cabbie, right? The guy from Shaversham Point?" Her voice sounded high and thin and stupid. "Look, I'm, like, so sorry about standing you up for that cab ride, but things got really crazy for me today! But I do owe you that fare, and a tip, so let me just get that for ya right now, 'kay?" She beamed, reached in her purse—

Whipped out the Mace can. *Squirt*. Sucker punched.

The man reeled back, clawing at his eyes. She twirled to meet the other guy, heaving her computer bag in an arc into his face. He whipped his arm up to block it. She used that split second to zap a front kick to his crotch. He stumbled back with a grunt of outrage.

She recognized the other guy as his leg snapped up and his boot heel cracked agonizingly against her wrist. The Mace can flew, bounced, rolled. She scrambled back into a cluster of garbage cans. Kicked one into his path. He bounded over it, blade glinting, slashing down—

Thud. She ran backward into a parked car, did a flying flip-'n'-roll over the hood, and hit the street at a dead run. She darted between cars, heedless of braying horns, squealing brakes. Guy Number Two was another cabbie from Shaversham Point. Normal reality had ripped open, releasing demons from hell. *Busy street*. She needed an avenue block, a subway stop. Witnesses. She groped for her phone. Gone.

Her legs pumped, past the Indian restaurant, the sushi bar, the Laundromat, the clothing boutique, the florist. No one in those places could defend her against knife-wielding demons while she called 911 and waited for the cops to sort it out. She'd be meat. So would they.

She peeked over her shoulder and *shit*, he was gaining. Subway stairs. She flew down the steps, praying that it was a turnstile one, not the revolving cage with no fare booth. It had turnstiles, thank God, but the fare booth was closed, just an automated machine. No one to see her plight, call the cops. A train pulled in, squealing. She leaped the turnstile like a jackrabbit, sped toward the train on the tracks, its doors agape. *Ping*, the doors were closing. She dove for it.

Crunch, the closing doors stuck on her shoulders and gnawed at her, burping and hiccupping in their efforts to close around her body. Pinned. She could only twist her head and watch death pounding down the stairs, straight toward her. The door lurched open. She tumbled inside, scrambled like a crab on the floor to the middle of the car. Her legs shook too much to get up. He was going to make it inside, too.

Whoosh, the doors slid closed in his face. *Thunk*, her attacker slammed into the train. He tried to pry his fingers into the rubberized closure, scrabbling. The train took off, smoothly gaining speed.

The guy jogged alongside, shouting something unintelligible. He bared his teeth, mouthed something vicious, grabbed at his crotch.

Lily huddled on the floor, breath rasping in and out. There was almost no one in the subway car. A teenage girl with earbuds, rocking out to her iPod, eyes shut. A homeless man, fast asleep and taking up a row of seats. An exhausted middle-aged woman, looking carefully away, wanting only to get home from work and put her butt into a chair.

Something warm and wet on her hand. Blood, dripping from a slash on her forearm. Heavy drops pattered onto the floor.

Wow. He'd cut her outside of Nina's apartment. She hadn't even noticed, she'd been so frantic. She stared at it stupidly for a moment, then pulled off her hoodie, wadded up the cloth of her sleeve, and applied direct pressure. She was chilly without the sweatshirt. Tremors racked her. She couldn't tell if it was shock or cold. Both, probably.

Outside Nina's apartment. How in the hell had they known she wasn't going straight home? She'd made her evening plans with Nina via cell phone, during the train ride. They were spying on her phone?

Or worse, they were spying on Nina's phone. That unleashed an even deeper, nastier thrill of dread. The killers knew all about her. They knew about her best friend. They probably knew everyone in the world she might call on for help. God knows, it was a short list, at this point.

She couldn't even call Nina, make sure she was OK. Any contact would put her friend in more danger. The blood on the floor made her think of Howard's shard of glass, and the anger and shock were sucked into the deeper, wider well of agonizing sadness.

When she came to her senses, she was huddled up, gasping for air. Rocking, like an autistic child. Like Howard before a suicidal pill binge. So this was why he did it. This was how it had felt to him.

She didn't know which direction the train was going. People got on and off, stepping around her. She wanted to get up, but her muscles wouldn't move. Fear had frozen her stiff.

She used to scold Howard for that obsessive rocking. It had infuriated her. It came across as so childish, so self-indulgent.

But he'd never been able to stop, once he'd started.

Now she knew why. Oh, Dad. Finally, she got it.

4

Portland, Oregon
Six weeks later

I have important things to do. You are not one of them.
The nonverbal message vibing off the hard-ass brunette's
haughtily turned back was impossible for Bruno to misinter-
pret. But perverse, self-flagellating idiot that he was, it went
straight to his dick.

She'd walked into Tony's Diner at 3:45 A.M., and he'd
swear to God, he'd felt her coming before she even turned
the corner and moved into the light under the awning outside. He was primed for her, after the last two nights of torture and titillation.

Fate had been kind. After hours of anticipation, finally
the follicles on his skin tightened, lifting hairs on end in a
breezy, ticklish rush of animal awareness. The bells over the
doors jingled. Ta-da.

His hair follicles weren't all that lifted and tightened.
Good thing he wore an apron over his jeans. When the chick
with the black pageboy sashayed into Tony's Diner, no matter how blitzed from lack of sleep he was, his glands promptly
pumped a substance into his body that made him want to
break into an old-time movie dance number. An incredible
rush. A tingling sense of infinite possibility combined with a
mega-boner. A huge, awestruck "wow" from the depths of
his being.

She'd chosen a table today, rather than the counter. Each
seating option offered different viewpoints, with varying advantages and disadvantages. He hadn't yet settled on his favorite. The back view was nice for legs, ass, the graceful
nipped-in curve of her back, the nape of her slender, soft-

looking neck, and he could do a lot of easy, blatant ogling while hustling around behind her back. When she took a table, he got more frontal scoping action but had to resort to old tricks from adolescence, developed before he'd discovered the ease and simplicity of mirrored sunglasses. Take it in, in one sweeping glance, and then pore over the gathered data in the privacy of his own dirty mind. He could never gulp enough of this girl in a single glance, though. He wanted to sit down across from her. Fix her with an unblinking, predatory stare.

Not that she'd notice, of course. She probably wouldn't even look up. Her powers of concentration were world-class.

He kept trying to pin down what it was about her that got to him. It was a thorny problem, requiring detailed, up-close research and analysis, he decided, preferably conducted in bed. Maybe the sharp, up-tilted angles of cheekbone and eyebrows, maybe the big, mysterious green-gold eyes, set at an exotic slant, accentuated with bold eyeliner, heavy with mascara. She wore cat-eye glasses with fake gems in the corners that should've made her look grotesque, but they didn't. They looked quirky, sassy, playful. They threw her beauty into sharp relief. She could wear anything and look great. Anything or nothing. Mmm.

And that mouth. She'd painted it a bright scarlet that was supposed to make her look super tough, but it didn't work. The fullness of the upper lip made her look vulnerable, almost childlike. And the severe jet black hair, all wrong for her luminous skin.

The look was Salvation Army sexpot. Shabby black stretch lace shirt, showcasing an enticing nipple hard-on. Frayed denim miniskirt, a little too tight for a luscious ass. Tiny bulge of snowy pale muffin top coming out the low-slung waistband where her shirt rode up that made him want to grab and squeeze. Scuffed red fuck-me peep toes with outrageous heels. Shapely legs in black stockings with so many rips and runs it had to be on purpose. He was usually good at decoding what girls said with their clothes, but he couldn't read this chick. She dressed like she wanted attention, and yet she stared into that netbook like her life depended on it, black-tipped fingers tapping in a ceaseless buzz. Eyes frozen wide. Glasses reflecting the screen's blue glow.

Denying Bruno's very existence upon this earth by the massive force of her indifference, even while ordering food from him. Bad tipper, too. But the nipple hard-on made up for that sin, abundantly.

There was that other quality, too, that he barely knew how to articulate. An intangible glow you could only see if you weren't looking at it. He'd grown sensitive to it hanging out with Kev. Who, mellow as he was, always carried a disquieting aura of danger about him. A sense of things about to happen. Good things, bad things. Big things.

But whatever big things were about to happen to the brunette, a romantic encounter with Bruno Ranieri was unlikely to be one of them. She'd been there every night for three nights, and she'd ignored him completely. Maybe he was an arrogant putz, but he was accustomed to getting attention from women. This girl could give a flying fuck.

Amazing that his glands were stirring at all, after covering the night shift for a month. Zia Rosa was AWOL, supervising the new McCloud kid's first month of life. Bruno couldn't remember which brother's kid it was. He couldn't keep any of Kev's long lost McCloud brothers or their spawn straight, not for the life of him. Dirty blond hair, bright green eyes everywhere you looked. And they bred like rats, so the problem was just going to get worse with time.

He'd tried to hire more staff, but one guy that he'd hired a couple weeks ago just got a call from an ex-girlfriend in Costa Rica and off he went to follow his heart. Then Elsa ripped a tendon in her knee skateboarding. So here he was, swathed in an apron, eyes burning from lack of sleep. Flipping burgers, dipping fries, bussing tables, and baking pies.

Just like old times. His current schedule involved a full day running his own outfit downtown, then an uneasy catnap, and working graveyard at the diner until dawn.

But hey, presto. Tonight's outfit zinged him into perfect wakefulness. Those holes in her tights just made his palms sweat.

Maybe she played for the other team. He didn't think so, though. He had lesbian friends, he knew the vibe. She didn't have it.

One thing she did have was a sweet tooth. She'd been working steadily through the dessert menu, limited though it was with Zia gone. Bruno was a fine short-order cook, and a good pastry chef when he put his mind to it, but Zia was the true pastry goddess, and she was off in Seattle, making beef broth for whichever McCloud wife had just reproduced. To promote lactation, like Nonna in Brancaleone used to do.

Sure enough, the thought of lactation made his eyes fall to the pert, here-I-am! jut of the brunette's nipples at the exact, fateful moment that her gaze darted up without warning. Yikes. Busted.

Oh, man. Eye contact. It was too much. Her gaze cut straight into his brain, like a hot knife through butter. He practically yelped.

Eye contact revealed fresh, fabulous details. Her eyes were hazel green, a hodgepodge of yellow and brown and green. She smiled, a hard, knock-you-back-on-your-ass smile. Not a come-on. A back-off smile.

She whipped the glasses off, laid them on the table. "Yes?"

He wanted to glance around himself for the man trap with the spikes. "Um, ah . . . what can I get for you?" What, was he *stammering?*

Her chin rose. "What have you got?"

Highly inappropriate answers whirled through his mind, like a swarm of crazed bees. He bit down hard, forced himself to act professional. "The menu's reduced right now, since Zia Rosa's gone. Tonight, we're down to rice pudding, banana cream pie, coconut cream pie, cheesecake, and brownie sundaes. But all of them are great."

Her stare was unblinking. A gunslinger in a high-noon duel. "And this Zia Rosa has been gone for how long now?"

The question taxed his brain severely, since all his blood had pooled elsewhere. "Ah. Um, I don't know. Five weeks?"

"That's how old the desserts are? Or did she fill the freezer?"

He recoiled in outrage. "Hell, no! The desserts are made fresh, all the time!"

Those big eyes got even bigger. "Ooh, cut you to the quick, did I?" she murmured. "Made fresh by who?"

His chest puffed out. "By me."

Her eyes narrowed to glittering slits. "No way."

He bristled. "Way! Why would I lie?"

She propped her chin on her hand and gazed up. "To impress me?" she suggested. "To distinguish yourself from the anonymous, sweating, teeming masses?"

Bruno considered that. "I didn't know I was competing with any anonymous teeming masses, sweaty or otherwise," he said. "And I've never had to work that hard to impress girls."

"Hmm." The eyelashes swept down as she pondered her next jab. "So you prefer to hang out with girls who are easy to please?"

Her attitude was starting to piss him off. "And why would it be a bad thing to be easily pleased?"

The eyes opened, wide and innocent. "Did I say it was bad?"

He closed his mouth. "Never mind," he said. "I'm lost in the maze of this conversation, and I can't find my way out, so I'm bailing. But if I actually were going to try to impress a girl, the first clever ploy that would come to my mind would not be lies about pastry making."

"I see," she said. "Well, that really begs the question.

What clever ploy would be the first one to come to your mind? I'd love to hear it."

He thought about it, shook his head. "I don't step into holes in the ground that big," he said. "Certainly not at four in the morning after a long shift. I'll pass."

"Suit yourself." Her X-ray gaze bored into his head so intently he practically started to blush. "I just can't see a guy like you making grandma food like rice pudding or banana cream pie. Brownie sundaes, maybe, but . . . no. Not unless you're gay, of course. Are you gay?"

He let out a slow breath, biting the insides of his cheeks to keep from smiling. "I'm an excellent pastry chef. My pie crust is better than my Zia Rosa's. Come on back to the kitchen. I'll make a chocolate cream pie before your very eyes. I'll feed a piece of it to you by hand. And by the time I'm done, you're not going to be asking me if I'm gay anymore."

She cleared her throat, gaze darting down. "Is that so."

"It is," he said. "On your feet. Come on back to the kitchen. I mean it. I'm dead serious. It's pie time. And I am so ready for you."

She chewed on one side of her soft red lower lip, peeking up at him. Her fabulous if somewhat gummy black eyelashes were at mysterious half-mast. "Um, no thanks. I'm sure you're very good at it."

Her provocative tone was gone. Her voice was quiet.

Bruno folded his arms over his chest, flipping the order pad nervously against his arm. She backed down, but too soon. He hadn't worked his mad out yet. "What the hell did you mean by that, anyway?"

She blinked, innocently. "Mean by what?"

"A guy like me," he repeated. "What kind of guy is that? What do you think you know about me? You have no clue who I am."

It was like she'd taken off a mask. She looked completely different. "I'm sorry," she said. "You're right. I made assumptions based on your looks, which is really shallow, and I hate it when guys do that to me. I don't know anything about you. Except for what you tell me."

Wow. He ran a flash analysis to decide what conversational road to travel next. Time to shift gears. A peace offering, maybe. "What do you want to know?" he asked, rashly. "I'll tell you anything."

Something flickered in her eyes. Her chin went back up. Her gaze raked over his body, assessing him. "For starters, tell me how you can make banana cream pie and chocolate brownies in industrial quantities and still look like that. And don't tell me about the thirty hours a week in the gym, because I don't want to hear it."

So it was back to brittle flirting. Whatever. "OK, I won't tell you that," he said easily. "I've just got one of those metabolisms. I can eat anything, anytime, as much as I want, with extra whipped cream on it. I know girls hate that, but we all have our gifts."

He headed for the dessert counter, where he proceeded to dish up a big bowl of rice pudding, dusting it with cinnamon. Then a huge, quivering slice of banana cream pie. He poured them both some coffee, buzzed and jittery though he already was. He needed something to do with his hands, if she was actually ready to acknowledge his existence.

Or he'd find himself panting. Wagging. Or worse, babbling.

He laid the desserts on the table. Her crooked smile faltered a little when he boldly slid into the seat facing her, the better to hide his hard-on. None of the other customers needed attention. Just as well. He would have ignored them if they had.

The silence stretched out taut as she sipped her coffee. Strong, fresh French roast, with a shot of real cream, no sugar. She liked it just the way he liked it.

Strange, to be sitting here quietly with a woman who turned him on so much and not be trying to show her how interesting or fascinating or unique or solvent he was. That's what he would've done in the old days. He'd cooled down on that, after his recent notoriety following his adopted brother Kev's mortal duel with the evil zombie masters, the gun battles, the bombs. Tony's death. All that shit.

That whole crazy goatfuck had culminated in Bruno doing a perp walk along with Kev and Kev's newly discovered biological brothers, in handcuffs in front of local news crews. They were found to be innocent of wrongdoing, but they'd had an uncomfortable time of it for a while.

That had put a big crimp in his social schedule. No more of that "Portland's Most Eligible Bachelor" hoo-hah. Just as well. That shit got old. He'd tried to convince Zia Rosa to take down that cover of the *Portland Monthly* she'd put up in the diner after the mag had done that "most eligible" article about him. It embarrassed him now. But Zia Rosa liked his dimples in that picture, and Zia Rosa could not be reasoned with.

Something about the zombie duels, Tony's death, had changed him. He wasn't sure what, but he'd started to shut up occasionally. Not all the time, and not for too long, but he was now capable of keeping his yap trap shut for a few minutes at a time.

So if this woman wanted to know something about him, she could ask. He wasn't going to run the Bruno Ranieri promo spiel anymore.

He gestured toward the rice pudding. "I put cinnamon on it. Cancels out the cholesterol. Read about it on the *Men's Health* Web site."

Her lips twitched. "That's bullshit." She eyed the banana cream pie. "What cheap pop-science justification have you got for that one?"

He contemplated the pie. "Well, bananas are good for you. Lots of potassium, which helps you shed water weight, right? And there's no trans fats in the crust. I can promise you that."

"Yeah?" Her lips pursed, suppressing a smile. "So what is in it?"

He grinned wickedly. "Lard," he announced. "Artery clogging, cholesterol-laden pig fat. Hope you're not a vegetarian."

Her smile broke free, and it was fucking blow-your-mind dazzling gorgeous. "At least you're honest," she commented.

"Always," he said.

"I hate liars," she told him.

"I don't blame you," he replied. "I don't like them, either."

More sipping, more silence, considering each other. He felt like he was under a blazing light, being silently interrogated. Except that instead of being a bad, scary feeling, it was . . . well, exciting. Like he was laid out naked. On the altar. Before the goddess.

Rigid and ready to serve. Yeah.

She picked up a spoon, let it dangle from her fingertips like a pendulum. The bowl of the spoon swung toward him, a blurred gleam in the foreground. He stared at the triangular arrangement of freckles on the bulge of her tit behind it. Where his gaze was helplessly focused.

"I can't eat all of this," she informed him.

"Try," he urged. "I think your metabolism's just fine."

She held out the spoon. "You help."

His cock jumped at the implied intimacy of the invitation. "No," he said. "It's for you."

"It's too much," she said. "And I hate waste."

He took the spoon, reluctantly, and waited. "You first."

She went for the rice pudding first. Her soft, crimson lips parted slowly to accept the creamy mouthful, then contracted in eager surprise around the spoon. Her body went rigid with pleasure, her eyes softened in momentary bliss. Oh, man. He shifted on his seat to get some relief.

"Wow," she whispered. "You made that?"

No need to repeat himself. He just waited for her to try the pie.

She forked up the tip of the triangle and stared at it, while the waiting silence took on an electrical charge that was almost unbearable.

She put it in her mouth, closed her eyes, savored it. Her eyelids twitched as she inhaled, sharply. "Oh, my God. That is delicious."

Bruno sipped his coffee, trying not to look smug. "Told you."

"A guy could rack up big points for desserts like this."

He dipped his spoon into the rice pudding. It was damn good, if he did say so himself. Zia Rosa was a good teacher. "That's good news," he said. "What else racks up points with you? Give me a list." He whipped out his order pad and pen. "I'll take notes."

She looked down into her coffee. "Honesty," she said.

He'd been hoping for more sexy repartee, but if she wanted to take this to the next level, that was fine. "No worries. I do honesty."

She rolled her eyes. "No worries, my ass."

"What, have you picked out some liars recently?"

She scooped up another bite, her gaze evading his. "Either that, or it's all men who are lying rat bastards."

"I don't lie," he assured her. "Ask me anything. I'll tell you the uncensored, uncut truth. I swear."

"Yeah? So tell me what you're thinking right now."

He was taken aback by the challenge. "Ah . . ."

"Don't lie." Her voice snapped like a whip. "Or I'll know."

She would. He could tell. She was smart, she had the eye, the ear. And he was a piss-poor liar in the best of circumstances.

He let out a sigh. "Thinking isn't really the word for it."

"Use whatever words work for you."

He braced himself. "I was imagining having sex with

you," he confessed. "I have been since I first saw you three nights ago."

Her gaze was unflinching. "Oh. Really."

"Yeah. I would never have told you that if you hadn't compelled me by brute force. Certainly not before introducing ourselves."

"I already knew," she said, matter-of-factly. "And like I said, I do appreciate honesty." She stuck out her hand. "Lily Torrance."

He took her hand. It was cool, smooth, and something electric zinged through him at the contact. "Bruno Ranieri," he said.

Lily. She had a name, finally. It suited her. Flowers were beautiful, feminine, tender. But a lily was no humble flower. Lilies had attitude. They were regal, queenlike. They took no shit off anybody. They demanded respect, worship. Tall, sensual, starkly elegant, even haughty. Flowers for church altars. Flowers for a goddess.

But something was off with her. She was too good to be true. Something was wrong with this picture. He studied her luminous skin, wondering if she was jailbait, maybe. A runaway. "How old are you?"

"Twenty-nine," she said.

That was total crap. She looked fully ten years younger. He looked her over, frowning. "You fucking with me?"

"Right after we've been introduced?" She handed him the spoon. "For the love of God, stop me before I hurt myself. Eat some of this."

"I value honesty, too," he told her, scooping up banana custard.

She stopped in the act of licking whipped cream off her thumb, chin going up in frosty hauteur. "I'm not a liar."

"Then answer one for me," he said. "And don't lie."

"I won't lie, but I don't promise to answer."

"Whatever." He reached across the table and grabbed her hand. "Just tell me. What's wrong with this picture?"

She jerked, like she'd gotten a shock, and tried to yank her hand back. Bruno hung on, grimly. Her fingers squirmed in his.

"What the hell is that supposed to mean?" she snapped.

"I'm not sure," he said. "You tell me. It's just that something's off with you. You're hot, you're sexy, you're smart, you're fascinating, yeah. But something's wrong. So what's the problem?"

She retrieved her hand with a yank. "I don't have a problem."

"Ding, ding. Gotcha," he said quietly. "That's a lie."

The color faded from her face, making her makeup look even more startling. Her eyes dropped. She grabbed the napkin, made a fuss over wiping some sweet goop or other off her chin. He waited.

"Have you run away from home?" he asked.

A bitter laugh jerked out of her. "I wish," she muttered, not looking at him. "At the moment, I don't have one to run from."

"Well, that's a problem all of itself." He reached for her hand again. She whipped it off the table and hid it in her lap. "Did someone hurt you? Your husband, your ex-boyfriend? Something like that?"

"No. No, it's . . ." Her throat bobbed. "Really. I'm fine." Her voice vibrated with tension. "Just stop, please. Or I'll have to leave."

He sipped his coffee, giving her a moment to get over her freak-out before he tried again. "Is there something I can do?"

"About what?" she snapped.

"About your problem," he persisted. "Does somebody's ass need kicking? I can take care of that for you. I kick good ass."

Her laughter rang out, sweet and bright and gorgeous. "Wow," she said. "You'd do that for me? After, what has it been now, a fifteen-minute acquaintance? Twenty, maybe, tops?"

He considered that, and opened his mouth, and the raw, uncut, uncensored truth just plopped right out. "Yeah," he said. "I would."

Her mouth hung a little open for a moment, totally flustered. And apparently charmed. "Supposing there were a whole lot of asses?"

He shrugged. "Then I'd just have to kick them all."

"Wow," she said. "That's bold. Whiz, bang, and suddenly you're my champion. That's really sweet of you. Not smart, but sweet."

Bruno sipped his coffee and let his statement stand. But her words did something to him. Doors, opening up inside him, letting in light. Things lighting up from the inside, coming into focus.

He'd been dead serious. He really would kick ass for her.

And she was right. It wasn't smart. Not smart at all. But there it was.

He scooped up more rice pudding, covered his embarrassment with chatter. Quick, before he turned red. "So what else can I be honest about? Any other secrets you want to know about the male mind?"

She rolled her eyes, snorting. "Never mind the male mind. Men are mostly dogs and pigs. Tell me about you."

"Tell you what?"

"Start at the beginning," she said. "And keep it simple."

"Not much to tell," he said. "I was born in Newark. Spent the first twelve years of my life there."

"Parents?" she asked crisply.

"I was raised mostly by my Uncle Tony and my Zia Rosa here in Portland," he said.

"And before, in Newark? Who raised you then?"

He flinched away from the question. "It's your turn, isn't it?"

"Who said we were taking turns?" She wound her fingers together and rested her chin on them. "You've evaded my question twice. Not very skillfully, but that means you're starting down the slippery slope toward dishonesty. So give up the goods."

He blew out the tension with a sharp sigh. "I don't know who my father was. I was a bastard. My mother never told me. Her family was ashamed of me, so it was just the two of us. She raised me alone."

She looked startled. "Ah. Um—"

"My mother was murdered by her fuckhead scum of a boyfriend when I was twelve. That was when I left Newark. I don't have anything else to say about Newark. If you don't mind."

Her eyes dropped. "No," she said. "I don't mind."

Another charged silence went on and on. He realized that she had absolutely no intention of breaking it. It was up to him.

What the fuck. He just went for it. "I didn't mean to be evasive," he said. "I was just really enjoying the conversation with you. And a piece of information like that is a real conversation stopper. It's like throwing a bomb on the table. Big downer."

Her lips looked tight. She wouldn't meet his eyes.

He sighed. Oh well. So much for this one. You win some, you lose some. Time to swallow the bitter pill of reality and get back to work.

He let the spoon drop and slid across the booth seat to get up.

She snagged his wrist. "I'm sorry I jerked you around," she said, her voice husky. Long, chipped black nails dug into the skin of his wrist like kitten claws. "And I'm sorry about your mom," she added, timidly.

He sat back down on the seat, silently jubilant. "What about my dad?" he asked. "Aren't you sorry about him, too?"

Her mouth curved. "What for? Fuck him. He provided the best of himself and disappeared before he could do any more damage. We've already established that men are dogs and pigs, right?"

"Most men," he said. He rolled his hand around beneath hers until he could clasp her hand from below. The contact was giving his palm a gazillion little mini-orgasms. "The day-shift guy will be here in about twenty-five minutes," he said. "Want to go out, take a walk? I'll tell you more about the awful, horrifying truth about men. Stuff you'll never learn in *Cosmo*. You could write a book. If you're interested."

"Strangely enough," she said. "I think I am."

5

Lily feigned not to see the smile he blazed at her before he went off about his business. Razzle-dazzle. The man was dangerous, but for none of the reasons she'd expected. She'd been through hell the last few weeks, but who'd think it to look at her? Giggling. Simpering. Fluttering, for God's sake. She must be suffering from hormonally induced brain damage to be acting this way. Hey, what's mortal danger next to a superlative piece of man meat, right?

Not that she could characterize Bruno Ranieri as meat. Far from it. He was special. He blew her mind, or what little was left of it, after the stress of the last six weeks. And she'd thought writing papers for cheating students had been stressful. Try life as a penniless fugitive.

Her first thought, during that dazed subway ride to nowhere, had been to go to the police, but something blocked her. A sense of looming danger, pervasive as a bad smell. The bad guys had been following her, listening to her. They'd known she was going to Nina's for dinner. And Nina's address. They'd murdered Howard and covered it up so easily.

No. No police. She was on her own. She scooped up more rice pudding, and her eyes dropped to the red scar curved across her forearm. She adjusted her arm to hide the wound. She probably should have worn long sleeves, but she didn't have many wardrobe options.

She was lucky she hadn't gotten tetanus. She'd bought gauze and disinfectant, and mopped up in a Starbucks bathroom, keenly aware of how much emergency rooms cost after all of Howard's near suicides. It would cost hundreds of bucks to get her cut stitched. Plus, anyone who could terrify Howie into silence, murder him the same day he broke that silence, and then put out an instant contract on her had the resources to watch emergency rooms. And cop shops.

Besides, what could cops do? Give her an armed guard? Send her to a safe house? Please. She was of no use to anyone. She wasn't poised to testify against a big mob boss. She'd end up filling out a report, and then she'd go home alone, and sit there, shivering. Waiting for the door to rattle, the window to shatter. Until it did.

So she'd stopped at a bank, taken as big a cash advance as her credit card would allow, bought a floppy hat, sunglasses, an oversized jacket. Caught a night bus for Philly at the Port Authority. She remembered the address of a women's shelter there, a relic from those nights when Nina used to rope her into volunteering to man the hotline.

Her cut and bruises corroborated her story about a jealous boyfriend attacking her with a knife. It got her a place to sleep, an offer of crisis counseling. But she couldn't tell those people anything, either. No more than she could call Nina. She'd put them in danger, too.

She'd run, as soon as she dared. She'd been running ever since.

She ached to call Nina, tell her friend she was safe. But she had to assume that they'd monitor Nina's snail mail, e-mail, landline, cell.

Besides. She wasn't safe. So why lie? Why say anything?

She didn't even know where to begin. She was so small and clueless, and her opponent so huge and mysterious. But Howard had given her a starting place. He'd paid for it with his life, too. So that cryptic clue had to mean something to somebody.

Magda Ranieri and her death were connected to this mess. God alone knew how. Or maybe, just maybe, her son Bruno knew.

Bruno walked by, flashed another mind-melting smile. She smiled back before she could stop herself. *Hard to get*, she reminded herself.

She'd done what research she could. Magda Ranieri had been murdered in 1993, in Newark, New Jersey. Her obit had stated that she was survived by her mother, Giuseppina Ranieri, and her son, Bruno Ranieri. No further mention of her murderer being found or prosecuted. No speculation as to why she'd been killed. That was as much as Lily had been able to glean from the library newspaper archives.

But Bruno might have a clue. He was supposed to "lock it," whatever "it" could conceivably be. So he must know what "it" was. And by association, who "they" were. What "they" wanted. Right?

Her search ended here, in Tony's Diner, where she ran up against a wall with a splat. Because asking Bruno if he had a clue was not a simple matter. In fact, it was flat out unthinkable. She pictured it.

Nice to meet you, Bruno! I've been stalking you for a while now. Someone is trying to kill me, and I think this is somehow related to the most traumatic event of your entire childhood, so would you please tell all the details of your mother's brutal murder to a complete stranger?

Right. Talk about a conversation stopper.

She'd considered just telling the truth, begging for his help, but she couldn't risk a flat "no." Or worse, a *get the hell away from me, or I'll get a restraining order.* Which was what she herself would have said, in her former life, if someone approached her with a request like that.

She had no other leads. She had to be sneaky, get close to him, gain his trust. That was the plan. But the perfectly defined shape of the guy's ass wiped her hard drive clean like a powerful magnet. This lust attack was so unlike her usual modality with the male sex, which was mostly fear and loathing. The men she'd hooked up with so far had been good for one thing only, and even that only on alternate bank holidays that happened to coincide with a blue moon.

She forked up another banana cream oral orgasm. She'd eaten more than half of both desserts. One would think running for one's life would be a real slimmer-downer, but no, disillusioned again. On the run meant convenience stores, bus stations, hot dogs, Mickey Dee's, pizza slices. It meant zero access to a decent kitchen, a stocked refrigerator, or any sort of vegetable. It meant all carbs, all the time. It meant desperate sugar compensation for loneliness and fear.

And here she was, compounding her sins with two desserts. The wretched man had not done his part in saving her from her own greed.

Bruno hadn't been hard to find. His business had a big, fancy interactive Web site. He was smeared all over Facebook and other social media. For God's sake, there was a magazine cover with his gorgeous, grinning face on it, framed and hanging right there in the diner. She'd read the article from the *Portland Monthly* probably a dozen times. It was one of the first hits she'd made on the Internet when she'd begun to research him. It was all out there on a silver platter, for anyone who wanted to know about him.

All except for the info that she needed. The monsters in his closet.

In any case, she was following him now for all the wrong reasons. Which was to say, just to get a better look. To see if it was a trick of the light, or if he really was that criminally hot. To check out that perfect build. Not swollen gym-rat bulk, which she abhorred, but sinewy, trim perfection. Pantherish power in his long legs, his defined thighs. The jut of his butt made her want to just sink her nails into his ass and palpate the wedges of muscle in his back with a feral squeal of delight.

Three nights ago, she'd risked The First Approach. She'd steeled herself for the close-up reality. Bad breath, enlarged pores, body odor, anything. She almost hoped for a fatal flaw, just to break the spell.

Nope. No flaws. The guy was perfect. She'd had to grit her teeth and look away when he took her order, and remind herself to breathe.

Information flooded in even while ignoring him. That big barrel chest. His black hair, buzzed very close, would be curly if he allowed it to be, but he was having none of that. His heavy-lidded Italian eyes were the velvet brown of rum truffles dusted in fine cocoa. His biceps distended the sleeves of a crisp white T-shirt. The sweeping pattern of body hair against sinewy golden forearms, the pattern of veins, tendons, the shape of his hands, it practically hypnotized her. And his smell. A knee-weakening blend of tapioca, coffee beans, and dish soap.

Fortunately, being speechless was part of the plan. She'd given a lot of thought to his handling, once she'd gotten a grip on his strange schedule, which did not include sleep. Fortunately, her schedule didn't include sleep, either. She'd broken it down. Fact: Any guy that fine-looking had to think he was God's gift. Therefore, frigid indifference was the way to go. It was guaranteed to pique his ego, spark his curiosity.

Of course, the corollary to this was that she herself had to be a stunning sex goddess. Yow. A tall order, on her budget.

Beauty and glamour were expensive, financially and emotionally. A constant I'm-so-smokin'-hot vibe took a lot of vital energy to project and maintain.

But she was highly motivated. She really wanted to live.

She had lots of practice at frigid indifference, but tonight she was bombing on it, big-time. She couldn't stop peeking at the sexy beard shadow that accented the angle of his jaw. Those jutting cheekbones, the creases of twin dimples. The throbbing force field of his sexual energy, bumping up against her personal space.

This crush was just a distraction her mind had grappled onto so that she didn't have to think about how lonely she was, how scared. So she wouldn't have one of her stress freak-outs, or start to obsess about Howard and his shard of glass. It was much less painful to obsess about Ranieri's luscious bod instead, and mull over The Approach.

Her problem was, once she'd hooked his attention, she wasn't quite sure what to do with it. Aside from the screamingly obvious.

She tried to breathe. She needed to get close to him. There was a tried and true way. Though sex did not necessarily mean closeness.

Ranieri was neither married nor engaged. Slut or no slut, there she drew the line. She supposed she could try to strike up a friendship, but how the hell was that even done? Like she had time to join his health club, chat him up at the juice bar, run into him at the bookstore. That kind of thing was so vague, so random. It could take years.

She didn't have years. She was going insane, treading water. Cocktail waitressing under the table, crashing at a squalid downtown youth hostel. Carrying her netbook everywhere because she had no safe place to leave it. Always looking over her shoulder for the guys in the SUV. Because eventually, they'd find her, and shove her into the back of their car, and skewer her. It was just a matter of time.

She had to find out what Bruno Ranieri knew, now. Ergo, they had to become best buddies, fast. Seducing a guy was a simple, step-by-step process that she could wrap her imagination around.

She would sacrifice her, well, call it virtue, for lack of a better word, in exchange for her life. She'd do penance later. If she had a later.

Then she saw his dimples, his ass, his eyes. Smelled his scent. She'd had that provocative, intimate conversation that she had actually started to enjoy. And suddenly, she couldn't remember what she was trying to accomplish anymore. Her agenda just flopped on its head.

She watched Bruno pour coffee for a guy hunched at the bar, and scraped up the last of her rice pudding. Wow. She was officially taking this to the next level, after a fifteen-minute conversation. She had to keep it light, playful, but how? Her hands shook. No, correction. Her whole body shook. He was going to notice that. It was hard to miss.

For God's sake. The man was not scary. In fact, he seemed really sweet. Who'd have thought that Dudley Do-Right vibe could be so arousing? Her champion, indeed. And he made a wicked banana cream pie, too. What a honey bear. A kissable, squeezable, positively lickable—

Cool it. She pressed her hand to her mouth, until her teeth bruised the inside of her lip. She could wait, of course. But for what? To get pissed off at him, and then alienate him with her hostility? This being as inevitable as springtime, death or taxes. Considering her track record with men.

Bruno glanced over. His dimples deepened the grooves bracketing his mouth. Something expanded in her chest, hot and breathless.

Worse yet, she could fall in love with the guy. God help her.

He pointed at the clock, held up five fingers. She clenched her thighs. Realized, to her dismay, that she was already wet. Her brain buzzed around in tight, frantic little circles. And the rest of her ignored her brain utterly and just kept staring at Bruno Ranieri. Salivating.

Wanting him for his own sake. Wanting to feel the way he made her feel. So alive. Burning with life force. Fierce, vital, hungry. Hopeful.

No rule says you have to fuck the guy, a dry voice in her mind said. *At least not until you know him better. He offered to help you. Protect you, even. How sweet. You have options.*

Shut up, she told the voice. She didn't want to think about her options right now. Her brain wasn't functioning anyway.

She might as well use the parts of her that were still operational.

The elegant young man dressed in a crisp white dress shirt and figure-hugging black trousers took away the cheese and fruit plate without making a sound. He presented new wine goblets, poured a new wine.

Neil King spared him an appraising glance, pegging him in time and vintage. Had the briefest of blank moments before retrieving the boy's name from his memory banks. Julian. Yes, that was it. Seventeen or so. Coming along nicely, if he was trusted to serve King a late supper.

Julian was one of King's special series trainees. His gaze lingered on the boy's height, the line of his jaw, his dimples. Handsome. And admirably self-possessed. Often the young, inexperienced ones got nervous and clumsy in King's presence. He found it annoying.

Today, he was in a benevolent mood and giving his full attention to Zoe, the young woman across the table. She'd earned it for her smooth handling of the Howard Parr affair. Or her part of it, anyway. It was not her fault the rest of it had gone so unexpectedly sour.

Zoe was one of his oldest operatives, from his first crop. In fact, she was the only one left alive of her pod. The cull rate had been much higher in the old days. It was impossible to pinpoint her exact age, since she had been scooped out of the slums of Rio de Janeiro as a toddler, in contrast to his younger trainees, who had begun their training in utero. Zoe had no last name, no birth certificate. Despite the deprivations of her early childhood, she'd shaped up beautifully. And like all his operatives, she was invisible, ready to assume any identity convenient to him. She was his, body and soul.

He'd kept Zoe waiting for this debrief dinner for almost four hours, primped and ready. It had been a busy day, and it was well past midnight, but when he finally walked into his private dining room, she'd leaped up in barely controlled delight.

Ah, yes. Control had always been Zoe's issue. Even so, he was cautiously pleased with her. Babysitting Howard had not been an easy assignment, requiring specialized training and years of tedious undercover work at Aingle Cliffs. But things had ended well. When Lily Parr institutionalized her father, he'd been very tempted to have Howard put down then and there. But something held him back. He hated to go back on a decision. And Howard was truly cowed. And a hit should always be matter of last resort. King wasn't a hamfisted Mafia thug, even if he was compelled to do business with them. He conducted his affairs with more delicacy than that. The extra cost was worth it.

Howard had been committed shortly after Zoe had almost bungled one of her assignments. She'd been in disgrace and in need of a long, teeth-grinding purgatory. What better than babysitting Howard? It was static, boring, possibly endless. Just the thing to teach Zoe a lesson in control while she put in the hours of hard reprogramming time.

His scheme had paid off. He had salvaged a multimillion dollar investment. Zoe had been patient, vigilant. She had executed her orders flawlessly, with only a few minutes' lead time. No one at Aingle Cliffs suspected foul play. He'd analyzed the issue of the word-rec bot and had judged that the technical delay had not been altogether Zoe's fault. Equipment failure. It was impossible to anticipate everything.

He studied her with pleasure as she chattered blithely on. She was giving him too much detail, but he was not inclined to be harsh. He lifted his eyes from contemplation of her décolleté—bony, but the lush swell of bosom was appealing, surgically enhanced though it probably was; he didn't remember from her file. And her gold skin tone and lush lips were lovely. He lifted his gaze to her animated face.

". . . thing that I was concerned about was my physiological responses, right after the job," she confided earnestly. "I tried, but I couldn't control my heart rate or my body temperature, and I started to sweat. It didn't affect my performance, but still . . . I've been doing the Group XIII Advanced KAM Biofeedback course again, both the A and B sections, but I wondered if you had any other suggestions for—"

"I'll tailor a new program for you personally," he said.

She flushed with delight. "Oh," she breathed. "I . . . I wasn't thinking that you should . . . I just—"

"I would be pleased," he told her. "I would consider it an investment well worth the time and thought."

"Oh, thank you!" she gushed. "It's the one thing I feel uneasy about, and I was hoping to find a permanent solution. In a way, the excess emotion came in handy, when it came time to discover the body. I needed to have a huge emotional reaction, so I channeled it all there."

She was over-congratulating herself, but he would let it pass. "Of course," he said. "Well, my dear. There you go. Balance is key, and positive attitude as well. You took what you thought was a weakness and turned it into a strength. Brava."

His phone made a discreet burble at that moment, while Zoe carried charmingly on about how she didn't want to waste his valuable time. The ring tone was muted, chosen not to be intrusive or irritating, but when he looked at the name on the display, he was irritated. Reggie. From his first special-series pod. He was so angry with Reggie. He gave Zoe a dismissive gesture that shut up her babble. "Yes?" he said into the phone.

"We've located Lily Parr." Reggie's voice was flat, but there was an underlying tension that hinted at relief. As if he thought by redressing his mistake, he'd be off the hook. How innocent of him.

"Really," King said. "Where?"

"Tony Ranieri's diner, in Portland."

"Ah." King made his voice crystal sharp. "So they have already made contact. You were not able to prevent that from happening."

"No," Reggie admitted. "They're together now. Inside."

King made the adjustment for the time difference. It was early morning in Oregon. "And are you there physically?"

"No," Reggie said, after an infinitesimal pause. "I'm driving from Seattle. But I'm close. I've sent people. Tom, Cal, Martin, and Nadia."

Oh, God. King stifled a groan. Cal, Reggie, and Nadia were all special series. He would not have chosen to bunch those three on this particular assignment, but it was too late. There were no other operatives close enough to replace them. "How did you find her?"

"It was a word-recognition app we rigged at Ranieri's diner. We got the signal about a half an hour ago. She was talking with Ranieri there, and some key words popped up. The bot caught them, and, ah . . ."

"A bot? A word-recognition app? You've been conducting a *passive* surveillance on Bruno Ranieri? With Lily Parr on the loose?"

Reggie struggled to reply. "I, ah . . . I had people following him for four weeks straight," he explained. "Then we decided to shift the focus of our search, so I redistributed manpower, and we—"

"Do you have a visual?" His voice chopped off the puling excuses.

"I will in a few minutes. I have people arriving in less than—"

"Is his car under surveillance?"

"Of course. Car, condo, diner, his business, everywhere," Reggie assured him. "Everything he says has been snarfed and sifted. He hasn't tripped the word-rec bots once since we rigged them. Until now."

"Don't trust those apps so blindly, Reggie," King lectured. "They're no substitution for human intelligence. Though you yourself might give that theory a run for its money."

He paused, waited for Reggie to come up with a reply.

Reggie coughed, hemmed and hawed miserably, until King's patience came to an abrupt end. He did not want to kill Bruno Ranieri. Yet. Not while there was still a chance to eliminate the danger of exposure that sneaky bitch Magda had threatened him with, years ago.

He loathed loose ends. Lily and Bruno could solve the puzzle Magda had set, tie those ends off for him, close that issue definitively.

But those two could not be out there loose, in circulation. Not now that they'd made contact. "Take them, and bring them to me," he said. "Do not injure them. And don't make any more mistakes."

"Sir, we've done all we could since she vanished, and we—"

"We? What's this 'we'? You were in charge, Reginald. You were team leader. Take responsibility. Say 'I.' It's what you would have done if things had gone as they goddamn well should have. Am I right?"

"But we . . . ah, but I—"

"One girl, alone," King mused. "No weapons but a can of Mace. And she evaded two of my agents, with their incredible training, their bottomless budget, their limitless resources.

For forty-two days. Do not expect a pat on the back for fixing this. Be grateful to stay alive."

King closed the connection, remembering Zoe's presence. Her eyes were speculative over the rim of her wineglass.

"So they found her," she said softly. "At last."

"At last," he said. "In Portland, at Ranieri's diner. Unbelievable incompetence. After decades of intensive training. So disappointing."

Zoe preened, perceiving the criticism of her peers, by reverse association, as a compliment to her. He decided to encourage the impression. It was a delicate balancing act, the application of carrot and stick. His elite cadre of operatives were spectacular specimens, but they required deft handling. Zoe had been a good girl. This time.

"I told them that Lily Parr was unusual," Zoe mused. "She struck me as extremely capable. Perhaps I didn't state it strongly enough. It was in the file. I made a report after every one of her visits."

"I should have sent you after her," he said. "Not those idiots."

Zoe's bare shoulders twitched in a modest shrug. "Reggie isn't an idiot," she murmured. "And I could only be in one place at one time."

"Pity," he said. "Your performance was truly exceptional."

Her face glowed. He became aware of a pleasant tingling sensation. He hadn't been consciously planning sexual indulgence in this debriefing session—in fact, he very rarely indulged, being naturally ascetic. But Zoe deserved a treat. He could exert himself for her.

He took pains not to consider his agents as sexual objects. It seemed extravagant to utilize an instrument in which he had invested tens of millions, decades of his life, for what amounted to a plumbing task that could be performed by a call girl for a few hundred dollars.

But Zoe's eyes were dilated. Her bosom heaved. She had emotional and physiological control issues, his critical diagnostic eye could not help but note. But now wasn't the time to scold her for them.

Zoe was as skilled as any courtesan, and he'd worked all his life to inculcate her fervid desire to please him. No call girl could provide that, no matter what she was paid. Since toddlerhood Zoe had been immersed in DeepWeave programming, a virtual world that was a product of his own psychological and pharmacological genius. Designed to augment and develop certain characteristics, and suppress others. Entirely free of any inconvenient ethical or moral oversight.

His experiments hadn't always worked out, but they had worked often enough for the project as a whole to be considered a resounding success. He had a winning recipe, now. After much trial and error.

Zoe's lashes fluttered. "May I ask a question?"

He chuckled. "I may not answer, but you can always ask."

"Why did you wait so long, sir?" she asked, eyes wide. "To finish Howard and the girl, and Bruno Ranieri?"

The question was not an unreasonable one, since Zoe might well end up replacing Reginald as team leader, tonight's results pending.

But she was not yet entitled to the whole truth. He lifted his glass, smiling. "Let us talk about you, my dear."

She flushed in embarrassment at her overstep. "Yes, of course. Please excuse me. I just wanted to be up to date, so that I'll be—"

"Ready to serve?" he supplied silkily. "Oh, but I have no doubt that you will be, my dear."

His throaty tone made her brown eyes dilate to pools of black.

Julian served their panna cotta, set out tiny cups of espresso.

"You may go," Neil told him.

Julian vanished. Zoe stirred a spoonful of sugar into her

coffee. He listened to the sputter of the candles while Zoe's heavy lashes swept low over her flushed cheeks, fluttering, shadowing the perfect curve.

"Shall I, ah, lock the door?" She sounded hesitant, girlish.

The glow upped to a throb. "No one here is stupid enough to open that door. And if they are, their death will be no great loss to us."

She giggled and rose to her feet, stumbling. Performance anxiety. She peeked, to see if he'd caught it. He smiled, letting her know that, of course, he had. But it was all right. No one was perfect. And with his help, she'd come closer to perfection than any other human creature.

But there was always room for improvement. Effort. Striving.

Her breath sped up. Her excitement was very real. He was an attractive man, youthful for his late fifties. Trim, fit, and strong. Aware of how attractive the mantle of immense wealth and power he wore was to women. Men, too, of course, but he'd never been so inclined, aside from some insignificant adventures involving drugs and group sex, back in his wild youth. The idea of using drugs in such a haphazard way now filled him with disgust. Drugs were an instrument of such power, such precision. Not to be flailed around like berserker idiots with a battle ax.

She took an unsteady step in his direction.

"The dress," he said.

She glanced down, artful locks of hair dangling around her face as she reached to struggle with her zipper. Bosom straining. The dress dropped, slowed by the lush curve of her hips, then fell around her ankles. She was naked beneath it, clad only in stiletto-heeled sandals and diamond drop earrings. The earrings were a gift given to all his female agents upon the occasion of their first outside assignment. The girls all treasured their earrings. Her breasts were full, high, and perfect. Her pubis was trimmed to a delicate swatch, as carefully shaped as an eyebrow. Her musculature was almost overly defined. Lean, taut.

King scooped the plates with their uneaten dessert carelessly to one side with his arm. "Put your foot up on the table," he demanded.

Zoe did so. He studied the elegant foot, nude in the scarlet peep toe. Her nails were lacquered a savage scarlet that matched her parted lips. Her eyes were heavy lidded, breasts heaving. She teetered on the single stiletto heel. The table wobbled, wineglasses trembling.

He did not steady her. She had to learn control.

"Do you want me to say it?" he crooned.

Her eyelids fluttered wildly. She sucked in a gasping breath. "Y-y-yes," she quavered. "P-p-please."

She shuddered, leg quivering as he slid his hand up the inside of her thigh, teasing his finger along the tender seam of her vulva. She was hot, damp, slick. He parted her naked, hairless labia, and thrust his fingers sharply into her slippery depths.

A sound came out of her that did not please him. Too strident. Zoe was an instrument that needed constant calibration. Perhaps he could make a tiny adjustment on her maintenance meds to make her more steady, more consistent. But he didn't want to dull her edge.

He would have to give the matter some thought.

Penetration was not strictly necessary to give her what she needed. His voice alone would suffice. In fact, he could perform this service for her over the phone, from another continent. He often gave remote rewards to his agents in the field, both male and female.

But not tonight. Tonight, he wanted to feel wet heat. Rippling contractions clutching his fingers as he exercised his power over her.

"Now?" he prompted.

Tears streaked with mascara streamed down her face. She could barely gasp out the word. "P-p-please."

He smiled, stroking her clitoris with his thumb, and recited one of the phrases that had been assigned to her. A verse of ancient Aramaic, from the Old Testament. His current criteria was that the code be in a dead language from a text at least eight hundred years old.

With each line, her tension tightened. She shook so violently, he was sure she would fall, or at least knock over the table. But she held together, stayed on her feet. On the final line, the wave crested. She threw her head back, shrieking as the climax wrenched through her.

Zoe swayed, staying upright by some miracle. She was flushed, damp with sweat. She sobbed silently. "I can't help it," she quavered.

He withdrew his hand from her body and wiped it with the snow white linen dinner napkin. "You'll learn," he assured her.

He considered what to do with her next, stroking his penis. He was erect, but it had been a long day. Intercourse was so strenuous.

Fellatio was a pleasant alternative. He tugged her until she sank to her knees. Buried his hands in her hair as she worked on the opening of his trousers. He'd just settled back into the experience and was admiring the inspiring spectacle of Zoe's full lips fastened around his penis when a knock sounded on the door. They froze, astonished.

Zoe's eyes went wide at this unheard-of presumption.

"Who is it?" he snarled.

"Sir, it's Julian." The boy's voice was tight with apology. "Please excuse me, sir, but Michael Ranieri is here to see you."

Oh, for God's sake. A hiss of annoyance escaped from between his teeth. He gestured for Zoe to get up, and tucked himself back into his trousers with a peevish glance at the clock. One twenty-seven A.M., what an ungodly time to show up. But Michael Ranieri was the one person on earth who could demand to be seen by King. Let alone at this hour.

Dealing with this thick-headed goon grew ever more intolerable. It bothered him that Michael Ranieri fancied himself King's equal.

Their fortunes had been linked since they'd met in college. Neil King's brilliance at cooking up recreational drugs and Michael Ranieri's huge appetite for them had guaranteed a long and profitable association. King bankrolled his graduate studies with the business that Michael provided, and with King's help, Michael Ranieri had slowly transformed his family's traditional mafioso prostitution and extortion rackets, and evolved the family business into something new. Michael was now acting head of the Ranieri family, marketing much-sought-after, limited-edition designer drugs that King created exclusively for him.

The net of avid users was ever expanding. As were the profits.

Even so, King always knew that he was destined for more than fueling the ego fantasies of the very rich. His dream was not merely to synthesize drugs that make people feel perfect. No, that fell far short.

He wanted to synthesize true perfection. In a human being. To actually improve on the normal human blueprint, with all its inherent flaws. A human was a haphazard rough draft. It needed molding. Careful, mindful sculpting, with an eye toward towering profit.

His project had grown and flowered into something extraordinary over the years. Zoe was a shining example. Arousal made her literally glow in the dark. His body hummed with frustrated sexual desire.

His operatives now made more money out in the field than Michael Ranieri ever dreamed of, discreetly shaping the history of the world while earning billions in fees. And every last cent belonged to King.

But this was none of Michael's business. The man knew of King's private creative project, in a vague way, but wasn't bright enough to grasp the true scope of King's work. So why burden him with it?

Zoe was pulling her dress back on. He held up his hand. "No, my dear. Stay exactly as you are."

The dress dropped. She straightened, ribcage tilted to show off her breasts to the best advantage as Julian pushed open the doors. He took note of Zoe's nudity and gave them a look that implored forgiveness before stepping aside to admit Michael Ranieri.

Michael was tall, stocky, in his fifties, like King, and blessed with the swarthy good looks that graced most of the Ranieri clan. He opened his mouth to complain. It froze open when he saw Zoe. Whatever he had been meaning to complain about evaporated from his mind.

King's mouth twitched. Michael was so predictable.

The man cleared his throat. "Ah . . . did I interrupt anything?"

Such a stupid, annoying question. King gave him a friendly smile. "Oh, nothing that won't keep and be perfectly enjoyable later. To what do I owe the pleasure of this visit, Michael? And at this unusual hour?"

"Can I speak in front of . . . ?" He pointed at Zoe.

"I trust Zoe absolutely," King said. Zoe's eyes shone with delight.

Michael flapped his hand. "I was at my father's eightieth birthday party," he said fretfully. "I couldn't get away until late. They've been busting my balls the whole past month. Ever since we heard about Parr killing himself in the nuthouse."

King's mouth tightened. "So sad, isn't it?"

"Hah." Michael snorted. "The only reason Howard Parr would die, and his daughter go missing, is because he talked. So did he talk?"

Every now and then, Michael showed a brief flash of inconvenient intelligence. "I'm taking care of it, Michael," King said.

"Oh, fuck," Michael snarled. "So he did talk. So, this Parr girl, what was her name, Lily? Is she dead? Tell me she's dead, Neil."

"I said, I'm taking care of it."

Michael threw his hands in the air. "That's just great. So she's on the loose, looking for Bruno Ranieri? You do remember that you can't touch Bruno. You know what would happen to us if you did, right?"

King sighed. "I'm not planning on killing them," he lied smoothly.

"So it's true, then? You were the one who did Howard?"

King gestured at Zoe, giving credit where it was due. "She did."

Zoe preened, displaying her perfect naked self with a queenly nonchalance that made Michael Ranieri tug at his collar.

King caught Zoe's eye, made a twirling gesture with his fingertip. Zoe gave him a smoky smile and spun on the balls of her feet. She did a three-sixty, and another half turn, placing her hands against the wall. Arching her back, legs parted. Oh, that naughty, slutty, clever girl.

Michael jerked his hypnotized regard away from Zoe's ass and shook himself like a wet dog. "So. About Bruno. You remember—"

"The famous letter, yes. More than a year has passed since Tony Ranieri was killed. They haven't sent it yet. Why are you so nervous?"

"Because Lily Parr is on the loose!" Michael yelled. "And if Howard spilled the beans to her, and she tells Bruno, then you're going to want to make a move, right? But if you do, we take it up the ass, Neil! Rosa Ranieri is a jealous bitch who'll fuck us just for spite!"

"Italian families," King said softly. "So colorful. Cousinly love."

"Second cousins." Michael stressed the distinction.

"They're only second cousins. And they're poison. I was the one that opened Tony's package twenty years ago, Neil, remember? With the severed fingers?"

King made his voice soothing, reasonable. "Michael, please. Think about it. Will anyone really care about that letter, after all these years?"

"Fuck, yes, they'll care! Didn't you hear about Sonny Franzese? He was put away at fucking ninety-three! I do not want my father to go to prison, Neil! He's eighty years old! And he's not well!"

It was clear from Michael's wine-flushed face that he was under the impression that this was all somehow King's problem. But now was perhaps not exactly the moment to make this clear. Perhaps Zoe could deliver the message some dark night. With a long knife.

And in the meantime, Zoe could also provide some badly needed distraction. "Zoe, my dove," he said. "Pour Michael a glass of wine."

Zoe obliged. Michael stared at her breasts, his face going hot and lumpish with lust. "Is she one of your, uh . . ." He trailed off, took the wine, his limited vocabulary failing him. "Will she, uh—"

"Do anything I ask?" King finished softly. "Yes, Michael. She will."

Michael gulped wine, staring. His erection was painfully evident.

King sighed, yielding to the inevitable. After all, Zoe was not made of soap. And at least this way, Michael could do the requisite grunting and sweating. King needed only to lean back and do the honors, reciting Zoe's reward codes. "Would you care to partake?" he offered politely.

Michael's eyes flashed. "Don't mind if I do. Is there a room—"

"Right here. I need to be close to her, so I can use her codes."

"Codes? What the fuck? You mean, do her right in front of you?" Michael shook his head. "That's sick, Neil. We're not eighteen anymore."

"The code gives her orgasms more powerful than anything you've ever felt," King coaxed. "Quite a sensation, for the man on the inside."

Michael's face reddened. "It's just too fucking kinky weird for me."

For Zoe's sake, King pulled out the book that held his sex drugs and selected a performance enhancer from the pages of transdermal dots. He stuck the dot on the inside of his business partner's wrist.

"Uh?" Michael stared at the green dot, suspiciously. "What's this?"

"A token of my esteem." King gestured at Zoe. "Feel free."

Zoe turned, bracing herself against the table and arching her perfect buttocks invitingly. Michael unfastened his pants, whipped out his stiff member. He took the plunge, with a piglike snort of satisfaction.

King sat down across from Zoe, gave her hand an encouraging pat, and recited another of her reward verses. She was squealing with pleasure in less than twenty seconds, shuddering with waves of delight as Michael pumped away heavily behind her, huffing and grunting.

Unpleasantly noisy, but King steeled himself and soldiered on.

6

Dawn was near, and the chick with the cat-eye specs was going for a walk with him. Or whatever that metaphorically entailed. Bruno's brain churned out a dizzying series of pornographic possibilities.

Down, boy. A walk is just a walk is just a walk.

That stern directive buzzed in Bruno's head like radio interference as he muscled his way through the rest of his shift.

This was way more than a walk. Everything about Lily was more than what it seemed. She had problems. He could smell them. He'd had plenty of trouble in his life. He'd started young, and he hadn't stopped yet. But her trouble vibe wasn't putting him off. Nope. On the contrary.

That was twisted. Sicko. Or at the very least, really, really stupid.

He was too wound up. He could feeling it coming over him, the perilous urge to babble. It was a self-defense mechanism, he figured. Consider his family. Silent lumps on a log, every one of them. Tony had just grunted orders and growled obscenities. Zia Rosa had mostly smacked him with a spoon and screeched Calabrese dialect. And Kev hadn't talked at all for the first year Bruno had known him, after Bruno came from Newark to live with Tony. He'd been too brain damaged.

Even now that Kev had gotten his life fixed, vanquished the evil zombie masters, found his biological family, and was wallowing in true love, he was no chatterbox. Nah, that was Bruno's God-given job.

Bruno took a peek at the outside thermometer. The coat crumpled on the booth seat next to Lily was too thin for this weather. He could get her into his car, he supposed. Turn on the chair heater. Let her inhale the scent of new leather upholstery. His car was made for seduction.

But he'd said a walk. A walk would keep him honest. His condo was across town, so he couldn't walk her to his home, bullshit central. The babe lair. The whole place carefully calculated to make girls wet. From the terrace with the stunning view of the Portland skyline and Mount Hood right down to the Jacuzzi, the high-tech appliances, the fridge full of gourmet goodies, and the stash of chocolate truffles, his rescue remedy for girls who displayed warning signs of hormonal imbalance. Oak floorboards, track lighting, Tuscan tiles in the huge kitchen, all of it was predicated on the ruthless law of the jungle; i.e., the female of the species will put out for the male who displays the largest and most up-to-date home entertainment system.

All bullshit. A cheap trick. Or come to think of it, hardly a cheap trick. A very, very expensive trick. But Lily would be wise to it.

He was uncomfortable in the place, now, especially since the Rudy dreams had come back. Must've been all that time spent sitting alone in the dark after Tony's death and the zombie masters debacle, contemplating his own desperate compensatory bullshit. Seeing it for what it was, shivering and naked and small. He'd spent a whole lot of money on a whole bunch of silly, extravagant shit that he did not really need to make himself feel safer. To scoot him back from that cliff's edge, where the smoke curled and the howls of the damned drifted up. But the edge was still right there. It didn't work. There was no such thing as safe.

Mamma's death had taught him that.

He brushed the thought away before it could dig its claws into his guts. Nah, he didn't want to bring Lily to his condo. She wouldn't be impressed by the espresso machine or the wet bar or the Tuscan tile. She'd look at him with those hard, blazing eyes, and see right through him. How hard he was trying. How futile it was.

He'd take her up to Tony's apartment, if he took her at all. There was little or no discernible bullshit in the shabby hole in the wall where Tony had lived since he had opened the diner. Bruno had lived there, too, from age twelve until he left home.

Sid had finally gotten himself in gear, and Leona stumbled in late, bleary eyed and sullen. He could not wait for Zia Rosa to get back and deal with them. He was not cut out to be a restaurateur. It was like herding fucking cats. He came out of the back room, shrugging on his leather bomber jacket. Lily got up, sliding her arms into her own shapeless thin canvas coat. It was baggy, wide shoulders drooping. So she didn't show that sexpot outfit off to just anyone. Good.

She belted her coat, caught him ogling. Her red lips curved. His face heated. He was so not smooth with her. His smoothness just fell off of him, *thud*. He became jerky, jagged. As dumb as a rock.

He held the door open for her and offered her his arm as they stepped out. She accepted it. The tingling buzz of contact penetrated layers of cloth and leather. The cold was damp and penetrating. Mist blurred the street, tinted orange by the streetlights, fuzzing the headlights of the cars that passed. They walked silently, Bruno scrabbling for a conversation starter and coming up blank.

She broke the silence first. "I must be keeping you from going home and getting some sleep."

He snorted. Yeah, sure. He'd forgotten what sleep meant. "Actually, my day's just beginning. Usually, I'd be heading home by now for a shower, and then it's right off to work again."

She shot him a curious glance. "Another job?"

"My real job," he explained. "I own a company that produces kites and educational toys." He read her puzzled expression. "Yeah, I know. So what's with the graveyard shift at a diner, right? I'm just covering for my aunt, Zia Rosa.

She runs the place, but she's not here right now, and we're short-staffed." He sighed. "So I'm up. Good old Bruno."

"This is the pastry-making aunt?" she asked.

"Yeah, the very one. Taught me everything I know. She's up in Seattle now. I don't know for how much longer. But if it's too much longer, I'm closing the place down, and to hell with it."

Yeah, right. Brave words. Zia Rosa was reveling in her surrogate grandmotherhood. It helped fill the hole her brother Tony's death had left in her life, which made it really hard to criticize her. Who was he to mess with anybody else's coping mechanisms?

"You must be so tired," she said.

He wasn't, actually. That point of contact where their arms touched was glowing, shooting impulses at random through his body. He'd be lucky if he didn't start twitching and jittering.

"You're not talkative anymore," she observed. "What happened?"

He smothered the howl of laughter so as not to sound psycho. "I'm nervous," he admitted in the spirit of total honesty, since she got off on that. "Too tense. It turns that faucet right off."

"Ah." The wings of her pageboy swung down to veil her face for a few yards. She turned to him again. "Don't be tense. I don't bite."

Like hell. He was covered with virtual tooth marks.

"What could I do that would make you relax?" she mused.

Oh, give him a fucking break. He stopped, making her lurch and stumble, clutching his arm. "Are you setting me up?" he demanded.

"Um. I actually don't have any ulterior—"

"Bullshit. You asked for total honesty. What do you think would relax me? Take a wild guess."

Her bright eyes narrowed. "So, what you're saying is, you want to just, ah, get right down to it?"

"No, that's not what I'm saying," he bitched. "You keep putting a sign on my forehead that says 'horndog asshole.' This might shock you, but I genuinely am interested in you as a person. I also have a hard-on. Under normal circumstances, the hard-on wouldn't matter. I'd take you to dinner, to the movies, strolling in the Rose Garden. I'd cook for you. Make pastry for you. We'd talk about spirituality and politics and food. I'd wait four or five dates before I even tried to kiss you. I'd let the tension build until you were ready to explode."

"Sounds nice," she murmured.

"Too bad!" he snapped. "Not going to happen! You've been yanking me around by the tail from the minute you opened your mouth! You're the one who's tense!"

"I see." Her hair hid her profile. "I suppose I am."

"You throw yourself in my path like a fucking grenade, at four in the morning, dressed like that, and start messing with my head! I don't know how to be with you, and I don't want to fuck this up. So help me out. What do you want from me, Lily? Spell it out. Don't make me guess."

She sucked in her lower lip. Trying not to smile, damn her. "Dressed like that?" she echoed. "How should I be dressed?"

She was jerking him around again, but he took the bait willingly enough. "A sweater," he informed her. "Flannel-lined jeans. Wool socks, warm shoes, a hat, scarf, and a thick down parka. As a matter of fact, you should be wearing a warm house with a locked door on top of that."

She was shivering, so he unlinked his arm from hers and wrapped it around her shoulders.

"I guess I am a little cold," she murmured.

Well, then. He'd go for it. In the name of gallantry. Or whatever.

"Do you want to go inside?" he asked.

"You mean, to your place?"

"No, my place is across town. But my uncle's apartment is right over the diner. I could make you a cup of tea or something."

"And your uncle?" she asked. "I don't want to disturb—"

"My late uncle," he clarified. "He died last year."

"I'm sorry to hear it," she said.

He didn't want to get anywhere near that, so he squeezed her shoulders. "So?" he urged. "You want to go up?"

She gave him a nod. He waited for more cues. For her to say something biting. For her to change her mind, flip-flop on him.

She didn't. They walked back the way they'd come, turning on to the side street behind the diner. Struck mute by mutual shyness.

He had an unpleasant moment as he led her up the shabby staircase, past scarred apartment doors badly in need of painting. The building was a dump, and Tony's apartment inside was no exception.

But the deal was struck. He unlocked the door and preceded her into an apartment as severe as a monk's cell but less attractive. Tony had been the ultimate minimalist. A bare overhead bulb. A crucifix on the wall. A color photo of Tony's parents, aged and scowling. A faded old sepia-toned photo of Tony's grandparents, clad in dusty black, also scowling. A sagging plaid couch, a beat-up coffee table, an antique TV. An ashtray still full of Tony's cigarette butts. That gave him a pang.

It smelled of dust, emptiness. It was frigidly cold, so he switched on the halogen space heater. The stench of burning dust fluff floated up to tease his nose as it flared eagerly to life. "Sorry," he said.

She laid her bag down and went to the window. "What for?"

He tried to turn on the lamp next to the couch, but the

bulb was burned out. The brutal overhead was the only light. It made his tired eyes water and sting. "That the place is so—"

"The place is fine. I am not fussy." She lifted the corner of the blackout shades and peered out. Nothing to see. Dawn was long in coming. Lily came back to stand over the heater, rubbing her hands. She wouldn't meet his eyes.

"I could heat some water for tea," he offered. "I could run down to the diner and get some—"

"No, I'm good."

That left him speechless, at a loss. Nothing to do, nothing to say. He considered and abandoned several ways to make her laugh. What came out of his mouth surprised him. "Is your hair dyed?" he blurted.

Her eyes narrowed. "Why? Does it look wrong?"

"Oh, no, no," he backpedaled. "It just seems, um, dark. For your skin. It's pretty. Sexy. It's just a really tough look. That's all."

Her chin went up. "I really am tough. Very tough."

"Never doubted it for a second," he said hastily.

She stared at him for a long moment. "It's a wig," she confessed.

Oh. A wig. Imagine that. "I see," he murmured, and gazed at the fake coif for a long moment before taking his courage in both hands.

"Can I, uh, see your real hair?" he asked.

She looked like she was about to refuse. Then she dropped her mascara-loaded eyelashes in a gummy black fan to hide her eyes, pulled off the cat-eye specs, and reached up to pluck out the pins.

No moment of revelation had ever been as sexy as the moment she pulled it off and faced him, her eyes defiant.

Her real hair was strawberry blond, curly wisps plastered fuzzily close to her head, like some retro, pin-curled twenties 'do.

She'd been stunning as a brunette. She blew his mind as a

red blonde. The harsh eye makeup and the violently red lipstick had made sense with the severe black bob, but their effect was different now. She looked vulnerable, delicate, lost. An innocent child who'd been all painted up. She'd lied about her age. He would swear to it.

She reached back and unwound the coil of tangled hair. Fluffing it loose so fuzzy corkscrews unwound, dangling voluptuously over her shoulders. So pretty, he could hardly breathe. His fingers itched to touch that flossy, soft mane. "Your real hair is beautiful," he said.

She let out a sniff. Unimpressed with his compliment.

He felt that prickle again. The buzz of wrongness, danger. Something wrong with this picture. She'd declined to answer before, but he tried again, with different words, in a different tone.

"What do you want from me, Lily?" he asked softly.

She took off her coat, tossed it on the back of the couch, and shook her hair loose. "Turn off the light," she said. "I'll show you."

He stared at her. This wasn't like him. Why couldn't he just take it at face value? A beautiful girl he hardly knew, hot for him and saying yes. It had happened before. "Yes" was good. "Yes" should not scare him to death. He played for time, lamely. "You mean, ah . . . you want . . ."

"You know exactly what I mean."

The blood in his body rushed to his groin, leaving his brain dangerously undermanned. Lighten up, he lectured himself. She was just a girl. Not a cosmic love goddess, wielding the power of life or death, dangling his destiny carelessly in her hand. He cleared his throat. "Are you sure . . . I mean, wouldn't it be better to wait until—"

"No," she said.

"Look, I don't want to come across like I don't want this—"

"You don't," she said. "I know you want it."

Her calm bothered him. So sure of herself, when he was a stammering mess. "Don't confuse me," he snapped. "I don't know why I'm resisting, because my dick is about to explode. But this thing with you is important. I don't want to start it off wrong."

She glanced at her wrist, miming looking at a watch. "Looks like we'll never start at all, if you have anything to say about it."

He tried again, doggedly. "If we just do it, then it's done. And we can't ever undo it. We can't ever do it over again."

"We can't?" She sucked in her lower lip, blinking. "Aw. How sad."

"Don't mock me," he ground out. "You know exactly what I mean. The first time is a one-time deal, and if we blow it—"

"Shut up, Bruno," she said. "This is actually harder for me than it may seem, and I'm reaching the end of my nerve. When that happens, I'll panic and disappear in a puff of smoke. Bye-bye. You get me?"

"Do not bully me," he snapped. "Here I am, trying to do the decent thing for once in my life, and you're giving me a hard time about it."

She took a step toward him. "Stop trying so hard," she said. "I didn't ask you to be decent. I asked you to turn out the light."

One last, flailing stab at caution. "It's like, with cooking," he blurted. "If you put too much salt in the stew, you can't take it out."

She considered that. "That's true," she said. "But you can put more food into the pot."

A massive flush started from around the center of the earth, encompassing his body as it rose up. The reaction appalled him. He wasn't like this with girls. He kept things light. He showed girls a great time, spent money on them, made them laugh, made them dream, made them come.

Until the moment arrived when they were no longer content with matters as they stood. At which point, it ended flat. Full stop.

So what was he doing, being terrified to put out for this girl for fear she wouldn't respect him in the morning. Afraid of giving her the milk for free. Afraid, in his gut, of giving her that much power over him.

Mamma and Rudy flashed through his mind, cramping his guts into knots. The man Mamma picked to father her son ran out on her before he was born. The last boyfriend she'd hooked up with had been a violent mafioso thug who had murdered her with his fists and his knife.

When it came to relationships, Bruno was genetically challenged.

Rudy hadn't been fit to scrape dog shit off Mamma's shoes. Bruno had known that, even at eleven. Rudy had been handsome, in a gold-chains-and-chest-hair sort of way, but that was all he had going for him. But Mamma had been beautiful, strong, smart.

Just not smart enough.

He didn't get it. Not then, not now. And in his rare moments of self-analysis, he'd figured that was probably the reason that he kept his love affairs so light. A guy just couldn't make mistakes that big if he kept things light enough. Featherlight. Light as air. Because what person could ever really guess at the depths of his own idiocy? Mamma hadn't had a clue about hers. And as for Bruno himself, well, hell. He certainly didn't have any great claim to self-knowledge. He just bumbled along as best he could. Hoping not to fuck up too badly along the way.

He went to the light switch by the door and flicked it off. When he turned, she glowed in the golden light from the space heater, and the shadow over her shoulders on the wall seemed a looming, black-cloaked figure. An ancient, mythical harbinger of doom and destruction.

He blinked. It turned into a pattern of blocked light again.

Jesus, what the hell was that about?

He was rattled, jittery, scared half to death. But he could no more say no to this girl than he could stop breathing.

7

He'd turned off the light just in time, right before the big, fat tears flashed down over her cheeks. Damn. Her makeup job was not tear-friendly, with all that coal black eyeliner and mascara. She'd gone with the unpredictable late-night vixen look, but it was a short step from that to a dripping raccoon mask. Vixens didn't cry.

She sniffed the tears back and gathered her courage. She was shivering, nipples poking out. The room was dim, just the glow of the halogen heater wavering and squiggling in her watery vision. Her legs wobbled as she sashayed toward him. She stopped to kick off the heels. She regretted the lost height, which she needed with this guy, but it wasn't worth taking a tumble.

The glow of the heater would be flattering for her skim-milk pallor, so she tossed her hair back and yanked the stretchy black lace shirt off over her head. Shoulders back. Boobs out, up. Ribcage tilted. Suck in the belly. Good posture did wonders for breast perkiness.

His eyes glittered. Suddenly the room seemed almost hot.

Lily kept her eyes open wide, hoping the tears would evaporate from her eyeballs. She wouldn't choke up now. She'd started this, and she would see it through. She struggled with the zipper on the denim skirt, got a grip, yanked it down. The skirt flumped ungracefully to the floor, denim studs clattering, leaving her clad in the black lace thong and the thigh highs with the rubberized thingies that were supposed to theoretically hold them up without garters but never quite managed the job. She hoped the rips and runs enhanced the ragged vixen effect. It wasn't just a look. Couldn't afford new ones.

He took a step closer. Her lungs locked. No air going in or out.

"I should take a shower," he said. "I smell like frying grease."

"No, you don't," she said. "You smell like coffee. And dish soap."

"Dish soap?" He looked rueful. "Wow. Seductive."

"It is," she assured him. And it was.

He was close enough to touch but taking his time about it, just vibrating at her, his very body heat a tender touch. He laid his hands on her shoulders. She gasped. His hands were so warm. How could they be so warm in this cold? A penetrating, tingling warmth, full of sparkles. It flowed into her body, stealing through her like a river of honey.

She'd just started to relax when he sank to his knees. She seized up again in a sudden panic. His hot breath tickled her navel. His hands clasped her hips.

"What the hell are you doing?" Her voice was shrill.

He hooked his pinkies into her thong and tugged it. "This."

Oh. That. Like she hadn't asked, begged, ordered him to get on with it. And now she was getting all sissy missy about it.

But she trembled as he pulled the garment down. It snagged, the crotch locked in the grip of her clamped, quivering thighs.

"You sure you're OK?" He tugged inquisitively at her thong.

Irrational anger gripped her like a charley horse. OK?

What did that word even mean? As if anything in her fucked-up world could ever be OK again in this lifetime. But it wasn't Bruno's fault. None of it.

And she'd die if he stopped. "I'm fine," she squeaked.

"Then relax," he coaxed.

Yeah. Like it was so easy. He petted her thighs, long, soothing strokes. She clutched the thick muscles of his shoulders to steady herself, and her legs unlocked, letting the gusset of her thong finally go.

He peeled it off one ankle, then the other, then lifted the scrap of black lace to his face, eyes crinkling from a hidden grin as he inhaled. He pressed his face against her navel, nuzzling. Slid down until his mouth rested against her muff. Just leaning there. The rhythmic swell of his breath was a subtle caress. "I want to make you come," he said.

She tried to laugh. The sound strangled itself. "So I should hope."

"No, I mean right now. With my mouth." He stroked the sides of her thighs, each caress coaxing her to relax, let him do his magic thing.

She cleared her throat. "Not now. Maybe later. If you're good."

"I'm very good." His voice vibrated deliciously through her groin.

He pulled her down onto the couch and slid between her legs, cupping her head to pull her close. To kiss her.

She arched away in panic. "No!"

He rocked back. It was hard to make out his expression in the dimness, silhouetted against the heater, but she could feel puzzlement and frustration coming off him in waves. "What the fuck?"

She was going to cry again. She didn't dare speak. She shook her head, blinking madly. Kissing would crack her along all the fault lines.

"You don't want foreplay or kissing? What the hell *do* you want?"

He was angry, and she didn't blame him. She was angry at herself. "Turn that thing off," she said, gesturing to the heater. "It makes too much light."

"What's wrong with light? Who are you hiding from? You'll freeze!"

"I won't freeze." As if. She felt feverish. She was going to combust.

Bruno gave the switch on the heater an angry slap. The light faded to a million shades of deep charcoal gray. He rose to his feet.

She grabbed his hand, terrified that she'd scared him off. "Where are you going?"

"If you don't want the heater, we need a blanket. There are springs coming through. I don't want you to get scratched."

It was so cold without Bruno to generate heat, but he was back a moment later, his arms full of fuzzy blanket. He arranged the blanket over the couch, half draped over the back, half draped over the seat.

He gestured sharply for her to sit. This was like an anxiety dream, only worse. Stark naked except for thigh highs, with a very large and volcanically hot sex god, who she'd cleverly wrangled into a really bad mood, looming over her in the dark. Nice move, Parr. Very smooth.

She tugged on the bottom of his jacket. "Won't you take that off?"

He shrugged the jacket off. Pried off shoes, socks, sent them flying. Yanked his T-shirt off over his head. She was transfixed as every sensual promise was abundantly fulfilled. He was ripped and beautiful, even in the dark. He wrenched his belt loose, shoved down his jeans. Kicked them off. Stood there, his cock jutting toward her.

Wow. She'd seen plenty of male sexual equipment, being as lusty and curious as the next girl, but she'd never seen anything like this guy. Not that she was a size queen, or anything. But even so. Oh, my.

He stood silently in that belligerent pose, legs wide, letting her look. Waiting for her to chicken out.

"Touch me," he said. "If you really want this. Touch my cock."

"My hands are freezing cold," she warned.

"They won't be for long."

She lifted her hands, tentatively. He grabbed them, wrapped them around the shaft of his cock. They gasped, him at the cold, her at the heat. Delicious, volcanic. The velvety supple softness, gliding over that hot, hard, urgent pulse of blood in his shaft. So thick, stiff, and ready. Her thighs tightened. Her hand barely closed around him.

Her body felt tight. Her skin felt too small. Bruno flung his head back. She wanted to kiss the taut tendons in his throat, but she was trapped in his tight grip. His fists clamped over her hand, guiding the long, squeezing strokes, the twisting swirls.

It was so quiet, just occasional night sounds of the city, their harsh breathing, the wet sounds of her hands moving on him. Rougher than she'd expected. Her lungs were squeezed small with excitement, thighs clenched around a hot glow. She pried a hand free and cupped his ass. Dug her nails into the taut dips and curves of his flanks, pulling him. She wanted to savor his slick, salty taste.

His hand blocked her face as she leaned closer. "No."

She was utterly taken aback. Men never refused blow jobs. The craving for fellatio was hardwired into them. "No?" she repeated.

He held her face firmly at a distance. "If I can't, you can't," he said. "Not unless it's mutual. It's my sexual code of conduct."

"Oh, come on!"

"Fair's fair," he said. "No compromise. Take me or leave me."

She squeezed his hot, pulsing rod, milking it. "I'll take you."

"Yeah?" He covered her hands with his around his cock. "I'm getting a weird feeling. I've been letting my dick do the thinking, but even with a nonfunctioning brain, I feel like you're messing with me."

"No." Panic twisted in her middle. "No, I'm not. Really."

"Oh, I'll still do it," he assured her. "I want it. But I'll tell you right now. If you try to make me feel bad afterward for having done it, it will piss me off like you would not believe."

"I won't," she assured him.

"Yeah? Good. If you have any doubts, this is your chance to put your clothes on and leave."

She grabbed his hand, pulling until he sank to his knees again. "No doubts," she said, pulling his hand between her legs. "Feel me."

His fingers dipped into the slick, hot moisture that bathed her pussy. Air hissed sharply out of his mouth.

He shoved her down onto the blanket. The lumpy cushions gave, aged springs creaking, and she shuddered with pleasure as he teased her pussy, sliding his fingers inside while his thumb sought out her clit.

He diddled her, dragging kisses up her belly that left a trail of wildly overstimulated flesh in their wake. When he reached her breasts, heat bloomed, unfolding from inside her chest and swelling helplessly to meet the call of his hot mouth. She made a shocked sound.

He lifted his head. "What? Don't tell me your tits are taboo, too."

The sour note in his voice made her giggle. "No."

"Thank God." He bent his head to her breasts again.

She usually got bored with foreplay, though she always awarded a guy points for the effort. But this was pleasure on a whole new scale.

She shook, straining, as each slow thrust caressed her sweet spots. His mouth coaxed her into a sparkling froth of sensation, until she was writhing, hips jerking, chest heaving against his hot mouth. "Enough," she gasped out. "Please . . . please. I want you."

"Give me one, first," he said.

She blinked in the dark, utterly lost. "Huh? Give you what?"

"Come for me. Before we do it."

She didn't have enough air in her lungs to laugh. Like orgasms were so easy to come by. "I can't do that on command," she explained. "It's not that easy for me to come, but I'm having a really great time, and you're doing everything right, so don't take it personally if I can't—"

"Shhh." He pressed his fingers to her lips. "It'll be OK. Just stop fighting. You're small. You need to relax. Trust me."

Trust him. Hah. She didn't even know what it would feel like to trust him, or anyone. He kept doing his thing, and the pleasure warped out of control, swelling into something huge, scary, something lethal—

It hit her, slamming her, with emotion, sensation, who the hell knew. It had no name, no precedent. It knocked her out.

She floated back after a while, limp and disoriented. Amazed she was still there at all. Still alive. Still herself.

Bruno was crouched on the floor, digging in the pocket of his jacket. A crinkle, the rip of foil. Good thing he was being responsible. She herself had forgotten all about that. Shocking. Stupid of her.

Bruno stretched her out on the couch. She shivered, boneless and soft. So vulnerable. Like a virgin on a sacrificial altar. He spread her legs wide, poised himself between them.

He started slowly, petting her slit with the head of his cock. The up-and-down swipe made her writhe with ticklish delight, wiggling to take more of him. He leaned back. Goddamn tease. She arched her back, reaching to grab his ass, pull him in where he belonged.

His white teeth flashed, and he swirled himself, lodging the head of his cock inside her, slowing down at the resistance he found there. Rocking, pushing. She arched, panting with eagerness. Wow, he was hard, blunt. But she was ready. Primed to screaming.

His weight bore down, his phallus driving deep, in a tight, delicious shove. She grabbed as much of his upper arms as she could wrap her fingers around and pressed back, arching her back, pulsing her hips against him greedily. Their eyes locked. His face was tense, all teasing gone. A muscle pulsing in his locked jaw.

He lowered himself, covering her body with his heat, his weight. The blanket he'd draped over the back of the couch fell down, covering his shoulders and the back of his head, blocking out what light there was. She was swaddled in a tight, breathless cocoon, with this big, hard, hot man all over her. Miles inside her.

He stared into her eyes and began to move. It blazed out of him, as clearly as words. Each lunge into her body said *mine, mine, mine.*

She hadn't signed up to be his, or anyone's, but it was happening anyway. It was too much. It was killing her, how good it was. Each stroke a hot, liquid lick of melting pleasure.

She started to fight again, just to make it back off enough so she could find her separate self again, but it was like fighting a mountain. His weight pinned her against the squishy couch. His cock pumped, slick and deep into the well of delicious sensation between her legs, twisting and swirling, finding so many madly lit-up sweet spots inside her and stroking over them, and over them, ah, God, *again* . . .

Her legs twined around his, trapping him deeper. She bucked and wiggled to get him exactly where she wanted him, and he followed every cue almost before she gave it. More tears slid out, but she no longer cared about the makeup mudslide. She whipped her head from side to side, whimpering with every heavy lunge.

He cupped her head, stared into her eyes, and kissed her.

A kiss to draw her soul out of her body, but he gave her his own in return. And the possessive, obsessive chorus of *mine, mine, mine* with each frenzied stroke—it was coming from her now, too. He was hers. All hers.

Things got incoherent after that, yet never had anything seemed so real, so vivid, so clear. They were gasping, yelling. The blanket tumbled with them as they slid off the couch and thudded to the floor, Bruno on the bottom. He slammed his arm into the coffee table, shoving it out of the way. It teetered, tipped.

She clawed the blanket off, wanting no barriers, and rode him hard, clutching his arms, her head flung back in pounding abandon. She was fever hot, glowing like a coal in the dark netherworld of that chilly apartment. He jolted upward against her, his fingers digging into her ass. Every thud of contact sharpened her wild, driving need.

He flipped her, pinned her, and she was on the bottom again, his tongue thrusting, twining with hers, his hips surging, heaving—

Pleasure ripped through them both, violent, relentless.

It left them a wreck of tangled, sweat-soaked limbs, gasping for breath. Flattened and limp. Sweet devastation.

Sometime later, the sweat had cooled. Bruno moved, feebly, to extricate himself. He slid out, leaving her collapsed, abandoned, alone.

And suddenly, horribly sad.

She braced herself for the moment of truth. What the truth was, she didn't know, but it was sure to be anticlimactic.

Bruno dropped his head into his hands. "Mother of God," he muttered. "That was . . . what just happened?"

She pushed herself up onto her knees. She'd lost a stocking in the frenzy. The other dangled off her ankle. "I, ah, don't know."

"Did I hurt you?" He sounded like he was holding his breath.

"No," she said hastily. "God, no. Not at all. On the contrary."

He heaved a sigh of relief. "Thank God."

She was hit by an unexpected wave of tenderness. Aw. He was an awfully sweet guy, totally apart from the celestial-sex-god thing. She reached to touch his face. He was so warm, the skin so supple, the stubble scraping her fingertips. She pulled away before he had a chance to reject the gesture. Didn't want to embarrass the man to death.

He caught her hand, yanked her close, and suddenly they were kissing again, like horny teenagers in a backseat. It made something ache and burn in her chest. He clamped her against him, silently demanding intimacy of a magnitude she'd never even known existed.

But she knew it now. Like an eye inside her had opened up, revealing unheard of emotions. Dangers, too. Like she needed new ones.

It didn't matter. She couldn't stop kissing him. Her arms were around his neck, strangling him, but he seemed to like it. She could feel his lips smiling as they moved over hers. "So we got rid of one dumb taboo," he said. "Want to take a run at the other one?"

She giggled, like a silly girl. "Um, ah . . . you mean—"

"Letting me go down on you. You wouldn't regret it."

She hid her red face, her out-of-control, shaking giggles against his neck, tasting the salt tang of his sweat. "You better let me catch my breath," she said. "That was intense."

His body stiffened. "Too rough, you mean."

"I didn't say that," she said. "Stop putting words in my mouth."

The silence sagged with the weight of all the things that were still too dangerous to say to him, but she had to find a way.

Her imagination just couldn't quite get past this wall.

She took a deep breath. All she could do was wait for the

right moment. God knows, it would be no chore to stick to him like glue.

"So. Ah. What now?" she asked, hesitantly.

His hand cupped her breast, lazily fondling her. The caress made shimmers of light move through her, sparkling inside her very skin. "I have some ideas," he said. "It depends on you."

"What depends on me?"

"Here's my proposal. I take you to my condo. I call in sick to work. We sit together in the Jacuzzi, you on my lap. Madly tongue kissing."

She giggled, weakly. "Um. Sounds good so far."

"Then, stark naked and fully erect, I cook you breakfast. An omelet with everything but the kitchen sink, pan-fried potatoes, sausages, fresh orange juice, cheddar scones, coffee. We eat and go into the bedroom. Then I spend the rest of the day making you come."

"Ah," she whispered. "Wow."

"And we take it from there," he concluded cheerfully.

She was smiling like an idiot. Happiness was bubbling up inside of her, and it scared her. She had no place to put it. It had nowhere to go, no room to grow. No right to exist in her life, as it currently was.

It would turn to pain soon enough. Everything did. But who the fuck cared right now? This might be the last fabulous time she ever had. Might as well go out on a high note.

"Sounds like a plan." Her voice a breathless squeak.

They dressed quietly, not looking at each other. Shyness had descended upon them again, and it felt odd, after such intense intimacy. He lifted an eyebrow as she stuffed her hair back up under the black wig and perched the cat-eye glasses back onto her nose.

They walked out onto the landing, and he took her hand.

She fought the warmth unfurling in her chest as she trailed him down the shabby, narrow staircase. This was so wrong, so foolish. She had to sharpen up. Her teeth clenched so hard, pain shot up her jaw.

Bruno sensed it and glanced back at her. "You OK?"

She manufactured a smile for him. "Yeah. Sure."

He frowned, worried, as he shoved his shoulder against the outside door. He stepped out backward, opening his mouth to speak.

She saw the SUV, door gaping. The dark figures, leaping at them.

8

Bruno was about to ask where her car was parked when she shoved him sharply to one side, and thunk, a baton thwacked down on her shoulder instead of his skull. Lily's leg whipped right up in a quick front kick. The guy swerved to evade it, snagged her leg. Her shoe flew off. She was yanked off her feet. Went down flailing.

Three attackers. Bruno blocked a punch, a kick, snagged an arm that held another baton, wrenching the attacker sideways with an arm twist. Had to let go, stumble back, block rapid-fire blows to his head and neck from the other guy. He got in a kick to the knee, spun to block the baton slashing toward his face from the other direction, but it caught him, a stinging blow that glanced off his temple. He caught the club, twirled, twisted, seized the arm. Pitched the guy forward and accompanied him in his short, hard flight, right into the brick wall.

A wet, nasty crunch, and he lay still.

The other guy was on top of Lily. The baton flashed down. She blocked with her elbow and fought madly, pale bare legs flailing wildly in the air. He dropped his guard to lure the third guy closer in, swerving to avoid a kick. Launched himself and put the first two knuckles of his right hand right through the guy's larynx. Turned before the prick even hit the ground to lunge for the guy on Lily. Got his arm around the bastard's neck, whipping his own face to the side to avoid getting popped. Wrench and twist. *Crack*. The man went limp.

Bruno flung him off Lily. The guy landed with a limp, heavy flop. Face toward them, mouth slack. Eyes empty.

Lily stared up, mouth wide, dragging in squeaking gasps. Her eyes glittered with terror. Her face was spattered with blood, which gave him a gut-wrenching scare until he moved and sprayed another shower all over her pale coat. His blood, not hers. He was leaking. His forehead.

He thudded down onto his knees, then onto his ass, legs splayed awkwardly beneath him. Trembling.

Holy fuck. He looked at the throat-smashed guy. At the guy he'd flung into the wall. Skull caved in, wide-open eyes full of blood.

Three dead guys. He had killed them in little over a minute. The shaking deepened, spread. Someone's bowels had opened. It stank.

He was a good fighter. Kev had seen to that. Lethal, many people had said, and he'd gotten off on the description, swaggering butthead that he was. Like it was a compliment. Lethal. How cool, right? Sexy.

Hah. He'd never considered the real meaning of the word. The description was literal now. It didn't feel cool or sexy. Holy. *Fuck*.

He'd never killed before. Or maybe he had, in that fire fight at Aaro's lair on the day of the zombie masters massacre. But spraying bullets from an Uzi into the woods was different than feeling bones crunch beneath your hands.

Self-defense. Not just his own. They would have killed Lily. Or would they? Strange, that they'd used clubs. Guns or knives would have been quicker. If the attackers had meant to kill them.

It hit him, full force. Oh, shit, *no*. He lurched away from Lily, lost the contents of his stomach. Coffee, rice pudding, banana cream pie, spattering all over a couple of fresh corpses. The heaves went on and on.

". . . have to go! Now!" Lily shook his shoulder. "Bruno!"

He spat the foul taste out of his mouth as best he could, wiped his shaking mouth on his jacket sleeve. He looked up at her, blank. Her words made no sense. "What? Go where?"

"Anywhere!" She grabbed his shoulder, shook it. "Come on!"

He hung on to himself, struggling for clarity. "Lily," he said, slowly and carefully. "Those guys are dead."

"Yeah! And we're not! So come on!"

He lifted his hand. "There are dead guys lying in the alley," he said. "I killed them. Killing people is frowned upon. It needs to be carefully explained. It's a crime, remember? Punishable by years in prison, at the very least? You with me here?"

"But it's not your fault! You were attacked! So let's—"

"The police will not know that unless I tell them," he went on grimly. "And you're going to have to tell them, too. Multiple times, until our brains are fried. And the forensics techs who analyze the scene will tell them. And our teams of lawyers will tell them. It's a long, tedious process, and it takes months, if not years, but there's no shortcut."

"We don't have time for that!" she wailed. She sank to her knees beside him. "Please, Bruno! We have to run."

"I've got no reason to run." He dug into his pocket, was almost surprised to find his cell still inside. He started punching numbers.

Lily grabbed his arm. "What are you doing?"

"Calling the cops, of course."

Lily grabbed his phone, hurled it against the brick wall. It shattered, plastic and metal exploding and joining with the rest of the debris. He stared, mouth agape. "What the fuck . . . ?"

"You can't call the cops! They are listening to you through that thing! They probably listened to what we just did, upstairs! That's how they found me! By watching you!"

"Who found you?" Even through the shock, he felt something inside him closing down in flat misery. "Oh, shit. I knew it. I fucking knew it, and I did you anyway."

"Knew what?" she yelled.

He waved his hands wildly. "That this was too good to be true!"

"This?" She gestured at the sprawled bodies. "You call this good?"

"No! Not them! You!" he shouted. "I might have known it! You're a black hole! You're a fucking head case!"

Lily clenched her hands into bloodied, shaking fists. Her hair was a wind-tossed lion's mane, makeup streaked to her chin. She was a fearsome sight, yet so fucking beautiful, she shone like a floodlight.

"I'm not crazy." She forced the words out, careful and clipped, as if her precision and self-control would prove her claim. "I'm not a black hole, either. I'm just unlucky, I guess you'd call it. I've been on the run. For about six weeks. From, ah . . ." She pointed at the bodies. "Them."

He struggled to his feet. "Ah," he said. "I see." Although he didn't.

"That guy, right there." She pointed at the one whose neck he had broken. "He tried to stab me in New York." She pulled up her sleeve, showed him an ugly scar slanting in an angry curve over her forearm.

"And you've been on the run since then?" he said.

Her throat bobbed as she tried to speak. She nodded.

Bruno pressed his bleeding forehead, felt blood drip through his fingers. "Did it occur to you to warn me that a squad of hit men were after your ass? You know, like, a gesture of common courtesy?"

Her face tightened. "Talk about a conversation stopper. What a turn-on, huh? Great banana cream pie, and by the way, I'm running for my life from a pack of cold-blooded killers. Way to chat a guy up."

"Chat me up?" He felt steam start to rise. "Are you for real? On the run for your life is not the best time to pick up a strange man off the street and fuck his brains out! Or is this how you handle stress?"

"No!" She pressed her hand against her mouth. "It wasn't about picking up any man. It was about picking up you. Specifically you."

Every moment they'd passed together reshuffled as he sought connections, explanations. "Lily," he said. "Do I know you?"

She shook her head. "No, but we have something in common."

"Yeah? What?"

She gestured at the bodies. "Them. For starters."

Bruno's teeth ground. "I'll tell you something about me," he said. "I'm a straight arrow. I make my money fair and square, I pay my taxes on time, contribute to homeless shelters, soup kitchens, the World Wildlife Fund. I do not lie, steal, or cheat. So whatever these guys were pissed about, it has nothing to do with me!"

"But I . . . but they—"

"I do not like this crap!" he roared. "I don't like getting punched, or jumped, or clubbed! It makes me tense! I do not like killing people before six A.M., even if they're hit men! I make a conscious, deliberate effort to steer clear of this kind of bullshit! You get me?"

"Don't yell. Please." She looked around, eyes darting nervously.

"Give me a good reason not to, Lily, because I'm not in a good place, and you're not helping!"

"I think . . . ah . . ." Her voice tightened. "I think it had to do with your mother."

The blood drained right out of Bruno's head.

The world expanded around him, vast and solitary. A wind-whipped wasteland. Lily still stood before him, eyes desperate, lips moving, but he could not hear her. Just cold wind, whistling in the void. The thrum of his heart hurt against his ribs.

That same old fucking pain. Completely intact and fresh, exactly as it had been in the bad old days. Like it had never really gone away, but had just hidden in the dark, waiting for its chance to leap out at him.

She grabbed his wrist, and the weird bubble popped. ". . . got to listen to me! My father was in the—"

He jerked back, sending her stumbling. "Don't touch me."

She shrank away. Bruno forced his numb lips to form words again. "Don't mention her again," he said hoarsely. "She's off-limits. Forever."

"Um, yes. But I—"

"Do not fuck with me," he said. "I'm right on the edge."

She twisted her hands together. "I'm not fucking with you," she whispered. "Please, understand. These people killed my father. The same ones who killed your, um . . ." Her courage failed her, and her voice trailed off.

He fought to keep his voice even. "My mother was killed by her asshole boyfriend. Decades ago. These guys would have been just kids."

She shook her head. "These guys are just hired muscle." Her gaze flicked over to the bodies. "Were, I mean."

This was great. Just great. A lifetime of struggle to create and maintain that precarious sense of normalcy after what had happened to Mamma, and this crazy girl blasted it to rubble with a few words.

"Listen, lady," he said. "I don't know what you've gotten yourself mixed up in. If you owe those guys money, if you're trying to get free of your pimp, if this is a drug thing, I do not fucking know or care. But you are bugfuck nuts, and I am having no part of it." He grabbed her arm and strode toward the diner, hauling her along behind him.

She struggled. "Hey! Where are you taking me?"

"To use the phone at the diner to call the cops," he said. "Since you killed my smartphone."

"No!" She twisted like an eel, but his grip was implacable. "Listen to me! Bruno, please, just stop one second and *listen!*"

He cursed himself for being a fucking fool, and stopped. "Make it quick."

"I have done nothing wrong! I'm not a prostitute, I don't sell or do drugs, and I've never borrowed money in my life except for college!"

The outrage in her voice almost made him smile. He channeled stone-faced Tony. "You could be lying."

"I don't lie!" she yelled back.

"No? You sure suck when it comes to omission of relevant truths. Like letting me know you've got a contract out on your life before throwing me down and fucking me blind, for instance?"

"Oh, shut up," she snapped. "I understand that you'd rather stay on the right side of the law. So would I, if I was given the luxury. But if you call the cops now, I'm going to die. And probably you will, too."

He snorted. "That's crazy."

"No, that's a mathematical certainty. The only way to stay alive is to fall off the map. That's where I've been for the last six weeks!"

He looked pointedly at the bodies strewn behind them. "You weren't quite as far off that map as you thought you were."

"I guess not," she said. "They must have been watching you. Waiting for me to make contact with you. Maybe they bugged your cell. Was it on you when you served me dessert?"

"Oh. So you've got this all figured out? A big conspiracy theory?"

Her eyes widened. "Does this look like a conspiracy theory?" She pointed at the bodies, finger shaking. "Those guys were not theoretical!"

"Maybe not, but when you start dragging me and my dead mamma, God rest her soul, into your personal problems with the criminal underworld, I call it a goddamn conspiracy theory!"

As if in answer, they were blinded by headlights as the SUV came to life, roaring toward them, front grill gleaming like a hideous metal grin. Bruno sent Lily flying and leaped. The SUV bounced over the bodies, glancing against the brick wall where they had been standing. Metal screeched, sparks flew. The SUV righted itself, cut the curb, jouncing and rattling. The taillights disappeared around the corner. He hadn't gotten the plates. Too dark, too fast. Too rattled.

He hadn't checked the vehicle. Christ, what a sloppy, pinheaded, cretinous asshole he was. He didn't deserve to still be alive. He ran to Lily, who was hunched, trembling on the ground. She'd acquired even more bloody scrapes on her legs. "You OK?" he asked.

She lifted her face, blinking, swallowing. "I think so."

Bullshit. She was terrified. Traumatized. No matter what she might have done to unleash this hell upon herself, he was still furious at the assholes who had done this to her. "I should call an ambulance for you," he said. "You need to be checked out. Here, let me—"

"No!" She pushed him, lost her balance, flopped back onto her knees. "The emergency room would be even worse than the cops. And I can't pay for it anyway. Those places are expensive. I understand if you can't believe me. But just let me go. Let me run as best I can."

Run? She couldn't even fucking walk. He stared down at the tangled fuzz of golden red curls on the top of her head. "I can't do that," he said helplessly. "How could I possibly do that?"

She looked up. Her face crumpled. Mascara tears tracked down her cheeks. "The cops can't save me from these people, whoever they are," she quavered. "I just want to keep on living. That's all."

"But you're all beat up! You need the cops! That's what they're for!"

"If you don't believe me, then it's not your problem," she said. "Just let me disappear." She tried again and struggled to her feet.

"Aw, fuck," he muttered. "Fuck, fuck, *fuck*." He kicked one of the swollen garbage bags, which split open, spilling out a foul, fermented slop. He stared up at the orange-tinted sky, releasing a stream of expletives in Calabrese that would have made Uncle Tony proud.

"Why, Lily?" he demanded. "Why is this happening to you?"

She scanned the street behind him, nervously. "Not here. I'll tell you everything I know, which isn't much, but not here. They'll be back."

Bruno felt trapped. The zombie masters massacre had shown him how unpleasant it was to be on the wrong side of the law, even for a short time. It had taken a while for the powers that be to sort out who had slaughtered whom. In the meantime, he and Kev and the rest of them had been locked down and examined from all sides. He remembered the stifled feel of it. Like a hand pressing down on his throat.

Jail would suck. He saw why Tony had run away from the life, many decades ago. Tony had used to work for his cousin, Don Gaetano Ranieri, a mafia boss back in Jersey. Tony had been his right-hand man. The protracted bloodbath of Vietnam had been preferable to that.

"If I go with you, I'm fleeing a crime scene," Bruno said.

"One that has my blood and vomit spattered all over it. Their first assumption will be that I murdered them, I guess. Since I'm not around to dispute it."

The cold wind blew her hair back from her ravaged, streaked but beautiful face. "But you'll be alive," she said. "That's good, isn't it?"

He grunted. He was being jerked around by a girl because she was pretty, and she was desperate, and he'd fucked her, so now of course he felt responsible. But Christ. Three big guys. One unarmed girl. Dickheads. He couldn't help it, pussy-whipped sucker that he was.

"I tell you what," he said. "I will get you some fresh clothes and get you someplace safe where you can rest. You take it from there. Then I go to the cops and I tell them absolutely everything. Understand?"

She gave him a tremulous smile. "Deal."

"Wait." He scuffed through the garbage scattered around the alley. Found the trashed remains of his smartphone and pried out the memory chip.

"Hey," she protested. "What are you doing? That thing—"

"Just the memory chip." He shoved it in his pocket. "It's mine. I want it." God knows, he intended for life to go back to what passed for normal as soon as possible. No way was he going to waste time scrounging all his contacts together again, sending out a new number. Hell with that.

He kept rummaging, kicking. There was her computer bag. He snagged it. There was one red shoe beside the Dumpster. The other was wedged between sacks of trash, next to one of the corpses. He retrieved them, knelt in front of her, placed her blood-smeared hand on his shoulder. Then he lifted one foot at a time to slip those pumps onto her clammy little feet. "Stupid shoes for a fugitive," he bitched. "You can't run in them. My car's parked up on—"

"No. Not your car."

"Huh?" He felt affronted. "What do you mean, not my car?"

"Not your car, your home or any of your places of employment, your phones, or your computers. Assume that they're all compromised."

"Ah." He was stymied. "So how are we supposed to—"

"We'll just have to be creative." She grabbed his hand and dragged him after her, deeper into the alley.

He let himself be towed along. "Where are we going?"

"I don't know, but if we stay in the alleyways, we're less likely to be seen when they come back looking for us. Can you hot-wire a car?"

He froze in his tracks. "Fuck, no!" he snarled. "I do not do shit like that! Haven't you been listening to me?"

"It's you who isn't paying attention! You know, about the mortal doom zooming toward you as we speak, like a heat-seeking missile?"

"Wow, Lily. With your sunny attitude and your sense of civic duty, I can see why you make so many friends."

Her eyes flashed. "Civic duty? It bums me when my father gets slaughtered. It burns my ass when thugs jump me and stab me and try to kill me! It's tough to maintain that glass-half-full vibe under those circumstances! So shoot me!" She grabbed a boulder from a wood-chipped lawn and lifted the rock over her head. "This one looks good," she said, walking toward an aging station wagon. "I like Volvos. They give me a sense of security."

He grabbed her shoulders. "What the fuck do you think you're—"

"Getting a car!" she yelled, lurching toward the car. "Watch me!"

"No." He jerked the rock away. "Let's think this through."

Her face crumpled. "There's no time," she said. "I'm out of ideas. I'm done. They're winning, Bruno. I'm fucked."

She was losing it. Damn. He pulled her into a hug. She wiggled in the confinement of his arms. "Let go of me!"

He didn't let go. "We're not stealing any cars," he told

her. "It's stupid, and it's rude, and it's also probably alarmed. And the cops will be looking for us soon enough anyhow."

She sniffed. "So what do you propose?"

"What's wrong with my car?" he asked, plaintively. "It's beautiful. Fast. Comfortable. And I have a key to it. And the legal right to use it."

"Your car is death," she said. "Sudden, certain death."

"God, you're harsh," he complained. "A cab, then?"

"They'll be listening. There will be a public record of where we went. They'll be watching anyone you know. Friends, family. Everyone."

"They? Who the fuck is this 'they'?"

Her mouth shook. "I don't know. I hoped to God you might have a clue, but you don't. I drew attention to you, and if they kill you now, it'll be all my fault. It was all a stupid . . . fucking . . . dead . . . *end!*"

"Hey!" He scowled. "Who you calling a dead end? I resent that!"

Snorting giggles vibrated against his chest. "Don't make me laugh, or I'll start to cry, and then you'll be in really deep shit."

"I believe you." Bruno stroked her slender, trembling back. Amazed at how delicate she was. Running for over six weeks from those goons, if what she said was true. And still kicking.

"You know, you're a pretty good fighter," he said.

She snorted. "Yeah? For a girl, you mean?"

"I didn't say that," he said. "But yeah. You're strong and quick, and you have nerve. Do you have martial arts training?"

"A little," she said. "Years ago, in college. Some of it stuck."

Which reminded him of something. "Hey. How's your shoulder?"

"What about it?" she muttered, soggily.

"You took a blow to the shoulder meant for my head. Let me see."

She flinched away as he reached for her lapel. "No, those blows were meant for me. You were just in the way. And you wouldn't have been, if I hadn't hunted you down and pinned a target to your chest!"

"Let me see it," he persisted.

She shoved him away. "We don't have time for a fucking tender moment, Ranieri!"

He held up his hands. "Wow. You're one tough bitch."

"Yeah!" she flung back. "That would be why I'm still alive!"

He pondered that. "Do you really know how to hot-wire a car?"

She sniffed. "Theoretically."

He looked dubious. "You do or you don't."

"I've studied how to do it on the Internet. I've seen diagrams. I know the principles. I'd figure it out. Eventually. I'm quite bright."

He was grinning, which clearly pissed her off. "Eventually," he repeated. "While the alarm squeals, and the owner comes racing out with a baseball bat. Come on. There's a gas station a few blocks over. We can clean up. Use the pay phone."

"To call who?" she demanded.

"If you want my help, you're going to have to trust me, OK?"

Trust him. What a concept.

Lily wobbled along, ankles quivering like rubber. She didn't even know what trust felt like, but look at her, trotting alongside this guy like his pet dog, not even looking at the street signs. Was that trust?

No, she concluded. It was exhaustion. Burnout. She had no executive energy, no ideas, nothing left. All she could do was glom on to someone else's strength and cling for dear life.

She'd never had the luxury before, not since Howard fell apart. If he was leading her to her doom, so be it. She'd almost welcome it.

She'd never relied on anyone else's strength before. She'd never seen anyone so strong, either. So quick on his feet and deadly with his hands. The way he fought was practically superhuman, and she hadn't even seen most of it, being busy fighting for her own life.

She'd seen high-level martial arts exhibitions, with Nina, back in their college roommate days, when they'd entertained fantasies of becoming women warriors. They'd put in a good bit of training in the dojo back then, and she'd loved it, though she'd been forced to give it up years ago. Dojo fees hadn't fit into her post–Aingle Cliffs budget.

But if there was one thing she had developed in her dojo training, it was an eye for the real deal. She could see it and feel it when someone was manipulating energy. Moving chi. Bruno was exploding with it.

Dawn had officially turned to daylight by the time they reached the gas station, albeit a dreary one. Cars streamed by as the workday geared up, and Lily felt horribly exposed walking around without sunglasses or a hat.

Bruno led her around back of the gas station to an unmarked door. The lock was broken, and when he opened it, the stench that wafted out was so foul Bruno flinched back, cursing. "Jesus," he muttered. "Can you stand to come in here for a couple minutes? I don't want to lose sight of you for one second. Hold your nose."

Lily dragged in the deepest breath she could and sidled into the foul little space. "This cannot be a hygienic place to wash a wound."

"I'm not going to wash the wound," he said, turning on the water. "I just want to splash off the blood smeared all over my face. Best not to draw attention to ourselves, right?"

"Something tells me that's not your biggest talent."

Bruno looked up from his position, bent over the small, filthy sink, and fixed on her eyes in the mirror as he splashed his chin. Pinkish water drained down from his cupped hands into the basin.

"What the fuck kind of comment is that?" he asked.

She silently kicked herself. "Not an insult."

"The hell it's not." He splashed again, still gazing at her. "What would you know about my talents, big or otherwise?"

A lot, after that incendiary half hour in his late uncle's apartment. She quelled the hysterical giggles and feigned her usual fuck-you nonchalance. "It's just an observation," she said. "A neutral one."

"Neutral, my ass." He wiped his chin. His long black eyelashes were tangled and gleaming with water. "Nothing about you is neutral, Lily. I bet you don't even know the meaning of the word."

She couldn't, in all honesty, deny that. So she didn't.

"So you've been observing me, then. For how long?"

She gulped air to calm the fluttering. Hands clenched, toes curled. Cool as a frozen mocha. "A few weeks," she admitted. "I checked you out online. And I've been tailing you physically for about a week now, as best I could, with no vehicle. You're not hard to find. The nights working at the diner made it easier."

Bruno wiped the water off his face with his hands. "That annoys the living shit out of me. That you've been observing me. Like some entomologist, studying a fucking bug under glass. Judging me."

"I haven't been judging you." At least, not in a bad way, she wanted to add, but the words were pinned down by his accusing glare.

He opened his jacket and ripped off the bottom strip of his T-shirt. It yielded him a long, limp strip of fabric. He pressed it against the still oozing wound at his hairline, wincing.

She couldn't help noticing, in the unwholesome glare of the fluorescent bulb, how the shortened T-shirt with its dangling threads showed off his tight abs, the glossy dark hair arrowing into his low-slung jeans. He had an innie. One of those taut, stretched ones like an eyelid, the kind you mostly saw on ripped models for men's health magazines. She'd missed a lot of juicy little details in the dark.

He looked her over, seized his T-shirt again, and ripped off still another strip, which left the garment barely covering his ribcage. He moistened it under the faucet. "Come here."

She shrank back. "I'm all right."

"No, you're not. You look like something out of a splatter film." He jerked her toward him and started to swipe at her face with the rag.

Huh. It actually felt kind of good to be groomed like a kitten.

"This is my blood, mostly," he told her. "But I've got no diseases."

"Me, neither," she offered. The wad in his hand was pinkish gray from blood and makeup. A glance in the mirror showed that she looked only shockingly bad, rather than like out-and-out road-kill.

"And besides, you're a fine one to talk," he said, still daubing.

She was so distracted by his scorching male vibes, she'd lost the thread of the conversation. "Huh? Talk about what?"

"Not drawing attention to yourself." He jerked her coat open, dabbing at the blood on her chest. "Look at your outfit. Every man who looks at you will look again, and then stare. Why the fuck not? You invited him to. And he will remember every last detail of your face and body. I guarantee it. If you don't want attention, dress down! Go drab!"

"But I did want you to notice me," she blurted.

His hand stilled, and he stared at her with a small, puzzled frown. "Yeah. Ah. About that. We need to talk about—"

"No, we don't. It's not the time or place," she said hastily.

"I shouldn't have mentioned it. I don't mean to pick a fight with you."

He grunted. "Yeah, right. You're always on the offensive, Lily. Every damn thing that comes out of your mouth is provocative."

She kept her gaze locked on the ragged edge of his T-shirt, staring at the threads dangling over his naked belly. "I guess so," she said. "I'm just made that way. That's probably why I'm single."

"Ah. Could that have anything to do with all these people who are trying to kill you, by any chance?"

She jerked away from him, stung. "No! It does not! I may be a mouthy bitch, but those scumbags have never even given me a chance to insult them properly! I have no idea why they're doing this!"

"Calm down," he said. "Don't yell. We'll draw attention."

She closed her scuffed, bloody coat with a jerk, belting it with numb, trembling hands. "Look, I understand your urge to scold me," she said. "I get that a lot from guys. But could we do it outside? I'd prefer a drive-by shooting at this point than another noseful of this air."

He got out of her way. "It's not necessary, you know."

"What?" She pushed out the door and inhaled the relatively sweet perfume of car exhaust and gasoline gratefully. "What's not necessary?"

"Being on the offensive," he said, following close behind. "You don't have to be. Not with me. I'm actually a pretty decent guy."

"I noticed that," she said tartly. "Otherwise I wouldn't have jumped your bones. I do have some standards, you know."

He stopped at the pay phone, dug in his pocket. "That's nice."

"It's just hard for me to switch out of offense mode. So don't take it personally. In fact, I might never be able to

switch out of it again, in this lifetime." Not that she expected
to live that long.

"That's a grim estimate," he said, counting quarters. "Good
thing I got some tips tonight. I don't usually have this much
change."

Lily charged on. "I'm going to piss you off again, probably soon," she told him. "So I'll just apologize in advance,
for the next, oh, say, five times. After that, we'll renegotiate.
OK?"

His mouth twitched, wryly. "You are a piece of work."

"That's why I—"

"Yeah, yeah. That's why you're still alive, and all that
doom and gloom shit. Now be quiet, and let me make this
call."

"What call? To who?" she demanded.

He rolled his eyes. "Remember what I said about trusting
me?"

"You're not calling Zia Rosa, are you? Or your employees
at the diner? Or your toy business? Or Kev McCloud, or his
brothers?"

Bruno set the receiver back on the hook, his face harden-
ing. "How do you know about the McClouds?"

She made an impatient sound. "Oh, come on. Don't be
such an ingenue! They're smeared all over your life. All you
have to do is look. And if I looked, you can damn well be
sure that *they* looked. It was all out there, for anyone to see.
And I'm not even that good at it!"

He gave her such a grim look, she started to twitch. "Stop
it, Bruno," she pleaded. "Don't give me that look."

"What else do you know?" he asked. "How's the ratio of
good to bad cholesterol on my last blood work? Do you
think my tax deductions last year were justifiable? Did you
read my text messages?"

She sighed. "You haven't done a damn thing to prevent
me."

"It never occurred to me that anyone would be interested!"

"Come on," Lily pleaded. "You can't stay mad."

"Watch me." His voice was hard.

"I already apologized, remember? For five future piss-offs?" she wheedled. "That leaves me four free ones."

"No way," he said sourly. "Spying counts for two. Maybe more."

"That's not fair! I wouldn't have done it if I hadn't—"

He put his finger to her lips. "Shut up. I have to concentrate hard to remember this number without the use of my electronic brain extensions, and I can't do it when I'm pissed off. So zip it."

"That's sad," she commented as soon as he lifted his hand. "Brain atrophy, and so young, too. There are things you can do for that, you know. Math problems, crossword puzzles."

He turned back to the phone. "You are now down by four. I'm dialing. We'll find someplace safe to exchange verbal barbs after, OK?"

Police sirens wailed in the distance, from the direction from which they had come. Bruno looked around, staring toward the sound.

"Looks like they found our buddies," he said.

"We've got to get out of here," she whispered.

"I'm working on it," he grumbled. "Stop bugging me."

He turned to the phone. His back was so broad, so graceful. She stared at the expanse of fine black leather draped between his big powerful shoulders. Turning his back on her was probably meant to be a snub, but in her current boggled state, it felt like an invitation.

She leaned against his back. He stiffened at the contact, but he didn't pull away. It felt good. She breathed in, leaning closer, pressing against his strength. Sucking it in. Vampire girl, glomming on to him.

A thought took form in her head. She should let it float

away. She didn't have the energy for data processing, particularly emotional stuff. But she followed it, letting it make connections, take on coherence.

About Bruno. It felt so right, the way they bopped each other around, bitching and snarking. Being with him was almost, well . . . fun.

How kinky was that. After that attack, the near-death experience, the blood. "Fun" was not a word one would usually associate with that type of adventure. She wondered if it was a conscious strategy, on his part, to keep her from falling to pieces. If he really was that smart, that intuitive, to figure her out so quickly, manage her so smoothly.

Or if it was just a random coincidence.

She huddled closer, not even bothering to eavesdrop on his whispered phone conversation. She wouldn't have made any sense of it anyhow. Not in brainless clinging leech mode.

She didn't want an answer to her half-formed question. Any answer would be disturbing, and she was disturbed enough.

Bruno was not her ally, shoulder to shoulder with her against the powers of darkness. No. He was helping out the poor sad crazy girl because he felt sorry for her. Pity did not an ally make. Neither did sex. Not even awesome, earth-shattering, mind-blowing sex.

She knew that. She really did. But even so. She pressed her nose against his vibrant warmth and inhaled. Mmmm. So nice.

What the hell. She was obscurely comforted anyway.

9

Reggie stared at the corpses. The team he'd sent to inter-cept Parr and Ranieri lay on the ground amid the garbage. Multiple witnesses milled around, talking excitedly into their cell phones. Cops were on the way, to catalog his error, put it on public record.

He was fucked. He pushed away the staggering finality of it, used DeepWeave Contingency 5.5.2 to calm and focus him, but the effects were muted. He knew what he was sup-posed to be doing, but he didn't move. He just stood there, paralyzed. Staring at the lifeless chunks of meat that had once been Martin, Tom, and Cal.

Cal had been from his family training pod. Like Nadia. A brother to him. Tom and Martin were younger, but Reggie studied with them both, sparred with them, worked with them ever since they'd been initiated as operatives. They were gifted with abilities normal people would take for superpowers. Now they were wasted. Bruno Ranieri had butchered them, and that sneaky little cunt Lily Parr along with him.

He wished that Nadia had shot them, but he'd told her to bail, rather than risk her dying, too. They hadn't been pre-pared for Ranieri's prowess. Nadia was good, but she would not have prevailed if Tom, Cal, and Martin had all fallen, not unless she'd used a firearm, and King had said explicitly not to kill them yet. Reggie stared at the bodies. So angry he could not control the shaking. Contingency 5.5.2 wasn't working.

Police sirens wailed in the distance. They were going to find him here, demand a statement, explanation, identifica-tion. He could not stay. Too late for damage control. He should spirit away the bodies, but blood was spattered everywhere, he had no idea whose. What an unspeakable mess. Someone would have to stretch out on the altar of responsibility and watch the knife plunge down. Guess who.

He had to move. He could not be taken into custody. His programming would not allow it. His own special series pod had undergone an experimental preventative imperative programming sequence. In a scenario like a police interrogation, he would die of convulsions in less than a minute, his body ripped apart from within.

King had deleted that element from the programming schedule with the subsequent pods, judging it too dangerous, and possibly wasteful. But for Reggie's pod, the deed was done. There was no undoing DeepWeave once it took.

He watched the idiots on the scene, wishing he could kill them just for the looks on their faces. Fear and shock foremost, but beneath it, excitement, unholy glee. An older woman indulged in an attack of hysterics. A younger woman tried to calm her. Attention-mongering bitches. Like they cared about his brothers. The hag was emotionally masturbating in public, for the fun of it. Normal people disgusted him. Their lack of discipline. Untrained animals, pissing on the floor. No idea what it meant to be born to serve, dedicated to the highest principle. A honed, deadly instrument in the hands of his god.

Of course, it was not their fault. They didn't have the benefit of meticulous selection and decades of DeepWeave programming to unlock their potential. They didn't have the grooming of a great genius. All they had was what grew wild in the weed-choked gardens of their stunted brains. The mental equivalent of dandelions, thistles, and ragweed.

Kill them all, the little voice whispered. *Just kill all the witnesses. Kill, kill, kill. Keep killing as they come.* It was the only thing that would give him relief. He'd give that squawking old bitch something real to squeal about, and then make squealing turn into sweet, sweet silence.

But it was too bright. Too late. There were too many people present. And the sirens were getting louder. *Move.*

Still couldn't. Some glitch in the way DeepWeave interacted with his emotions. Not the fault of King's programming, of course. Never that. The intrinsic imperfection of human beings was the problem. That was why so few of them survived the culling process. And even the chosen few who did were never perfect. One of King's great sorrows.

Shame galvanized him, enough to make his hand move. He stuck it, stiff and shaking, into his pocket. Pulled out a sheet of transdermal emergency patches. Calitran-R35, specifically calibrated for his body to damp down any faulty processing of excess emotions. He peeled one off, stuck it on the inside of his wrist, where the skin was thinnest.

The relief was immediate. In seconds, the rictus softened. He backed up, gaining coordination with each step. Turned, and took off at a lope back toward the car he'd left parked on the next block.

Reggie started the car, drove to the house he'd been instructed to use, which was only ten minutes away. He parked the car on a side street, not bothering to lock it. In fact, he left the keys in the ignition. He would not be using the car again. It would not be recovered. It was untraceable, as was the vehicle the team at the diner had used. He should probably call Nadia, he thought, vaguely.

But why? It was over. Too late to try to take control. He was over the cliff. Falling straight down. He caught a glimpse of himself in the beveled glass panes in the door, surprised to see that he looked much as he always did. Swarthy, good-looking. Curly dark hair, chiseled features, dark eyes, dimples even when not smiling.

He wasn't sure what he'd expected to see. A naked skull. A rotting corpse. Nothing at all. Yes, that was it. He was nothing. All his identities forged, all his passports false. Only for King did he exist. Only the name King had given him defined him. And now he was nothing. No one at all.

Grief gripped him. Cramps were beginning. He rummaged for more Calitran, stuck another patch next to the first. It summed up to a dangerously large dose, but it hardly mattered now.

He went up to the master bedroom, and slowly, methodically began to take off his clothes. He pulled off garments and folded them with meticulous care until he was entirely naked.

He folded back the coverlet and sat upon the smooth white sheet, placing his smartphone on one side, his Sig 229 on the other. A small, faraway part of his mind scuttled like a rat in a maze, making and discarding far-fetched plans. Running away, buying a new identity. He spoke fifteen languages fluently. He could go anywhere and sell his abilities to the highest bidder. Live as free as a bird, as rich as a king—

The King. Everything led back to King. His idol. His god.

Cramps jerked his abdomen. Tears poured down his face. He couldn't live without King's approval. The part of him that hungered for freedom wasn't strong enough to send an electric impulse to his muscles. It was just a faraway, idle thought. Blasphemous flickers on the edge of his consciousness that made him feel guilty and unclean.

He tried to clear his mind. To wait, with dignity and serenity, as befitted one of King's elite operatives. But the grief was agonizing. He doubled over, began to rock. His throat tightened until the moaning coming out of him became a breathless, keening wheeze.

It felt like hours, but it wasn't more than four minutes before the phone buzzed, spinning on the sheet next to his thigh. There was no question of not picking it up. Just the mere flash of such a heretical thought through his head sent splinters of agony through his skull.

Reggie flipped open the delicate, flexible fold-screen, quadrupling the viewing field. King's benevolent face filled the screen. The sight of him triggered a longing that made Reggie cry out loud.

Shame followed the outburst. King was displeased by uncontrolled emotion, even devotion. They all struggled to control it.

"Well, Reginald?" King's soothing baritone, sparkling with velvety harmonics, stroked Reggie's nerve endings like silk. Reggie shuddered as emotions ripped through him. He steeled himself to be strong, to face the end with dignity. It was all that he could offer King now.

Even in failure and despair, one had to hold oneself to standards.

Reggie opened his dry mouth. "Ranieri and Parr fought off the team I sent to subdue them," he said. "They've escaped."

King's eyes widened. His silence filled Reggie's mind, widening, spreading with each second, like a pool of blood from an opened artery.

"And the team?" The sharp tone in King's voice made Reggie jerk as if he'd been slapped. "Their status?"

"Martin, Cal, and Tom are dead," Reggie said. "Nadia is still alive." There was hardly any point in drawing in more oxygen, but his lungs did it anyway. His body was a dumb machine, grinding stupidly on.

"The bodies? You recovered them?" King's eyes glittered.

Tears ran down Reggie's face, but his programming did not allow him to blink in King's presence. His pupils dilated automatically at the sight of his maker. "No," he began. "There were eight witnesses. Police were arriving momentarily. I heard the sirens. I would have had to—"

"Do not presume to explain yourself to me."

Reggie flinched as if stung by a flail.

"You know what happens now, Reggie?" King said. "Your poor decision making has lost us three operatives. Four, including yourself. It has exposed me. This is unacceptable. Do you understand?"

"Yes." Reggie's voice cracked. "I understand." Tears blinded his eyes. He dashed them away so that he could see that beloved face for the last few moments allowed to him. Even when King's eyes blazed with disapproval, he could not look away. The cramps were so intense, they were tearing his muscles loose. Crushing his organs.

"Prepare yourself." King's stern voice was unrelenting. "Hold the phone up, so I can see you."

Reggie did so. King began to recite. The text was in ancient Greek, a passage from the *Iliad*. Reggie's body shook. Tension built with each phrase. The culminating line made something give way inside him.

He relaxed, thinking of nothing. A blank slate, awaiting orders.

"Pick up the gun, Reginald. Put it in your mouth."

He did so without hesitation.

"Fire," King said.

Reggie kept his eyes fixed on the beloved face as he pulled the trigg—

Detective Sam Petrie stared at the last of the bodies as the transport company guys hoisted it onto the gurney for its final journey to the medical examiner, and tried not to breathe. The combined effluvia of fermenting garbage and recent death was potent.

The criminalists were still busy collecting and logging evidence. His friend Trish was one of them. She was organizing for the blood-smeared batons to be taken to a drying locker, and filling out all the form 49's to get the blood samples analyzed for DNA.

This was a weird one. Three big guys armed with knives and guns had inexplicably opted to use batons to defend themselves while an unknown assailant or assailants had beaten them to death, apparently using only bare hands. This pending forensic analysis, but Petrie had a feel for it. He was sure.

Two batons were bloodied. Blood was splattered over the asphalt. One man's neck was snapped, one's larynx was crushed and collapsed, and the third's skull had been bashed in. No witnesses.

Whoever did it had to have been immensely strong, huge, and/or hopped up on a performance-enhancing drug. A drug deal gone bad?

One thing it probably wasn't was a hardened professional. Not with vomit spattered everywhere. Vomit said raw beginner. But what raw beginner killed three big guys with his bare hands? Why hadn't the three big guys defended themselves with the guns, or knives? Very *X-Files*. A pack of aliens? A sucker-mouthed sewer monster? Yeah. Right.

The team of criminalists were wrapping it up. Trish, a petite blonde with a thick tawny braid hanging down over her police jacket, ducked beneath the yellow tape and jerked her chin in the direction of the diner. "Coffee?" she asked. "Got called too early to get my caffeine fix."

"Don't you have to go back to the crime lab?" he asked.

"Nah, I'm not on the primary team today," she replied. "They just needed some extra bodies." Her eyes flicked to the gurney being rolled up into the transport company vehicle. "Warm bodies, that is to say. So? Coffee?"

"Yeah, sure." He could use some coffee. He followed her around the corner and back into the diner, which was a mishmash of bright chrome, pink plastic, and weird art. Garish landscapes, strangely interspersed with austere, Japanesy pen-and-ink nature drawings.

Petrie had left his partner, J. D., to interview the employees of the diner, all of whom looked shaken. The cook, Julio, a grizzled Hispanic guy, was behind the counter, propped on his elbows. The waiters sat on counter stools; a big, balding blond guy hunched over his coffee and a thirtysomething redhead with Pocahontas braids, crying noisily while instinctively propping up her bulbous cleavage with her elbows.

Julio poured them coffee without being asked as they approached the counter, and shoved a plate of pastries their way with ill grace. Trish took a cruller and bit in, sighing with delight.

"He took off at about a quarter to five," Julio was saying to J. D. " 'Bout fifteen minutes after Sid and Leona here finally dragged their asses in here, half an hour late. As usual."

Sid slanted Julio a dark look, but Leona, the Pocahontas chick, didn't seem to notice the dig. "I cannot believe that was happening right next to me!" she trilled. "Murderers, right on the other side of the wall! What if I'd gone out the kitchen door? I could have gotten killed!"

"Who took off at a quarter to five?" Petrie asked.

"Bruno Ranieri," J. D. told him. "Grandnephew of Rosa Ranieri, the lady who owns the place. She's up in Seattle right now, visiting family. He was working night shift. Left probably right before it happened."

"You talked to him yet?" Petrie asked.

J. D. shrugged. "Not answering his cell, or at home. His other work number is still after hours. I left messages everywhere."

" 'Course he's not answering," Sid said. "He's with that girl."

J. D. and Petrie both whipped their gaze around. "What girl?"

"The girl he left the diner with," Sid explained. "She'd been here when I came in to work for the last few nights. This morning, she gets up and leaves with him. Something tells me he's not gonna answer his phone for a while." He waggled his eyebrows. "I wouldn't, if I was him."

J. D. and Petrie exchanged glances. "Who is she?" Petrie asked. "Do you know her name?"

"Nope. She was hot, though. Black hair. Glasses. Nice tits."

"Don't be gross, Sid," Leona roused herself to snap. "God, I wish Bruno were here. I'd feel safer if I had a black belt ninja type like him around right now."

Petrie studied her. "Who's a black belt ninja type?"

"Oh, Bruno's amazing," she said, mistily. "He's got, like, these muscles that just go on and on, and he does kung fu, like what you see on TV. Kev does, too, but he's older, and he's taken."

"So Bruno Ranieri is a trained martial artist?" Petrie said.

"Leona!" Julio hissed. "Stop being a goddamn cow!"

Leona's eyes got big, her gummy lashes fluttering as her gaze darted from here to there. "Oh, my God," she squeaked. "You don't think that . . . oh, my God, no! No way! Bruno would never . . . he's, like, only the sweetest guy in the whole world! He would never—"

"Don't get upset," Petrie soothed. "We just want to get all the facts. So, this Kev you mentioned. This is another Ranieri? A relative?"

"Sort of," Julio said reluctantly. "Adopted. His last name is McCloud, now. Used to be Larsen. Long story. But you can forget about him. He's out of the country, traveling with his girlfriend. Australia, New Zealand, someplace like that. So leave him be."

"I don't mean to bug anybody," Petrie said mildly. "But can I have the phone numbers? Rosa Ranieri, Bruno. Kev McCloud, too, please."

Julio roused himself, grumbling, and went to the phone on the wall near the kitchen entrance. He tore off a scrap of paper that had been taped to the bottom of it, slapped it down on the counter. "Home, work, and cell for Bruno. Home, cell, and all the McClouds' numbers for Rosa. And this one here's Kev's cell number. But he's gone."

Petrie slid the slip of paper into his pocket. "Thanks."

"This is Bruno, right? Nice." They all turned at Trish's voice. She was looking at a framed magazine cover that graced the wall over the dessert counter, sipping her coffee and gnawing her cruller.

"Yeah, that's Bruno," Julio said reluctantly.

Petrie strolled over. A good-looking dark-haired guy flashed a charming, dimpled smile at him from the cover of the *Portland Monthly*.

"I remember this cover," Trish told him. "The guy is mega-cute. Most eligible bachelor? Yum. I'd take him."

Petrie leaned closer. "Wait a second, I've seen this guy. He was mixed up in that weird shit that came down in Beaverton last year, right? When that billionaire got offed, what was that guy's name?"

"Parrish," J. D. supplied, joining them and staring at the photo. "None of them ended up being charged with a crime, though."

"Huh," Petrie muttered, staring at the guy's very white teeth, all of which were prominently featured in the picture. "Interesting."

Trish's phone buzzed, and she whipped it out. "Yeah? . . . Uh-huh . . . no shit . . . yeah, OK. I'll be there right away." She dropped the phone into her pocket, rolling her eyes. "Duty calls. Suicide, over on Wygant. Some clown blew his brains out and managed somehow to set off some kind of explosive device and shoot out the neighbor's bedroom window at the same time. Big mess."

"Wow. Takes talent," Petrie observed.

"Big-time." Trish kissed her fingertips and pressed them to the glass over the magazine cover. "Bye-bye, dimples," she crooned.

"You do know those are just a genetically inherited defect in the underlying facial muscle tissue, right?" Petrie told her.

Trish popped the last bite of cruller into her mouth and chewed it, her face blank. "Come again?"

"Dimples," he explained. "It's just a bifid major zigomaticus. The muscle attached to your cheekbone." He indicated on his own face.

Trish gave his cheek a condescending pat. "Aw. You're just jealous because you don't have any. Don't worry, Sam. You're still cute."

"It was just an observation," he called after her.

She turned and winked at him. "Bruno didn't do it," she said. "It's not possible. Those bifid zigomaticus are just too adorable."

The bell tinkled as the door fell shut behind her. Julio let out a grunt in the sudden silence that followed. "Women," he said.

The image on the view screen spun and blurred. The device came to rest sideways, showing a partial view of Reginald's big toe. A rivulet of blood trickled down between it and the second digit.

Neil counted the seconds until the picture disintegrated.

That was that. When Reggie's heart stopped, the device erased itself, and detonated. A small explosion, just a safety feature to ensure that the coms were thoroughly destroyed and never fell into the wrong hands. He used it with only his own personal operatives.

The feature had never been put into use before. This entire scenario was unprecedented. King had considered his mature, trained adult operatives to be 99.9 percent infallible.

Bruno Ranieri represented that .1 percent of uncertainty. It should hardly surprise him. But Bruno had never had the benefit of decades of intensive training, nor long-term DeepWeave. Neil had written the boy off long ago as an evolutionary dead end. More trouble than he was worth, considering his pit bull relatives.

But he'd managed, in his own crude way, to become exceptional.

King was furious. At Bruno, for slaughtering his agents. At Howard and Lily, for lighting the fuse. At Reginald, for being his shining star, and then daring to fail. It was dangerous to get attached, but he was only human. And Reggie had been special series, too. That entire pod had been the very first of his special series, and with their natural genetic advantages, he'd always expected a bit more from them.

Neil had no choice but to terminate Reginald's life. He had to be rigorous, or what message would he send to his other operatives? He could undermine their psychological stability and destroy them all.

Zoe was huddled on the floor, still naked and gasping. He felt an urge to kick her until she was quiet. He controlled it. One did not kick a finely tuned machine worth tens of millions.

He could understand her being upset, but for God's sake, she hadn't even been podmates with the dead agents. Neil fostered the development of familial feelings, raising his trainees in small family groupings. Experience had taught him that family bonding fostered intellectual and emotional health as well as esprit de corps. But Reggie, Cal, Martin, and Tom were years younger than Zoe. She'd never even been assigned with them. No, she was just carrying on. As usual.

Anger piled up on anger as he pondered the logistical nightmare he now faced. He'd already leased Reginald's services over the next two years to the Amesbury Group, a wealthy multinational corporation, for a staggering sum of money. Now he had to renegotiate the contract. Failure would mean a loss of revenues of well over three hundred million over the course of the next two years alone.

First, basic housecleaning. He punched Nadia's code into his com. She responded instantly. "Yes, sir?"

"What is your position?" he demanded.

"I'm driving on Airport Way," she said, her voice very subdued. "I was waiting for Reggie to give me further—"

"Reggie is dead," he said harshly.

Nadia let out a thin squeak, then a strained silence.

"Nadia?" he prodded. "Are you there?"

A wet sniff and a wobbling voice. "Awaiting orders, sir."

His teeth ground. Nadia, too. Nauseating. But Nadia at least was justified in being devastated, having lost two pod-mates in one blow. The fourth of their pod quartet, another female, had been culled ten years ago, at the age of fourteen. Only Reggie, Cal, and Nadia had made it.

Poor Nadia. Bereft of her pod. So sad. But that was no excuse for wallowing in self-pity. "Go to the house on Wygant Street and dispose of his body," he ordered. "I want no trace of him for the authorities to find. Not so much as a hair or a skin flake."

"Sir, ah, how do you want me to—"

"Be creative," he snapped. God, was no one displaying any powers of independent cognition today? "Use acid, use the food processor, use the garbage disposal, use whatever you want! Just be thorough! It's bad enough that all the others are headed for the morgue!"

"Yes, sir," she murmured. "Ah . . . sir, are you . . . am I . . ."

He sighed, sharply. "No, Nadia. You are not in disgrace. You followed your team leader's orders. He was the one at fault, and he has paid for the error in full. Understood? Now go do as I said."

"Yes, sir," she murmured. "Thank you."

He wished that Nadia had had the initiative to defy orders and put bullets into Parr's and Ranieri's brain stems on the spot. But he could hardly fault her for doing as her team leader had directed.

Zoe's snorting and whimpering grated on him. She needed aggressive behavioral modification and changes in her meds. To be fair, he had perhaps overdone it in the sexual rewards. To show off for Michael, he'd basically inflicted a twenty-minute orgasm on the poor girl. She could barely stand up. It would be no wonder if her brain chemistry was somewhat altered.

It occurred to him, staring down at her, that Zoe might do for Reginald's contract, assuming they would accept a female. Zoe's skills were formidable, and her flaws were easy to downplay. He gazed at her dewy, writhing body. Zoe could offer frills to the Amesbury Group CEO that Reginald could not. At least not to this client, who favored women.

King had been acquainted with Michal LeFevre, the CEO of the Amesbury Group, for years. In spite of LeFevre's three hundred pounds of quivering bulk, his greasy comb-over, liver spots, and his seventy-four years, the man had an insatiable appetite for beautiful young women.

King wondered if the man knew how it would feel to have the young woman's passion be unfeigned, the orgasms real. If LeFevre had Zoe's DeepWeave sexual imprint commands, he could experience that wonder firsthand. Zoe would be his adoring slave.

LeFevre would never be able to refuse. In fact, King might even up the price. He'd never factored his operatives' sexual programming into his contracts. It was risky, uncertain, and he preferred to keep the Levels Eight, Nine, and Ten mortal control commands, such as the one he'd just issued to Reginald, strictly to himself. But Zoe might not work out in the long run anyway. Her overheated sexuality and helpless sobbing hinted at deep inner instability. It might be best to use her up all at once. Recoup what he could of his investment. Cut his losses.

But first, Zoe would rid the world of Lily Parr and Bruno Ranieri.

Fury flared afresh. Reginald, Cal, Tom, Martin. Four of his mature male operatives. Two from the special series. It was a staggering loss.

Watching Reginald blow his own brains out had not even begun to soothe his anger. He only wished he could kill that incompetent piece of shit more than once. King looked down, noticed that he was erect. Anger often had an energizing effect on him. He stroked his penis thoughtfully as he approached the sobbing woman on the floor.

But Michael had left scarcely ten minutes before, sweaty

and spent, and Zoe had not even washed. It would be unhygienic.

The com buzzed. Nadia. Too soon to be reporting on the successful completion of her task. Which meant there was a problem.

"What is it?" he barked.

"Sir, I'm outside the Wygant Street house," she said. "The police were here when I arrived."

King was so appalled, he had nothing to say. "How . . ."

"It seems that the bullet Reggie fired went through the bedroom window." Nadia's voice was apologetic. "It also went through the bedroom window of the neighbor's house across the street. The woman who lives there called the police. She's being treated by the EMTs for cuts from the broken glass. They're wheeling Reggie's body out now."

King closed his eyes. His blood pressure was climbing, his ears roaring. Reggie had managed to fuck up, even in death.

"What do you want me to do, sir?" Nadia's voice swam through the haze of red with a few seconds of delay. "Sir? Are you still there?"

"Go to headquarters. I'll send you a new team leader tomorrow."

"Yes, sir. I am so—"

He cut off the connection, uninterested in whatever else she had to say. He nudged Zoe with his toe. "Get up."

She gazed up, tear-blinded, nose running. "But, sir, Reggie—"

"Shut up, and get on your feet. Or are you too emotionally destroyed to take Reggie's place as team leader?"

Zoe gasped and scrambled to her feet with gratifying swiftness. "I'm ready," she said, her voice suddenly clear as a bell.

Finally. The attitude he liked to see. "I want Parr and Ranieri gone. Vanished. No trace. No witnesses, no publicity, no bodies. Fast."

"Yes, sir."

He stared at her, panting with rage. On impulse, he swept the table clear. Dessert plates, coffee service, wineglasses, burning candles, all crashed to the floor. He wrenched his pants open, shoved Zoe back against the table. She draped herself back eagerly, opening wide.

It was a relief at first, but after a while, the pounding began to bore him. Zoe's moist, quivering body was so wet, so eager, so yielding. She perceived his brutality as pleasure. If he lashed her with a whip, she would beg for more. He needed resistance tonight. Conquest.

He was losing his erection. It made him want to strangle her.

He pulled away, leaving her whimpering, on the verge of her fifth orgasm. And he had not even used the programmed phrases to elicit them. This was pure spillover. Innate sexual heat and emotional excess. Typical of Zoe. Dirty little slut. "Get dressed," he ordered her.

She jerked up onto her elbows. "But I . . . but please, can't I—"

"No." He buttoned his pants, did up his belt. "You've had enough for tonight. You must earn your treats."

"Yes, sir." She struggled into her tight dress as he entered commands that would give her a higher level of access to relevant files.

"Go wash," he said. "The car will be waiting in twenty minutes to take you to the airport. Study the files en route."

Zoe was looking confused. King manufactured a smile to settle her nerves. "If your assignment is a success, we will dine again, and I will give you a full Level Ten reward sequence. The whole thirty verses."

Her eyes went wide, dazzled. "Oh, sir," she whispered. "Really?"

It was a bit iffy to overuse sexual rewards. In fact, such an overwhelming experience could actually damage her. But sex seemed to be Zoe's most powerful motivating force. And matters were very urgent.

"I've never given the whole sequence to any of my agents before," he said throatily, stroking her cheek. "But you, my lovely Zoe, are special. A real treasure. So finish this business. And hurry back."

Zoe scurried to comply.

10

"Pull over here," Bruno said. "At the mall."

"Here?" Alex Aaro scowled over his shoulder at them. "You're being pursued by hit men, and you want an Egg McMuffin?"

Bruno exhaled through his teeth. He bitterly regretted having called the guy. Aaro was not his friend, nor even Kev's friend. He was Kev's brother Davy McCloud's friend, an old Army Rangers buddy. He'd helped them out in the zombie masters debacle and gotten the shit blown out of his property in the process, so he'd racked up pity points to offset his terminally bad attitude. Plus, he'd helped the McCloud brothers and their friends on other strange exploits, the tales of which were so improbable, Bruno still couldn't bring himself to believe them. Nutzoid McClouds. They baffled him. But Kev fit right in, even after an eighteen-year hiatus. Which, of course, only pissed Bruno off all the more.

Yep, Aaro was resoundingly not his friend, but that was what made this dickface the safest one to call, if Lily was to be believed about the apocalyptic surveillance bullshit. He had his doubts, but those attackers had been focused, trained professionals. Not drug-addled street scum. It was weird enough to make him very careful.

In spite of the explosions and the pitched gun battle at his remote forest home, Aaro had, amazingly, stayed out of the press. He kept a low profile, being freakishly paranoid, the McClouds said.

And that meant something, coming from those guys.

"We need clothes," he said. "At the Gresham outlet mall. We're a mess."

"Retail therapy for the stress? What'll it be, Victoria's Secret?"

He was not rising to the bait. "Clothes," he said evenly. "Normal, warm winter clothes. I can't use my cards until I know what the fuck is going on, so you'll have to front me."

Aaro swerved into the mall entrance. "Let me get this straight. You call at the crack of dawn with a story about bodies on the streets of Portland. You demand taxi service, because out of nowhere, the whole world wants to kill you and your schizo girlfriend, too."

Lily bristled. "I am not schizo!"

"And now we're going for a shopping spree at the mall, at my expense. Shall we get a latte and a ginger current scone at the coffee bar? An acupuncture treatment? A massage?"

Bruno stared at the guy. "I can't drag her up to Tony's cabin in a miniskirt and heels. There might be snow up there."

"Bruno, he's right. Stopping for clothes would be silly," Lily said. "Let's just save that for when we—"

"You're spattered with blood!" he yelled. "Your coat is canvas, with no lining! You don't even have any goddamn underwear!"

Lily jerked loose of his encircling arm. "You bastard!" she hissed. "I do, too!"

"That thong you're wearing does not count," Bruno retorted.

Aaro jerked to a stop and gave them a knowing look. "Glad to hear the hit men haven't cramped your sex life any."

"That was before!" he snarled back. "The hit men came after!"

Aaro flinched, lifting his hands. "Don't give me the blow-by-blow. God, look at me, in my sad celibate state. Forced to buy hot lingerie for Bruno's bare-assed girlfriend."

"Don't bother," Lily told him. "I'd rather die than wear it."

Aaro turned his sharp, narrow gaze on her. "If death is what you wanted, your new fancy boy fucked that up for you back at the diner. So what would make you feel like living again? Culottes? Tap pants? Stretch lace? Red satin? Go wild, honey. You like thongs?"

"Watch it, Aaro," Bruno said.

Aaro's eyes flicked to Lily's crotch. It was hidden by the folds of her blood-spattered canvas coat, but Lily's battered knees still snapped smartly together. "Oh, I do," he said. "Whenever I get the chance."

She gave him a thin smile. "When hell freezes over, buddy."

"Ooh. Scary," Aaro murmured. "You tell her, man, because I'm way too intimidated to say it to her face, but she should keep her panties on in these dangerous times."

"Up yours, asshole," Lily retorted.

Bruno put his finger over Lily's mouth. Anger had given her a nice rosy glow, which had to be a good thing, up to a point. He held up his hand to forestall whatever snide and hateful thing Aaro was opening his mouth to say. "You are out of line, man," he said quietly. "Shut up."

Aaro's mouth tightened. "I knew it," he said. "I knew, as soon as I saw who was calling, that this would be another massive goatfuck with international implications. It always is, with McClouds."

"I'm not a McCloud. I share no genetic material with those freaks!"

Aaro dismissed that with a wave of his hand. "You might as well be. The curse rubs off on anyone they hang out with. You've been exposed, so you're already fucked. And so am I." He glanced at Lily, not without sympathy. "You too, from the looks of things."

"That's stupid," Bruno muttered.

"Yeah? My home, my vehicle and my privacy got bombed to rubble the last time I answered a phone call from one of you clowns!"

"You were reimbursed in full! They threw money at your head to make up for that! You have no reason to feel sorry for yourself!"

"You can't reimburse privacy," Aaro said darkly. "Doing favors for you guys is costly on a whole lot of levels."

"Look at it this way," Bruno said. "I'm a client, OK? Bill me by the hour. Name your fucking rate. Save your receipts. I'm not asking any favors, so I won't unleash the curse. No favors, no curse. Simple."

"Nothing's simple about broken bodies on the street."

"I told you," Bruno protested. "They were trying to kill—"

"Yeah, I get the white knight thing, but was it necessary to snuff the guys? Was your brain functioning at all? You've got no idea who they were, what they want, or from what direction they'll come the next time." His eyes cut to Lily. "Or do you?"

She shook her head, her lips tight.

"Great. So now, instead of having somebody to interrogate, you've got a possible murder rap. What a trade-off. Why didn't you just beat the shit out of them? You, my friend, have fucked up."

Bruno bit back a snotty retort. He was still afraid to think about the entity that had taken over his body during that fight. And he didn't want to get mired in explanations and self-justification. Waste of time and breath. There was nothing he could say to Aaro that wouldn't be whining, or excuse mongering. He shook his head. Later for that.

"OK, then," Aaro said sourly. "Whatever. By the hour, up the ass, receipts itemized. What do you want me to buy?"

"Sensible winter shoes." Bruno turned to Lily. "What's your size?"

"Six, but seriously, I really don't want—"

"A big sweater for her, some drab color. A wool knit cap. A winter coat. Down, with a hood. Black nylon, something big and puffy. Jeans for both of us. I'm about your size, and for her . . ." He looked her over appraisingly. "Ten for her. And get me a sweatshirt."

She jumped. "Hey. That's not my—"

"Yeah, I know you're more like an eight, but I want them loose," he snapped. "This is not about showcasing your ass."

"Speaking of her ass," Aaro interjected. "You haven't told me how you want the underwear." He eyed her, chewing his lip.

Lily lunged for the door. "I'm done. Have a nice life, gentlemen."

Bruno caught her as she grabbed the handle, and yanked her back. His arm locked around her, clamped over her heaving ribcage.

"Let go of me," she said. "Right now."

"I can't," he said. And it was the literal truth.

Aaro made a disgusted sound. "You're cooked, buddy. Your judgment is deep-fried in testosterone. Not a pretty sight."

"Go earn your hourly fee and get out of my face," Bruno said.

The slam of the van door cut off a string of obscenities, which then faded away into the distance.

The silence in the van was punctuated by Lily's rapid breathing. The thrum of her pulse was too fast. She was shorting out. Muscling her around probably wasn't helping, but he couldn't stop. He was shaking, too. His heart banging just as hard.

She pried at his wrist. Her hand was icy cold. He covered

it with his and opened his jacket, pulling her back so she could soak up some skin-on-skin heat. The contact had its predictable effect.

He tried to keep his lust locked up in the privacy of his own head, but Lily could pluck horndog impulses right out of the airwaves with the precision of a pair of surgical tweezers. She shifted against him, moving uneasily against the throbbing heaviness in his groin.

"Sorry," he offered. "All that talk about asses and underwear. I'm suggestible. Plus there's the combat buzz. Gets you every time."

She scowled at him through tangles of bright hair. "Just a physiological phenomenon? Nothing personal? Gee, that's so flattering."

He started to laugh. She winced when his hand tightened on her shoulder. He lifted it, angry at himself for having forgotten the bruise.

He pushed her coat open and plucked the shirt down. Oh, ouch. It was bruising already. He laid his hand over it. No pressure, just warmth. "I'm sorry about this," he said. "I wish I had some ice for you."

She started to shrug, thought better of it. "I'm not sorry. If they'd hit your skull, you'd have gone down, and we'd both be dead. Or worse."

"There's worse?" He smiled. "That's a positive way of looking at a big hematoma. You working on that glass-half-full attitude?"

She snorted. "Hardly. Speaking of attitudes. Aaro? Holy shit, Bruno. Where did you dig this guy up? He's horrible!"

"Sorry about that," Bruno said ruefully. "He was always sort of a clam, but today he's totally on the rag. Still, he has the resources that I need. And did you come across his name from your research on me?"

"Nope," she said. "Never heard of the guy."

"That means he was the right one to call."

They stared into each other's eyes. The energy buzzed,

hot and strained. It was wrong, stupid, irresponsible, but he leaned forward, breathing her in. Her lips parted. Her eyes had a wild, misty glow.

He kissed her. The zing of contact knocked the cage door wide open, and something big and muscular came barreling out, snorting and pawing. Something that wanted what it wanted and didn't give a shit about doing the right thing. He tugged down the tattered stretch lace of her shirt, pulling until the points of her soft, perfect tits popped out. Took a whap to the face. Barely noticed it, he was so intent on tasting her nipples. Sweet and taut in his mouth. He flicked his tongue over the rigid buds and suckled until her fingernails dug into his jacket.

He pushed her leg up onto the seat, shoved up the skirt. Didn't have far to go. Sexy woman smell, mixed with perfumed girly bath products. Her pussy glowed from their exploits in Tony's apartment. The gusset of the thong was lost in her plump, juicy folds. She made a breathless sound as he plucked the gusset away and took a long look at damp ringlets, her pussy lips poking out like a hothouse flower.

"Stop this," she said. "I thought you wanted answers."

"I thought I did, too," he said. "Then I looked under your skirt."

He wooed her into another kiss for a couple of honey-sweet, wet, sticky minutes, until she gathered her wits and shoved at him again.

"Now is not the time, Bruno! If that guy Aaro came back while we were involved, and saw us, I'd have to kill myself just to save face!"

"How about I kill him, instead?" he suggested. "We'll just take his van, dump him, and run. What's one more body, more or less?"

Lily blinked at him for a few seconds. "Um. You're kidding, right?"

Aw, shit. He flung his head against the seat and shut his

eyes. So, he really was that terrifying. How fucking depressing was that.

"Now is a really bad time to joke about that stuff, Bruno."

"Fine. I won't kill him." He brushed his knuckle over the smudged mascara on her cheekbone. "Don't be scared of me. I'm not dangerous."

"No? Three dead guys on the ground in barely over a minute?"

He rocked back, jarred. That event had nothing to do with the person he thought he was. A good fighter, yes, but he approached martial arts more as a sport than anything else. He wasn't dangerous. He was the class clown, the smart-ass, the charmer who would do anything for a laugh. Not a killer.

But those guys were dead. He could call it self-defense, but he hadn't been thinking self-defense. He hadn't thought at all.

He'd just killed. So easily. Smoothly. Like some part of him was used to it.

He stared at her lips, her tangle of glossy hair. He tended to distract himself from uncomfortable feelings as quickly and forcibly as possible. Sex was an awesome distraction.

He tried to look harmless. "I'm not dangerous to you," he told her.

"Bullshit," she whispered. "You could destroy me."

He winced. "Stop being so apocalyptic. It bugs me."

She giggled, which he took as a good sign. "Can you blame me?"

He thudded down, off the seat, onto the floor. So. Didn't look like he was going to score. Not unless he forced the issue, which would make the disconnect complete. The old Bruno, the new Bruno. The Bruno who could slaughter three guys was hard enough to integrate with his self-image. A Bruno who forced a woman into sex . . . nah.

God, it was hard, though. He shoved Lily's knees together, hard, and dropped his head down to the tops of her thighs, pressing his hot cheek against the grubby coat. The tryst in Tony's apartment played in his head. Every hot, silken clutch of her pussy around his aching prong, burned forever into his memory. He ground his fists against his eyes until kaleidoscopic sparks swirled and spun in his inner vision.

Red like blood. Spattering Lily's coat. Trickling out of the mouth of the guy on the ground. Oozing from the crushed skull of the other man.

So familiar. Fighting like a robot. Losing control, being taken over. Like his Rudy dreams. Except that the opponents had been real this time, and could die. Had died. Broken and bleeding.

Lily's hands came to rest on his head. She bent over and laid her face against the back of his head. The hot rhythm of her breath had transformed his scalp into an erogenous zone. He endured it in a state of razor-edged sensual overload. Pure heavenly bliss. Fucking torture.

Click. They jerked apart as the door slid open. Aaro stuck his head in. "I saw that," he growled.

"Saw what?" Bruno asked, defensive.

Aaro tossed assorted shopping bags into the van. "You owe me three hundred and ninety bucks so far." He held out a paper food bag.

Bruno took it. "Oh. Ah, thanks."

"Don't thank me. No favors means no thanks."

"Yeah, right." Bruno dug for the coffee.

"I thought you should get some caffeine and sugar into her before her blood pressure went south." Aaro looked Lily over. "But she's glowing. Looks like you've successfully regulated her blood pressure in other, more pleasurable ways."

"Shut up, Aaro," Bruno growled.

"Just get this straight, loverboy. No boinking in my van."

"Fuck off," Lily's voice rang out. "We didn't do anything."

"That would explain why his head was in your lap." Aaro reached into the bag, fished out coffee and held it out. "Enjoy. You're welcome."

She stared at him for a moment. "I don't have to thank you, remember?" she said. "You're not doing me any favors."

"True. I'm so crushed. Now drink some coffee, dollface."

Her eyes widened. "Did you just call me *dollface?*"

"No." Bruno snatched the cup out of Aaro's hand and passed it to her. "It was an aural hallucination. Have your breakfast sandwich."

"Yeah, ignore me." Aaro pawed through the bags until he found one with stenciled hearts on it. "By the way, you never did tell me your size. Hope nothing binds or pinches your tender pink places, babe."

He let the bag fly. It landed on Lily's lap. She shrank back as if it were a venomous snake. It hit the floor. Fuck-me-please panties spilled out. A tangle of satin, lace, and silk. Red, black, peach, flesh-tone.

Bruno growled expletives in a Calabrese dialect as he shoved underwear into the bag. It was his standard tension reliever. None of the people he insulted knew he was commenting on their grandmother's predilection for sex with sheep.

"I am not wearing that slutty, disgusting stuff." Lily's voice was haughty. "Certainly not after you've pawed it. Dog."

"Arf, arf." Aaro's tone was more cheerful than it had been so far at any time this morning. "I love it when she spits bile."

11

The van door slid open. A blast of cold, intensely sweet air swept in, along with a noise that took a while to decipher. Birdsong. And air. So clean and sweet. Lily lingered under the surface, reluctant to come up. It had been so long. Sleep felt so good. She rubbed her eyes.

Bruno peered in. "You OK? You've been out for hours."

"I'm fine," she said through chattering teeth.

"Out you come, then." His jacket swung open as he helped her out, showing off washboard abs, that taut belly button, the arrowing trail of dark belly hair, bare to the elements. He must be cold, too, but he didn't look it. He had a nuclear furnace raging inside him.

He set her on her feet, and she wobbled on the unsteady ground. Icy wind lifted her snarled hair into a wind-whipped halo. The absence of noise pollution, burnt ozone, hydrocarbons, smoke, or particulate matter was weirdly alien. The wind moaned. Only a jet plume proved that civilization existed. "Where the *hell* are we?" she demanded.

"About twenty miles out of White Salmon, as the crow flies," Bruno said. "My uncle had a cabin."

"I never saw anything about a cabin in the property records!"

"Of course you didn't," Bruno said. "He fixed it that way himself, thirty-five years ago. He had a checkered past, before Vietnam. Tony wanted a place where he could disappear, from the law or the Ranieris, whoever was out for his blood." He looked around. "In fact, Kev and I don't have a clue what the hell to do about this place. The paperwork, I mean. Who the fuck knows whose name it's in? Tony never told."

"That doesn't explain what we're doing here!" Lily's voice shook.

Bruno frowned. "I told you I'd find you someplace safe to rest, remember? Without using my credit cards, this is the best I can do."

"But we're cornered here! Does this place have Internet? Phone service, taxis? Wireless?"

His face answered her. "Oh, God," she moaned. "You've dropped me into the bottom of a well. This is just freaking perfect!"

Aaro edged away. "I'll be on my way. You'll be getting my bill soon. Not that I know where to send it, since you're a fucking fugitive."

Bruno grunted. "You'll get your money."

"You mean, you're leaving us here?" Lily's voice squeaked with horror. "You're driving away, and leaving us here with no vehicle?"

"Like shit through a goose." Aaro sidled toward the driver's side door. "See ya, babe. Be good."

"No! I'm coming back with you! I am not staying here!"

Aaro got into his van, eyes wary. "Keep your distance, lady."

"Don't you dare drive away!" She tottered toward the van.

Aaro revved the engine and rolled his window down an inch to deliver his parting shot at Bruno. "Never would have thought I'd say this, man, but your girlfriend makes celibacy look good."

"You *asshole!*" Lily grabbed the handle, which locked with an audible *thunk* an instant before she touched it. Tires spat dirt and pebbles. Aaro peered out his window, trying not to drive over her feet.

She hung on, but Aaro did not stop. There was no question of running in those heels. She stumbled, sliding to her knees as the van rounded the curve, roared down the hill, rattling over a narrow plank bridge laid over a dry creek bed. It turned a corner and was gone.

Oh, *ouch*. That knee had already taken a lot of abuse.

Bruno pulled her to her feet and tried to hug her, the sneaky son of a bitch, but she was in freak-out mode, arms windmilling, tottering on the useless shoes. She pitched and swayed in the gusts of wind.

"Calm down," he was repeating, over and over, his tone pleading. "Calm down. Just calm down. This is a safe place."

He looked worried, scared, gorgeous. She tried to breathe. Safe place, her milk white ass. She laughed so hard it started her crying. He ended up hugging her, and she was too far gone to fight him off.

"I just can't be in a place like this," she gasped out. "I'll go crazy."

He glanced around at the terrifying, appalling nothing around them. Trees, bugs, rocks, sky. "What's this?" he asked. "A place that's wild, clean? Safe? What the fuck is not to like about this place?"

"The reason I've survived is because I've stayed on the move!" she yelled. "I'm like a shark that can't stop swimming or I'll die! I can't just look at the view while I wait for them to come beat me to death!"

"They won't." His voice was low, soothing. "I won't let them. No one knows about it. No one saw us come. My friends will come get us. I have a plan. We can have a meal, a shower. A nap. Is a nap so terrible?"

"I don't have time for a fucking nap!" she howled.

"You needed that one you took just now," he said triumphantly. "And you could use another one, where someone is sitting by the bed with a loaded gun. How long has it been since you relaxed?"

She goggled at him. "Loaded gun? Excuse me? You mean to say you have one of those? On your person?"

He looked impatient. "Of course, thanks to Aaro. More than one."

"And you know how to use them?"

His chest vibrated, plastered against hers. "Spare me, Lily."

"When pigs fly! Loaded guns are not items that I find relaxing!"

"You are so fucking hard to please. I don't know if it came across in your research, but I'm actually above average in intelligence. I can think my way out of a paper bag, and I can handle a gun. So chill."

"But if I'm not doing something, I'll go crazy!"

"So I'll just keep you really busy," he said.

She wasn't sure quite how to take that statement, so she ignored it entirely. "I'm just so goddamn scared," she whispered.

"Trust me," he said, unexpectedly, and scooped her into his arms.

"Hey! Stop that!" She flopped and twisted.

"You can't walk in those shoes, and you can't go barefoot, either," he said. "You'll freeze your feet. Stop wiggling."

He set her down on the small porch and fiddled with the padlocks on the doors. He'd done it again. Teased her through a screaming meltdown and out the other side. And he'd known her for, what, a few hours? They'd found their groove. He wasn't afraid of her.

Wouldn't last long, though. It never did. She never made it easy for guys. She eventually scared them or intimidated them or pissed them off or threatened their masculinity. She was a difficult proposition for a relationship in the best of times. And this was the very worst.

Look what a prize she'd been so far. Jerking him around, lying to him, spying on him, using him. Leading hit men to him. Getting him attacked, almost killed. Getting him in trouble with the law. Costing him shocking amounts of money. He was going to get sick of it.

How depressing. It made her guts feel sour. Hah. Like she

had the requisite brain cells to stress about her romantic prospects right now.

At least, the sex was, well, incendiary. A point in her favor. Guys weighed sex heavily in the balance. It was a big priority for them.

That thought perked her right up.

Snick, the lock gave. Bruno pushed the door open into a black, stifling cave. She was blinded as she stepped inside to the scent of woodsmoke and dust. Bruno opened the shutters, jerked a curtain aside, revealing a double bed swathed in plastic. Bedding was bound up in plastic bags as well. Her eyes adjusted to see him dragging blankets out of one of the bags. Laying one down on top of the plastic bed cover.

"Lie down," he said. "Cover yourself up while I get things going. The fire, the propane water heater. Some food."

"I can help," she offered.

"It'll go quicker if I do it alone. I've got the choreography of this place down. You rest, get warm. Relax."

Relax, her ass. Like she ever had, in her whole life, with her complicated baggage. And this was even before killers closed in. She sat on the bed. Bruno plucked off her shoes, scooping her legs up. He tossed another blanket on top of her.

He got to work on making the place habitable.

The blankets were fuzzy and thick, but she was stone cold from the inside. She huddled into a ball and watched him, teeth chattering.

Bruno kept looking over at her as he built a fire in the stove. When the flames were crackling, he came over to the bed, flung off his jacket, kicked off his shoes, and slid under the blanket with her.

Her glands went bananas. The bed creaked under his weight. Plastic crackled. He smelled like salt, sweat, the coppery tang of blood, and under that, his own special Bruno smell. He hugged her. The release of tension in her body was cataclysmic. It felt so good, so hot.

"You're freezing," he said, his voice disapproving.

"Yeah, well," she said. "You're helping."

"Not fast enough." He rolled over right on top of her, squashing the breath out of her. The bed sagged, creaked. "That better?"

A flush rose, like a hot cloud, until her whole body felt red. She wanted to say something offhand. Sure. No biggie, having a gorgeous sex god who held all the keys to her destiny, squishing her onto a bed.

He propped himself onto his elbows so that she could drag in some air. She didn't do it consciously, but suddenly, she'd moved so he was resting the stiff bulge of his crotch against the vee of her opened thighs. The wind moaned, singing of a vast empty solitude outside that made it so much more intimate within. The last two lovers in the world.

There was no reason in the world for him not to just open his jeans, twitch the gusset of her thong aside and have her. She ached for it. A hot pull of mindless yearning that actually hurt, it was so strong.

He answered her silent call, settling into an incredibly slow, sensual pulse. Her face got hotter, her breath shallow. They couldn't break their eye contact. It blazed out of her like light, how badly she needed him to press against that sweet ache, just like that, again . . .

She lifted herself against him. He seconded her every move with such grace, such perfect swirling pressure and the slow . . . firm pulse and push, and oh, God, yes . . . *yes* . . .

She exploded, energy pumping down to her fingers and toes. Beyond. Extending out into infinity, fused with him, with everything.

When she got enough presence of mind back to be mortally embarrassed, he was kissing her. Tender, coaxing kisses, wordlessly asking for something from her that she didn't even dare put a name to. Let alone grant him. She just didn't have it to give. She turned her face away, but Bruno was having none of that. He cupped her face, forced her gaze back until their eyes locked. "You warmed up?" he asked.

She nodded.

"I just meant to get you warm. I swear to God. I didn't mean to dry hump you. That just sort of happened."

He lifted himself up. Before she knew what she was doing, she'd yanked him back down. He landed on his elbows, wary. "Huh?"

"Don't you want . . . ?" She couldn't say it. She wound her legs around his thighs and let her body ask the question.

He gave her an are-you-kidding look. "Of course I want it. But you've been skating on the edge of a breakdown ever since those guys attacked us. You almost had one right outside. It's not a good time."

"I'd be OK," she assured him.

He shook his head. "You can't be sure how you'd feel. And if I started, I wouldn't be able to stop."

So? Who wanted him to stop? She wanted to scream, slap him, force him to stop trying so hard to be a good guy. But that would make her seem crazier. Push him further away.

"Get warmed up," he said. "Get on your new clothes, get some food into you, then we can talk about everything you know, suspect, or guess, or fear about what's happening to you. Then we hike up to the bluff."

She jerked up onto her elbow. "Are you kidding? Is this a time for a flipping nature walk, Ranieri?"

"It's the only place with cell reception," he said. "I can use the phone Aaro gave me, with encryption software."

"To call who?"

"My brother's brothers. My adopted brother Kev recently hooked up with his biological family a few months ago. Real eventful, you might say. But you know all about that, right?"

She dropped her gaze. "Um. Some of it."

His eyebrow tilted. "I figured that. Anyhow. Once I've talked to them, I can make some decisions."

She blinked. "Um. Excuse me? *You* will make the decisions?"

"Yes." He stared her straight in the eyes. "Me. It's your own fault, Lily, for dragging me into this. Now you have to deal with me."

"Don't get masterful on me, Ranieri. I don't respond well to that."

"You need someone to make some decisions for you, babe," he said. "Just a few. For a little while. Just rest. And trust me."

She shook her head. "Don't ask me to trust you, because I can't. It's nothing personal, I swear to God. I just don't have the equipment."

"You don't have a choice," he said.

It was true, she realized. She'd put herself smack-dab in someone's else's power. Alone in a cabin in the armpit of the universe, with a guy who could pick her up and twirl her on his pinkie if he felt like it. But there was no reasoning with her urge to micromanage.

"They'll be listening to the McClouds," she said stubbornly.

"The phone calls will be encrypted," he repeated. "These people run a security company, Lily. They're ex-military, ex-special forces, ex-everything. Plus, they were raised by a paranoid survivalist freak with global conspiracy theories." He blinked. "You know, your kind of guy."

She bristled. "Smart-ass."

He got back to work. Lily stared at dust motes dancing in the beam of light that sliced through the window, determined to stay alert.

Next thing she knew, the smell of coffee and frying onions was dragging her out of sleep. She forced herself up onto her elbow, trying not to wince. The shoulder hurt, a lot. The room was warm. The angle of the light had changed, moved up the wall.

Bruno stood over a gas range, stirring onions that sizzled

in a cast-iron skillet. They smelled amazing. He looked different. A fresh black sweatshirt. Wet, clean hair, no bloodstains. He looked yummy.

She rubbed her eyes. "Hey."

He gave her a smile that would bend metal with its sheer charm load. "Water's hot in the shower tank. You like steak?"

"Wow." Her stomach rumbled. She hadn't been able to afford anything with that much protein in it since D-day, and rarely enough before that, either. The rich scent made her dizzy. "Where did all this food come from?"

"Aaro got some groceries for us, in Bingen. I call it ten minutes to sit-down. Can you shower in that time?"

"I'll try." She got to her feet, took the battered terrycloth bathrobe he offered her, and closeted herself in the miniscule bathroom.

The shower was heaven. She stayed under until it turned tepid, then chilly, then glacial. It took that much scrubbing to get the makeup off. But afterward, the face in the mirror was her own. Not Mata Hari. Or the mascara-smeared hell-hag.

When she came out, the table was set for two and loaded with fragrant, steaming food. "Sit," he said.

She was intensely conscious of her nudity under the damp terrycloth. "Shouldn't I dress?"

"The room's warm. And the food's hot. And it's just me."

True enough. She sat down and dug in. The steak was pan seared, pink and juicy and melting, and heaped with caramelized onions. He'd done cheesy buttered noodles, some sort of long pasta with frilly edges, dripping and rich. A heap of peppery coleslaw. Slices of hothouse tomatoes. Crisp, warty sour pickles. Fresh sourdough bread to sop up drippings. Mmm. He kept refilling her plate. She kept eating.

"I'd offer you a beer, but it's not a great idea," he said. "It would take the starch out of you for the hike. So it's water, for now."

"That's OK," she said. "I don't drink."

"Oh?" He buttered a hunk of his bread. "Not ever, or not now?"

"Not ever." She looked down, wishing she hadn't said anything.

"Any reason for that?"

"Does there have to be?"

His shrug was elaborately casual. "You're the one who was flapping it in front of my face."

She sighed. It was relevant, she supposed, in a painful, oblique sort of way, so whatever. "My dad was an alcoholic, and a junkie."

He took it in, his face impassive. "This would be the father who—"

"Yes. The father who was murdered six weeks ago, by those guys who attacked us, I assume. Or whatever organization hired them."

"Ah." He got up, rummaged on the shelves. He found a plastic box and knelt in front of her, pushing the robe open over her knees.

She shrank away. "What the hell are you doing?"

"Disinfecting the scrapes on your legs. While I do that, you talk."

"I'll do it myself! Just give me the stuff! I can take care of it!"

"Shhh." He batted her hands away. "Let me."

Lily stared down at the top of his dark head and fished around for a starting point. "Well, my name is Lily Parr, not Torrance," she began. "I guess I'll start when my dad fell apart. I was ten. Which would have made it 1993."

His eyes flicked up when she mentioned the year that his mother had died. "Fell apart how?"

She clenched her teeth as he swabbed with the alcohol-soaked wad of cotton. "Like I said, he started drinking heavily. Then he started in on the opiates. Heroin, mostly, I think, although one white powder looks pretty much like another to me. Ouch, goddamnit, that hurts!"

"Hold still." He leaned in with the tweezers. "There's grit in here."

She hissed and cursed as he tortured her with tweezers. He was unmoved, intent upon his task. "What work did he do?" he asked.

"He was a fertility specialist," she said. "A researcher, in IVF technology. He got early retirement not long after his breakdown. He was barely fifty, but he got a pension. A good one, but not generous enough to fund a drug habit. I started swiping the checks before he saw them. I paid the bills so they wouldn't turn off the lights, the gas. So we could eat. Not that he was that interested in food anymore."

He nodded, frowning in concentration as he taped gauze over her knees. His eyes flicked up, waiting while she struggled for words.

It sounded so sad, and flat, when she laid the facts out. Howard's string of suicide attempts. The decision to commit him to an institution. The search for the perfect clinic that would keep him alive. And then, that last, awful visit. Howard's cryptic warning, and his message, about Magda Ranieri and her son. The mysterious thing that needed to be locked, whatever it might be. Miriam's interruption.

Then the call from Dr. Stark, and Howard's so-called suicide. And the guys waiting outside Nina's apartment with knives. And that was it.

It wasn't enough for him. She could feel that in the air. Strongly.

"I tried to research you, while I was on the run," she told him. "I tried to find out more about the nurse, Miriam Vargas, too, but she seemed to check out. At least, I found records of her going to nursing school in Baltimore. I tried to find out more about Magda, but I got nowhere with that. Just statistics, the newspaper articles, the obit. The only next step was to talk to you. So, um. I made my way here."

He placed his big, warm hands gently over her knees. The

soothing warmth felt good, over the stings and scrapes and boo-boos.

So, at last. Here it was. The question that had been burning in her mind for six weeks. The one she'd almost given up hope of asking.

"Do you have any information?" she asked. "Any insights?"

He met her eyes. Her heart tumbled, thudded, three stories down.

"Babe, I haven't got a fucking clue," he said.

She shivered and tugged the robe tighter. "But I . . . didn't you—"

"It was exactly like I told you," he said. "I didn't misrepresent what happened at all. My mamma was killed. It was a banal incident of domestic violence. She had really bad taste in men. She didn't give me instructions to lock anything. She didn't give me anything, or tell me anything. She put me on a bus to Portland one night to keep me from getting killed. That's all there is to that story."

Lily nodded. Her throat was too tight to speak.

Bruno went on. "The only big question is why she didn't climb on that bus with me. That's what I will never understand."

She brightened. "Well, maybe that's it. Maybe this is the answer to that question. If we could figure out what she was—"

"No." His voice cut her off. "Don't do it, Lily."

"Do what? I'm just speculating—"

"Don't speculate," he said. "Don't try and lay your crazy agenda over what happened to my mamma. It won't hold the weight."

Oh, shit. She'd hit a nerve. She backpedaled, nervously. "Bruno, I'm only trying to—"

"There is no mystery to solve. I faced that, a long time ago. It was bad enough the first time. I'm not going back to do it again."

She twisted her hands in the damp terrycloth and tried to face it.

"So, looks like you tracked me down and lured me into your honeyed trap for nothing," he said, after a while. "I'm sorry I don't have any better recompense to offer you for all that effort."

She bristled. "What do you mean by that?"

He shrugged, without meeting her eyes. "Just wondering if you regret having gone through with it."

"With what?" she asked, apprehensively.

"Fucking me," he said. "You know, now that you've discovered that the cupboard is bare. Does that kill the buzz?"

Oh, ouch. She got up and backed away from him. "Is it necessary to make me feel like a whore?"

"You said the word, not me."

She tried to marshal her argument, but it kept slipping apart in her head like a wet paper bag. To her own ears, her story now sounded preposterous, ridiculous. A pack of over-heated, disconnected lies.

"But what about what Howard said?" she asked. "Why would he mention you and your mother if there wasn't a connection?"

"I've never heard of a guy named Howard Parr," Bruno said.

"But why would they kill him, right after telling me if he—"

"Because they didn't," Bruno said. "By your own account, your father had severe mental health problems. Don't ask me to rip my life apart based on the ramblings of a suicidal heroin junkie who'd been confined to a locked ward for, what, how many years now?"

"Almost six, when I add them all up," she said. "But you don't understand. I know he was murdered."

He shook his head. She wanted to scream at him. To slap that sad, sad look off his face. "Face it, Lily," he said quietly. "Get real."

"Goddamnit, it is real! I knew him! He was terrified of blood! He would never have cut himself, not in a million years!"

"Depends on how much pain he was in," Bruno said. "Maybe you can't even imagine how bad it was. It might have been worth it to him to face his fear. He saw his opportunity, gritted his teeth, and took it."

"No, it's not possible. Not him." She hid her face. It hurt, so bad, that he didn't believe her. Even though she'd never really hoped that he would, she still felt so betrayed. Hurt to the depths of her being.

"Nobody knows better than me how much it hurts to swallow this down," he said. "But sometimes stupid, random, bad things just happen. They have no meaning. There's no mystery, no explanation. Just shit luck. I've accepted mine. I'm not going to redo the work I did."

Lily kept shaking her head. She couldn't stop shaking it.

"I'm very sorry about what happened to you," he said. "It's awful. Terrible. But it's not connected to my mamma. Or to me."

"Then how did they find me? They found me because they were watching you. Why would they if there's no connection?"

"They found you because they found you." His voice was harsher now. "You slipped up. It's that shit luck again. You've had a stinking big dose of it. I understand your desire for company, but don't pin your shit luck on me. I've already had my share."

"Then why?" she yelled. "What the hell do they want with me?"

He just gazed at her, looking miserable and uncomfortable.

A horrible realization began to unfold. "Oh, my God." Her belly clenched. She regretted having eaten so much. "You think I'm a liar?"

He stared into her eyes for a long moment. Trying to read

her mind. "No," he said softly. "I don't think that. God help me, but I don't."

She pressed both arms against her belly. "Well, that's good, at least. But then how do you justify . . ." Her voice trailed off, as it slowly, painfully sank in. "Ah. I see. So you think I'm crazy, right?"

His mouth was a flat, unhappy line. "I think you're confused, and scared, and sleep deprived. And stressed to the fucking max."

It was the truth, but his gentle tone and careful word choice were still offensive to her. "I see," she said, bitterly. "So, I'm a couple cans short of a six-pack, right?"

Bruno dropped his face into his hands, shoulders slumped. "Fuck if I know," he muttered. "But those killers are real."

The silence was unbearably heavy. Lily straightened her shoulders. Time to suck it up and move on. "Fortunately for you, it's no longer your problem." She sidled past him to the bed, where he'd piled the shopping bags. "I apologize for wasting your time. And I'll just, ah, get the hell out of your way now."

"You can't do that now, Lily," he said.

"I'll need the stuff you bought." She dumped clothes onto the bed, pawed through them. "I'll reimburse you. What did Aaro say? Four hundred?" She rifled through the panties, picked out the least offensive of the lot. Peach lace. She pulled them on. Struggled into the jeans.

"I don't give a shit about the money," he said.

"I don't really care what you give a shit about. How much did you spend on gas? You'll have to let me know whatever Aaro bills you, too."

"How about my legal bills, when somebody gets around to charging me with murder two?"

That was way too big a bite to chomp down on right then. "Let's stick with simple stuff for now." She pulled out the T-shirt, the sweater. She couldn't put them on without getting naked, and she hesitated to do that in front of a guy who thought she was a lying opportunist. But he'd seen it all, so what the hell. Off with the robe.

She wrenched on the tee. The sweater was huge, sleeves flopping sadly off her shoulders. She sat on the bed and got to work on socks, shoes. She felt so stupid. Embarrassed to exist. She shrugged on the coat. The clothes were comforting in their stiff bulk. Like armor.

"I'll just hike down to civilization now," she said. "This stuff should keep me plenty warm. Thanks for everything."

"It would take a day to walk down from here, even if you knew the terrain and could take shortcuts, which you don't. Don't be stupid."

"It's crazy, not stupid, buddy. Crazy has a better ring to it. And like I said, no longer your problem. Please forget I ever bothered you."

"No," he said. "You're in danger."

"Tell me something I don't know. Let me out of here before I die of embarrassment." At the moment, death by exposure or being eaten by a cougar was preferable to having Bruno look so sorry for her.

She wasn't even to the door before he grabbed her from behind. He pulled her against his body, which reminded her of a lot of things she would rather forget right now.

"Sunset is two hours away," he said roughly. "Please, Lily. Don't be both crazy and stupid. Just don't."

"You can't stop me." She immediately wished she hadn't said it. Because of course, he could. Easily.

To his credit, he didn't say it. She was very glad she was facing away from him. He didn't have to watch the crazy girl start to snivel.

So damn stupid. After all those dire warnings to herself, all her stern pep talks, she'd suckered herself into the fantasy of Lily and Bruno, the intrepid team. Lily and Bruno together, pitted against ultimate evil, had been a way different vibe than Loser Lily, pitted against it all by herself.

Bruno released her cautiously, like he was afraid she was going to bolt. "Let's hike up to the bluff, since you've got your coat on already," he said brusquely. "I have to make those calls."

She shook her head. "You've established my status as a lunatic. So cut me loose! Focus on your own problems!"

"I still have to figure out what to do with you. Just because your bad guys aren't connected to me doesn't mean they're not deadly."

"Oh, no!" She shook a frantic finger. "No, you don't have to 'do' anything with me. I can take care of myself."

He pulled his jacket on, ignoring her. It pissed her off to the point of screaming. "Look, I'm mentally ill, right? Cut me loose! Simplify your life! If I get killed, it's not your fault! You don't even have to feel guilty! I release you from all responsibility! I'll sign a fucking waiver!"

"I need you as a witness, for what happened outside the diner."

It was a good try, and a convincing argument, but she didn't buy it for one second. "It's because you had sex with me, isn't it?"

Hah. She'd nailed it. She could see it, all over his face.

"Shut up, Lily," he muttered.

"Ah, yes! I get it! You feel guilty, right? So sorry for the stressed-out crazy girl who can't keep straight why people are trying to kill her? You feel bad, for taking advantage of a vulnerable, deeply disturbed person in her hour of need? You feel like bottom-feeding slime for abusing the handicapped? Well, fuck you, Bruno Ranieri. Fuck you."

He shoved her grimly toward the door. "Shut up and walk."

12

Unfair, Miles reflected glumly as he tailed Zia Rosa through the baby supplies store. The crapola errands always fell to him. Got scut work? Something mind numbing, time consuming? Call good old Miles.

He stared at the rectangular block of Zia Rosa's back draped in a leopard-print tent of a blouse, gold chain link necklaces jingling cheerfully over it all, a tiger-striped plastic purse. Cruising down the aisle with her broad, stumpy gait like she owned the place.

He'd asked her four times if she'd gotten everything on her list, and if not, could he please, please just run and fetch it for her, but she had to run her eye over every last damn product in the aisles to make sure she hadn't forgotten anything. He felt like a yipping Chihuahua, dragged behind her on a leash. She gave about that much attention to anything he said. Zia Rosa had very selective comprehension.

Had to be today that she had to get the bouncy seat for little Eamon and the foam wedgies for the crib of tiny Helena, Davy and Margot's newest addition. Today, when Cindy's band's recording session had been canceled due to tech problems in the studio. Which would have led to her being home all afternoon. With him. Naked, going at it like a couple of crazed bunnies. But not today, because of a mysterious phone call from Aaro. It seemed Kev's prickly, problematic adopted brother Bruno had gotten himself into some sort of bizarre trouble. And whiz-bang, the McCloud clan went to red alert. That meant everybody was grounded until the situation was clarified. But explain that to Zia Rosa. Even the McClouds, with their combined testosterone, could not intimidate that woman out of doing whatever the fuck she wanted. The McClouds had met their match. It would've been funny, if they hadn't been using Miles to solve their problem.

Nothing had been the same since Zia had showed up, a package deal along with Kev McCloud's triumphal return. She'd proceeded to camp out all over the McCloud clan's lives, or at least, those that were reproducing, which was most of them, at this point. She'd earned Liv's and Margot's and Erin's undying devotion for her help with the babies. The kids adored her. Tam was terrified of her. That said it all.

And there was the food. God-kissed, orgasmic Italian food in industrial quantities. Everybody got themselves invited to dinner when Aunt Rosa was cooking, and then went around surreptitiously pinching their gut afterward, resolving to put in a few more hours in the gym to burn off the baked ziti or the cream custard pinoli tart, or whatever.

Miles had been bitching about the latest Zia Rosa lecture, something along the lines of "have those babies while you're young or you'll be sorry," while Davy changed the oil in his truck. He'd wondered out loud to Davy why they didn't just tell her to get gone, so everyone could breathe easy again. Davy stood up, frowning up into the sky, wiping oil off his hands, and explained things with his usual brevity.

"You have a mom," he said. "You can afford to be fussy. When you have kids, they'll have a grandma. We don't. Here's a turbocharged super-grandma, readymade and available for use. So what the hell. We'll take her. In a heartbeat. We'd be stupid not to."

That had reduced him to an abashed silence. It was true. Not many grandparents in the McCloud milieu, besides Erin's mom. Liv's scary mother definitely did not count, and Raine's mom gave everyone hives, particularly Raine's husband, Seth, so just as well she spent most of her time in London. No benevolent, diaper-changing, ziti-baking grandma energy from that direction. So since then, he'd held his tongue, kept his Zia Rosa bitching between himself and himself.

He was jerked out of his reverie when he almost ran into Zia Rosa's back. She'd braked to coo over twin toddlers in a tandem stroller and was gurgling Italian endearments. *"Dio mio,"* she murmured. *"Uguali. Ugualissimi. Incredibile."*

She looked up at Miles, eyes spilling over, clearly expecting some sort of a comment, but he didn't speak Italian, except for food names. They were all learning food names now.

"What?" he asked. "Huh?"

She sniffed, her jowls quivering. "The *bimbi*," she said. *"Pazzesco*. The girl is just like my niece Magdalena when she was little, *angeletto mio*, may she rest in *santa pace*. And the little boy, he's Bruno. Exactly like my Bruno. *Mi fa brividi*." She crossed herself and then dug into her purse, fishing a couple battered photos out of her wallet.

The mom of the toddlers was a good sport about it. She was young and pretty, and she got all gooey and did the requisite *oh, my God, you're right, that's, like, incredible, they really do look just alike, that's so totally wild* when she looked at Aunt Rosa's photos. Her eyes got misty, her voice got froggy, and then, oh horrors, she said the words Miles had been dreading. "Would you like to hold them?"

Oh, fuck him. He tried not to clap his brow and curse the day.

Of course, Zia Rosa's reply was along the lines of *is a bean green, does the pope shit in the woods*, yada yada. She cooed and tickled and pinched, and told the mom her convoluted story of why she'd concluded that Eamon needed the bouncy chair and Helena needed the foam wedgies, which sparked off the mom's story of how she needed mesh crib covers to keep the twins in their cribs at night. That sparked tales of Bruno's adventuresome babyhood, which was a well with no bottom.

The young mom's husband exchanged can-you-believe-this-shit glances with Miles as the minutes ticked by, and then wandered off, clearly bored out of his mind, leaving Miles to his solitary fate. Thanks, dude. He appreciated the solidarity. Zia Rosa and the mom ranged over a broad array of baby-themed topics and had settled enthusiastically into the benefits of pure lanolin for cracked nipples, ooh, tasty, when the little girl started to squawk. Which necessitated pulling out yogurt, Goldfish crackers, a binkie, in their efforts to comfort her. Meanwhile, the other twin, released from his bonds, wandered off to wreak mayhem in the baby food aisle. After some ominous crashing, Zia Rosa fluttered her hand at him. "Miles, go watch over that *bimbo*," she commanded.

So off he went, chasing the little monster through the formula aisle. Trying to explain that the lactose-free baby formula was not meant to be used for a soccer ball. The kid laughed in his face. A store employee came along just as the box burst open and released its cloud of white dust. The woman started shrilly lecturing Miles, like he was the dad, and where the fuck had the kid's real dad disappeared to? Hello? Anyone? In the meantime, Zia Rosa and the mom discovered that the little girl's problem was a poopy diaper. Evidently a two-woman job.

Jesus, he was glad Cindy was in no rush to procreate. He loved the little McCloud hellions, every last one of them, but he also loved getting into his truck and driving away, stereo blasting. Free at last.

Finally the mom came to rescue her son. She turned to Zia Rosa to start the "great to chat with you" part of the conversation, and "thanks for the tip about the amazing flushable swippie wippie soggy-wipes for poopy butts," or whatever they were gabbing on about. At last, they broke free and headed for the checkout line. *Yes*. Heavenly choruses swelled. Light broke through the cloud-choked sky.

Miles shoved the loaded cart doggedly through the parking lot. Zia Rosa was fiercely supervising the loading of her baby booty into the back when a shout rang out. "Hey! Excuse me!"

It was the dad of the twins, loping toward them, holding up a phone. "We found this in Hayden's stroller," the guy explained. "Must have rolled out when you were helping Kate change Hayden's pants."

Zia Rosa took her phone, smiling mistily as the man sprinted away. "Lovely family," she said wistfully.

Miles opened her door, bracing for what he knew was next.

She was ready for him as soon as he got into the driver's seat. "So when are you and Cindy having a little *bambino?*"

"Never." Miles punctuated that statement by slamming his door.

"Never say never, *giovanotto*," she intoned. "What's written is written. You will have *bambini*. Soon. Very soon."

Oh, man, she was hexing him. He made the sign with his hand against the evil eye, the one that she'd taught him herself, learned from her old grandma back in Brancaleone, in the old country.

She opened up her purse and fished out her wallet as he fired up the engine. She pulled out the photos she'd showed to the mom. "It gave me *brividi*," she said. "Cold shivers. Just look. Exactly like my little Magda and my little Bruno. Look at them."

What else could he do? He braked. Looked. And looked again.

Holy . . . fucking . . . *shit*. They really did look like those kids.

And not just like. *Exactly* like. Weird. He was getting *brividi* himself. He'd had plenty of opportunities to observe the kids, especially the boy. He peered more closely. One was a black-and-white, taken in the late fifties or early sixties, maybe. A formal portrait. The little girl was solemn, unsmiling. The boy was in an informal color photo, taken in the eighties by the looks of it, and exactly, in every detail, identical to the hellion from the pit, right down to the dimples in the fat cheeks and the fuck-you-you-pathetic-pencil-dick-chump gleam in the kid's eyes.

It was completely creepy.

Miles glanced into the old lady's triumphant face. She'd caught the shock-and-awe vibe and was very satisfied with herself.

He put the truck in gear. Babies, for the love of God. They all looked alike, right? Round heavy cheeks, bright sparkling eyes, pouty rosy lips, soft silky curls, cute button noses? The kids couldn't have been that similar. Power of suggestion. He was spending too much time defending his childless state while shopping for swippie wippies soggy wipes. The constant, grating stress had softened his brain.

Into the approximate consistency of baby shit.

Petrie glanced at his watch as he got himself logged into the medical examiner's office. Trish was waiting for him, tapping her foot. As if she were the one who'd dragged her ass all the way to Clackamas because of someone's inexplicable whim.

"I'll be late for lunch with my grandmother because of this," he groused, with ill grace. "I was supposed to meet her at the London Grill at the Benson, and I'm not going to make it in time. Not even close. She's going to make me pay for it. In blood."

Trish clipped the visitor's badge onto the lapel of his jacket and gazed at him, her big blue eyes limpid and absolutely pitiless. "Trust me," she said. "It's worth it. You have to see this, Sam."

"Why not just tell me about it on the phone? Why the mysterious build up? Why make me schlep all the way over here from downtown?"

"It's a visual thing," she said, without turning. "You'll see."

Trish led him through the office and into the rear area where the autopsies were done. She stopped at one of the examining tables and drew the cover off the cadaver, with an almost imperceptible flourish.

Petrie took a look. And froze. Mouth hanging open.

"They called me in to take pictures," Trish said. "That suicide on Wygant this morning, remember? He'd put the gun in his mouth. It took out the back of his skull, but left his face intact."

Petrie looked up. Trish's face was somber, but her eyes had a glint of excitement. "It's him, isn't it?" she prompted.

He just stared down at the dead man's face. It was Bruno Ranieri. Feature for feature. His hair was an inch or so longer than it had been in the photo, but it was him, right down to the dimples. Trish indicated them with a blue fingernail. "Check out those bifid zigomaticus, huh?"

"Yeah," he said. "Who caught this one?"

"Barlow," she said.

"You tell him?"

"Not yet. Wasn't quite sure. Wanted you to see it first."

He looked into her eyes. "OK," he said. "I'll tell Barlow. I guess I have to call Rosa Ranieri to come ID him for us."

He stood outside, in the chilly October rain for a long time afterward. Immobile, even with Grandmam waiting at the restaurant. Staring at the slip of paper that held Rosa Ranieri's contact info.

This was the part he hated. Telling a person that someone they loved had died, badly. He never got used to that. It never got easier.

He punched in one of the McCloud numbers and waited. A young woman's voice answered. "Hello, McCloud residence."

"Hello, this is Detective Samuel Petrie, of the Portland Police Bureau," he said. "I'd like to speak to Rosa Ranieri, please."

13

Bruno massaged Lily's naked ankle. She winced and flinched like she had a multiple compound fracture that was gushing blood, for God's sake. What a wuss. Odd, knowing how tough she actually was.

"It's not swelling," he said for the tenth time. "It's not sprained."

"Well, it hurts! I'm the one inside my body, OK?"

"For Christ's sake, Lily. What part of 'the sun will go down soon, leaving us stranded in pitch-black, sub-zero cold and hundred-mile-an-hour wind gusts if you don't get off your ass' do you *not* understand?"

"So leave me here! Collect me on the way down! I won't move, I promise. I'd get eaten by a grizzly or instantly lost. So just go!" She flapped her hand at him, in a "be off" gesture. "Buh-bye! See ya!"

He stared at her, stony. "You're sticking to me. Like glue."

Her eyes burned. She was furious, with good reason. He could see it, and feel it, too, from her point of view. It made him feel like shit. But he couldn't follow her to the realm of bugfuck lunacy. Mamma, involved in a sinister plot with an evil mastermind? Not. She'd just had bad taste in boyfriends. And in any case, the subject was charged with such lethal emotional voltage, a single touch would fry him.

So he wasn't touching it.

But if he couldn't support her version of reality, the next best thing was to try to keep those shitheads from killing her until she could get the help she needed. That help was out of his depth, maybe. But kicking shitheads' asses, that was a job he could wrap himself around.

He wrapped both hands around her delicate ankle, trying to impart some of his body heat, and started inserting her clammy foot back into her sock. She responded by kicking his chest, knocking him onto his ass. Ouch. Ingrate.

"I'm capable of putting on my own sock, thanks," she snipped.

"Do it, then," he growled. "And hurry."

She shook his arm off when he tried to help her up.

He stopped at the turnoff, debating whether to do the pilgrimage. Didn't seem like a great idea under the circumstances, but as soon as he thought the sensible decision was made, and tried to proceed on up to the bluff, the impulse sank in and forced him right off the path. So. That was how it was going to be. He gave in and struck off horizontally across a long, treacherous slope of broken rock.

"Hey! " she yelled. "Didn't you say the cell reception is at the top of the bluff?"

"Quick detour. Something I have to do first. Come on. Keep up."

"Detour?" Her voice cracked in disbelief. "What the hell could you possibly have to do up here in the frozen wastes?"

He didn't bother to turn. "It's personal."

"Is it, now! Well, excuse me for wondering why I'm being dragged across a goddamn rockslide!"

He could estimate how far behind him she was from her labored breathing, and she was doing all right, so he just pushed on, scrambled up the steep part, and crawled over the lip of the small hanging valley.

It was almost level up there, a long, gentle slope, with a broad swath of trees, larger and taller than the scrawny malformed ones on the more exposed, wind-whipped side of the bluff. It was a pretty place.

He walked over to Tony's silver pine, laid his hand on it. The contact calmed him down. He'd been up here maybe four or five times since he'd lost Tony. He'd found that it helped. For a little while.

Lily clambered over into the valley, plainly uncharmed by the beauty of the place. She glared as she leaned over to pant, bracing her hands against her knees. So much for the calming aspect of this side trip.

"Would you mind turning around for just a second?" he asked.

Her brows snapped together. "Come again?"

"I asked you to turn around."

She looked affronted. "I got that part. What I don't get is why."

He sighed. "I have to take a leak," he explained. "Do you mind?"

"What? You're kidding me. You dragged me all the way over that so that you could piss on your favorite *tree?*"

He turned his back and got down to business, letting her mutter and fume. It was a long one, after all the coffee. By the time he was done and all buttoned up, he'd decided she deserved an explanation.

"Tony used to bring me and Kev up here, when I was a kid," he said. "When it wasn't snowed in, we'd come up on weekends. Every time we came, we would hike up here and take a piss under that tree. It was, I don't know. A thing, with us. With Tony. A ritual, I guess."

Her expressed softened. "Ah."

"Anyhow. That's why. Sorry for dragging you along."

She didn't have a single sharp word for him as she struggled across the rockfall back to the winding deer path.

"So peeing there makes you feel closer to him?" she asked.

He shrugged. Didn't really want to examine it. Impulse

was impulse. You squelched it or you followed it. A guy could twist his brain into knots if he thought too much about that stuff.

"At home, there was this place in Riverside Park," Lily said. "My dad and I used to go there before . . . what happened to him. We'd play cards. He'd do his work stuff, I'd read comic books. We ate salami on hard rolls from the deli on Ninth Avenue. Mint Milanos and Snapple."

"Yeah," Bruno said, warily. "And this is relevant exactly why?"

"I go there, once in a while, to the park," she said. "I buy Mint Milanos and Snapple, and sit there with my laptop, with whatever term paper I'm writing." She forced out a breath. "When I can stand it."

Bruno stared at her. His throat was getting tight. "Let's go."

"It's OK, if it makes you feel better," she said softly. "I get that. It connects me to him. My memories, anyway. Of how he was."

"Don't get all misty on me," he said. "It's not the same thing."

"No? How do you figure?"

"Oh, gee." He snorted. "Snapple? Urine? World of difference."

"Because you're a guy. They are connected bodily functions, right? Depends on which end of the mechanism you're looking at."

He held up his hand. "Don't go any further with that. Please."

"You're the one waving it in my face. Like a flag." Her eyes dropped to his crotch. "So to speak."

He set off, hoping she'd let it go at that. At least feeling sorry for him had put her in a softer place. That had to be a good thing.

"Why that tree?" she called up. "What was special about it?"

"That wasn't the kind of question you could ask Uncle Tony," he replied. "Two possible answers. Best-case scenario was a grunt."

"Ah." She scrambled behind him, panting. "Worst-case scenario?"

"The back of his hand across my face."

Her crunching footsteps stopped. "Sounds like a swell guy."

He stopped to let her catch up, thinking about Tony. How he'd pitched out of a window hugging a bomb to save them. How he'd made Rudy and his thugs disappear. Yeah, Tony had been a bad-tempered, violent man. And even so. "Yeah," he said quietly. "He was a swell guy."

She stumbled, thudding to her knees with a gasp, and no wonder with those oozing scabs. He lunged down the slope, grabbing her elbow.

She yanked it back, almost rocking off balance again. "Hands off!"

What the fuck? "You're still mad?" he asked. He felt almost hurt. "I thought we were having a tender moment."

A grin flashed on her face as she struggled back up to her feet. "We were. Just don't touch me with that grubby paw until you wash it."

Oh, for God's sake. He struck off again, but the stupid grin on his face lasted him almost all the way to the top of the bluff.

Mt. Adams was fogged in. A froth of gray clouds were piled up like dirty cobwebs in the canyon between the bluff and the slope of the nearby volcano. Bummer. Seeing the mountain was the payoff for all that effort. He led her to the lee of the cliff, where the worst of the wind would miss her, and left her huddled there to find the next best spot.

There were text messages for him on the Virgin phone. The first was from Aaro. Short, succinct, rude. A phone number, and then:

Det. Sam Petrie, PPB. Knock yrslf out butthead

The next was from Kev. Even briefer.

WTF? call me now

And another, from Sean McCloud.

W8ting 4 news ??

Scariest call first. He hunkered down, pulled out one of the new cell phones that Aaro had brought for him, stuck in his own chip. True, once the cop had a warrant out for his arrest, he'd be able to identify where the signal had originated, but by that time, he and Lily would be long gone. And hopefully this whole situation would be already resolved.

He sucked in air, dialed the detective's number.

It might be suicide, but damn it, he was not a criminal, and he would not behave like one. It was his civic duty to let the cops know how matters really stood. They were doing a tough job as best they could, protecting the citizens of Portland. It was the right thing to do.

Whether or not he was fucking himself up the ass by doing it was another matter entirely. His jaw twitched, clenching painfully.

The call connected and the guy picked up. "Sam Petrie here."

"Hello, Detective," he said. "My name is Bruno Ranieri. I'm calling about one of your cases."

There was a dead silent, blank moment. "This is *who?*"

"Ah, Bruno Ranieri," he repeated. "I'm calling about the three dead guys behind Tony's Diner on Sandy Boulevard this morning."

There was another pause, and then, "I'm listening."

"So, uh, I was coming out the door of the apartment

building, and those men attacked me. In the process of defending myself, I, uh . . ."

"Killed them," the cop finished, heavily. "And left them there. On the ground. For your neighbors to find."

Oh, shit. This wasn't going the way he'd hoped. "It was legitimate self-defense," he said, trying to keep his voice calm, even. "They were armed, I was not. There's blood spattered around the scene, some of it's mine. Vomit, too. Also mine. Just, ah, so you know."

"Why didn't you call us? Why didn't you stay at the scene?"

Bruno forced the trapped breath out of his lungs. "I had reason to believe that we were still in danger," he said tightly.

"We?" Petrie repeated and waited. "Tell me about this reason."

"I don't know much yet," he hedged. "I wish I did, believe me."

"Let's take this a step at a time. Who is 'we,' Mr. Ranieri?"

Bruno decided there was no reason to be coy. Lily had claimed not to be in trouble with the law. And the bad guys already knew her identity. Maybe this guy could help find answers for her.

"Her name's Lily Parr," he said. "She's from New York City. These people are trying to kill her. They're highly skilled and well organized. She's been fleeing them for six weeks now."

"Ah." Petrie's voice was relentlessly bland. "Who are these people? Can you identify them?"

He gritted his teeth. "No, I can't. And neither can she."

"Neither can she," Petrie repeated slowly. "That's fascinating. Does she know why they're pursuing her?"

"No," he said. And it sounded so very wrong to him. A big, fat lie that only a pussy-whipped idiot like himself would believe.

Petrie grunted, clearly no idiot. "You'd think she'd have an idea."

"Well, she doesn't," he said, trying not to sound belligerent. "She's trying to find out every way she can, but she doesn't."

"What is Lily Parr's relationship to you, Mr. Ranieri?"

Whee, haw. Who the fuck knew. "We met early this morning."

"And you killed three men defending her? And you believe that she has no idea why they attacked her?"

He swallowed. "That's correct."

"She must be a very persuasive woman."

Bruno cursed himself for making this call. "The forensic analysis of the scene will bear up everything that I say. Talk to the techs."

"I usually do," Petrie said, mildly. "In any case, you and Ms. Parr are urgently wanted for questioning. How soon can you get here?"

"I'm not sure," he hedged. "Right now, I'm stranded with no vehicle. And I have to make sure Lily gets someplace safe first."

"Did you not hear what I said, Mr. Ranieri? Ms. Parr is wanted for questioning, too. We can come and pick you up. Where are you?"

"Look, she did nothing! All she did was get attacked!"

"We'll see," Petrie said. "Mr. Ranieri, do you have a twin brother?"

The question took him by surprise. "No. Why?"

"No brothers at all?"

He squinted into the wind, which was whipping tears from his eyes and then threatening to freeze them. "No. None. What the hell?"

"You might be interested to know that until you called me just now, you were presumed dead."

Bruno scowled in total bafflement. "What? Dead? How? I never—"

"A man committed suicide this morning," Petrie said. "He looked exactly like you. In fact, I suggest you call your great-aunt Rosa right away and tell her you're alive, since I just got in touch with her and requested that she come down here to identify your body."

Bruno jolted up to his feet. "What the *fuck?*"

"Hey, mistakes happen when you flee the scene of a triple homicide," Petrie said. "Call her, please. She's upset."

"It's not a triple homicide!" Bruno protested. "I didn't commit a crime! I just prevented them from killing us!"

"Yes, of course," Petrie said. "Call your aunt, and then come in, and tell us all about it. You'll probably need to give us a DNA swab, too, so we can rule you out—"

"You guys already have one," Bruno said. "From some stuff that happened last year."

Petrie was silent for a moment. "I see. And might this situation have any connection to what happened last year?"

"Absolutely not," he said. "No chance in hell."

"Huh. You have a really eventful life, Mr. Ranieri. And I want to talk about this all further. Come on in, soon. And please keep in mind: The longer I wait, the worse your prospects become."

"I can't do that right now," Bruno said. "I'm truly sorry. I'm not doing this to make trouble for you. I'll be in touch."

He broke the connection and dropped his face into his hands.

It was snowballing. A dead lookalike suicide, a hysterical Zia Rosa. And staying square with the law and trying to help Lily Parr seemed to be mutually exclusive. He didn't relish the thought of life as a fugitive. Much less did he relish the thought of life in prison.

He had to call Zia, but that was going to be an emotionally punishing yell fest. He was too rattled to face it, at least for another minute or two. Sean, next. He pulled out the dedicated phone Aaro had given him, enabled the encryption function, dialed.

"About goddamn time," Sean said tersely. "What the fuck is going on? With this cop calling to tell Zia Rosa that you blew your brains out? She practically had a stroke on us, man! It was ugly!"

"I don't know," Bruno said helplessly. "All I can say is, I didn't do it. I still have my brains in there, such as they are."

Sean grunted, clearly unimpressed with Bruno's brains, whether located inside his skull or elsewhere. "So? What's the deal? Aaro called after that and told us what he knew, which wasn't much, but at least he told us you were still alive up there, so Zia could calm down a little. He told me about finding Petrie's number for you. Did you call the guy?"

"Yes. It didn't go well. But he knows who the corpse is not."

"Huh. So what the hell happened?"

"Like Aaro told you," Bruno said wearily. "These guys attacked me and this girl I hooked up with this morning. I defended myself, and—"

"Snuffed them in the process." Sean's voice was heavy with disapproval. "Heard about that part."

"On the bright side, I'm alive, and so is she," Bruno snarled.

"Yeah. The only positive thing you can say about the situation."

"I did not call you for a lecture, so fuck off."

"The lecture is the price you pay for my help," Sean informed him. "Back to the problem. The guys you killed. Any ideas?"

"It's about Lily," he admitted. "She wasn't surprised."

"Ah." Sean pondered that for a beat. "What did she do to them?"

"Nothing," he snapped. "She did *nothing*."

"Wow, aren't we defensive." Sean waited for more and huffed with impatience. "Bruno. I need a little more collaboration here from you."

"She doesn't know! That is to say, she has suspicions, but . . ."

"But what?" Sean prompted.

"But they're not helpful ones," he forced out.

"Define helpful."

"She thinks it's connected to me," Bruno admitted. "Her dad committed suicide in a locked psych ward over a month ago. She says it's murder. She also thinks it was connected to my mamma's murder. We're talking way back, when my mamma, ah . . . Did you know about her getting killed? The Mafia goons who came after me?"

"Yeah, Kev mentioned that," Sean said.

Yeah. Right. Kev "mentioned it." Like that horrible event was something you could just "mention." Only Kev. Only the McClouds.

"And what do you think?" Sean insisted.

He looked over at Lily. She was huddled against the face of the cliff. Shoulders slumped, face hidden. Two locks of hair fluttered out of her hood on either side of her hands. The brightest point in the picture.

He steeled himself. "I think it's a load of crap," he said. "I think what happened to my mamma was exactly what it seemed."

"So. What's the deal, then? With the girl?" Sean asked delicately.

"I don't think she's lying. She's convinced of what she says."

"She must be pissed at you," Sean said. "For holding out on her."

Duh. Bruno swallowed back a rude and unhelpful comment.

"So." Sean's voice was brisk. "What do you need from us?"

"Help securing Lily. Help figuring out who's attacking her."

Sean paused. "You're taking on the cross, then? Wow, man. Sure you're up for it? Looks like a big ol' fucking shit storm."

"I don't know what else to do!" he exploded. "The guys

who attacked her were coordinated, trained. They meant business."

"Have you considered the possibility that this chick is, um . . ."

"Sure I have," he snapped. "I've made my judgment call. I'm helping her. So you can help me do that, or you can fuck off."

"I sense the effects of excessive sexual hormones on your brain."

Bruno's nostrils flared. "So I take it you're fucking off, then?"

"Calm down. I'm not one to criticize when it comes to sexual hormones. I'm not judging you, man. Really."

"Fuck if you're not," Bruno growled.

"Don't get testy," Sean soothed. "I'll collect you guys tomorrow. We'll find a safe place to stash your girlfriend—"

"She is *not* my girlfriend—"

"Seth and Raine's island would be good," Sean mused. "And we'll start to dig for answers. Sound good to you?"

"Yeah. How soon can you get here?"

"I'll leave tonight, late. I'm thinking a dawn arrival."

"Another thing," Bruno said, apologetically. "Lily's convinced you guys are under surveillance. I have no clue whether this is true or not—"

"But in the interests of covering our asses, we've got a plan in place," Sean supplied. "I booked a room at the Marriott downtown. At midnight, Miles meets us. I take his rig and head down to you guys. Then Miles drives Liv and Eamon to Tam's the next day. So even if they're tracking our vehicle, I won't have to worry about them."

Bruno sighed in relief. Sometimes the innate paranoia of the McCloud clan was actually convenient. "Yeah. Thank you."

"Why didn't you crash at Aaro's?" Sean complained. "Sandy would've been so much easier to get to. There are real roads up there."

"He didn't invite us," Bruno said.

"Since when do you need an invitation to trash someone's life, property, and livelihood?"

"That's a McCloud creed," Bruno said sourly. "Not mine."

"Is that so?" Sean sounded amused. "We'll see how it shakes down in the end. Wait, wait. Hold on. Zia Rosa wants to talk to you."

Bruno jumped, as if stuck by a pin. He wasn't psychologically prepared for Zia yet. "What the hell is she doing there?"

"I'm at Davy's house." Sean was enjoying himself way too much. "She's here now, since Davy and Margot have the littlest baby. Helena's number one. Eamon's been demoted, poor squirt."

"No! Don't put her on the phone yet! Wait—"

"Here he is," he heard Sean say, and Zia's voice blared over the line at triple volume.

"Eh, Bruno? *Che cazz' stai a fare?* Who's this cop who's callin' me, tellin' me you was dead?"

"I'm sorry about that, Zia, but I'm not dead, so—"

"*Che cazzo*, Bruno! I practically had a heart attack!"

"I know, Zia, but I swear to God, I didn't—"

"I don' wanna hear about you shootin' yourself in the head no more, OK? I got high blood pressure! I coulda had a stroke!"

"I'm really sorry. It won't happen again," he repeated, for all the world like he was apologizing for having blown his brains out for real.

"And what's this I hear 'bout these dead guys? You kill these guys, Bruno? Outside the diner? That ain't smart, honey."

"I didn't mean to," Bruno explained. "I was just trying to—"

"And this girl? They tell me there's a girl. Who's this girl, eh?"

Trust Zia to cut to the chase. "I just met her, so I don't really—"

"She a nice girl, honey?"

His eyes flashed to where Lily had been—and got a nasty shock to find her gone. He looked around, frantically. Spotted her, up high.

She'd clambered all the way up to the tip-top of the crumbling granite cliff tower and was looking out over the canyon piled full of stormy fog. A ragged window had opened up, showing her a breathtaking glimpse of Mr. Adams' stark, snowy shoulder. She stared at it, hair whipping like a bright flag against the wintry palette of whites and grays. Beautiful and lonely. Proud. And tough.

"Yeah, Zia," he said quietly. "I think she is a nice girl. She needs help, though. She's being messed with pretty bad."

"Well, you help her, then. Nobody messes with a Ranieri," Zia said. "Kick them dirty sonzabitches' asses, hmm? Make Tony proud."

Zia Rosa's bloodthirsty encouragement made him grin. "You bet, Zia," he promised. "I'll try. I promise.

"This girl, she like babies?"

Bruno rolled his eyes. Only a matter of time with Zia Rosa. "We haven't gotten that far. We've been distracted by killers on our tail."

Zia Rosa clucked. "You young folks, you too easily distracted," she lectured. "You forget what's important. You gotta—"

"Not going there, Zia," he said loudly. "I'm busy, OK? I'm hanging up now. *Ti voglio tanto, tanto bene*, OK? Goodbye."

He closed the line in midsquawk and sat, listening to the relatively soothing shriek of wind around the jagged rocks. He thought of calling Kev, but why? What could he do but scold?

He looked at Lily, up there on her granite pedestal. A

fortress of solitude. Her body's whole proud, defiant stance
was a silent reproach in itself.

Hell with it. Kev could wait. There was only so much
abuse a guy could take. That chick was not done with him
yet tonight.

Not by a mile.

14

Zoe crossed one long leg over the other and listened again
to the recorded conversations that had taken place in
Davy McCloud's living room. She squeezed her thighs together as she did so, privately relishing the deep, throbbing
ache.

Melanie, one of the agents who had handled the job at the
baby store this afternoon, tapped at the keyboard, manipulating the filtering program that enhanced the sound. Nadia
and Hobart looked on.

The ploy had worked. The source of sound was a remote-
activated speakerphone in the phone buried inside Rosa
Ranieri's purse, crowded with junk and tossed who knew
where in the McCloud house. So many variables, but she'd
decided to risk it, and the risk had paid off.

Zoe felt surprisingly fresh and alert, considering how
long it had been since she'd slept. She'd coordinated Melanie
and Hobart's baby store gambit from the plane, as soon as
she'd seen the old woman and her handler, Miles Davenport,
coming out of the McCloud residence on the long-range hid-

den surveillance cam. She was pleased with herself. So was King. He'd told her she was special. Made her team leader. He'd promised to read her one of her reward texts tonight over the phone.

Her thighs and buttocks contracted, provoking a spontaneous orgasm that pumped tingling heat down her thighs. Fortunately, the climax was not powerful enough to startle her into vocalizing, but she did miss a few seconds of the recording.

"Run it back, please," she ordered. "The last twenty seconds."

Melanie looked puzzled, but she did as she was told. The voice came through again. Sean McCloud spoke, his voice tinny through a cloud of static fuzz, but the one-sided conversation was audible.

"... *booked a room at the Marriott downtown. At midnight, Miles meets us. I take his rig and head down to you guys. Then Miles drives Liv and Eamon to Tam's the next day. So even if they're tracking our vehicle, I won't have to worry about . . .*"

The sound of a newborn baby swelled into the foreground, and the voice of an older woman, speaking Italian. "*Dai piccina non piangere, dai . . .*"

"Can't you filter that baby stuff out?" Zoe snapped, irritated.

Melanie's fingers drummed madly on the keys. "Working on it."

McCloud's voice came back into focus. "*. . . when do you need an invitation to trash someone's life, property, and livelihood? . . . Is that so? We'll see how it shakes down in the end. Wait, wait. Hold on. Zia Rosa wants to talk to you.*"

"Stop it there," Zoe said. "Have you arranged for Miles Davenport's vehicle to be tagged?"

"Manfred went up to cover it right away," Melanie said.

"And Seth and Raine's island? Who are Seth and Raine?"

"Seth Mackey and Raine Lazar," Hobart supplied promptly.

"Mackey is a colleague of the McClouds. They have a private island in the San Juans. Stone Island. Here's the map. And a satellite picture."

Zoe glanced at the printouts Hobart was holding out and waved them away with a finger flutter. "Later. What do you have on Aaro?"

"Not as much as I'd like," Hobart said. "He did a stint in the Army Rangers with Davy McCloud. It was very difficult to find any info on him before that, because he had changed his name. His original surname was Arbatov. From Coney Island, New York. Ukrainian in origin. His family was famous for arms trafficking, but they wound down after the patriarch Oleg Arbatov was diagnosed with cancer. The current boss is Alex's cousin, Dimitri Arbatov."

"Alex hasn't been involved in the family business since before the army, and not much then, either," Nadia said, eager to be seen as useful, though from the look Hobart gave her, he'd done all the work. "They consider him a black sheep, it seems. He appears to have gone legit."

"How admirable of him," Zoe said. "And now?"

"He runs a one-man security consultancy," Hobart broke in as Nadia began to reply. "Private referrals. Cyber security stuff for private corporations. It's extremely difficult to find personal data on him."

"But you managed," Zoe purred. "Of course?"

Hobart's smile was smug. "Of course."

"Is someone on it?" Though it was hardly necessary to ask.

"I'm on it," Nadia broke in eagerly. "I'll head to Portland now."

"And Detective Sam Petrie? Is anyone assigned to him?"

Melanie's mouth hung open, clearly taken by surprise. "Ah . . ."

"I need the same software loaded onto his phone that you put on the Ranieri woman's," Zoe said. "I would have assumed that was self-evident. Bruno Ranieri spoke to Petrie today, and I would have loved to have heard that conversation. They have the cadavers of four of our operatives. Is it just me? Is this not painfully obvious? To anyone?"

Melanie's mouth worked. "Ah . . . I'll just go down tonight, and—"

"No" Zoe said to her sharply. "Not you."

"But I can—"

"No." Zoe raked the woman with her eyes. "You don't have the look. You're the one we use when we need the fresh-faced suburban mom. But you don't do a convincing slut." Her eyes cut to Nadia. Nadia's chin tilted up, proud to be the slut of choice. Zoe had never liked the bitch. Special series twats. Thought they were such hot shit.

Melanie sputtered, reddening. "I could, too!"

"Probably it will just be a matter of breaking into his house and loading the software onto his phone while he sleeps. But if a personal approach is necessary . . ." Zoe's voice trailed off. "I'll do it myself. You take care of getting smart tags on all the McCloud vehicles. Bug-sweep proof." Zoe tapped her long fingernails on the desktop.

"Manfred did that weeks ago," Melanie said sullenly. "We've been logging every last move those people make. Would you like to see the—"

"No. I'm sure you're being extremely efficient." Zoe dismissed her with a wave. Melanie looked hurt. Zoe was being harsh, but she had to establish her authority as team leader. Which meant being ruthless.

"We're lucky that the Ranieri woman put her purse down right in the common room," Melanie said, trying to draw attention back to her successes, not her shortcomings. "And just in time to hear of Sean McCloud's travel plans tonight. If it wasn't for their kids making all that noise, we would barely have needed to filter the recording at all."

"Speaking of kids." Zoe glanced at the door to the adjoining room, where Melanie had left the tandem stroller. The toddlers had been asleep, but the boy had just woken up and was exercising his lungs. The sound was irritating. She required a calm environment for optimal concentration. Then the girl woke up, too. The sound redoubled. The operatives stared at the stroller and its shrieking occupants, at a loss.

"What's wrong with them?" Zoe asked. "Are they hungry? Make them shut up. Do you have food? Bottles?"

"That's the pod leader's job." Melanie sounded defensive. "Not ours. And they've got bottles in their strollers if they want them."

Hobart glanced at his watch. "She was supposed to have been here by now to pick them up. She's forty minutes late."

"Call her," Zoe said. "In the meantime, do something about that noise. Drug them or something. I can't stand the sound."

Melanie looked uncertain. "That's forbidden in the protocols. They've had less than optimal results in the past using sedatives."

"So?" Zoe said impatiently. "Do something else, then. I don't care what you do, just solve the problem."

"I can put the stroller into the bathroom," Nadia suggested. "If we shut the connecting door, we'll have two doors to block the sound."

"The tandem won't fit through the bathroom door," Hobart said.

"The supply closet, then," Nadia said. "The door's wider. It'll go if we wiggle it in sideways. Come on, Hobart. Help me lift it."

Zoe watched as Nadia and Hobart wrestled the double stroller with its shrieking cargo into the dark maw of the supply closet. The door swung shut. The volume cut by two-thirds. When the suite door closed, the sound was blocked almost completely. Ah. Much better.

"Good," Zoe said. "Jeremy, Hal, and Manfred will make up my team tomorrow when we follow Sean McCloud. I'll hook up with them in Portland, after I take care of Petrie." She looked at Melanie, then Hobart. "You two stay here. To monitor us." She glanced at Nadia. "You concentrate on Aaro. Get going."

Nadia scampered away, eager to get to work as the super-slut. Melanie's mouth tightened, face red. Zoe observed this with satisfaction. It was the stupid bitch's punishment for not even thinking of including Petrie in the surveillance net. Hers and Hobart's. They would stay at headquarters, in disgrace. That would teach them. She'd chosen every available agent in the area for her team, except those two. Idiots.

Hobart turned to face the computer screen without comment. Probably relieved to be spared combat duty. Gutless egghead geek.

"I've sent a list of supplies to your comms. Add anything else you think would be useful, have it assembled and packed by early this evening. I will brief the team here, at nine P.M."

"Ah, one small problem." Hobart was looking at his list.

Zoe spun on him. "I don't want to hear about problems," she said.

Hobart looked up, apologetically. "I can't get an armored SUV for you in that amount of time. I had no idea . . . these things need just a little lead time. Maybe I could get one by tomorrow afternoon—"

"I can't believe you didn't anticipate this. We can't wait. Our window of opportunity will close. Are you too stupid to see that?"

"Um, maybe by midmorning, if I offered them an extra—"

"Just give me a normal SUV," Zoe snarled. "We'll have to manage without the armor. Is everything clear? Good. Get to work."

They got to it.

Finally alone, Zoe placed her long golden legs up on the desk, admiring how graceful they were, right down to her slender feet in the white wedged sandals. She clicked the mouse until she set the recording to run from the beginning. Rosa Ranieri's triumphal return from the baby supplies store, followed by the phone call from Petrie, which had involved much wailing and carrying on in Italian.

She tried not to let herself get distracted by the thrills of anticipation, thinking about that phone call tonight in the privacy of her room. Lying on her bed, telling King about her excellent progress.

Too bad about the armored SUV. She would have preferred to play it safe, but truly, it was probably overkill.

Tomorrow, she would complete the task he had assigned her. She would undo all the damage Reginald had done. She would be brilliant.

King would be so very pleased. And when he showed her what a full Level Ten reward sequence felt like, all thirty verses . . . oh, my.

She would be pleased, too. Oh, so very pleased.

Lily shifted on the chair by the stove. The tender moment up on the mountainside hadn't lasted. Since his cell conversations on the bluff, which he'd taken great pains not to let her hear, Bruno had been stonily silent. She'd been appalled, on the mountain, to find out that the descent was even more excruciating than the ascent. A contradiction of natural laws. Physics reversed, just to insult her. Water flowing uphill. What was up with that? Her knees and ankles still shook like jelly.

But her life lately had been nothing but a series of contradictions of natural law. By the laws of emotional physics, it made no sense that a mild-mannered—well, maybe not so mild, but certainly relatively harmless—chick who wrote essays for a living should end up being the target of brutal assassins. If Bruno was right, and there really was no connection to Magda, then what the hell did they want with her? Like water, flowing uphill for no good reason. Why would water bother? Why expend the effort? It wasn't like there was any money to be made in killing her. And yeah, she did tend to speak her mind, true, but she'd never been quite that bitchy to anybody. She was almost certain of it.

And Bruno, being silent. Wow, that felt like another contradiction of natural laws. At the cabin, he was a blur of activity, but scarily quiet the whole time. He built up the fire, cleaned and loaded three different handguns, made up the bed, restoked the fire. He cooked a delicious meal, which they ate in strangled silence. He washed dishes. He would not let her help with these activities. Evidently, her mental instability would be dangerously exacerbated by the stress of rinsing lettuce or tucking a sheet over a mattress. She'd tried to insist, but he'd turned her down so hard she'd ended up huddled in the chair, wishing she was small enough to slide under the door. The silence was deafening.

She tried to lose herself in the twisting, dancing flames while Bruno sloshed and clanked at the sink. Then, quiet.

Her neck prickled. She twisted around. He was holding a six-pack. He looked at the beer, he looked at her, and he put it back into the refrigerator. "Feel free," she said. "It's my own personal choice not to drink. I'd never judge anyone else for having a beer. It's OK."

"It's not that," he said. "Kev would kick my ass if he caught me drinking alcohol while stuff like this is happening. He'd say, 'Lack of vigilance will get you killed.'" He shrugged. "He doesn't say it so much now that he's in love. Guess the world seems less dangerous now."

"The bad guys aren't here tonight. Go ahead," she urged.

He sank down onto a stool near the fire. "Nah. I don't know where they are, how many, what their resources are. Makes me fucking tense."

"I noticed," she murmured.

"That bad, huh?"

"Terrible," she informed him. "Like toxic waste."

He laughed, but the sound petered out fast. "Sorry about that."

"It's OK," she said. "I'm being a little more bitchy than usual, too."

He slanted her an eyebrow-tilted glance. "Just a little?"

"Just a little," she said resolutely. "Cannot tell a lie. I'm snarky and difficult even under normal circumstances. Just so you know."

His dimples flashed. "Good of you to warn me."

She blew out a sharp breath. "I try to be good."

They listened to the fire crackling for a while.

"Normal circumstances," he echoed. "What are those, for you?"

"Huh?" His keen gaze scrambled her thoughts into mush. "What?"

"Your 'normal.' I have no idea what that is," he said. "I met you in a really weird time in your life. So clue me in. What's normal, for you?"

She hesitated for so long he started to look worried. Like she was going to confess to being an escort, or cooking meth in her basement.

Oh, hell. Out with it. "I write term papers," she said.

His brows knitted together. "Yeah? For what? About what?"

"About anything. On any topic. For whoever can pay my fees."

The puzzlement on his face was replaced by surprise. "Huh? Oh. You mean . . . for people who are cheating? In school?"

"Yeah." She braced herself for the judgment that was coming.

But he just looked fascinated. He tilted his head to the side, studying her intently. "Who hires you? College kids?"

"Lots of different types," she said. "Foreign students who can't manage the English. Non-foreign students who can't manage it, either. Rich kids who are too busy partying. They all keep me busy."

"No shit," he murmured. "So what's your own degree in?"

She shook her head. "Don't have one. Never made it all the way."

He frowned. "But how . . . but if you're so good at writing—"

"I was going to Columbia," she began. "Full scholarship. I was going to get my BA and my masters both in four years. I had one year to go, my thesis to write. Then I discovered that Howard hadn't paid the property taxes on his house. He'd spaced it, for years. I had to come up with eighteen thousand dollars, or he'd have lost the house."

"Whoa," he murmured. "Ouch."

"Bad enough, him being a junkie," she said. "But him being a junkie under a bridge, or in the subway, well. That I could not face."

"I hear you," he said.

"So there was this Greek guy I knew who was struggling with his doctoral thesis in history of medicine. He offered me three thousand bucks to write it for him." She shrugged. "I couldn't turn it down."

"Of course you couldn't," he said. "I wouldn't have, either."

She blinked. Wow. Nice of him to be so understanding. "So, word got around," she continued. "I started getting referrals."

"Did you pay the property taxes?"

"Yes. But I never managed to finish my own degree. There was no time. I was at it twelve hours a day. Then Howard had another episode."

"Episode?" Bruno repeated gently.

"Overdose. Suicide attempt. I decided to put him in a clinic, since I'd finally found a way to pay for it. And if someone was watching him, I figured, I might even be able to sleep at night. When I wasn't working."

"Sounds tough," he murmured. "I'm sorry that you—"

"I'm not trolling for sympathy," she said, abruptly.

He held up his hands. "God, no. Never that."

The fire crackled in the heavy silence. Lily decided it was time to conclude the touchy subject and move on. "I was stuck, once Howard was committed," she said. "It was the only work I could do that earned me enough to live, plus fork out eleven thousand bucks a month."

He winced. "A month? Good God."

"And that was one of the more reasonable places. So, that's normal, for me. Writing for cheaters. Go ahead. I'm braced for it."

"You are?" He actually looked like he was trying not to smile, the smart-ass bastard. "Braced for what? What am I supposed to say?"

"You don't have to say it. I've heard it all," she said. "Wasted potential. Pearls before swine. Prostituting my gifts. Bad karma. It broke my friend Nina's heart. She thought I should have just pulled the plug on Howard and let whatever happened to him happen. But I just . . . couldn't." She looked down. "The joke was on me, though. The worst happened anyway. He's dead. All that effort. Down the drain."

"No." Bruno's voice was resolute. "Your friend was right in that it wasn't the smartest thing to do. But I still admire you for trying."

She was taken aback. "Ah. Um, thanks. I guess."

"I read somewhere, if you do something for love, the effort is never wasted."

The memory flashed through her mind. Those long-ago Sundays in Riverside Park, playing cards, joking around, laughing and people-watching with Howard. She looked away from Bruno, eyes stinging.

"Sappy greeting-card platitudes like that bite my ass," she said.

He choked off muffled laughter. "Tough bitch."

"Yep, that's me." She didn't want to go any deeper, but she couldn't bear the silence. "And you? What's normal for you?"

"Why ask? You know everything there is to know about me."

She felt absurdly hurt. "That's not true! I know you have a part ownership in the diner. I know you own a business selling kites and educational toys. And that's all. It's a very superficial level of knowing."

"What else is there?"

"You're being deliberately stupid and annoying," she snapped.

"Yeah, about that. Just to be fair. I'm stupid and annoying even under normal circumstances. So what do you want to know, anyhow?"

"How you feel about it," she said, crabbily. "If you like it. If you're satisfied. If it's what you dreamed about when you were a kid."

He stared into the fire. "I don't know." He sounded reluctant. "It's a good business. I like that I call the shots, that I own the outfit. But it's not something I set out to do with a clear plan. It just grew. I saw profit potential in Kev's designs, and I went for it. I just wanted to make money. I thought it would make me feel . . ."

"What?" she urged, after he petered out. "Make you feel what?"

He flapped his hand. "I don't know. Safe, maybe."

"From what?" she prodded.

He frowned. "I don't know. I'm just talking out my ass, Lily. Safe from feeling like shit, I guess. Safe from feeling scared."

It took her a minute to work up the nerve to ask. "Does it work?"

His face was like a stone mask. "No," he said.

It took a while to breathe down the tears. "What pathetic schlubs we both are," she said. "Going after the moon with a butterfly net."

His dimples flashed. "That's a poetic way of describing pathetic schlub behavior."

"Hey, you know us crazy poet types."

The c-word wiped the smile right off his face. He shot up to his feet, his face a stone mask again. "It's late. Tomorrow's a big day. You should get some sleep. Dealing with McClouds takes a lot of energy."

Aw, crap. She'd accidentally killed the tender moment. But no way was she going to be dismissed like this. "You look like you're chewing Excedrin tablets whenever you mention the McClouds," she said. "What's your deal with those guys? Do you dislike them so much?"

Bruno looked uncomfortable. "No. They're OK."

"You're lying," she said baldly. "Out with it."

"No. Really. They're fine," he insisted. "I'm the problem, not them. You know that thing that happened, with the Parrishes, last year? Kev's amnesia, and all that? Him finding his biological brothers?"

"I read everything that was in the papers," she said.

"Well, there they are. Kev's brothers. They look like him. They're smart, like him. They know all this crazy shit that nobody else knows, like him. He's got this wacky childhood in common with them, and he remembers it all. How do you expect me to feel about them?"

"Um . . . you could try being happy for him?" she ventured.

"Awww." He held up his hand, rubbed his thumb and forefinger together. "Here's the world's smallest violin, playing a sappy tune."

"Ouch," she murmured. "That bad?"

"Oh, yeah," he said. "It's that bad. He's the only brother I have. Then, one day, he gets three new, improved brothers. Guns drawn, muscles flexed, saving his ass when the shit came down. More than I could. And afterward, there's the tender family reunion, right? And the lovely wives are covering him with kisses, and babies are tumbling, and kids are swarming, all the nephews and nieces jumping all over long-lost Uncle Kevvie. And I'm, like, great, dude. Yay for you. Good on you."

"So you feel like chopped liver?" she asked. "Is that the problem?"

"Fuck, Lily. I never claimed to be Mr. Mature. Could we change the subject? Because the further you go with this one, the more badly it's going to reflect on me. I'm a selfish dickhead. End of story."

"No you are not," she said. "Anyone would feel that way, whether they admitted it or not. You just say how you feel, that's all."

"Well, that's the definition of a dickhead," he said sourly. "A guy who isn't smart enough to shut his big mouth in time."

"No. That's not the definition of a dickhead," she said quietly.

"No? In any case, I'm using the McClouds in spite of feeling like chopped liver. They can't say no to me, for Kev's sake, so I'll exploit them for my own selfish purposes. Sounds dick-headed to me."

"Exploit them how?"

"Making them help you. Kev's twin is coming to get us. They'll find a place for you to hide. Help me find who's gunning for you. They may bug me, but they might as well make themselves useful in the process."

She stared at him. "Bruno," she said. "These people don't know me. They don't owe me favors. I have no money to pay them for their time and resources. How long will they realistically put up with this?"

He looked obdurate. "Until I say it's enough."

"You have that kind of clout with them?"

"I'll use up what clout I have. Might as well be good for something, right? When they're sick of helping, I'll think of something else."

He stared back at her, belligerent. Daring her to argue.

"Another thing," she said quietly. "You just met me. You don't know me, either. Not really. How long can you put up with this?"

He shrugged, dismissively. "I guess we'll find out, huh?"

She shook her head. "No. Waiting to find out would destroy me. I appreciate your willingness to help, but I have a way better idea. Drive me to a bus station, lend me enough cash for a sandwich and a bus ticket to Anywhere, USA, and wish me luck."

"I can't do that," he said.

She covered her face. "Oh, Bruno. For God's sake—"

"You don't understand, Lily." His voice cut through hers. "I'm not just being difficult or stubborn. I literally cannot . . . do . . . that. I can't cut you loose, put you on a fucking bus. Not an option. Sorry."

"And if I just, you know, disappeared?" she offered. "Would that release you from this compulsion?"

"No," he said. "I'd come after you. And I'd be sorely pissed."

"I've had enough of pissed people coming after me lately," she flared. "I don't need it from you, too."

"Fine. Shut the fuck up and accept my help with no back talk. You don't have any choice." He walked over to her, put his hands on her shoulders, looming. His energy overwhelming her. "I'm bigger than you."

She stared up at him for a moment, eyes narrowing. "Don't you dare try to intimidate me," she said through her teeth.

"Just trying to find out what works with you."

"That won't work, ever," she informed him. "It'll just piss me off. So, this compulsion to protect me, it's because we had sex, right? So now you think you're somehow responsible for me?"

His fingers tightened. "Don't start, Lily."

"That's stupid, you know. And wrong. Antique bullshit."

The dim room seemed suddenly smaller, hotter. She shoved

his hands off her shoulders and tried to stare him down. But she was falling in, getting lost in the fathomless darkness of his hooded eyes.

"Let's not go anywhere near that," Bruno said.

"Sorry, but I'm no better at keeping my mouth shut than you are," she said. "You're letting out a really scary god-king-of-the-universe vibe, and it bugs me. Being bullied does not make me shiver with sexual excitement, Bruno. It just makes me say sarcastic things, which then escalate to screaming obscenities until the offending behavior stops."

"Oh, man. I'm in for it then," Bruno said. "Lucky me."

He'd retreated behind some wall in his head. She hated the way it felt. So conscious of herself as a woman, and yet so incredibly alone.

"You can't make these decisions for me," she told him. "I owe you my life, and I'll be grateful forever. But as soon as you turn your back, I'll be out of here, like the whack job that I am."

"So I just won't turn my back on you," he said. "Ever."

She clenched her jaw until it throbbed. "You are hopeless."

"And you are tired. You should sleep," he said. "We can't resolve this argument tonight anyhow. Go on, lie down."

She glanced over at the bed and bit her lip.

"Don't worry," he said. "You get it all to yourself."

Dismay congealed in a cold, gluey lump in her belly. She hadn't realized how much she'd been counting on physical intimacy. Anything would do. A hug, a back rub, a cuddle. Or anything else he could dream up. Sign her up for that. She was strung out on the way he made her feel. Had been for weeks, ever since she'd started, well, stalking him.

"Where are you going to sleep?" she asked.

"Don't worry about it," he said gruffly.

"As fucking if! That's ridiculous! There's only one bed! As tired as you are, you're sleeping in a straight-back chair? Am I so scary?"

A muscle in his jaw twitched. "Pretty much."

"For God's sake, Bruno! Relax! Your virtue is safe with me!"

"Virtue, my ass. Somebody stays awake. It ain't gonna be you."

Lily tried for a reasonable tone. "I'm not going to be able to sleep if you're sitting on a chair, clutching your gun and glowering."

"I'll clutch and glower quietly."

She shook her head. "I won't lie down unless you do. That's final."

He shook his head, frowning into the fire. She put her hand on his shoulder. His muscles jumped and twitched beneath her hand.

"Please, Bruno," she whispered. "Please, rest, too."

He rubbed his eyes. "Fine, whatever," he growled.

So it was that half an hour later, they were both stretched out on the bed, fully clothed but for their shoes. Bruno had insisted that she lay inside the comforter with himself outside of it, leather jacket draped over his shoulders, his back to her.

She stared at the bulwark of his shoulder. He wasn't asleep. He was motionless, but she sensed the frantic mental activity in his head.

She was beyond sleep. Punch-drunk. Weirdly, she no longer really cared what he thought of her. Why stress about it? She had nothing to hide. He knew things about her no one else knew, not even Nina. Things she hadn't even known herself, until she seduced him. Like that she was a wild hellcat in bed with him, for instance. Wow. Who'd have guessed? Hard to reconcile with her self-image. Lustful Lily, sex maniac. And the fact that he thought she was a fruitcake, and therefore, no longer eligible for wild hellcat sex. Damn. That really stung.

She didn't want to think about it, but the thoughts were thinking her. Howard had been diagnosed as schizophrenic.

She'd known he was crazy for years. His madness was part of the landscape of her life.

But where did that leave her with these knife-wielding assassins? If Howie's Magda story was bullshit, then what reason could there be for those guys to chase her . . . unless there was something that she didn't remember? Had she somehow managed to piss off dangerous people . . . and couldn't remember why? Say, blackouts? A split personality?

No. Not possible. That was absurd. Howard was crazy, but not her. Not logical Lily. No woo-woo crapola for her, thank you very much.

Right. Crazy people never allowed for the possibility of being crazy. That lack of mental flexibility was a hallmark of craziness.

And oh, man. If she stayed on this train of thought any longer, it would take her over the broken railway bridge and dump her in the abyss. She had to derail, or she'd have to metabolize all the sleep-killing fear and dread chemicals now dumping into her blood.

So she did the one thing that she knew would wipe her brain squeaky clean of all thought, rational or otherwise.

She reached out and touched Bruno's shoulder.

15

Bruno arched like she'd slapped him with electric paddles. "Jesus, Lily," he hissed. "You startled me."

"You shouldn't turn your back on me if I'm so terrifying."

He let out a sigh. Shook his head. And did not turn.

"You need to relax," she said, stroking him. "I can't imagine that would be easy, though. Being in bed with a madwoman and all."

"Goddamnit, Lily. Shut up with that crap."

"Um, no. I can't. Sorry," she murmured. "I'm just stressed. Makes me do that nervous-talking thing. You know. You do it, too, right?"

"Sometimes. Lately, I've been working on keeping my yap shut. The results look promising. I recommend it."

She cuddled closer. He stiffened. "You, advocating self-control?" She slid her hand beneath his jacket. "That's kind of funny."

"Don't," he muttered. "Please."

But she couldn't resist. She found the bottom of his sweatshirt and slid her hand inside. Her breath caught as she connected with hot, smooth skin, the big, graceful contours of his back, the ridges of bone, the slabs of muscle. Powerful and ripped. His body was superdeluxe.

He arched back with a gasp as she explored the curve of his shoulder blade, the small, bumpy muscles that overlaid his ribs. She let her fingers slide up his spine until they touched the cowlick at his nape. It was shaved almost to stubble to tame the curl, but she could see the tender swirl, the circular pattern. It filled her with yearning.

She wanted to kiss it. And didn't have the nerve. Tormenting him was one thing. She could brace herself for him to be stern, to make her be good. But she'd shrivel and die of shame if he rejected her tenderness.

Her hand slid to his waistband. Inside, to the cleft of his ass.

"What do you think you're doing?" His voice was strangled.

"Oh, Bruno. That's just sad. If you have to ask."

"Christ." His voice was pleading. "Don't do this."

She snuggled closer. "In a way, it's liberating." She

pressed her lips against the curve of his neck, breathing in his hot male musk.

"What's liberating?"

She nipped him gently. "That you already think I'm deranged."

He twisted to glare at her. "I never said that!"

"Actions speak louder than words. The point is, since I'm crazy, I'm not responsible for anything. I can do, well, anything. Wow." She slid her hand around his front, let her fingers trail down that silken arrow of chest hair. "It opens up my horizons like never before."

He grabbed her hand, clamping it against his belly so that it couldn't creep lower. "Don't."

"And this situation forces you to be the grown-up at all costs. Mr. Mature. It's a role you're not used to playing, right?"

"What exactly do you mean by that?"

"Nothing bad," she soothed. "You don't deny yourself much. Who could blame you? You have money. You're good-looking. You enjoy women. They enjoy you back. You avoid responsibility."

He sat up, glaring. "So I'm a frivolous playboy asshole?"

"Shhh," she soothed. "Don't yell at me, Bruno. I'm unstable, remember? I might freak out on you." She stuck her thumbs in her ears, waggled her fingers. "Stay very calm. Don't set me off."

He got up, turning away from her. "Stop pushing me. Please."

The vibrating tension in his voice sobered her giddy mood. "I can't," she whispered. "I'm sorry. I just can't seem to do that."

He turned to her. "You want me to fuck you now."

It wasn't a question. She didn't have to answer it. A good thing, because she couldn't speak. She just gulped and waited. Hopefully.

"I don't have any condoms," he announced. "I just had the one, in my pocket this morning. That's it."

Oh. Geez. She was taken aback. Such a prosaic reason.

"I would have had to ask Aaro to buy condoms for us this morning when we stopped for groceries to be prepared for sex," he said. "And I just didn't have the stomach for it."

She cleared her throat. "I, ah, don't blame you one little bit."

"I assume you're not on the pill. Being on the run and all that." He paused, hopefully. "Unless you have an implant, or something."

"No," she said quietly. "No implant. No something."

He blew out a heavy sigh. "So there we are."

"Can't we just . . ." She flapped her hands eloquently. "You know."

"Yeah, I know. In a normal universe I'd say, sure we could. I'm usually good when it comes to sexual control. But not with you."

She wondered if she should be offended. "Why?" she asked. "What's so special about me?"

"I don't know," he said. "Going to bed with you is like getting on the ultimate fun house carnival ride. The door closes, and the ride starts, and it's bigger than I am. And it ain't over 'til it's over."

"Oh. I, um, see." She was blushing, abashed.

"If it went like it did at Tony's apartment, I'd come inside you. I won't remember why I shouldn't. I won't remember my own name. Sex with you turns me into a mindless, screaming fuck machine."

Ooh. Wow. Her lower body clenched deliciously at the thought.

"Well," she said delicately. "I think you're exaggerating a tiny bit."

He shook his head. "No. Not at all. Not even a tiny bit."

They stared at each other. The prickles on the back of her neck turned into racking shivers. Shimmering heat pooled low in her body. Thoughts, hopes, possibilities shifted between them. Into probabilities.

Then, into a certainty. She felt the moment it happened. The energy, changing all by itself. Without moving a muscle, without saying a word, his male energy was suddenly blasting out at her, unchecked.

"Listen to me, Lily." His voice was low. "Decide if you really want to get on that fun house ride. You're right. I'm not Mr. Mature. I can't resist you, because I don't really want to. You know the risks."

"Will you at least, you know, try to not—"

"Yes, or no. I can't promise anything. Get it through your head."

She stared at him. Some small, faraway part of her brain was appalled at how stupid, how irresponsible, how insane this was.

She was acting like an addict. Strung out on her drug of choice. After all the fear and howling emptiness, she could not resist the bright, glowing way he made her feel. In his arms, she felt free. Powerful. He was the only thing on earth that made her feel that way. She'd heard junkies describe their highs like that. And she didn't even care.

She folded the comforter down on his side, inviting him in.

Bruno's leather jacket hit the floor with a thud. He peeled off his sweatshirt, yanked off his socks, with jerks that seemed almost angry. He shoved his jeans down and stepped out of them, naked and beautiful. Offering himself, but not with arrogance. In spite of his strength, some subtle part of him had surrendered to her.

He needed her, too. She saw it in his face, his eyes. No matter what he thought about her problems. She wasn't alone in this fear, this hunger. Heat swelled in her throat. Tear fog swirled in her eyes. She got up, faced away from him. Silly to get gooey and emotional just because he was taking her up on her aggressive offer of sex. Any normal guy would do that. In a heartbeat. It wouldn't change things one bit. But at least he'd come down off his high horse. He wasn't trying to protect the crazy girl from her own folly. That was something.

She wiped her face, sniffed back tears, and walked around the bed, taking a long, hungry look. He was dazzling. Every detail so specific, so inevitable, so perfect. Every hair on his body, lovingly designed and placed just so, adding up to a perfect synthesis of male beauty. And she couldn't wait to grab that thick, hard cock pointing at her so urgently. To make good, athletic, prolonged use of it.

She flicked tears off her face with her fingers and struggled to stay on top of herself. It was impossible, but it was foreign to her nature not to try. Bruno waited. The silence was so full. Thick, like honey. Palpable and heavy and sensual. She swam through it, moving closer to him with the slow drift of utter inevitability.

Barely an inch of space between them now. The heat throbbing off his body touched her, caressed her. She contemplated the brown oblongs of his nipples adorning his thick pecs. The pattern of his treasure trail. The placement of the moles on his shoulders and chest.

He took her hands, held them to his face. Pressing his mouth against her palm, the pad of her thumb. He placed them against his chest, and they gasped at the rippling jolt of exchanged energy. It crackled through her, lighting her up like a star.

The kiss was inevitable, but they waited for it, circling it slowly like they were afraid of it. Once their lips touched, that carnival ride would start. Good-bye, rational thought. Not that she felt all that rational now.

He grabbed handfuls of her sweater, peeling that and her undershirt off, leaving her tousled, shivering. Covering her breasts with her arms, feeling foolish. Flustered and shy, even now.

He tossed the sweater away, brushed her hair off her face.

Her nipples barely touched his chest, but they lit up as if they'd been kissed, suckled. His cock bobbed against her jeans. He brushed hair behind her ears, tracing her cheekbone. He pulled the band off her braid, unraveled the kinky, fuzzy mass of her hair.

"Great hair," he murmured, rubbing his face in it. "Love the hair."

Her giggle choked into a gasp when he shoved down her jeans without bothering to unbutton them. He helped her step out of the jean shackles, leaving them in a tangle on the floor. "Nice panties," he murmured, cupping her ass. "Very hot."

She rolled her eyes. "Don't remind me."

He jerked the garment down. "OK, fine. Lose the panties."

She peeled them off her ankles and basked naked in his heat. If snowflakes fell on them, they'd dance and hiss, like drops on a griddle.

Snap, something gave in. He grabbed her, or she grabbed him, she couldn't tell who initiated what, and the fraught silence exploded.

It was like they'd attacked each other. She felt so uniquely, specifically naked wrapped around him, straining. A live wire, thoughts and feelings exposed. Their mouths moved, opened, tongues twining, moaning. She thrummed, burned, with a need that had no name. Not just sex, but a heart-splitting ache, a sharp yearning for something far deeper. She craved him. Wanted to crawl inside him, body and mind, heart and soul. She wanted to walk inside his dreams. She was jealous of his past, possessive of his future. She wanted to wrap herself in him like a blanket, twine herself through his body, braid herself into his life. Into his very veins and blood, until they could never be untangled.

The world shifted and spun, pulling at her body. She barely noticed him bearing her down onto the bed. She was wrapped around him, tears spilling over. His pleading mouth called them forth like a fountain, a cleansing rush that left her fresh, clear, and still more desperate for his big body arching possessively over hers. Pinning her onto the bed while his mouth drew forth her soul and claimed it.

She gave it up so eagerly. As if to withhold it would kill her.

His lips moved down her throat, leaving a path like moonlight on water. Slid to her chest, cupping her breasts, lapping and suckling, and forget moonlight, it was the sun now, shining right out of her chest. She was blinded by the intensity, almost frightened as the light in her brightened, the sensation swelled, sharpened, and . . . *what* . . . ?

Energy pumped through her, each jolt a blinding explosion . . .

When she came to, she shook. He was hugging her so tightly, air could barely enter her lungs. Ah. OK. An orgasm. A huge one. And he'd only been touching her breasts. Whoa. This really was a fun house ride.

As if that wasn't enough, he rubbed his scratchy chin tenderly against her breasts, as if to console them for moving on, and slid lower.

She grabbed his face to stop his downward progress. "Stop."

He lifted his head. "Why?"

She sank her fingernails into his big, muscular shoulders. "I'm not getting on that fun house ride alone," she said. "I want company."

"I'm not going anywhere." He pushed her thighs wider, placed his palm over her pussy, cupping her pubic fuzz. "I'm right here for you."

"No. I mean, I want it to be mutual."

He looked distressed. "Aw, what's with the complicated rules? Let me make you come a few more times before I go off the deep end, OK?"

"Let me touch you, too," she insisted, still shoving.

He fought for a while but gave in with a growl of amused

acquiescence. She spun around until they were sixty-nined, and there he was, in all his glory. That big cock, bobbing in her face, dripping precome. His earthy, warm male musk made her mouth water.

He waited while she got herself organized. It took some wiggling to find the angle. She needed both hands to handle him, and when she got down to it, he was so broad, velvety hot, rock hard. She gripped his shaft, feeling the veins taut and throbbing beneath her hands. Her hands tingled like sexual organs themselves as she went at him, lustily licking up every last salty gleam of precome, milking him to squeeze out more. Slow, swirling, tongue-lashing the head of his cock. Sucking him deeper as her mouth got used to his girth. She slid her hands up his stalk, fluttered her tongue. She could never get enough of making him quiver and groan and writhe. It made her feel powerful, like a goddess.

It made her feel . . . well . . . happy.

Happy? She had no business being happy. She was setting herself up to get her heart crushed under the wheels of a cement truck.

A stab of panic almost quenched her arousal, but Bruno wouldn't let that happen, with his perfect instincts. He just put his head between her thighs, put his mouth to her, and proceeded to drive her wild.

She had to stop what she was doing, just lie back and gasp at the unbearable pleasure. His mouth moved tenderly over her clit, lips caressing, tongue plunging, swirling and trilling and sucking. Licking up her lube as if he were starving for it.

After a while, they found their groove, and she grabbed his hips and sucked him deep, her thighs wrapped around his head. She could sense the grin on his face as he licked and lashed at her. She, of course, didn't have the luxury of a smile with that huge phallus to deal with. It was all she could do to accommodate him at all. But she managed.

They rode surging waves of voluptuous mutual pleasure,

a perfect balance of power and trust, but he won the first round. He pushed her until she had to give in, sprawl back, and be washed tenderly away on wave after shining wave of surrender.

She drifted back through the rainbow haze of aftershocks and found him sitting cross-legged next to her, stroking her hair.

The look in his eyes scared her. It made her feel so raw. Hopeful.

"You're so beautiful, when you let go," he said.

She had to clear her throat before the mechanism would work. "Don't get mushy on me, Ranieri. I'm not through with you yet."

He grinned. "I should hope not. My head would explode."

She gripped his cock, pulling him into her mouth again. Bruno wound the fingers of one hand into her hair and clamped the other around her hand where she gripped the base of his cock, his breath sawing harshly in and out of his mouth at each deep pull.

It didn't take long. His balls tightened, his taste changed, and he exploded with hot bursts of energy, like light strobing against her eyes.

He shouted as heavy jets of come spurted out. Almost too much to keep in her mouth. She kept him inside until the last lingering pulses ended, and milked out every creamy drop.

He flopped down beside her. They stared at each other, speechless, in the flicker of the lamplight. Sounds of the night came to the foreground as her heartbeat slowed. The *whoo* of the owls, the crackle of the dying fire. The murmur and sigh of wind-tossed trees.

Bruno unwound himself and got up. He crouched to poke another couple of logs into the stove. Then he pulled a glass from the cupboard and filled it with water. He came back to bed, offering her the glass. She accepted it gratefully. He ran his fingers slowly through the fuzzy coil of hair that snaked over her arm as she drank.

She smiled at him when she was done. "So. Looks like we did OK, right? As far as dangerous carnival rides go, I mean."

He shook his head, took the glass, put it on the floor, and pulled her hand onto his lap, curling her fingers around the breadth of his penis. He was hard again. Very. His heart throbbed under her hand.

"That wasn't the ride," he said. "That was just the lead-in."

Her breath got caught in her constricted lungs. "Ah. I, uh, see."

He splayed her knees open and slid his hand up her inner thigh until he reached her muff, and then slid two fingers inside her pussy, tenderly parting the gleaming folds. "That was just to soften you up."

Her chest hitched with nervous laughter. "I had no idea that I needed, ah, softening up. What, am I too hard? Too tough?"

"No." He piled pillows behind her shoulders and rolled onto her body, settling between her thighs, shoving them apart wider. "Just tight," he murmured. "Just small. You hug me." He nudged the head of his cock between her pussy lips, teasing it deeper, lazily swirling himself until he was slick and gleaming. "But you'll take me now. Right?"

She arched, wordlessly trying to take in more of him.

He grabbed her chin, forced her to stare into his eyes. "Right?"

She could only nod, but even that evidently wasn't enough for him. He still waited. She swallowed. "Right," she whispered.

"Good." He thrust inside her, a slow, wonderful, tight slide.

His cock stroked and squeezed and caressed her inside

parts, surging deliciously in and out. Every swirling move a sweet, wet, candy-lick kiss. She bucked and squirmed in delight, straining for more.

He kissed her ravenously as her legs twined, trapping him closer.

He surged in deep, his hips jarring hers. She gasped with delight.

"Now's when the carnival ride begins," he said.

Nadia waited in the dark, her vehicle hidden by boughs of evergreen and darkness. She was in an altered state, as alert as a coiled snake, repeating DeepWeave DeepCalm sequences. She'd doubled her dose of the endorphin and serotonin regulators, too, to guard against inconvenient surges of emotion for Reggie and Cal. She felt their loss, but after taking the patches, it felt very far away.

Headlights sliced and flickered through dense trees. She pressed down on the excitement before it unsettled her. She had gotten lucky. Only two hours, and her target was on the move.

It had taken Hobart forever to drag together what scraps of information were available about Alex Aaro, and Hobart was the absolute best at information mining. They'd pinpointed his residence, but she knew better than to get physically within a mile of the place. If it took that long to get dirt on him, then he was very good. Careful to the point of pathologically paranoid. Ex-Ranger, raised in an arms-dealing Mafia family, security specialist. She would be very careful.

The approach had to be subtle. It required luck, patience, cunning. And here he was. Crawling out of his den, after only two hours. Her heart rate kicked up as she saw the vehicle turn, and she lifted the infrared binocs to check the vehicle. He drove a Chevy Tahoe, a bland is-it-gray-or-is-it-bronze color. And yes . . . the figure in the driver's seat was him, and he was alone. More luck. *Yes.*

Hope thrilled her. This could be the successfully com-

pleted mission that would get her noticed by King. Maybe
more than noticed.

Like Zoe. She wondered if the rumors were true. That
Zoe had been so blessed, so graced. It wasn't fair, after the
way the stupid bitch had fucked up four years ago. She'd
been buried at the nuthouse to pose as a nurse, and now he
was rewarding her? Making her team leader? While Nadia
was special series, with a string of successful missions under
her belt. A spotless assignment history. Unfair. Particularly
since Zoe was putting on airs now, as team leader. Carrying
on like the favored concubine. Stupid, arrogant cow.

Her tires crunched as she drove through the blind of pine
boughs and pulled onto the road after Aaro. Maybe her time
would come. Maybe it wouldn't. None of them were worthy
of that supreme blessing. She would do her duty, with all her
heart, expecting nothing in return.

Although she did have an uneasy feeling that she might
have to prove herself all over again, after what had happened
to Reggie and Cal. King might be wondering about the via-
bility of the entire pod.

In truth, Nadia had a guilty secret that tormented her
dreams. She had not betrayed her podmate, but she'd known
about Reggie's secret rebellion. Natasha's, too. Both of her
podmates had actually sneaked outside books and read
them, for almost a year before the all-important age fourteen
testing date. It was an unspeakable offense that called for instant culling. Reggie had pulled himself together, covered
his ass, avoided the cull. Natasha had not been so lucky. On
her, it had shown.

But she, Nadia. She had never done such a wrong, stupid
thing. Never. She had stayed pure, absolutely obedient. Perfect.

Her intense awareness of her own virtue made her almost
giddy.

She used night vision goggles as she drove, keeping a
careful visual on his taillights. As soon as he reached a

major intersection and turned, she flipped her lights on and hurried to keep up.

He was pulling in at . . . oh, God, yes. Thank you, thank you, *yes!* A bar. Couldn't be better. She was being tongue-kissed by Fate tonight.

She pulled over, waiting for him to get out of his vehicle and go inside before pulling into the parking lot. She parked and opened her purse to organize herself. She had to get him alone, preferably at his home, to download the software onto his phone. If Fate continued to be amorous, perhaps she could plant some other devices as well. She had the spray kit, the quick-acting knock-out pill, and a tasteless, odorless hypnotic pill with aphrodisiac properties. If she was lucky, she wouldn't need any of them. After all, she herself was the aphrodisiac.

She preened in the mirror, dug for her lipstick. Freshened up with a glossy crimson that made her full lips even more seductive. Another pass with the mascara brush. She rearranged the bustier, propping up her cleavage. Fluffed her long, glossy chestnut hair.

Nadia stuck the two pills, using weak glue, beneath the false nails on her index fingers, perfect for discreet flicking into a drink. She peeled adhesive backs from the slap-on GPS tags for his vehicle. She got out of the car, sauntered past his vehicle. Stumbled, crouched to adjust the strap of her four-inch heels, lost her balance. Caught herself on the bumper of his Chevy. Oops! She rose gracefully to her feet. Performing to no one felt silly, but at least no one could accuse her of being sloppy.

Onward, to part two. She sashayed in a slow, hip-swinging walk into the place, letting her eyes adjust. The fuck-me-please outfit was a double-edged sword. She had to get right to him, or she'd end up fending off every horny lout who wandered into the place.

Aaro sat at the end of the bar. Nadia weaved her way between jostling bodies and hot-eyed gazes. She slid into the seat next to his and fluttered her mascara-loaded lashes at him. She gave him her best slow, curving, just-imagine-what-I-can-do-with-these-lips smile.

"Buy a girl a drink?" she murmured.

He glanced at her, gaze bouncing off and then, a half second later, sucked right back. She deepened the smile. Arched to accentuate the cleavage as his gaze dropped, checking out the whole picture.

"I'm on a budget," he said.

Her smile froze. Fury rushed in. That rude, humorless dickhead.

She gestured at the bartender. "Gin and tonic, please," she called. She turned back to Aaro. "I can buy my own."

"That's fortunate."

Well, well. She might actually need the drugs wedged beneath her fingernails. But never let it be said that one of King's operatives wasn't up for a challenge. She propped her elbows on the bar, cupped her chin in her hands, gave the bastard a kittenish stare.

She liked what she saw, from a purely physical point of view. Aaro was tall, strong, muscular. She liked that as much as any girl. Thick shoulders, barrel chest, narrow waist, good ass. And his face intrigued her. Sharp, high, slanted cheekbones, caved in cheeks, heavy-lidded green eyes, the arrowing slash of his dark brows. His nose a craggy, bumpy hook that had seen some breakage. Long hair, dragged back into a cheap elastic band. A non-descript brown, but it was glossy and thick. His mouth a stern hyphen, cruelly flat. Dangerous. Very bad attitude. Hmmm.

This could be fun. Nothing wrong with mixing business with pleasure, if pleasure served her ends. And King's. Of course.

She decided on blatant provocation. "You're not too friendly," she observed. "Makes a girl wonder why you're here at all. You could sulk alone in the dark at home, if you wanted. It costs less."

His mouth hardened. "You're wasting your time, sweetheart. Whatever you're looking for tonight, I don't have any."

Her gaze dropped to his black T-shirt, his faded jeans. The bulge at the crotch that hinted that just maybe, he might not be quite as unfriendly as his words suggested. "You have plenty," she murmured.

He took a swallow of his whiskey and set the glass down with a sharp thud. "I don't think so." His voice was brusque.

"Aww." She pursed her lips in an exaggerated, gleaming pout. "Why are you being so difficult?"

"Because I'm not what ladies like. I don't call the next day, I don't send flowers, I don't want to meet your kid, I don't want to fight with your husband. I just want a glass of fucking bourbon."

She put one of her crimson nails against his hand. He froze. "I don't want flowers." She punctuated each word with a jab of her nail. "I won't give you my number. I don't have kids. Let me tell you why I'm here tonight."

He rolled his eyes. "I'm really not interested in—"

"I don't care," she said. "I'm telling you anyway."

After a moment, he jerked his chin at her to go on. Curious.

Nadia improvised on the spot. "I just met with a private investigator who I hired to follow my husband. He had pictures of my husband's affair. With my sister. Graphic pictures." She let her lip quiver, ever so slightly, then ruthlessly tightened them. Trying to be strong.

He shrugged. "That sucks. And this pertains to me . . . how?"

"I'll tell you how." Nadia let her voice harden. "I shouldn't call or see either one of those shitheads tonight. I need distraction. You'd be doing a great service to humanity, and you would single-handedly decrease this year's violent crime rate of the greater Portland metropolitan area if you provided me with that distraction."

He gazed at her expressionlessly over the rim of his glass.

"I'm not in the habit of putting myself at the service of humanity," he said.

"Then put yourself at the service of something more basic." She reached under the bar. He caught her before she could grab his crotch.

"Uh-uh," he growled. "Don't touch."

"Let me." She let her voice drop to a throaty whisper. "You look so strong. You could make me forget."

His eyes were dilated, his cheekbones flushed. She almost had him, but he still shook his head. "No," he said. "You're trouble."

"What if I am?" she asked. "It won't matter. I'll be long gone. I already know you're a cheap, rude, woman-hating bastard, so I won't expect manners, or gentleness, or clever conversation, or sweet talk." She leaned closer to breathe the words in his ear. "I'll be happy with inarticulate grunts. While you fuck me hard . . . from behind."

He rocked back, looking almost shocked. "Jesus, lady."

"Yes, I know," she crooned. "I'm a very nasty girl tonight."

This time, he let her hand connect with the denim at his crotch. She almost squealed at what she found there. Big, hot. And rock hard.

"Is that what your husband did with your sister in the pictures?" he asked. "He fucked her from behind?"

She flinched and looked away, letting her hair fall forward to hide tears she could generate on command. She let the silence stretch out for a minute, sipping her drink as she got her emotions under control.

Sniff. Oh, that perfidious snake of a husband. Oh, that lying, treacherous slut of a sister. They both deserved to die. They really did.

She shook her hair back and took a huge, terrifying risk. "I'll show you the pictures, if you want," she said, brushing tears away with her knuckles, so as not to smear her mascara. "They're in my purse."

She held her breath, heart thudding, as he considered looking at the sexually explicit photographs that she did not have.

"I'll pass," he finally said. "I don't need that kind of stimulation."

Tears of relief sprang into her eyes. She sniffed them back, theatrically. "Suit yourself. I don't need to look at them again, either."

He looked almost . . . sorry for her. God, she was good. The best.

"Take it or leave it," she said. "No strings."

"Women say that a lot," he replied. "It's never true."

"You mean women actually talk to you that often?"

The corner of his mouth curved up. She followed up her advantage, leaning close. "Believe me, big guy," she whispered. "I don't even want to know your name. Don't tell me. I am *so* not interested."

They stared into each other's eyes. He raised his drink. Her hand tightened greedily on his cock as he drained it. She could feel his pulse, a strong, rapid throb in his stiff rod. "Take me home," she whispered.

His eyes hardened. "I don't take anybody to my home."

Course correct. She hid her irritation with a smile. "Better still," she said smoothly. "The hotel across the highway?"

He nodded and rose to his feet. Up, and up. Mmm. So tall. She got up, too, picturing herself reporting a successful mission and maybe even getting The Call, from King. An invitation to tell him all about it over dinner . . . and then, if he thought she'd been good enough . . .

Thinking about it made her wet, which had the happy effect of making her even hotter for rough, mindless sex with Aaro. A breathless, squirming, sexy feedback loop. She took Aaro's muscular arm.

Goodness, he was huge. She might have to double dose him, she thought, palpating his bicep. She could administer it in something from the minibar. If not, there was always the vapor. Three squirts, for such a massive man. But not quite yet, though. Oh, no, not yet.

She'd go a few rounds with this one before she brought him down.

16

*B*runo *ducked under the swing of the studded iron ball that swung on Rudy's mace. There were three Rudys, inexplicably wearing medieval chain mail. The second was armed with an ax, and the third with a broadsword. Bruno jerked back. The broadsword swooshed by his Adam's apple. He stumbled to the side to avoid the ax, dove to bring down the mace-wielding Rudy.*

Then he saw the dais.

Lily was bound to a pole. She wore a long white gown, torn and mud stained. She was blindfolded. Oil-soaked wood was piled around her. Her ragged skirt flapped in the wind. So did her skeins of hair.

Terror tore him open inside. He sprang up to fight, but now there were six Rudys, a mass of suffocating bodies driving him back as one of them sauntered toward Lily, waving a burning branch. He glanced back, his sweaty face split by a mocking grin. Thrust the flame into the fuel.

The wood ignited instantly, flames leaping to lick at Lily's ragged skirt. Bruno struggled, shoving, punching, howling Lily's name.

She yelled back, but the sound came from so far away—

The image splintered. *Thud*, he was on a floor in the

dark. Naked, sweaty. He looked around frantically for his attackers—

Lily was huddled against the wall, naked. Her hands were over her nose. Her eyes were huge. Oh God. What the fuck had he done?

It took him about six attempts to get words out, his voice shook so hard. "You . . . all right?"

She lifted her hand, looked at it. Blood trickled from her nose. His horror soured into shame. "Oh, fuck," he muttered. "Did I do that?"

"I'm OK." She touched her nose. Blood reddened her fingers.

"That wasn't the question." He tried to get up. Thudded down onto his ass, still shaking. He hadn't even thought about the nightmares. How dangerous they might be for her. Hadn't even warned her. Fucking idiot. He'd just drifted off in a post-coital haze. La-di-dah. Zzzz.

"It's my own fault," she said softly. "I should have known better. You were having the mother of all nightmares, and yelling my name, and I, um . . . tried to grab you. To wake you up. Big mistake."

He cringed. "Oh, God, Lily. I'm sorry."

"It's OK, really," she assured him. "I'm not—"

"I could have fucking killed you!" he roared. "Do you realize that? How close you came?"

She shrank back. "You didn't," she said. "So chill. No harm done."

"No harm done?" His voice cracked. "You've got a fucking broken nose, and you have the nerve to say *no harm done?*"

She palpated her nose. "Not broken. Just, you know. Bumped."

"By my *fist?* That's not a bump! I *slugged* you, goddamnit!"

"Well, and so? You're not helping matters by yelling at

me. You were dreaming. It's not your fault. Get the fuck over it."

Her attitude was so calm in the face of all the apocalyptic doom he was feeling. It had a weird effect on him. Like a knot, slipping loose.

He fell into pieces. Shaking with silent sobs. He dropped his face into his hands, mortified. Lily grabbed him, but he flinched away, flinging her arms off. "Don't touch me!"

"No way!" she yelled back. "You can't do that to me! You can't push me away! I won't let you! Not anymore!"

"I just don't want you to get hurt!" he bellowed.

She grabbed him again, and what could he do? Slug her again?

Aw, fuck it. Let her hug him if she wanted to risk it. It was her skin. He kept his face covered and just endured the silent, racking sobs. He couldn't make any sound. Pressure in his throat kept building. His voice box was imploding. A burning, crushing ache. He didn't even try to stop crying. He knew when he was pounded.

After a while, the weight of her arm across his shuddering back came into focus. Her cheek was pressed against his shoulder. Drops of moisture tickled, cold against his back. She was crying, too. Did not help. Not that he had any right to complain, after scaring her, popping her in the nose. Letting her watch his nervous breakdown up close.

Lily went into the bathroom, came out again a moment later. The bed sagged as she sat again, her warm body pressed against his. Thigh to thigh, shoulder to shoulder. She shoved tissues into his hand. He mopped up the snot, keeping his face averted. He felt like a helpless kid again, on those nights when he rolled into a ball and put a pillow over his head, when Rudy and Mamma were having at it.

She threaded her cold fingers through his. "Will you tell me?"

"Tell you what?" He was channeling his sullen, truculent

Uncle Tony again. Hardwired to act like a butthead when he was stressed.

Lily was unfazed. "The nightmare."

He shook his head, but she tugged his hand. "Tell me."

A shudder rippled down his spine. "It's old," he muttered. "Had it since I was a kid. When I was thirteen, Kev put a spell on me. Talked me into a trance every night. They finally eased off." He tried to swallow. A diamond-hard lump lacerated his throat. "Now they're back."

"What's the dream about?"

He shrugged. "Fighting. I'm in a white virtual space, like a video game. Monsters come at me. And I fight them."

She harrumphed. "Scary."

"Oh, yeah." The words exploded out of him. "Because it's not like other nightmares. I wake up feeling . . ." He trailed off. It was too weird.

"Like what?" she prodded. "Come on, Bruno."

"Like it's real," he concluded, feeling ashamed. "I mean, physically real. Like I'd really been fighting. Pulled muscles, sweat, bruising. Sprains, even. Maybe because I hit stuff while I flop around. I end up on the floor sometimes, like now. I don't fucking know."

"Wow," she murmured. "What kind of monsters?"

"My mom's boyfriend. The one who murdered her."

Her soft cheek pressed his shoulder. "That's so horrible."

"Yeah, it is," he said. "But he was not what particularly sucked about tonight's dream, believe it or not."

She nudged him after a few moments. "So? What was, then?"

"You," he said. "You were there. Everybody in costume. Medieval armor, like a goddamn Arthurian pageant. You wore a fancy white gown. You were bound to a stake. And they held me down while Rudy . . ." His throat closed up. "He stuck a burning branch into the wood."

"Don't tell me, let me guess," she said. "That was the moment when I tried to wake you up, right?"

"Yeah." He waited for more. She just hugged him. "So, uh . . ." He cleared his throat. "I gather you are not as freaked out by this as I am."

"My threshold for freak-outs has gotten higher lately," Lily said. "I can only be scared of so much at one time, and I'm sorry, but your dream just doesn't make the cut."

"Oh," he muttered, vaguely embarrassed. "Gee."

"Don't take it personally," she urged. "It's, like, a triage thing. I just don't have the juice. I know it must be really awful for you."

"Whatever." He felt an urge to laugh, but that was too close to sobbing. "What the fuck were the crusading knight outfits about? Ye olde renaissance fair from hell? My subconscious decided the dream needed dressing up? What's next, flamenco outfits?"

"No," she said quietly. "It's about saving the princess."

He went still. Her words reverberated in his head. "Come again?"

"It's a classic theme, right? In fairy tales, in movies. Video games you played as a kid. Didn't you ever play to save the princess?"

"Yeah, but . . ." His voice trailed off. He was unnerved. It was true, he'd played in video arcades as a really young kid. But after the dreams started, he'd stopped. He hated video games.

Lily draped herself over him so that his head was tucked under her chin, her gorgeous, mouth-watering tits were right in his face, in all their succulent, springy softness. Right up there to distract him.

"You really are my champion," she said. "Even in your dreams. Like you were this morning."

"I, ah . . . but I—"

"I've never had one before," she said. "I always had to fight alone. It feels nice. Thank you."

"Hello. Lily," he said, his voice vibrating with tension. "I failed. In the dream. They torched you. It wasn't nice."

She tilted his head back. Her eyes shimmered with tears. "They didn't get me this morning," she said. She ran her finger across his brow, then through his hair. "And you tried. I could see you were trying. Heart and soul. That's enough for me. That's more than I've ever had."

His arms clamped around her. She melted into his embrace.

"It's not enough," he blurted out, harshly. "I want more."

She just gazed up at him, looking confused. He gave her an impatient little shake. "I want more," he repeated, louder.

She looked bewildered but willing. "Ah . . . OK," she offered, timidly. "Take it, then. You can have it all. It's yours. Everything."

All. Everything. That was good. He could work with that.

Then they were kissing, dying for more of that magical whatever it was that they made together, out of nothing, out of nowhere. A mystery made of energy and heat, out of ache and want.

He pushed her down onto the bed, lips locked, fitting his body to hers. Feeling her silent welcome as she arched and spread, wiggling against him until his cock could find its way in, then the long clinging slide. Arms clutching, legs twining as they rocked and plunged, sighing, gasping. No technique or style, just raw emotion. The bite of her nails in his back were points of light in the heaving turbulence. They thundered over the top and down, into the heart of a violent climax.

Reality crept back, with relentless marching steps. His sweat cooled, trickled down his back, into his ear. The first few times they'd had sex, he'd managed somehow to keep from coming inside her.

Well, hell. He'd warned her. And he still felt like an opportunistic asshole. He pulled away, rolled onto his side. She glowed in the dim light of the kerosene lamp he'd left burning. So beautiful he could start up and make this same mistake again, right now.

"I'm sorry." The words rasped out. Hoarse from all the sobbing.

She just nodded, as if it were no big deal. Too used to danger. Her threshold was high. It took a lot of juice to be constantly terrified. There was nothing to say. She touched his cheek. She didn't say, "No problem." They had nothing but problems. She didn't say, "It's OK." It wasn't.

You're my champion.

That scared him to his bones. He'd always avoided responsibility. Now he knew why he'd steered clear. It was a ten-ton weight of cold rock. Stark fear, of failing her, losing her. Fear that could break him.

But all he could do was keep fighting. Hell, he had lots of practice.

This was ridiculously easy. Zoe was irritated. She could have sent that brain-dead sow Melanie after all. Petrie didn't even have an alarm. There was a tree that would allow an intruder with no technique at all to clamber onto the kitchen roof and steal over to the bathroom window. Evidently, Samuel Petrie was not as paranoid as a normal cop.

Zoe felt practically insulted.

She slid the window open and slithered in like a slim shadow. She realized that he just hadn't gotten around to putting his paranoia into practice. Boxes were piled everywhere. The rooms were empty.

Research had revealed that Petrie was twenty-nine, unmarried. Wealthy family. Ivy League school. He'd decided after graduating to go into police work, to his family's distress. He'd recently bought his first home in a middling shabby North Portland neighborhood.

The master bedroom was at the end of the hall. Light and chatter of the TV came out, even at three A.M. She'd waited until the last minute to creep in, but soon she had to rendezvous with the team following McCloud down from Seattle. If he was still awake, she would melt away the way she came. Lots of cops had trouble sleeping. Tomorrow was another day. She angled a tiny mirror around the door and peeked.

Ah, yes. He was sprawled on the bed, a sheet wound around his hips. Mouth open. Fast asleep as the TV gabbled. She drifted toward the bed, smiling behind her mask, silent as a whorl of smoke.

She angled the bottle close to his face, admiring the jutting angle of his stubble-shadowed jaw, and *squirt—squirt—squirt*.

He murmured, but the stuff worked instantly. He wouldn't stir for hours. In fact, with such a heavy dose, he was liable to sleep through his alarm and wake with a nasty headache tomorrow. Poor baby.

Zoe sat down on the bed next to him. The large bed and low dresser were the only articles of furniture in the room, and they stank of newness. No mirror. Dead giveaway that there was no woman in his life. Only a man could make do with just the mirror above a bathroom sink.

Boxes of clothes were stacked against the wall. A Glock 19 sat on the bedside table, well within reach. So he wasn't so fearless after all.

His smartphone sat next to the gun. She took it, hooked it up to her own, running Hobart's superfast password-cracking program.

It only took about ten minutes before the program sifted out his code and she was in, downloading the remote spy program. Copying the contents of his device to her own phone to pore over at her leisure. Hacking was not her specialty. That was how eggheads like Hobart justified their existence. Even so, her level of expertise was higher than that of a normal cyber criminal. She checked the time. There were a few minutes to kill, so she got into his SMS register for that day. She formed a grid, plugged the times and messages in it into her head, toggling between SMSs sent and those received. She found a series that warranted interest, an exchange with a colleague named Trish.

Petrie: need a favor

Trish: don't u always

Petrie: will be walking blood samples over from ME's to crime lab tomorrow 4 dna testing. Meet me there?

Trish: whose dna?

Petrie: Bifid zigomaticus + 3 john does from diner. Cd u do ur magic thing, get them fast tracked?

Trish: what's the rush

Petrie: got a bad feeling. pls Trish. I love u will be ur slave 4ever

Trish: chill out prettyboy. get ur tongue out of my ass it tickles

Hmm. So, the results of genetic testing on today's disaster would soon be known to all. Zoe tucked her phone away, put Petrie's precisely where he'd left it, and wondered if she should do anything more.

She studied Petrie himself. Tasty. Thick, unruly chestnut hair, spiking every which way. Strong jaw, virile beard shadow, bold Roman nose. She wondered what color eyes he had. He was long, lean. His naked torso was taut, with the whippet-thin, wiry musculature that she liked. It looked streamlined, efficient. Better than beefcake bulk. She ran her leather-gloved hand over his cut pecs. Dragged the sheet down over his hip. He slept naked. Mmm, nice. She cupped his balls. Stroked her gloved fingers over the penis draped across his thigh.

It jerked in her hand and swelled. A shame to waste an erection like that. Three expert strokes brought him to an admirable state of hardness. And drugged, too, with respiration and blood pressure at their absolute lowest. Imagine what he could do when awake.

Zoe slung her thigh over him, straddling him on the bed. Reached for his gun in her leather-gloved hand and placed the barrel under his chin, scraping it along his stiff beard stubble as she squeezed his cock.

She could be Petrie's naughty succubus. She saw herself sheathing him in latex, mounting up, and closing her eyes and dreaming of King and reward phrases as she rode herself to juicy completion.

But she was team leader. She had to set the example. There was no justifiable reason to fuck Petrie. It would be self-indulgent, and King would disapprove. She dismounted, lay the gun back down in the exact place and position it had been, and tugged the sheet back up, after giving that beautiful, thick, stiff cock a final regretful farewell pat.

No, her work here was done. Petrie's involvement was peripheral. Nothing to be gained wasting some operative's time processing useless data. Monitoring his smartphone should be more than sufficient. She left him as she had found him and drifted down the corridor, uncomfortably distracted by unfulfilled sexual impulses. She should have assigned Nadia to Petrie and taken on Aaro herself. But it was that greedy whore Nadia, bucking and squealing in some hotel room.

So unfair.

17

Bruno was grumpy the following morning, speaking only in imperative grunts. *Get dressed. Eat this. Drink the coffee. Hurry up.* He kept peering out a tiny crack in the cabin's curtain, gun in hand.

She heard the murmur of a car engine, the crunch of a car pulling to a stop, and suddenly, his battle tension relaxed.

So. It was the right car. The right visitor.

She followed Bruno out into the icy cold, conifer-perfumed half-light of dawn. A tall, brawny guy wearing a long sheepskin coat stood next to a red Jeep Wrangler. A wool watch cap was pulled low over his forehead. His face was lean— sharp cheekbones, hawk nose, grim mouth. His jaw was covered with glittering gold and silver beard stubble. His pale eyes fastened on hers, bright with curiosity. "Morning," he said.

She gave him a cautious smile. "Thanks for coming all this way to pick us up," she offered.

He slanted a glance at Bruno. "No problem. Thanks for the pretty manners. Guess I didn't drive all night for nothing."

Bruno grunted. The wind swirled bits of snow around them. The tension made the hairs on Lily's nape prickle.

"Talked to Kev a couple hours ago," Sean McCloud said.

"Good for you," was Bruno's rejoinder.

"He called from Christchurch," McCloud went on. "He and Edie were looking for the first flight they could find for Portland or Seattle."

Bruno cleared his throat. "That's nice."

"You think?" Sean's voice hardened. "He said you didn't call."

Bruno shrugged. "You know there's no cell coverage here."

"He was scared shitless for you."

"What's between me and Kev is private," Bruno said.

Sean's eyes flickered. "Whatever. But I think you should get that bug out of your ass before you start walking funny."

Bruno stuck the gun inside his jacket. "Let's get going."

"Anytime, man," McCloud murmured. "Anytime."

Bruno walked to the edge of the ravine and raised a pair

of binoculars to his eyes. He stared down at the mountainside. When he lowered the binoculars, his face had changed. "They're coming."

The dead-calm quality of his voice made Lily shiver.

McCloud looked startled. "Who's coming?"

"You were followed," Bruno stated. "They've got us. Pinned."

"No way. That's not possible. This car is clean. We talked about this business over encrypted phones. I went to insane lengths to make sure that nobody tagged Miles' rig. Give me those things!" Sean snatched the binoculars away and peered down at the road. "I don't see anything," he complained. "Where?"

"Look where the creek curves at the level of that spur on the bluff over there," Bruno directed. "Now follow it up to the second switchback from the bottom. No headlights. Look for movement. They just turned the hairpin. Heading back up in this direction. See it?"

Sean McCloud was silent for a moment as he searched, and then he sucked in air. "Son of a bitch. How the hell did they know—"

"Because they know everything," Lily blurted, feeling sick.

There was a brief moment of blank dismay, and then Sean McCloud seemed to shake himself, as if throwing off a spell. "Come on, then." He sounded so casual, it was almost bizarre. "Let's get to it."

"To what?" Lily demanded.

"Our plan. How long you figure it'll take them to get up here?"

Bruno peered down, calculating. "At that speed, twenty-five minutes, maybe. I've got some pistols and ammo Aaro lent me. A Glock 19, a Beretta 92, an H&K USP. Got anything with you?"

"Hell, yeah," McCloud said absently. He crossed his arms again, tapping his fingers. "Only one vehicle," he murmured.

"Arrogant sons of bitches. Who the fuck do they think they're dealing with?" He stared down the hill, eyes slitted. "You got that little bridge down there, at two hundred meters. That's the best place to rig it. Got a chain?"

"Best place to rig what?" Lily demanded.

"The bomb," McCloud said, as if it were obvious. "We could go with ammonium nitrate and fuel oil. Diesel or kerosene. I've got some Tovex in the truck to boost it. Did Kev ever store any fertilizer up here?"

Bruno looked bemused. "Uh . . . uh . . ."

"Never mind, forget it. Flame fougasse, then." McCloud pushed on. "We dig a hole on the road, hide a container of fuel wired to some explosives. Boom, problem solved. Until the next dickheads find you."

"You can rig it that fast?" Bruno said.

"If you stop jerking off."

"Wait!" Lily yelled as the men leaped into action. "One quick second. Please."

The men lurched to a stop and spun, with identical what-the-fuck-is-your-problem-lady looks on their faces.

"We don't have a lot of time," McCloud said. "Make it fast."

"What if the people in that vehicle are not our bad guys? What if they're, you know, just innocent passersby?"

Bruno and Sean exchanged glances. "Lily," Bruno said, as if speaking to a slow-witted child. "People do not innocently pass by this place at dawn with their headlights turned off. It's the last property on the road. The road runs out into a deer track three hundred meters farther on. This is the furry, pimply ass-end of fucking nowhere."

She gestured at McCloud. "He said himself it would have been impossible for them to follow him! You can't risk killing innocent people!"

"You want to go wait by the road?" Sean McCloud's voice sounded only mildly curious. "Offer them coffee and Danish?"

She waved her hands. "I just don't want people to die because they're on the wrong road at the wrong time! That would suck!"

Sean shrugged. "OK. Plan B," he said. "I dig in up the hill at a hundred meters with my M21, check them out with my scope. It'll magnify the ambient light enough to see inside. If it's Great-aunt Betty, we give her coffee and Danish. If they're the bad guys, we fuck them up, take one of them alive, and interrogate the living shit out of him."

Bruno's face cleared. "Sounds good."

"Plus, we can deliver our survivors to the cops afterward," Sean went on. "A blood gift to appease their wrath."

"Even better," Bruno said, with growing enthusiasm.

Sean McCloud gave her a hard look. "If there's more than two, I'm capping them, straight off," he said flatly. "This is too fucking risky as it is. I don't want to die today. I've got a kid."

Lily gulped and nodded. No arguing with that position.

"So, how about that chain?" McCloud was all business again.

"Down by the bridge," Bruno said. "Tony always used to chain the road when he left."

"String it. I'll gather supplies."

Bruno loped off down the road. Lily watched him go and aimed the nervous question at Sean McCloud's back as he rummaged through the back of the Jeep for supplies. "How do you intend to, ah, take some of them prisoner without killing them?"

McCloud flashed a grin over his shoulder. He held up handfuls of small, dark cylindrical objects. "Watch and learn," he said. "This is gonna be fun. Promise you won't tell my wife. She's funny that way."

She studied them in trepidation. "What the hell are those?"

"Flashbangs. Stun grenades. Now be quiet and let me work."

* * *

There was an art to feigning sleep. Aaro was good at it. His standard method of not dealing with whatever female he'd just had sex with. Breathing was key. Deep, slow, and steady. Mouth slack, open, face relaxed. And calm. No mental buzz, no static. Chicks picked up on that. Bright ones, anyhow, and this one was bright. He could tell in spite of their deliberate dearth of conversation.

He was justified in the sleep he was feigning, after the fuck marathon she'd put him through. Not that he'd complained. He'd been fine with the hard, uncomplicated pounding that she'd wanted. Up, down, backward, forward, bring it on, he wasn't fussy. She liked it rough; she came easily and often. But she kept wanting more.

After six bouts, he caught on. She was a sexual black hole. A guy could kill himself trying to satisfy her. But it had been a long time, so what the fuck, he put out. She was gorgeous. High, bouncing tits. Ass taut and perfect. Snug, hot pink pussy, waxed and plucked and groomed. A walking wet dream. His dick stiffened thinking of it. So why was he feigning sleep instead of mounting back up, giving her more?

It was the clenched feeling in his belly. Like a tiny fist. After ejaculating that many times, he should be comatose, but her febrile desperation made him nervous. Even while she was climaxing, she was always clawing for something more. Something she just couldn't have.

Maybe it had to do with the asshole husband screwing the slut sister. In any case, it was depressing, and he was depressed all on his own, thanks. He'd avoid the whole sticky mess of sex altogether, if he could. Steer clear of females, with their incomprehensible demands. Live the life of a monk, tranquil, solitary. But he had a functioning dick that wanted what it wanted, and it had to be periodically appeased, or he got testosterone backup. Toxic. Very bad scene.

So he was good at feigning sleep. Biofeedback training

helped. He had control over his heartbeat, blood pressure. He projected the vibe *sleeping, sleeping,* while following her every move. The rustle of sheets, the roll and dip of the bed. Feet padding toward the bathroom. Water running. Click, a beam of light, a cloud of steam. He listened to her dressing, relief warring with caution. She was bailing for real. *Yes.*

She rummaged in her purse for a moment. A few beats of pure silence. His small hairs prickled. What was up? She was just standing there, staring? Wondering if she should wake him, say good-bye?

Please, don't. Just go. Take your problems and vanish. Write a note if you have to. And then . . . just . . . go.

She was tiptoeing closer. The balls of her feet shushed against the carpet fibers. Next to the bed. He felt her body heat, smelled her shower gel, her shoe leather. But no breathing. She was holding her breath.

He almost twitched with the need to open his eyes, but then he'd have to talk to her. Even fuck her again, maybe.

The silence was strange. It quivered in the air. Like indecision.

Or . . . anticipation.

His heart sped up. He'd have to drag in air soon. Something was off. Either she'd lean over, kiss him good-bye, God forbid . . . or else . . .

Or else she was holding a knife to his throat.

His body contracted. He jerked, knocked whatever she was holding away from his face. It went flying.

She landed a punch to his jaw. Her elbow stabbed his ribs. *Fuck.* He barely blocked the knee to his balls. Lunged for her as she scuttled back. She was fast, but he had the weight and reach. He blocked her punch, seized her arm, flipped her. Landed on top of her, all two hundred and forty pounds of him. Knocked out her air. Felt no remorse.

She bucked, choked for air. He pinned her wrists, looked around. He was naked, and a hotel room didn't have much in the way of ligature lying around, so he groped under her top with one hand, unhooked her bra. He ripped the straps loose, yanked the lacy garment off her torso. Used it to bind her wrists. Twisting hard, knotting tight. No mercy.

He rolled her onto her back, on top of her bound hands, and leaned until her face paled and sweat popped out on her forehead.

"I've rethought this no-names rule," he remarked. "Considering this development, I think you should tell me who you are."

Her eyes glittered, her chest heaved. "Fuck you."

He leaned harder, forcing a high-pitched wheeze out of her, and without taking his eyes off hers, snagged the object he'd batted out of her hand. A little spray bottle. Son of a bitch.

"What's this? A knock-out drug?" he asked. "What's it for?"

She shook her head.

He studied her. "I have a hundred and eighty bucks on me in cash," he said. "Bet you spent five times that amount on those shoes alone. If you want money, you should be cruising the casinos on the Indian reservations. Not slumming in roadhouses with losers like me."

She stared back, defiant. She was no junkie in search of a quick fix. She glowed with health. And with a face and body like that, she could bilk men out of all their money without having to resort to knock-out drugs. So what the fuck? If she hadn't picked him for money, she'd picked him for some other reason. Two things came to mind.

Neither of them were good.

He leaned on her again and gave Hypothesis Number One a spin.

"My father sent you, ney?" he asked in Ukrainian.

Her eyelids fluttered, but he saw no comprehension. He had a lifetime of practice reading fleeting expressions of stone-faced people. A family survival skill. He got nothing from her. Not a twinge, not a flash, not a flicker. He swatted her face, made his voice even harsher. "Talk, you stupid whore," he snarled in the same language. "My father? My uncle? Tell me, or I'll rip your tongue right out of your head!"

She spat at him, but that was payback for the slap.

He could be wrong, had been often, but he had to call it. She didn't understand Ukrainian. She wasn't sent by his family. So much for Hypothesis One. Sending a beautiful woman to fuck his brains out was hardly Oleg Arbatov's style, anyhow. The way the old man hated his firstborn, he'd be more likely to send six big guys with blackjacks.

He jerked open her fallen purse. Makeup, wallet, two blister packs of tiny pills, distinguished only by colored dots on the foil. A phone, some sleek design he didn't recognize. He flipped through the wallet. A driver's license made out to Naomi Hillier of Bellingham, Washington. Credit cars, department store cards in the same name. A wad of cash. He leafed through it. Eight thousand, hoo-hah. The wallet had none of the detritus of a normal life. No parking tickets, receipts, scribbled numbers, dry-cleaning pickup slips. No manila envelope full of pictures of the cheating husband and the slut sister going at it doggy style, either.

He brandished the spray bottle in her face. She bucked like a bronco. Maybe the stuff was lethal. But Jesus, why? Granted, he tended to piss people off just by existing, but if someone was that mad at him, one would think he'd have half a clue. Time for Hypothesis Two.

He lifted himself slowly off her. "Listen, Naomi," he said. "You move one millimeter in any direction I don't order you to move, and you get a faceful of whatever the fuck is in this bottle. Got that?"

She nodded.

Pulling clothes on was tricky, one handed. He didn't bother with his T-shirt, since it would require a split second of being blind, which was one split second too long. He pulled on his jeans, shrugged the jacket over his naked torso, shoved the shirt into his pocket. Slid his feet into his boots without bothering to lace them. "On your feet."

She struggled awkwardly to her feet. "Where are we going?"

"The police," he said.

She started to laugh. "Because I'm not playing nice? Aw! I'm sure they'll feel sorry for you, after you tell them how you spent your night."

He twisted her bound hands up behind her. "Shut up and move."

"I'll tell them I was raped. Why do you think I wanted it rough, you stupid fuck? I got one of your condoms out of the trash and put some of your spunk into myself. I have you cold, asshole."

Here it was. The money question. "I'm not taking you to the Sandy cops. I'm taking you to downtown Portland. To the Justice Center. We're going to talk to Detective Petrie."

It was subtle, but he caught the zing of tension. The eyelid flutter, her pupils contracting. All he needed to know. Son of a *bitch*. Hypothesis Two won, ding, ding, ding. This was about Bruno and his schizo girlfriend. Hit men jumping out of cars, dead bodies strewn on the streets of North Portland. Big trouble, and idiot that he was, he'd stuck his nose right into it. No, worse. He'd stuck his dick into it. Repeatedly.

He grabbed the girl by the throat and pushed her onto the bed, pulling his knife out of his pocket. He snapped it open, twirled it.

Her eyes fixed on the flashing blade, frozen wide.

"You have a beautiful face," he said softly. "You want it to stay beautiful? Tell me what you want from Bruno Ranieri, bitch."

"I don't know what you're talking about."

"We both know that's a fucking lie," he hissed. "Where shall I start?" He caressed her cheek with the point of the blade. "How about an eyelid? That's a toughie for the reconstructive surgeon to fix." He traced patterns on the skin under her eye. Smiled evilly, like a guy who actually enjoyed torturing women. He knew guys like that. He'd seen what their smiles looked like when they were working on their victims.

It didn't feel good on his own face.

Veins throbbed in her temples. Her lips tightened, quivered, drawing back from her teeth. Seconds passed. She'd called his bluff.

He put his knife down, like the limp dick his father had always mocked him for being. He couldn't convince her that he was capable of cutting her. He had no credibility. In some circles, he'd been told, this failure would be to his credit. Right now, it was fucking inconvenient.

He jabbed the spray bottle under her chin, but she didn't react this time. "Let's go," he growled. "If I hear you inhale, I spray you."

She stumbled beside him, stiff but unresisting. Into the cinder block stairwell. Out into the hotel parking lot, where dawn was threatening the horizon. She was shaking, hard, by the time he shoved her into the passenger seat of his Chevy and strapped her in.

He stopped, took a second to yank on his shirt, since it didn't look like she was going to attack him. Those racking shudders did not look like an act. She'd forgotten that he existed. She was fucked up.

He cut off the bra knotted around her hands. Draped his jacket over her, tucking it under her chin. Thus thoroughly shoring up his persona as a real badass motherfucker. He blasted heat on her as they drove. He'd expected a shrill scolding, a string of inventive lies, or at least some slick, jive-ass rant. All he heard was teeth chattering.

He went back and forth in his head on what to do with Naomi about a thousand times as he drove. The more miles that went by, the worse she looked. And the more his options narrowed.

He hated sticking his neck out, getting squashed onto an examining glass under blazing light and powerful lenses. He'd rather lose a limb. But what the fuck else could he do right now? With her? He couldn't just dump her by the side of the road somewhere. Particularly now with his genetic material inside her bodily orifices.

He clenched his jaw, grabbed his cell phone, dialed the number he'd found for Detective Sam Petrie the day before.

The guy picked up quickly, considering that it wasn't quite eight o'clock yet. "Detective Sam Petrie here," he said.

"Detective Petrie, my name is Alex Aaro," he said. "I have with me a person of interest in your case, involving the three dead guys that turned up behind Tony's Diner yesterday."

"Ah." Petrie paused expectantly. "And? Why is this person interesting?"

"She just tried to kill me," he blurted.

Petrie made an encouraging sound. "Tell me more."

"I will, but I've got to take this girl somewhere. Are you at the Justice Center now?"

"Ah, almost," the guy replied. "Just have to park. Where are you?"

"About ten minutes away. Look, could you meet me right out front, or in the lobby? I don't want to have to look for parking with her."

"Ah . . ." Petrie hesitated, sensing the swiftly rising level of weirdness. "What's wrong with this girl? Is she hurt?"

"Just get her some coffee, would you? Or a pastry." Aaro stared at Naomi's grayish face, her chattering teeth. "Something with lots of sugar."

"Mr. Aaro, do you—"

Aaro cut the connection and thumbed off the phone. His jacket had slid off her again and hit the floor. She vibrated against the seat belt. Maybe she actually was a junkie, and she'd mixed her fix.

He picked up speed, racing through red lights. God, how he wanted this to be over. He hoped Petrie would show up on time.

He jerked to a stop on SW Third, right outside the imposing main entrance of the Justice Center, figuring he'd unload the girl and leave her with Petrie while he re-parked. Please, God. He took her purse for Petrie's benefit, but the phone he wanted to look at himself, so he tossed it into the front seat for future study.

He hustled her up the broad stairs of the entryway, through the bank of glass doors. She weaved and wobbled, dangerously unsteady.

He glanced wildly around the place, trying not to look as desperate and harried as he felt, scanning for someone whose body type fit the voice from the phone conversation. There. Tall guy, thirtyish, big jaw, tousled hair. Lots of stubble. He held a paper coffee cup, a white paper bag. Good man. He'd brought sugar. His eyes asked Aaro the question. Aaro's feet answered it, forcefully steering Naomi's body toward the other man. "Detective Petrie?" he asked.

The guy's eyes flicked over Naomi, who was breathing with a strange, audible wheezing sound now. "Yeah, that's me. Hey, looks like your friend there needs the emergency room."

"She's not my friend," Aaro snapped. "She just tried to kill me."

Suddenly, Naomi jerked, so violently she wrenched herself out of his grip. She vomited, a projectile fountain that rose into the air and spewed around in a nasty arc as she twisted, flailing her arms, her body jackknifing. The people nearby leaped back from the splatter with shouts of disgust. She thudded heavily to her knees, and then fell flat, her body twitching.

Aaro knelt next to her, placed his finger on her carotid artery. He saw Petrie in his peripheral vision, crouched on the other side. He felt an irregular flutter . . . and then nothing. For many long seconds. Dead.

The convulsions had snapped her spine.

Someone elbowed him roughly aside as people gathered around Naomi's curled-up body. Someone was pumping on her chest. Others were shouting instructions, suggestions. One guy was calling for EMTs on his cell. A woman was crying, noisily.

Boom. The sound jolted him. From outside. Shouts, screams. Alarms began to squeal, at every pitch, a crazy, cacophonous chorus.

Aaro staggered to his feet with the others and went to look out the door. He stared, barely surprised at what he saw, right outside, in the street. His Chevy. Windows blown out. Smoke pouring. Blown up.

A hand touched his shoulder. He turned, looked into Petrie's bloodshot eyes.

"Is that your vehicle?" Petrie asked.

Aaro nodded. "Second time in six months," he said, for no reason that he could fathom. Like it was any of Petrie's goddamn business.

A short, fat guy who'd come to the door to gawk whistled appreciatively. "Oh, man. That's gotta hurt. You must have an exciting life."

Aaro let out a long sigh. "You have no idea," he muttered.

"They are going to fuck you up the ass on the insurance now, you know that?" the short guy informed him, with unseemly relish.

"Yeah," murmured Aaro, bleakly. "I do know that."

"Let's go have a talk while the EMT people come for your friend," Petrie suggested.

"She's not my friend," he said again. "She just tried to kill me."

Petrie gazed at him. "OK," he said. "Let's go discuss how this relates to my case, then. You might as well take this coffee." He held out the paper cup. "You're going to be here for a while."

Bruno huddled in the brush, ears straining for the hum of the engine on the switchback. Sean McCloud hadn't said much once they'd established radio communication. The guy was in his hiding place up the hill, in the zone, peering through his scope. Soon the purported bad guys would turn the hairpin and make the last pass to the bridge. And then, showtime.

Stay up there. Be good. Do as you're told for once in your life. Bruno punched the telepathic message toward the place where he'd left Lily, swathed in the smallest body armor that Sean had, which still swamped her, and a big camo poncho draped over it. He'd given Lily the Glock 19, with a full magazine and a chambered round, and strict instructions to hightail it up the mountain, and put distance between herself and the stunt that he and Sean were about to pull.

She was supposed to wait on the bluff. If they didn't come collect her, well, that was a real shame. In that sad case, she kept her head down and called Sean's brothers on Bruno's encrypted, dedicated cell.

It comforted him that she had on some Dragon Skin body armor.

Lily didn't like being stashed. Too bad. She was the one who'd nixed the flame fougasse option. He'd liked that scenario, the finality of it. Watching the full vehicle rise up into the air and gracefully explode, ah. Take that, you fuckers. But no. Couldn't be that simple.

The motor rumbled. He heard tires crunch. He gathered himself into a state of focused calm. He had a sense that Sean was in that state naturally. That part of his brain was permanently switched on, like Kev's was. One of those weird McCloud things. Like being able to rig an ANFO bomb or a fougasse in fifteen minutes. Crazy shit.

The last quarter hour had been a whirlwind tutorial in do-it-yourself explosives. Under Sean's direction, he'd fever-ishly taped and wired a stack of nine-volt batteries together in a series to multiply their voltage, rigged stun grenades with blasting caps, daisy-chained them with telephone wire to the battery and the cell phone. They'd duct taped the packed batteries and Sean's doctored cell phone under the bridge, which spanned a dried-up torrent that splashed down the hill in the springtime, two hundred meters from the cabin. The flashbangs were hidden in dirt on the section of road between the bridge and the chain. A drift of pine nee-dles barely covered them and the wire.

Wheels crunched on rock. An engine revved, lifting the loaded vehicle over bumps, wells, and ruts. The vehicle ap-peared, a dark SUV, easing around the last narrow turn. It slowed, steering onto the narrow bridge, which consisted only of thick planks laid long-wise, just wide enough to perch the wheels of a vehicle upon them. The wood groaned at the weight, bowing and creaking as if the four-by-sixes would snap.

The SUV cleared the bridge and slowed to a stop, blocked by the heavy chain, thick as a man's wrist, that Bruno had strung across the road.

The chain was attached to rings driven into two big posts made from creosote-soaked railroad ties. They'd been sunk into wells of cement, and over the years the ground had eroded around the wells so that they stuck out like grubby, warty pedestals. A gate had once hung upon them, but the hinges had rusted off long ago. Tony hadn't bothered with a gate. He'd just strung the chain when he left. It wasn't like there was anything to defend. Just the humble cabin.

Bruno's cell phone was in his hand, which was cold, shak-ing. Sean's number glowed on the screen. The guy had con-tributed his cell to the cause, cutting a hole right over the vibrating device to insert the wires. When he pushed "call," the tumblers would turn, the wires would make contact . . . *boom*. And the dance began.

Even without a scope, he saw through the tinted windows that the SUV was full of people, heatedly conferring. The chain made them nervous. They didn't like the road, either. The only spot on the road wide enough to turn was beyond that chain. Behind was just a narrow, crumbling track barely as wide as the SUV's axel, and sheer drop-offs all the way down to the switchback. They had to go forward or else back all the way down in reverse. The rear driver's side door popped open. A guy got out, wearing camo. Definitely not Great-aunt Betty out for a picnic.

The radio crackled. "He's packing an M4." Sean's voice was calm. "Three more inside. I'm taking the driver. Ready?"

"Yes," Bruno said.

"On my signal," Sean said.

One second. Two. Three—

Bam. A bullet punched through the windshield. Red spattered the windows. Bruno hit "call," covered his ears.

The vehicle doors burst open. Armed assholes came boiling out.

Bam, one of them slammed hard against the SUV, bouncing—

Boom-boom-boom. The stun grenades went off. Blinding flashes.

The guy who'd fallen against the SUV stumbled and pitched into the ravine, sprawling against the tumbled boulders. *Bam*, the guy who had investigated the chain was suddenly flat on the ground at the roadside, clutching his leg.

"Body armor," Sean said tersely into his ear. "Go for the thigh."

Bam. *Bam*. Sean kept firing, but Bruno couldn't tell at who.

He stared at the wounded guys on his side of the vehicle.

The guy who'd checked the chain was clutching a wet red wound in his thigh. The other was trying to climb up to the roadway. Bruno took a breath, let it out, aiming for the climbing guy's leg . . . squeezed the trigger. *Bam*. The guy shrieked. He'd hit his target, amazingly.

Now the hard part. "Going to cuff them," he muttered.

He hauled the plastic cuffs out and burst out of his hiding place, leaping, skidding, and sliding down the slope toward the fallen men.

18

Zoe scrambled for cover, gasping. She'd taken a shot to the SAPI trauma plate that had slammed her down and knocked out her wind. Cracked a rib or two, maybe. It hurt to breathe.

Those scheming *pricks*. She was so angry she could bite out her own tongue. Her neck had been prickling since they stopped at the chain. Now Hal was dead, his head half gone. She was splattered with his blood and brain tissue. The rest of the team was likewise fucked.

Jeremy and Manfred were down, whimpering. So accustomed to being unbeatable, they had no idea how to manage themselves when compromised. She wanted to shoot them herself to make them shut up. She peeked around a boulder, scanning for movement.

Yes. There, in a camo poncho, oozing toward her downed team members. She squeezed off a shot. Ranieri jerked but kept scrambling.

Zinggghh, the sniper returned fire and forced her back down.

They had body armor, too. The cunts. She should have known when she saw the chain. She hadn't seen a chain in the satellite photos.

Of course not. That's because there hadn't been one, bitch.

So arrogant. So stupid of her to think she could manage without an armored SUV. So sure her elite, superbly competent team could handle it, with all their firepower. And now they'd been slammed.

She'd thought this through so carefully, weighing the need for speed against the safety of a larger team. The only other trained operatives in the area were the losers Hobart and Melanie, and that opportunistic whore Nadia, who was in any case too busy fucking Aaro. It would have taken days to get more people, and it was so important to move today, while Parr and Ranieri were alone, relatively exposed. If she'd waited, they'd have been swept behind the protective wall of the McCloud family, which raised the stakes, the price tag, and the risk of exposure exponentially.

And look at her. Wasting time justifying her mistakes.

She'd felt so superior to Reggie, but she'd made his exact error. Underestimating those sneaky, steaming pieces of shit. *Again.*

She'd had several different possible plans in place. She'd been ready to jump in any direction, but she'd favored the simplicity of positioning snipers above the road to pick them off like rats.

Exactly like they'd just done to her own team.

She slithered through wells between huge tumbled boulders and found a crevice to peer through. Ranieri was already jerking plastic cuffs tight around Jeremy's wrists. She estimated him at forty-five meters. She leaped up, took aim.

Bam. Her aim was off. The shot caught him on the torso, center mass. With body armor, that did nothing more than knock him backward. He hit the ground, scrambled for cover.

Bam, bam, McCloud forced her back down while Ranieri crawled toward Manfred. Her best chance was the thicket in the ravine.

She crawled into the brush-choked gully, scrabbling in rocks and roots and spiny foliage. Up over the edge of the drop-off. She wiggled through scrubby brush until she found a place to look down. A hundred meters, maybe a little more. Fuck, her chest hurt.

Jeremy lay on the ground, trussed and helpless in a pool of blood, but still writhing. Ranieri had cuffed Manfred, too, but he was bleeding out. It was a very long shot from here with a Beretta Px4 pistol, but the other M4s and the M110s had been packed into the vehicle out of reach. She'd improvise. She focused on Ranieri's dirt-smeared face, took careful aim, relaxing, focusing, but the filthy bastard was a blur of constant, restless movement. She dogged Ranieri with the Baretta as he hoisted the writhing Jeremy under his armpits, dragging him over and throwing him right next to Manfred. Jeremy saw his colleague, the gaping leg wound, the blood. Manfred's slack face, his staring eyes.

The realization of what was about to happen hit Jeremy the same moment it hit Zoe. He jerked up, arching and straining—

Boom. She flinched as Manfred's cell phone blew up, flipping his and Jeremy's bodies both into the air. The cell had self-destructed shortly after the cessation of Manfred's heartbeat.

That blast had to have killed Jeremy, too. Zoe braced herself.

Boom, the other phone went off as well. She peeked out. Only the still, broken bodies of her team were lying there. So Ranieri had not been killed. He'd taken cover. Hiding like a lizard in the rocks. Cowed.

He must be so bewildered. So confused.

Her body shook with silent giggles. So funny. She hadn't even considered those phone self-destruct mechanisms as a danger at all. They were accustomed to easy, smooth victories. No losses. No contest.

What a shame Ranieri hadn't been crouching over her colleagues when they blew. That would have been so funny, she could hardly . . . even . . . *stand* it. And the laughter was hurting her broken ribs. She groped for her personalized dose of Calitran-Z. Peeled off the adhesive, pushed the business side against her wrist.

She was alone now and cut off. She carried only the pistol, the thermal goggles around her neck, and—*wait*. Hold everything.

Excitement pumped hotly through her body. Parr wasn't with the men. They wouldn't have left her in the cabin. They would have given her an escape route to maximize her chances of survival. But Parr was emotional. She'd bonded with Ranieri. Probably fucked him left, right, and sideways already. And she was tough, too. No rabbit.

Parr had heard the shots and explosions. She'd creep back, worried and curious. The woods were thick, and she was probably shrouded in camo. No problem. Zoe lifted the thermal goggles and quartered the hillside, scanning for that rainbow-tinted glow. If she could cut Parr off, she could pick off Ranieri and McCloud when they came running to Parr's aid.

Yes. Fifty meters up. Invisible to the naked eye, but Zoe's eyes were anything but naked. Parr glowed in the woods like an opal.

Zoe's blood-spattered cheeks hurt from grinning.

Keep it together, Parr. It was hard to follow her own stern advice. Her hands were slick with sweat, clamped on the butt of the Glock that Bruno had given her along with terse instructions. *Point and click. If you don't want it to go bang, don't pull the trigger.* Clear enough, but her heart thudded so fast she was dizzy. She hadn't been this scared on her own account, but the thought of Bruno, lying on the ground, bleeding—oh, God. Her knees almost buckled.

She couldn't do what Bruno had ordered her. She couldn't run and hide. Not after she heard the noise. She had a gun, she could pull the trigger, like anybody else.

She shuffled down the hill, scared to her guts of what she might find there. She crawled down below the cliff's edge, under a crumbling overhang, looking for a good vantage point with cover.

The long silence was scaring the crap out of her.

Wind sighed in the scrubby trees that clung to the rocky slope. She huddled under the overhang, and—oh *God*—

Bats burst out, fluttering. She jerked back, almost lost her balance—

Zhingg, a bullet smacked the rock wall, right where her head had been. She slid and tripped. One leg slid off the ledge, sending a shower of dirt clods and rocks bouncing down the hill. Where the *hell* . . . ?

Lily stared out at the grayish brown foliage. She leaned forward—

Zhhingg, another bullet whizzed past her ear, hit the cliff face, exploding in a stinging shower of rock and dirt. So close.

She was pissed. Enough of acting like prey. She'd hunt that dirty rat bastard right back. She slithered on her belly, one hand awkwardly clutching the pistol, and dragged herself up between two big towers of striated black granite. She spotted the gunman scrambling up the hill.

Smaller than she'd expected, dressed in camo gear. Loping up the steep mountainside with the grace of an Olympic gymnast doing a medal-winning routine. He looked up. Their eyes met.

Holy *shit!* That was no man. That was Miriam! Howard's nurse!

Miriam gave her a big smile and swung up her gun. Lily ducked. *Zzhhing,* a bullet ricocheted off the rock where her head had been.

Lily clenched muscle, teeth, fists. *Not today, bitch. You're not going to get me today.*

Miriam was crawling hand over hand. Lily scrambled to use the moment of grace, crawling frantically up over the ledge and into the trees. She belly crawled, as quietly as she could, but still snapped twigs and thwacked boughs. Her heartbeat alone had to sound like distant thunder. An ancient tree had fallen years ago, and its whitened root system towered into the air like a skeletal fan. Best cover she could find. Also the most obvious. Too bad. Miriam would arrive any minute.

Her heart's drumbeat made it hard to hear anything. She coiled herself behind the base of the fallen trunk and strained to listen.

A soft crunch, a *shush-shush.* Her ears reached for the sounds, straining to catch more sound waves out of the air. She wondered if those goggles Miriam wore could see her behind the spreading tangle of roots.

She pretended to be empty air. There were ragged holes in the splayed root system, she noticed, where the roots were smaller and finer. She could see the sky through them. Like lace.

"I know you're there, Lily." Miriam's tone was gently mocking, maybe five yards away. "Behind that fallen tree root. Just stand up. Let's finish this. I promise I'll make it quick."

Lily dragged in a slow breath through chattering teeth.

Think. Think. The woman was a cat type. Cats played with their prey, disemboweling them before they ate. It was a big, fat lie that she meant to kill Lily quickly. She would want her fun.

"W-w-will y-you t-t-tell me one th-thing first?" She made her voice small, pathetic. Cowering mouse. Whiskers quivering.

Miriam chuckled, indulgent. "Sure, honey. Ask me anything."

Lily positioned the Glock pointing straight up, under one of the holes in the root system, and rose until her face showed.

The woman waited, attentive, her gun leveled at Lily.

"I just, um, wanted to know . . ." She blinked, rabbitlike.

Miriam's full, sensual lips curved. "Yes?"

Lily tilted the gun horizontal, pulled the trigger. *Bam*.

The recoil flung her arms up, sent her stumbling back, tripping over rocks. She hit the ground, scrambled to her feet, took aim again. *Bam*. Miriam lay on the ground, struggling to rise.

Lily tried again. *Bam. Bam. Bam*. Twigs and leaves and trees snapped. *Bam*. The bullet tore a hole in the fallen tree. Wood chips flew. Her arms shook. Her fingers were numb.

And Miriam rose up, like some immortal demon spawn. "Is that all you've got for me?" she wheezed. "You stupid fucking whore!" She laughed, her lips peeled back from her teeth, and swung her gun up.

Bam. A huge blow to Lily's chest slammed her to the ground.

The gun flew from her hand. She struggled to rise, groping in the underbrush for the Glock, her chest a well of fiery agony. "You crazy bitch," she gasped out, fighting for air. "What's your problem with me?"

Miriam aimed. "Just that you're still breathing."

Crack, crack. Lily jerked, stumbled.

It took a beat to realize that she wasn't shot. It was Miriam who spun and was flung down onto her side. Her gun hit a dead branch, flew into the bushes. The woman lurched to her feet, looking around for it wildly. She spotted Lily's Glock the same moment Lily lunged for it.

She let out a shriek and ran at Lily like a charging bull.

The impact knocked her backward, and they tumbled over the rounded edge of the ravine, sliding in a clawing, screaming, grappling ball, thudding, rolling, jolting down that rough, steep slope.

Closer and closer to the edge of a sheer rock face below, where it was ten yards of freefall to the creek bed below.

Lily snatched at small trees as they rolled by, but hers and Miriam's combined weight made them rip and shred through her hands, thwapping at her face. They fetched up against an outcropping at the edge of the cliff. Miriam's back hit it first. Lily took advantage of that stunned second to tear herself loose, scrabbling for something to hold.

The first thing her groping hands could clutch was an old root from some ancient tree, still jutting from the hillside. Her other hand grasped a bunch of saplings, no more than two feet high. Shallow, tender root systems on a hard rock face. They wouldn't hold for long.

Miriam lunged for Lily's ankles. Lily hung on grimly, wrists and shoulders screaming at the strain. Miriam dangled from her feet, slowly clawing her way up Lily's leg. Her nails dug in painfully as she grabbed handfuls of Lily's jeans, which were sliding down over her hips.

Lily kicked, twisted, trying to knock the woman loose. The root systems started to give. One pulled loose. The others were straining. Miriam was dead weight, and clad in heavy body armor just as Lily was. Swinging on Lily's knees, like a horrible ripe fruit that would not drop.

Crack, crack. Gunfire echoed through the canyon. Miriam let go, slid over the edge of the cliff. Her long, wailing cry cut off abruptly.

Lily dangled, staring at a wall of frozen mud and rock. She was intensely conscious of the cold smell of the icy earth. Blood on her hands trickled down into her sleeves. Her jeans were twisted around her thighs. The icy rocks scratched and bumped against her naked hips.

Her tormenter was gone. And she could not move.

It could have been hours, hanging there, before the sound penetrated. Somebody shouting her name. Yelling it, over and over.

". . . goddamnit, are you OK? Lily! Answer me! Lily!"

Bruno's voice, rough with fear.

Lily pulled in air to respond, but it all wheezed out in a useless squeak. Her lips felt numb, cold. They wouldn't seal to form words.

He kept calling. She kept trying. Finally, she got it out. Small, but audible. "B-b-b-bruno?"

Silence for a stunned moment, and then an excited clattering shower of small stones tumbled down onto her head. Dirt showered into her already stinging eyes, and she flinched, trying to blink the stuff away. "Lily?" he yelled again. "Lily? You OK?"

She looked up again, eyes streaming. There was his big silhouette against the blinding white sky, clinging to the hillside above. "Y-y-yeah."

"You're too far down." His voice shook. "I can't reach you. Christ, I wish I had some rope, but it would take twenty minutes to get to the cabin and back. Can you hang on for a few? I'll find a way to get closer."

"Um." Too complicated a question to answer. Hanging on. That was the thing. She'd concentrate on doing it, not talking about it.

Seconds ground by while Bruno struggled and cursed, sending down a constant stream of rocks and dirt onto her. Then she heard him calling again. She concentrated to put his words together.

". . . best I can do to pull you up. Try, OK? Just let go, see if you can stretch up at least about eight, ten inches? Lily, goddamnit, answer me! Can you hear me? Hey! Lily!"

She coughed, cleared her throat. "Yeah," she croaked out.

"Yeah, what?" he snarled.

She sucked in air, gritting her teeth. "Yeah, I'll try."

Her bleeding hands hurt, but she started scrabbling against the slippery rock face, trying to get her numb feet up over the edge of the cliff. Neat trick, with knees shackled by slipping-down jeans. She finally found a lip of rock that didn't crumble. Wedged her foot against it.

She lifted herself, almost screaming as pain redistributed itself in her arms, shoulders, hands, as blood enthusiastically pumped into new, hurt places. She scrambled up, reached . . .

Bruno's big, warm hand fastened around her wrist and pulled.

She yelped, she couldn't help it, but followed where his hand pulled her, supporting herself with her feet whenever she could.

And when she couldn't, his strong grip never wavered.

Then they were crawling on a slope no longer a sheer cliff face. He pulled her up next to him on a narrow, almost flat ledge where they could both perch and yanked her jeans up over her hips with a jerk. "You have a tough time keeping your clothes on," he complained.

"Your own fault." Her voice was a ragged thread.

His teeth flashed. "You ain't seen nothing yet, babe."

"That's not what I meant, you oversexed doofus. I meant, it's your own fault for buying my jeans too big. I told you I was a six."

He jerked her close and gave her a long, hard, breath-stealing kiss. She leaned into it like he was the fountain of life itself.

He drew away. "Speaking of oversexed doofuses," he said. "You gotta love those panties. That red lace is so dramatic against the wintery landscape. And your ass, wow. It glows. Like a full moon."

She stifled the giggles. They hurt too much. "Shut up about my ass, dog. Now is not the time."

He kissed her again. "You're really special, Lily."

"Oh, really? Gee. I'm touched."

"Most of the women I date, if it lasts all night, it ends

with coffee and pastry, maybe exchanged phone numbers, if I'm feeling really brave. But mornings with you, I mostly end up just killing people."

She shrugged, and holy God, it hurt. "You should have put me on the bus to Anywhere, USA, while you had the chance."

He tilted up her chin. "Too late. You're under my skin."

"Hello?" McCloud's voice punched in from above, sharp with disapproval. "Get a fucking room, would you? Move it, people!"

Bruno dragged her up the hill. She didn't really understand the words he said. It was the tone, a comforting, low-pitched hum that tingled in her ears, pulling her as firmly and gently as his hands did. *Put this hand here. This foot there. Stretch to the right, just a little farther, there you go. Good job . . .* It wasn't that far in terms of distance, but it took a shaking eternity to creep sideways along the gorge wall.

Finally, they got to ground even enough for him to scoop her up like a sack of potatoes. She wrapped her arms around his neck. So glad he was still alive. All of them were. How incredibly improbable to have survived that.

He set her down on a stump near the bridge. McCloud held a big, scary-looking rifle in his arms. He looked her over, appraisingly.

"Not shot?" he asked. "Nothing broken?"

She shook her head. Torn, swollen, sprained, maybe, and bruised to a flipping pulp, but not shot or broken. "You guys?"

"Fine," Bruno said. "Both lucky."

She rubbed at the dirt and grit in her eyes. "Thanks for the sharpshooting," she offered. "Saved my butt."

Bruno jerked his thumb toward Sean. "That was all him," he said brusquely. "I don't have that kind of aim."

"Oh. Um." She blinked at McCloud. "Well. Thanks."

He nodded gravely. "At your service."

"And, ah . . ." She gestured toward the SUV. "Them?"

"Three are dead," Bruno said. "Two of them had cell phones that blew up. I assume your guy is still alive down there, or we would have heard a kaboom from the creek. Assuming they all carry those fucking things. The driver didn't."

"Not a guy," Lily said. "It was the nurse."

Bruno looked baffled. "What nurse?"

"Miriam. My father's nurse," she explained. "At the mental hospital. She must have been the one who murdered him."

McCloud grunted. "This is so fucked up. Let's get out of here."

"They're probably watching us from a satellite," Lily said. "We can't run from them."

Bruno lifted his hand and gave the sky the finger. "Up your ass," he said, mouthing the words with exaggerated care. "Let 'em watch."

"We can't leave unless we move their rig," McCloud observed. "I can't off-road here."

"So we roll it off the road," Bruno said.

Sean looked dubious. "They could blow us up."

Bruno stared up at the sky. He held up a blackened, bloodied hand, felt the snowflakes swirling down. He looked at Lily.

"It's nine miles to the nearest big highway," he said. "They'd have all the time in the world to come and finish us off if we were on foot."

McCloud nodded. He glanced at the SUV. "Flip a coin for it?"

"No," Bruno said. "I'll do it. You take Lily. Move back."

Lily shot up off the stump, panicked. "No! Bruno, don't, please—"

"Let's get this done." Bruno headed toward the SUV.

She burst into tears as McCloud led her away.

Bruno leaned over the dead driver, put the vehicle into reverse, and took off the emergency brake. He came around to the hood and pushed, shoving it off the edge and over. It slid, rolled, bounced, crashing through trees until it finally came to rest. Far, far down.

Sean and Lily walked to the edge of the road and looked down.

"Wow." Sean sounded impressed. "That was stern."

"I want the cops to be able to look at it," Bruno said. "I don't want those bastards to be able to retrieve it. And I don't want that nurse bitch to have an easy ride. Let her hike in the snow if she's still alive. Let's go, before they come down on us."

"Who the fuck is 'they'?" Sean's voice was harsh with frustration.

"If I knew, I'd cut the head off the snake and burn it," Bruno said.

They took off the chain, hiked up the steep road to the cabin. Bruno bundled her into the back of Sean's Jeep, then pushed her to the middle seat and got in himself, fastening the seat belt over her.

Sean's bright gaze did not miss the proprietary way that Bruno pulled her close to lay on his shoulder. "Rest," he said.

McCloud's grin flashed. "If you can. I'm going to go way too fast for the driving conditions."

"Punch it," Bruno said fervently.

Lily's head rocked back as the vehicle leaped forward.

Bruno leaned forward as they rattled and bounced. "Hey."

"Yeah?" McCloud shouted back. "Speak up."

"Thanks, for helping," Bruno blurted. "Sorry. About before."

McCloud slewed the vehicle around the hairpin curve and gunned the engine as soon as they were on the straight stretch. "Wait until we're safe to thank me. I'll enjoy it better when I can gloat."

"Don't wait," Lily said. "Get it while you can."

The men glanced at her. She looked back. Like it had to be said.

There wasn't any safe, anymore. Ever again.

"Try her again," King rapped out.

"I just did," Hobart told him. "She's not responding. And I can't—"

"If I hear you say the words 'I can't' one more time, I will pull up your Level Ten mortal command sequences right now. Is that clear?"

"Yes, sir." Hobart's frantic typing filtered through the microphone.

King stared at the large screen. There were insets on the side, one of which displayed Hobart's pinched face. The agent who had been, along with Melanie, inexplicably left behind. The other insets were charts showing the vital signs of the four operatives who had gone on this ill-fated mission. Three were flatlined. The other was close.

His anger was crippling. It was difficult even to breathe, let alone think. He could not believe that mistakes this huge could be made by his own operatives. How in the *hell* . . . ? It made his brain hurt.

The rest of the screen was filled with a satellite image that showed a dense, waving mass of conifers. The microchip in Zoe's clavicle blipped in a mass of rocks near a creek. She was not visible. Her chart showed an erratic heartbeat, a falling temperature. Manfred, Jeremy, and Hal were cooling fast. Three hundred million dollars, turned into buzzard bait. "Show me the view from Zoe's com," he barked.

"Yes, sir." Desperate tapping, and the picture transformed into an indistinct blur. Rocks covered with waving fronds of fuzz.

Oh, for God's sake. It was underwater. Of course Zoe was not answering her com. It had been dropped in the creek.

"Sir?" a timid voice offered. "Here is the coffee that you—"

"Get away from me while I'm busy," he snarled at Julian, who was presenting the coffee and the plate of cookies dipped in dark chocolate.

Julian scuttled away. It occurred to King that he had, in fact, ordered the snack. But a special series trainee so close to the end of his training should have the sensitivity to intuit a good moment to serve it.

"Explain to me again why you and Melanie are in Tacoma, thumbs fully inserted up your asses, a six-hour drive away from this disaster."

Hobart passed the buck. "Ah . . . ah . . . well, Zoe was team leader, and I . . . ah . . . she'd decided that speed was crucial, so she, ah . . . well, our intelligence indicated that McCloud was going to be—"

"Do not speak of intelligence," King cut in. "That quality has not been demonstrated to me, certainly not by you. No one else available? What about Nadia? She's had three times as much combat experience as you, Hal, or Jeremy. Why was she not on the team?"

"Uh . . . uh . . . well, Zoe assigned her to Aaro, and he—"

"Who the hell is Aaro?" he bellowed.

"An associate of the McClouds. He transported Ranieri and Parr to the cabin after the fight at the diner. Zoe wanted Nadia to plant tracking and spy software on Aaro's phone, and the only way—"

"Planting *tracking software* took precedence over this mission? How far is she from the cabin? Patch her in to me immediately."

"Um . . . there's a problem. With Nadia."

"What?" he roared.

"Well, uh . . . she's dead." Hobart's voice was a miserable croak.

King went very cold. Several seconds ticked by. "Explain."

"She, ah . . . her cell phone just exploded. Twenty minutes ago."

King struggled for self-control. "It took you twenty minutes to come to the conclusion that this fact might be of interest to me?"

Hobart began a gabbling litany of excuses. King called up Nadia's signal to see for himself. Sure enough. Flatlined. "Where is her body?"

Hobart hesitated. King exerted effort not to call Hobart's Level Ten command sequences and make him stop using oxygen he did not deserve to breathe, since he had no brain cells to nourish.

"She was at the Justice Center, at Southwest Third Avenue," Hobart said. "Her tag is moving now. I imagine she's being transported to the county medical examiner."

Another body in the ME's office, keeping Reggie, Cal, Tom, and Martin company. No way to clean up. No damage control. Again.

"Show me the satellite shot over Zoe again," he said.

Waving conifers filled the screen. King stared at them in silence, as if he could find some pattern, some plan in the wintry forest.

Then he saw it. A torso, barely visible in camo fabric, emerging from under an overhanging cliff. Crawling out onto tumbled rocks.

Zoe struggled to her feet, stumbled toward the creek, and waded into the water. King winced as she lost her balance, splashing full length. She struggled upright, swaying. Lifting her face to the sky, her big, dark eyes imploring. She held the com. She lifted it to her ear.

"Patch her through to me," he commanded.

The sound quality changed. He heard the static buzz, and beyond, birds, water, wind rushing in the device's microphone.

"Zoe?" he asked, and then yelled. "Zoe! Do you hear me?"

"I'm ready." Zoe's voice was barely audible, a froglike croak.

"Ready for what?" he snapped, irritated.

She blinked up at the sky. "I failed you," she said. "I'm ready." She closed her eyes, waiting for her Level Ten death command.

The martyred look on Zoe's ravaged face made King's teeth grind. As if she could have it so easy. Watching Zoe die was a luxury he could not afford. For now. "No, Zoe," he said sharply. "Get out of the water."

She gaped at him, stupidly. It infuriated him. The one tool he had on the ground was blue-lipped, standing in icy water like a shit-brained lump. "Move, Zoe," he commanded. "You must fix this."

She stepped forward, fell to her knees. Icy water sloshed over her chest, her shoulder. She half crawled, half swam to the bank. *Hold the com to your ear, bitch. Do it.* She crawled onto the rocks, lifted the phone. Her ragged panting became audible.

"Zoe, listen to me." He used the deep voice he'd assumed in DeepWeave audio, which Zoe had absorbed for hours every day as a child. "Take out the Melimitrex and inject it into your thigh."

He was repeating instructions that had been drilled into her already, but he needed any excuse to keep her bound to the sound of his voice. Her hands shook violently, but she managed to pry the syringe out of the foam case. She flicked a drop from the needle. Tap, tap. She'd worked as a nurse, after all. She stabbed it into her thigh, through the water-logged cloth, and flung her head back, baring her teeth.

He watched her vital signs. Melimitrex VIII was always a gamble, albeit a better one than it had been in the previous seven generations of the drug. It was the result of decades of trial and error. Calibrated to the individual's height, weight, and body chemistry, each dose stimulated the glands with a brutal kick. Other components included a powerful painkiller and a mood enhancer similar to cocaine. He only administered that drug in the most dire of circumstances. Its success rate hovered around 60 percent. The fate of the unlucky 40 percent, well, suffice to say that it was painful to watch, and blessedly short.

Not that he had any choice. Zoe would be unconscious in minutes without an intervention. He saw the moment that the drug started to work. Her breathing deepened, her heart rate steadied.

She flung her head toward the sky again, nostrils flaring. Trust Zoe to make a fuss and carry on as if she were on stage.

He made his voice solicitous. "Do you feel better, my dear?"

"Oh, yes," she told him. "I feel wonderful now."

"Excellent. Listen, Zoe. I will recite a verse to you now. It will give you strength to do it. Are you ready?"

"Yes." Her voice quivered with emotion. "Oh, yes. Please."

He slowly recited Zoe's Level Ten endurance verses. King was very proud of his Level Ten endurance commands. They unlocked hidden reserves of energy and mental acuity, releasing endorphins that had the same effect as a passionate emotion. The strength one read about in *Reader's Digest* articles, say, an eighty-year-old crone lifting a car off her stricken grandchild. But what was the difference between chemically simulated passion and real passion? Nothing. It was all chemistry.

"Listen carefully," he told her. "Go to the vehicle, and—"

"I have no weapons," Zoe blurted. "They disarmed me. Ranieri—"

"Is gone," he cut in. "Ranieri is no longer your concern. They rolled the vehicle off the road. Take what you can carry, hide the rest. Hide Hal's, Jeremy's, and Manfred's bodies as best you can. I don't want them found before our cleanup crew arrives. Mark the spot with a tag. We'll calculate the best route for you to the rendezvous point. No one will be able to meet you for a few hours yet." *On account of your bad planning, you cretin*.

She hemmed and hawed. "But what . . . but I—"

"You must be strong, Zoe," he told her. "When the extraction team comes to get you, they will put you on a plane and bring you to me."

She blinked rapidly as she stared up into the sky, eyes welling full of tears. "They will?" Her voice was that of a lost, hopeful child.

"Of course. You've been very brave. You'll be rewarded. I promised." There was only so much a satellite could pick up. But he fancied he saw Zoe's eyes dilate, her cheeks flush. "Now go!"

She leaped to obey, climbing like a mountain goat. The promise of a Level Ten reward series could move mountains.

Whatever worked. At the moment, he could not afford to be fussy.

19

Lily glanced around at the people gathered in the room lit with mellow lamps and crowded with big squishy couches. She felt shy and on the spot.

"He has to lock it," Lily repeated. "That's what Howard said. That Bruno has to lock something. That he'd understand when he saw it."

"But you didn't. So what the hell are you supposed to lock?" Sean gave Bruno a look that was almost accusing.

Bruno shook his head. "Not a fucking clue."

"Strange," Sean mused. "It would make more sense if he was supposed to unlock something. A code, a door, a safe, a password?"

"That's all Howard said." Lily felt as if she'd failed them somehow. "I didn't get it, either. Then the nurse interrupted us. The one who murdered him." She hugged her knees, sank deep into the plushy couch. After weeks spent trying to avoid notice, the relentless, concentrated attention of this group of people made her feel like she was going to collapse in on herself, twitching and babbling.

Their attitudes didn't help, either. Not that they were rude. Far from it. They'd saved her ass, patched her up, fed her, clothed her, given her painkillers and antibiotics and anti-inflammatories, plied her with caffeine and sugar. But even so, she sensed a wary wait-and-see feeling in the air. The vote was still out on Lily Parr.

Bruno sensed it, too. It made him defensive. He sat right next to her, his arm flung possessively across her shoulders, daring them all to disbelieve a word she said. Touching, since yesterday he hadn't believed her, either. Who would? She wouldn't, if she were them.

All of the McCloud brothers except for Kev were there, Davy and Con and Sean, as well as Sean's wife Liv. Their hostess, the terrifyingly beautiful Tam Steele, was the owner of the house perched on the cliff over the Washington coast near the coastal hamlet of Cray's Cove.

Aaro was there, too, looking sullen and traumatized after his ugly morning adventure. His eyes were haunted shadows. He wouldn't meet anyone's gaze. There was an ethereally beautiful, dark-haired girl named Sveti who sat in a corner, listening. She had sad eyes, a faint accent. Lily hadn't yet puzzled out her relationship to the others. And Miles, a muscular, shy guy with a big nose. And Zia Rosa dominated the room like an out-sized Paleolithic goddess. Bruno's great aunt resembled a huge bulldog, with black bouffant hair and a shirt with fuchsia polka dots and a pink plastic-bead neck-lace. Zia Rosa scrutinized Lily with an expression that could only be described as avid. It was unsettling.

"Lily's exhausted and injured," Bruno said. "She needs sleep—"

"Your father said that Bruno would understand." Sean's older brother Davy broke in, his gaze inwardly focused. "But what was he supposed to understand? What was 'it'? An object? A place?"

Lily laced her fingers together, examining the memory again. She hoped she hadn't revised it herself in having thrashed over it so many times. She addressed the oldest McCloud, a lantern-jawed guy with the same keen, bright green gaze as his brothers. "He said Magda told him that her son would understand when he saw it. But Howie never had a chance to say what 'it' was. That was when Miriam inter-rupted us."

"Miriam, the nurse. Who then morphed into Miriam, commando warrior," Connor McCloud said.

Bruno bristled. "What are you implying? I saw that bitch in action, and believe me, she was bad news."

"I'm not implying anything. I'm just getting this all straight."

"We've got it as straight as we can get it tonight," Bruno said. "Sean was there. Rehash it all with him if you've got doubts."

"Hey." Lily patted his tense, knotted forearm. "It's OK," she told him. "I'm not sleepy after all that coffee. Chill."

"I don't want them hounding you," he fretted.

"There's hounding, and there's help," said Tam quietly.

Lily turned to the other woman, whose arms were draped over her very pregnant belly. "That's for sure," she said. "Hound away. Finally I have other brains to work with be-sides my own. It feels good."

It was difficult to hold Tam's gaze. A trait that many people in the room shared. These people had been through a lot, and survived. Their eyes saw past masks to the cringing stuff she would rather hide.

Tam Steele was so beautiful, one's eyes got sucked to her like a magnet at first, but soon after came a strange desire to let one's eyes skitter away from that golden laser slice of comprehension.

The paneled sliding doors opened. Another man she hadn't met walked in. Good-looking, with raven hair, chiseled features, dark eyes with an exotic gypsy slant. He gave a nod of greeting to everyone, eyes resting on Lily and Bruno for the X-ray once-over that she was almost getting used to, and then he wove across the room to crouch behind Tam.

He slid his arms around her, cradled her belly, nuzzling her neck.

Lily noticed Bruno's sidewise stare. "What?" she whispered.

"Just wondering how you'd react," he said. "To Val, I mean. Most straight women drop their teeth when he walks into a room."

The off-the-charts weirdness of that statement rocked her back.

"Are you kidding me?" she hissed. "You think I have enough functioning neurons left in my head to ogle strange guys? *Now?*"

He shrugged. "You don't need a lot of neurons to ogle," he said. "I'm not overloaded with extra neurons, and I ogle all the time."

She poked him in the ribs. "Stop it! I can't believe you even have the energy to be a pinheaded, insecure asshole at a time like this!"

"Me, neither," added Liv, the voluptuous brunette who was married to Sean. She cuddled a baby to an opening in her loose denim shirt and peered sternly over the tops of her horn-rimmed glasses at Sean, who was slumped beside her, exhausted, his hand clamped around his son's chubby leg.

"I'll add that to a long list of unbelievable things. Like, how you told me you were going down to the Gorge to do Kev's other brother some innocuous favor that involved a lot of driving. And now, I find out about gun battles and dead bodies exploding."

"Hey! It *was* an innocuous favor! I was planning to pick them up and drive them here!" Sean looked wounded. "What did I know about the gun battles and the exploding bodies? You're wronging me!"

"Hah. So innocuous you had Miles load his Jeep with eight different firearms, artillery rounds, stun grenades, blasting caps, Tovex, and tear gas?"

"You can't blame me for being prepared!" Sean protested. "I can't help it. It's on account of my upbringing."

Tam flapped her hand at them. "Have this argument later, in bed. So, a recap. This started six weeks ago, when your father began to—"

"No," Lily broke in. "It started eighteen years ago, when my father went from being a successful research physician to being a drunk and a heroin addict, in a matter of days. Something bad happened to him. I never knew what. He was finally starting to tell me, and they killed him for it. All I know is that it involved Bruno's mother, who died a violent death at about the same time. I find that a very odd coincidence."

Tam spoke up after a moment's reflective pause. "And let's not forget Aaro's fabulous self-destructing sex toy, who also had one of these exploding phones in her purse. Another odd coincidence."

Aaro shot her a dark glance but was clearly too drained to radiate true malevolence. Zia Rosa, who sat beside him, clucked her tongue and patted his thigh. "You know what your problem is, Alex, honey?"

He looked trapped. "Don't tell me. Please."

"Your problem is, you ain't picked out some nice lady. Look at all these people here. They're happy, see? They all got somebody. You don't got nobody. If you had a nice girl to go home to, you wouldn't have got caught with your pants off by that nasty *puttanella*, eh?"

"Zia, now's not the time for the family-values lecture," Bruno said.

Zia Rosa waved him down. "Shhh. Like my old *nonna* back in Brancaleone used to say," she intoned. *"Attent' a le fosse."*

Lily leaned over to Bruno. "What does that mean?"

Bruno sighed and translated. "Beware of the holes."

Aaro buried his face in his hands. "Tell me about it," he muttered.

Zia Rosa patted Aaro's thigh again, palpating his quadriceps muscle appreciatively. "The time's come, I guess," she announced, her voice heavy. "We oughta have a talk with those Ranieri cousins."

"Ranieri cousins?" Lily said. "Which cousins are those?"

"They're second cousins, actually. We got the same *bisnonni*. One of the big crime families in Jersey. Don Gaetano's papa was a Mafia don back in Calabria. Tony, Bruno's great uncle, he was don Gaetano's right-hand man, back in the day. But Tony didn't like the life. He ran off."

Lily waited for more. Zia Rosa just looked at her expectantly.

"Well, um . . . what do these other Ranieris in Jersey have to do with me?" she asked. "I don't know them."

Zia Rosa shrugged. "They sure as hell knew Magda."

Bruno shot up off the couch. "What the fuck are you saying? It was Rudy who worked for the Ranieris! Not Mamma!"

"Don't you use them dirty *parolaccie* with me, *stronzetto*," Zia Rosa scolded. "Be respectful. I'm guessin' it's time to send Tony's letter. Them dirty sonzabitches broke the bargain. And they are goin' down."

Her words dropped into a pool of absolute silence. The

room suddenly felt like it got smaller as everyone shifted forward in their seats, craning their necks to stare at the older woman.

"What bargain, Zia?" Bruno's voice was tight.

She shrugged. "The letter Tony sent to Michael Ranieri, years ago. Tony chopped the fingers offa them mobster thugs who come after you, remember? He wrapped the letter around 'em and sent 'em to Michael."

Bruno felt his voice coming from far away. "I remember mobster thugs. I didn't know anything about chopped fingers. Or a letter."

"I guess not. Tony didn't talk about stuff like that. But he had to tell me, so I'd know who to send the letter to if they whacked him."

Everyone was perched on the edge of the cushions, except for Liv, who was still nursing her baby. Even Sean had jolted bolt upright.

"Tell us about the letter, Zia," Davy encouraged.

She fluttered plump, beringed hands. "Ah, well. Tony knew where a lot of bodies were buried. The hows, and the wheres, and where the money went. He dug some of them holes himself, see. You know how it is." She glanced around the room. "Well. Maybe you don't."

"I do," said Aaro quietly.

Zia Rosa patted his thigh again. "He wrote it all down," she went on. "And the deal was, if them Ranieri *coglioni* whacked Tony, or tried to come after you again, I was to send the letters out. To the press, to the prosecuting attorneys, the DA in Newark, the current DA, too." She cackled. "Those guys'd come in their pants if they read Tony's letter."

"You never sent it?" Connor said. "You still have it?"

"So far. Tony told Michael that he'd left the copies with a lawyer, who was supposed to mail 'em out if Tony died. But Tony didn't trust no lawyers. He kept 'em in a safe deposit box. I was supposed to send 'em, if anything happened. But when something finally did . . ." She shrugged, her face sagging with sorrow. "It didn't have nothin' to do with the Ranieris. I figured it was over. But I guess it ain't over." Zia Rosa dug a tissue out of her purse and blew her nose into it, sniffing.

"Where's the safe deposit box, Zia?" Connor asked gently.

She dabbed her eyes. "Eh? Oh, there ain't no safe deposit box no more. I took the letter out after Tony died. I figured, if they was gonna make a move on Bruno, it would be when Tony kicked the bucket. I didn't want to have to worry about no stupid banking hours."

"So?" Val was prompting her now. His face, resting on Tam's shoulder, was keen with interest. "Where is the letter?"

"In my purse," Zia Rosa said, as if it should be obvious.

Bruno was in front of his great-aunt before being aware of having moved. He sank to his knees and held out his hand. "Let me see it."

She stared at him, troubled. "Tony didn't want you to read this letter," she said. "He didn't want you to know the bad stuff he done."

"I would never judge him. He saved my life. Let me see it, Zia."

She sighed heavily and unsnapped the clasp on her huge purse. The room was silent but for her muttering and rummaging.

Finally, she pulled out a battered envelope and handed it to him.

Bruno pulled out a sheaf of thin, crackling onion-skin typing paper covered with hand-typed, single-spaced words. He felt light in the head. There were about ten pages. He ran his eyes over the first page and could hear Tony's gruff, smoke-roughened voice in his head.

To Whom It May Concern: This is the true and factual account of Antonio Ranieri, born in Brancaleone, Calabria,

Italy, on November 14, 1938, and my dealings with Mafia bosses Gaetano and Michael Ranieri, from the years of 1955 through 1968. This document was made on this day of January 16, 1987, in Portland, Oregon, before witnesses . . ."

Wait. This was off. He read it again.

"No. Zia, this can't be right," he said. "This date is 1987, not 1993. The thugs came in '93. I didn't even come to Portland until 1993. Remember? I was twelve when I got here."

She snatched the letter back and squinted through her bifocals. "No, honey. This is right. This one's the original, see? In '93, he was just sending a photocopy of the one he'd sent before. With the fingers added on. To remind Michael and Gaetano that the bargain was still in effect."

He was baffled. "What bargain? Why did he send it in '87?"

Zia Rosa looked blank, and then her eyes got very big. *"O Cristo Santissimo,"* she breathed. "You mean, you don't remember, honey?"

Bruno fought the urge to scream in her face. "Remember what?"

No one seemed to want to breathe. Zia Rosa crossed herself.

"Some bastard took you away from your mamma, when you was seven, honey," Zia said. "It took your mamma and Tony over a month to get you back. I figured you was old enough to remember that."

Bruno shook his head. He did not remember that. But he did not like the way his insides felt, hearing about it. Shivering, cold. Small.

"Magda called Tony for help," Zia went on. "It was a guy who was in bed with that junkie shithead, Michael. Some drug pusher business partner of his."

"But who?" Bruno burst out. "What was his name? What the hell did he want with me? It wasn't like Mamma had any money."

Zia Rosa shook her head. "Tony didn't tell me details. He figured it was safer that way. Magda got Tony to write that letter to put pressure on Michael to get you back."

Bruno swayed there, searching in his memory for something that corresponded to this new information. All he found was a blankness and a creeping sensation of fear. He shook it off. Pulled the letter back.

"But if Tony held this over the Ranieris, then how could they let Rudy kill her?" he demanded. "Wasn't she protected by it, too?"

The light in Zia Rosa's eyes faded. She suddenly looked very old. "He couldn't do nothin' for her, honey. She broke the bargain, see?"

"What bargain?" he yelled. "You're not making any fucking sense!"

"*Zitto*. Don't you use that tone with your auntie." But she patted his cheek as she spoke to soften the scold. "The deal Tony struck was that Magda got her boy back and kept her nose out of it. She and her boy got left alone, Tony hung on to the letter, and everybody played nice. But Magda was too pissed. She wouldn't stop digging."

"Digging for what?" His voice cracked. "What was she digging for?"

Zia Rosa shook her head. "All's I know is that Tony was worried, because Magda kept goin' after that dirty prick. She wanted to make him pay for what he did to you. And they got her. At least she was smart enough to send you away. Only smart thing that girl ever did, God rest her sweet soul."

"But I . . . but she . . ." His mouth worked, his mind whirling for a way to avoid conclusions that made his guts churn.

"Tony told her to stop. But she couldn't. She loved you so much. Not that I blame her for bein' pissed, after what that *testa di cazzo* did. She said you wouldn't talk for months after she got you back." She sniffed. "Hard to imagine, you not talking, but it's true. Not a peep, except at night. You screamed the place down. Almost got her evicted."

"Oh, God," Lily whispered. "Bruno. Your nightmares."

Bruno recoiled from that. One thing at a time. "But I was supposed to testify against Rudy in the trial. Remember? Rudy killed her. There was evidence, but the dirty cops contaminated it."

A flip of Zia Rosa's plump hand dismissed Rudy. "Rudy took the fall, sure. But it wasn't him who ordered the hit. Rudy was just a dumb-ass *scagnozzo*. Why do you think she took up with that low-life in the first place, honey? My Magda, who coulda had any man she wanted? You think she was hanging around with that slob for her health?"

No, not her health. He thought of the black eyes, the bruises.

"She did it for you," Zia said. "She was using Rudy to infiltrate."

He shook his head. It made him sick, guilty. He held up the letter. "Why didn't Tony use this? Why didn't he ram this up their asses?"

"He was trying to keep you alive," she said simply. "If he'd sent it, sure, it woulda messed them up. But they woulda killed him, and probably you, too. He loved that girl, but she was gone, and he had to cover your ass. Don't blame Tony. He did the best he could."

"You should have told me," he said.

"You had enough problems. What point was there in telling you?"

"All these years, I thought the guy who killed my mother was dead," he said. "That it was over. And it's not. That's a problem."

"Yeah," she agreed. "But what would you have done if you knew?"

He stared down at the letter. "I would've hunted down that piece of shit and ground him into paste."

"Well." Zia Rosa looked triumphant. "There you go. That's why we didn't say nothin', honey. That's exactly why."

He stared at her, uncomprehending. "Huh?"

Zia Rosa made an impatient sound. "Think about it. We didn't want you caught up in a whole new revenge cycle with those scumbags. You were doin' good, honey. You got past it. You started that company with Kev, you were making good money, you had a nice place, a good life. Why throw that away? For what? Past is past. What's done is done."

"But it's not done," he said. "It's not done at all." He glanced up, suddenly noticing the rapt attention of all the people in the room.

Many pairs of eyes slid abruptly away from his.

His anger flared afresh. "This is a great way to find out my life is based on a lie. Turn it into a sideshow act to entertain the masses."

Zia Rosa clucked her tongue. "Don't be silly. They're just family."

"Kev's family, Zia," he reminded her. "Not my family."

Flat silence. Sean spoke up. "You're walking funny again, buddy."

"Piss off," Bruno replied through set teeth.

"Family is whoever you're left with after everybody else is sick of your bullshit," Tam said. "We'll see who hangs around for you, Bruno."

A rude retort rose up, but Zia Rosa sensed it and cut him off. "*Stai zitto, idiota,*" she hissed. "Kev would be so embarrassed!"

He subsided, with some difficulty. His face felt hot. His jaw tight.

"Well, I know what to do next," Zia said briskly. "I gotta have me a talk with don Gaetano and Michael. Since Tony's not around to do it."

"No, you don't," Bruno said swiftly. "I'll take care of that, Zia."

"No way. He won't talk to you," she scoffed. "He'll just

have his thugs dump you in the river. I'm the one's got clout with don Gaetano. He still feels guilty. Can't look me in the eye, the old pig. *Brutto maiale.*"

"Because of Mamma?" Bruno asked.

"Nah. Because he was supposed to marry me."

Everyone swiveled and stared at Zia Rosa. Zia Rosa and marriage were ideas so far removed from each other it was cognitively jarring.

Zia preened a bit, enjoying the attention. "My *papà* set it up. *Un matrimonio combinato.* I was in the old country, seventeen. I didn't want to go. There was a guy in Brancaleone who liked me." She looked wistful. "But he didn't have no money, and Papà, well. You didn't argue with him. So I go to America to get married, but when I get there, what do I find? I find my cousin Constantina's got herself pregnant with that pig Gaetano. Dirty little *troia.* She had Michael. Her oldest boy."

"The current boss, right?" Bruno said.

"Yeah. Costantina had been in America for years. She wasn't fresh off the boat like me. She spoke English, she wore the right clothes, she knew the right dances." Zia shrugged. "And she was pretty."

Everyone looked away.

Zia Rosa cleared her throat. "So, anyway. I'm the one who has to talk to the old bastard if we want to get anywhere."

"Forget it," Bruno said. "You're not going anywhere." Zia Rosa patted his cheek, which made him frantic with anxiety. "I'm serious!"

"I'm sure you are, honey," she soothed. She pulled Tony's letter from his hand, smoothing it against her knee. "It broke Tony's heart, what happened to Magda." Her voice frogged up. "Such a beautiful girl. You look so much like her, it makes my heart hurt. Look at her." She dug for her wallet and peeled a photo out, leaning to show it to Davy and Connor. They made sympathetic noises. Then she showed it to

Aaro. "This is my Magda. Bruno's mamma. Wasn't she gorgeous?"

Aaro looked and sucked in air. "Oh. *Fuck*."

He snatched the photo from Zia Rosa and stared at it. His voice was not loud, but it had a quality that stopped the buzz in the room.

"What?" Bruno rapped out.

"The girl I met," Aaro said. "The one who died." He held up the photo. "She looked just like this, except for the hair. This could be her."

Bruno stared down at the other man. Murmurs swelled around them. "My mamma's been dead eighteen years," Bruno said. "I saw her dead body. I saw it put into the ground. Don't mess with my head."

"Christ, no. I didn't mean to say I thought this woman was your mother," Aaro said hastily. "The girl I met was in her early twenties."

"A coincidence, then," Con said as if offering up a vain hope.

Voices swelled. Someone grabbed Tony's letter. Zia Rosa was crying, noisily. People were talking all at once. And Bruno was done. The voices were a jangle of meaningless sound. His heart thumped like a big bass drum. He kept seeing the image of Mamma in her casket, her dead face painted with makeup to cover her bruises. It was fixed in his mind in all its bleak detail. It did not fade or soften with time.

All this time, he'd gotten it wrong. Tony and Kev had taken care of Rudy and his goons. He'd told himself that justice had been done.

But he'd always known in his heart justice had fallen way short.

A hand tugged his arm. Lily. He got obediently to his feet, let himself be led out of the room. He was grateful to her for taking charge.

The sliding doors clicked shut behind them. Lily slid her arms around his waist and pulled him close. He tucked her head under his chin and tried not to squeeze. She was injured, bruised. Fragile.

And he wanted to cling to her, like a child. He looked at the circles under Lily's eyes. Her hair was smoothed into a corkscrewing red-gold ponytail. Most of her bruises were hidden under the sweater. Except for the purple line under her eye that he'd given her when he popped her in the nose during his dream freak-out.

He hated how fragile she looked. How exhausted. Hated how powerless he was to protect her. He tried like a maniac, with everything he had. And all his efforts were utterly inadequate.

The door slid open and Tam came out. "Either of you need anything else?" she asked. "Painkiller? Something to help you sleep?"

They both shook their heads.

"OK, then. The freshest lovebirds always get the dove-cote," she said. "Follow me. There's lots of stair climbing, but who gets tired with all those endorphins pumping through your body?" She nudged Bruno. "The bedside table is always stocked with latex."

"Mind your own business," he snapped.

She chuckled as she touched a panel, which slid into the wall, revealing a spiral staircase.

"Don't you dare walk up those stairs, *carissima*."

It was Val in the pool of light spilling from the noisy living room.

Tam turned to him, her eyes gleaming. "Don't be such a hen," she said. "As if I would. I'm not that kind of hostess."

"I have to watch you like an eagle." Val's faintly accented voice was silky with mock menace.

Tam tilted her head, a small smile playing about her lips. "A hawk," she said. "The correct expression is 'watch you like a hawk.'"

"Eagle," Val repeated stubbornly. "Eagles are bigger."

Tam chuckled. "Ah. And bigger is better?"

"Yes. I use every advantage I can with you. Always."

"Men," Tam scoffed and turned to Lily and Bruno. "You'll find towels in the cabinet outside the bathroom door. Good night."

"Thank you for everything," Lily said.

But they weren't listening. Val had swept Tam into his protective embrace and was murmuring to her in some language Bruno couldn't place. She smothered laughter behind her hand. Every gesture, every smile and glance created a bubble of intimacy around them. A magic private space, where both of them felt safe.

He'd never even been aware of such a thing before.

And all of a sudden, here he was, envious of it.

20

The spiral staircase dumped them into a room that under any other circumstances would have blown his mind. Octagonal, with big triangular windows in each side, each with a different amazing view in the daytime. Gleaming wood paneling, a grouping of chairs and couches around a coffee table and a flat-screen TV, luxurious and understated and comfortable. A wrought-iron spiral staircase led up to a loft bed.

He went to the window, stared out into the night. The moon was peeking through a hole in the clouds, illuminating the undulating patterns of glowing white foam spread across the huge beach far below.

Lily wrapped her arm around his waist. "Want to talk about it?"

"No." It snapped out. Not what he wanted to say. It was just hardwired in there, popping out to shove away intruders. Like an alarm system, buzzing when it was breached. He could hear the gears grind as Lily tried to puzzle out how to manage him. Didn't envy her the task. He couldn't manage his own self. Why should she have more luck?

"I never knew my own mother," she said.

Aw, Christ. He was in for it now. He clenched his teeth. "No?"

"She and my father tried for years to get pregnant. That was in the early days of fertility medicine. My dad did research in it, like I told you. My mom did seven cycles of IVF before they conceived me."

"Yay," he muttered. "Glad she did."

Her arm tightened around his waist. "Sweet of you to say so," she said. "They were, too. At first."

She paused, gathering her thoughts. Bruno wanted to scream. If it was going to hurt, he wanted to power through it. "Let's have it."

"Have what?"

"The zinger," he said. "Tonight's all about the zingers, one after another, straight to the liver. Whatever you're going to zing me with, have at it. Please. Get it over with."

She stiffened, turning away. "Never mind. You're right. Now's not the time for this conversation."

He spun her around to face him. "No, really," he said. "It's the only time we've got. Just tell me, goddamnit. I want to hear it."

"She died," Lily said. "In labor. A big blood vessel had formed across her cervix. She hemorrhaged. Bled out in a couple of minutes. If they'd done an early C-section, she'd have lived. But they didn't know."

He pulled her closer, nuzzled her hair. It smelled like lavender.

"My father felt guilty all my life," she said. "If he hadn't moved heaven and earth to get her pregnant . . ." She shrugged. "I felt guilty, too. I know it's stupid, but there it is."

They swayed, locked together, as he tried to take in what she was trying to tell him. "It's not the same," he said. "You were a baby. Your parents made their decisions and took the risk. Both of them."

"So did Magda. How is it different?" Her voice was muffled against his shirt. "She must have been hell on wheels."

"Oh, yeah. That, she was." Laughter shook him, the tight, high-frequency kind of laughter that could all too suddenly turn into tears.

"She must have loved you so much," Lily whispered.

"I wish she'd loved me less," he blurted.

"Oh, baby." Her voice was fogged up. "Don't say that."

"All these years . . ." His voice was blocked by a hot, aching lump in his throat. "It never made sense that a woman like her would . . . aw, shit. She was special, you know? Having me messed up her life, but she never complained. Her own mother gave her no end of hell. Grandma Pina, raving superbitch. Rosa and Tony didn't speak to Pina for thirty years because of that. But Mamma was beautiful. Smart. Not a doormat. She was the opposite of a doormat. Kind of like you."

The sound she made was half laugh, half sob. "Thank you."

He pushed on. "She was tough, you know? I couldn't understand why she took it. The way Rudy talked down to her, the way he hit her. And being intimate with him, oh, Christ." He blew out a breath, as if he were trying to expel toxic gas. "Now I get it. And I can't take it."

"Bruno," she whispered. "Sweetie. It's not—"

"It makes me want to vomit," he burst out. "I'd rather it

was that she was stupid about men, or she had self-esteem issues. Or that she was lonely, or that any man was better than being alone. But doing it for me? Oh, Jesus. That's a gift I don't want. That's a curse, not a gift."

Lily grabbed his hands. Her eyes blazed. "I'd do it," she said. "If I were her, and you were my son? Hell, yes. I'd do it for you."

"Don't even say it. She shouldn't have had to do that. No one should ever have to. Someone should have helped her. Saved her."

Lily lifted his trembling, knotted fists and dropped a gentle kiss onto each of them in turn. "And you think it should have been you?"

He didn't answer. He didn't need to.

"You were a child!" she raged. "Up against an organized crime syndicate! Get real! Give yourself a break!"

Laughter shook him again. "I'm eighteen years older now, and guess what, babe? I'm not doing a whole lot better than when I was twelve! It's fucking déjà vu. In the past thirty-six hours, you've been clubbed, shot at, and thrown off a cliff. And there wasn't a damn thing I could do to stop it."

"You saved me, you moron!" she yelled. "You're being deliberately stupid and dense about this! My God, you ask a lot of yourself!"

He touched his forehead to hers. "I can't help it," he blurted. "I love you."

She went very still. He realized, with a stab of pure, white-hot panic, that he meant it. He really did. Body, soul, blood, bones, teeth, and guts, he meant it. He loved Lily Parr. Period.

Oh, shit. And he had to run off his mouth about it.

He tightened his fingers around her cold ones. Fear gripped him, deep and hard. What a loser. His timing. It sucked. "Don't say anything," he begged. "I know it's too soon. Things are too crazy."

She tilted her head up, kissed him. Little, flowerlike kisses, blooming against the corner of his mouth. But she evaded his returning kiss, drawing back, swaying away. Not ready for it.

"I won't hold you to it," she whispered.

That didn't sound promising, but what the hell, he'd taken the plunge. "You don't have to hold me to it. It is what it is."

She slid her arms around his neck. He kissed the corners of her eyes. Sure enough. Wet. Hot. Salt. He kissed the tears away, making it a ritual. Each tear he licked away was a magic spell, holding her to him.

"Can I say something . . . ? Without making you mad?" she asked.

He went right on guard. "I don't make dumb promises like that."

"Then I'll have to risk it." She kissed his jaw. "The way you felt scared, because you couldn't protect your mother? And me?"

"It sucks. Literally. Like a vortex underneath my guts. So?"

"That was the way she felt about you," Lily said.

Bruno shut that out. He just had no place to put it. He shook his head, not sure what he was negating. Subject closed.

Lily waited but wisely concluded that she wasn't going to get a coherent response from him. She padded into the bathroom, leaving him alone with his thoughts and the moon. He leaned his forehead against the cold glass, watching his breath fog it up. The white patch of steam, swelling and retreating. The bathroom door clicked open. Light spilled out into the dark room. Lily came up behind him, stroking his back. Perfumed steam wafted along with her.

He turned to look at her, realized that she was naked.

It bowled him over how beautiful her perfect curving silhouette was backlit by the glow from the bathroom. So graceful. His throat tightened. His cock sprang to attention. His balls were heavy, throbbing.

"Lily," he warned. "You're covered with bruises."

She tilted her head. The light caught the sly gleam in her eyes. "Shhh," she murmured, getting to work on the buttons of the fleece shirt he'd borrowed from some McCloud or other. "I'm fine. But I won't pressure you. I know how tired you are, particularly after that meeting. Let's just, you know. Cuddle. Skin to skin. It feels so good."

A sound burst out, hurting his throat. "Fat fucking chance."

"We could," she said stubbornly. "We really could. Men are so weird about that." She shoved the shirt off his shoulders and started in on his belt. "Nothing's stopping us." She shoved his pants down.

"Ya think?" His cock leaped out, *sproing*, like it was spring-loaded.

She gazed at it. "Ah," she murmured. "Just out of curiosity, are you in this condition in spite of all your stress? Or because of it?"

"Does it matter?" He tried and failed not to sound belligerent as he kicked off his shoes, wrenched his jeans the rest of the way down.

She shrugged. "Just wondering."

"One, I'm jacked up and totally out of my mind. Two, you're gorgeous, and you drive me wild. That still doesn't make it a good idea."

She took his hand, led him toward the stairs. "Well, gee. Maybe you're right. Let's just take this upstairs and have this argument while we're warming up the sheets." She glanced down at his turgid dick. "We can discuss all the, um, ramifications under a cuddly comforter."

He held back. "It's not just that," he said, miserably. "The dreams. You shouldn't sleep with me, Lily. It's not safe. I'll sleep on that couch."

"Fuck if you will." Her voice was as sharp as glass. "Come up those stairs with me, right here, right now. Or. Else."

Well, damn. She had him by the dumb handle. He followed along up that winding staircase like a docile hound, helpless to resist the spectacular view of her ass. It was so round, accented with velvety shadows deepening the cleft and pooling in the twin dimples at the top, collecting under the lush, pearlike under-curve of her butt cheeks. He wanted to cup and stroke and pet and kiss. Hours of worship.

He didn't have the strength to do the right thing. Even to protect her. And he loved her. What a dickhead. Weak and selfish.

"If I dream, you know to get the hell away from me, right?" he persisted. "Don't try to wake me, don't try to touch me. Clear? Got it?"

"Sure." She smiled mysteriously over her shoulder. "I promise. No physical contact of any kind. Scout's honor."

He squinted at her. "You're messing with me."

She started to laugh. "This isn't fair. What good is it to have a man tell me he loves me if he won't touch me, and won't sleep with me, and won't put out? Screw that!"

"You haven't told me if you love me back," he said.

Fuck. He chickened out as soon as the words were out of his mouth and lunged to put his hand over her mouth. "Sorry. I didn't mean to do that to you. It just popped out."

She yanked his hand down. "But I—"

"Sometimes I talk too much." He kissed her as he pushed her down onto the cold iron steps of the spiral staircase, caged by the curving bars of the railing. He pushed her legs open. "It's an impulse-control thing. I'm working on it. And I'll put out, big-time. Believe me."

He sank down, put his mouth to her. She protested, giggling and squirming, but he was fiercely intent upon knocking her off whatever train of thought she might have been traveling.

He cupped her mound with the V of his index finger and forefinger and lifted it, parting her pussy lips and making the taut, rosy bud of her clit pop pertly out of its hood. Ready for worship and giddy distraction from thinking. Thinking was a bad idea for stressed-out girls. Better to be whimpering, thrashing, coming. Getting a clue of the advantages of being loved by him, one of those being lots of prolonged, enthusiastic tongue action. He just could not get enough of her. Her taste and texture and scent. The softness of her inner thigh against his cheek. Plump, tender pussy folds, drenched with salt-sweet girl juice. He suckled her clit, finger fucking her, delving for secret hot spots.

It took a few minutes, but he felt when the tension in her body changed from resistance to urgency. Her quivering thighs were clamped around his head; her snug channel squeezed hungrily around his fingers. He put on the brakes a couple times, made her wait, fingernails raking his shoulders. It made him smile against her juicy muff.

And then, the strong, eager pulse of her pussy throbbed around his fingers as pleasure jolted through her. Sweet satisfaction.

He wiped his face. "So. We were going to discuss ramifications?"

She could not move. He scooped her up, tossing her over his shoulder. Her body vibrated with silent laughter.

The bed at the top of the stairs was recessed into a space with three big windows on each side, so that one would feel like they were in a bed that was floating on air. He tossed the comforter back and set her down on the snowy white expanse of the sheet.

He sat down beside her. Slid his hand into hers. Waited.

She sat there, catching her breath and hiding her face against his shoulders. After a few minutes, she looked up. "It occurs to me that this crazy situation might just have a silver lining," she announced.

He gripped her thigh, high up, where he could circle his

fingertip delicately around the top of her sensitive slit. "No! Really?"

"I didn't mean just sex," she said tartly. "Believe it or not."

"Guess I'm not trying hard enough," he remarked.

She batted his hand away. "Shhh. What I mean is, you finally have a chance to put it right. To straighten out the great painful dilemmas of your existence. When do people ever get to do that? Never, Bruno. Most of us just have to suck it up. Whatever our baggage is."

Suck it up. Yeah, that's what he'd done, for eighteen years. "Aside from the question of whether we survive this great opportunity, what the hell's with you? You working on that glass-half-full attitude again?"

She slid off the bed and to her knees, facing him. "You bet I am," she said throatily. "And I am going to help you do the same thing."

His blood thundered, looking into those lovely eyes, at those hot, soft lips. "Oh, yeah? And how are you going to do that?"

"Like this." She leaned forward and sucked his cock into her mouth.

She'd meant for it to be playful, to lighten the mood, make him laugh. But her sensual assault had the opposite effect.

He dragged in a ragged gulp of air and arched over her, clenching handfuls of the sheet. He shook, his body as taut as a mass of high-tension cables. She caressed him, voluptuous twisting strokes and swirls with her hands and tongue, but his quivering tension worried her.

She looked up. "Hey, Bruno," she urged. "Relax. Breathe."

He cupped her face and kissed her. Sweet, desperate kisses, so tender and pleading, they undid her utterly. Any plan she might have had of cajoling him into a better head space fell apart. He was seething with raw feeling. No games, no tricks. Just two naked souls, trying to knot themselves together for all eternity.

It made her heart flower, hot and helplessly yearning. Expanding into something bigger, wider, someone who could maybe take in the world and accept it. Love it, even. Good and bad.

He spread her out, and she stretched and arched for him in total trust. His weight pinned her down against the cool linen, the boundaries of her universe exquisitely defined by his body. His mouth moving over hers, drinking her in.

He poised himself over her, tongue thrusting and twining with hers while he stroked the bulb of his penis between her pussy lips. Up and down, dipping tenderly into the well of lube, and then up, over. More moist, sliding, licking strokes, teasing and swirling himself juicily around her clit. She shuddered and jerked, raising her hips. Silently begging for him to thrust inside and be done with it.

He lifted his head, letting her gasp in some badly needed air. His face was shrouded in shadows, but she felt the raw hunger, barely controlled. It made her heart swell until it hurt. She arched, pushed, forcing his cock inside, crying out with delight at the slow invasion.

They gasped, sighed, with each slow drag out and plunge back in.

She rocked and heaved to get him deeper. She felt flushed and throbbing inside, clenching and moaning as he stirred her around with his thick, hot club. Every squeeze pumped pleasure through her body.

It didn't matter who was on top, who beneath, who gave, who took. They each gave and took everything, with frantic tenderness. The storm took them, tossed them, like leaves and twigs in wild water.

It washed them up finally, limp and helpless on the other side.

Lily was lying on top of him when she floated back.

Sweat cooled on her back, but she was warmed by the scorching heat of his body, the thick presence of his cock, still wedged deep inside her. His heartbeat throbbed, slow and heavy against her womb. Against her heart, too. She rose and fell with the rhythm of his breath.

Only when the chilled sweat made her start to shiver did she lift herself carefully off, sliding his half-hard penis out of her body.

And found herself awash with come.

Hello. She sucked in air. Reality slammed back. She flopped onto her side next to him, trying to breathe. The bedside table had been stocked with condoms, Tam had told them, pointedly.

And they'd just jumped off that cliff without a thought. Again.

Her brain was fried with sex hormones. By now, they were spoiled rotten for skin on skin, hot and wet and intimate. And once a barrier was breached, it was so hard to go back and reestablish it.

God knows, if she ever wanted to conceive a baby, he was the man she wanted to father it. They belonged together. If Fate would just stop smashing at them with a sledgehammer, they'd be fine. They could make it work. That scenario had never been even remotely imaginable to her before. But with Bruno, it was. It really was.

She'd do anything to make that a reality. She would try so hard.

But that didn't make the timing any less horrific, considering recent events. Or she herself any less irresponsible and stupid.

She snagged the duvet with her toe, yanked it up to cover them both. Entertained a vague notion of going downstairs to wash, but her legs were so limp. She'd probably tumble down that staircase and break her neck. Her body pulsed, glowed. The sore parts that she'd hurt in the last couple of days were tender, but the glow was stronger.

She leaned close to him, just staring. He was so beautiful, it just blew her mind. The sweeping design of dark eyebrows, those smile crinkles at the corners of his eyes, the noble shape of his nose. His chiseled cheekbones and jaw, that sexy beard shadow. Those sensual lips. Her eyes were famished for him, no matter how long she gazed.

He was fast asleep, but what the hell. She said it, right out loud. "I love you, too."

He didn't move. The words didn't technically count if they didn't reach their target, so she'd say it to his face in the morning. She'd say it, and say it, and say it. She'd shout it and sing it. It made her feel stronger. Like, maybe she could beat this crazy thing and come out the other side. Into something more real and beautiful and special than she'd ever dreamed of. It was possible. Anything felt possible.

She started to giggle, and then silently sob, huddled under the duvet, tears soaking into the sheets. Wow. Look at her, morphing into a weeping optimist. The power of sex hormones was miraculous.

And love, of course. And love.

21

The little kid was making him nervous.

Bruno fidgeted at the breakfast table, hiding behind his coffee mug. Six-year-old Rachel, Tam and Val's little girl, eyed him intently. She was a pretty thing, thin and wiry, her pointy face dominated by huge, heavily lashed eyes, a rosebud mouth, and a tangle of gleaming dark ringlets. She wore pink-framed glasses and slurped pink-tinted milk out of her cereal bowl. She studied Bruno as if he were some fascinating swamp creature that she wanted to catalog and dissect.

The kitchen was a crowded, noisy place, packed with hungry people. Davy sat beside him, chowing down on steak, eggs, and bagels. Getting Davy to talk was like prying rusted nails out of a board, which made him the perfect breakfast companion for Bruno that morning. Zia Rosa was in hog heaven, gleefully presiding over sizzling frying pans as she tossed out short orders right and left.

Bruno sat sullenly in the midst of that loud, banging, clinking, laughing swirl of activity. All he could think about was what a cowardly thing it was to sneak out of bed while Lily was still asleep, but he didn't know if he'd dreamed what he'd heard her say the night before.

I love you, too.

It might have been real. It really might, and in that case, he could just go ahead and let his head explode. But if it were not, he'd have to open a wormhole and tunnel into a parallel universe in which he had never been born. He was also jazzed by the strange fact that he hadn't had one of his fight dreams last night. First time in months.

". . . me that cereal?"

He wrenched his attention to Rachel, who was yelling in a way that suggested it was not the first time she'd spoken. "Huh?"

"The cereal," Rachel said impatiently. "Pass me the cereal box!"

Bruno looked where she was pointing on the shelf. Looked back, at the open cereal box in front of Rachel's bowl, some of which was still floating in the pink milk. It was the same exact type of cereal.

He leaned across the table, hefted the box, rattling its contents. It was almost completely full. "Use the open box. There's plenty in there."

The little girl gave him a calculating look and glanced furtively to the right and left. "I want the prize," she confided. She pointed to the undersea scene pictured on the box, which sported cartoon fish and a treasure chest dripping with jewels, festooned with ropes of pearls. "I already have the ring and two of the bracelets. But I don't have the necklace yet. Maybe there's one in that box." She paused, made an impatient but still furtive gesture. "Well? Get it!"

Bruno glanced around the kitchen for her parents. Not there. He was probably committing a huge faux pas, but hell. One look at the kid, and a guy knew he didn't want to get on her bad side.

He snagged the cereal box and passed it to Rachel, who tore into it with feral eagerness. The inner bag got torn, cereal flew right and left, scattering over the table and floor as she dug for her prize. Yikes.

He was relieved when she unearthed the plastic bag with a shriek of delight. It was a heart-shaped locket, painted plastic, studded with big fake jewels. Then the energy in the room changed. The sound level dropped. Everyone took a simultaneous breath in their conversation. The fine hairs prickled up on the back of Bruno's neck. Heat raced under his skin as he turned to look. God. He was *blushing*, for God's sake.

Lily was framed in the doorway, offering shy smiles and nods. She glanced at him. He couldn't breathe. Her hair was damp, spiraling in lush corkscrewing waves. Her lips were soft, luscious. She had color.

A shriek of chair legs scraping, and Davy McCloud wiped his mouth, shoved a last chunk of bagel into his mouth, and piled up his plate, glass, cup, and silverware. He vacated his place, gesturing with his chin for Lily to take his chair and sit next to Bruno.

She smiled her thanks and slid into the chair, looking at everything except for him. Zia Rosa headed over with a cup of coffee and set it before her, having already administered sugar and cream for Lily according to her own personal and inflexible criteria.

"You eat a big breakfast, honey," she announced. "Watcha want, omelet, pancakes, French toast? Over easy, scrambled, ham, bacon?"

Lily looked bewildered. "Ah, whatever's around is fine. A piece of toast, if there is some. I can do it myself. Please don't worry about it."

Zia snorted. "Girls these days! What are you gonna make babies out of if you don't eat? What are they s'posed to be built out of, air?"

Lily choked on her coffee.

"Zia, you start in on her, and I'm wrapping duct tape around your head," he warned her, but the damage was done.

"You shut up, boy. I wasn't talkin' to you." Zia barreled back to the stove to dish Lily up, a woman on a mission.

"Sorry about that," he muttered. "Should have warned you. She's got this thing about grandkids. Huge pain in the ass."

Lily started to reply, but Zia Rosa came marching back, bearing a platter of food that made their eyes widen in awe. A huge omelet was splayed over the plate, stuffed with cheese, vegetables, and sliced ham. A mountainous heap of fried potatoes teetered over it. Three pieces of toast. She laid it down, crossed her arms over her bosom, dark eyes narrowed. Daring them to defy her. *"Mangia,"* she said, her voice steely.

Lily looked intimidated. "You'll help, right?" she asked him.

"Sure." Looking at her at that close, intimate range, smelling her shampoo, it made his body stir. Gave a man an appetite.

There was a commotion outside the kitchen, and voices outside, one of which made his heart jump. *Kev.* Bruno's chair shot back. He leaped up as his adopted brother strode into the room.

Kev's dull green canvas raincoat billowed around his knees. His dirty blond hair had grown out past his shoulders, loose and tousled. He looked grim and as tired as a guy ought to look after flying from New Zealand, but even so, he looked better than Bruno had ever seen him.

Months of traveling the world with Edie, his bride-to-be, had agreed with him. He was filled out, had color. He looked a lot more like Sean now, his biological identical twin, than he ever had before. Except for the scars that seamed half of his face from cheekbone to jaw.

Edie was making the rounds of hugs, but Kev cut through the crowd. He made his way to Bruno, grabbed the front of his sweatshirt, and jerked him up until their faces were inches apart. "What the fuck is going on?" His voice suddenly silenced all other conversation.

"Uh . . . long story," Bruno said.

Thud. Kev shoved him against the wall, which made the various bruises on Bruno's ribs hurt like hell. "I hear you met some femme fatale and started slaughtering people for her? Dead bodies on the streets? Posses of commandos coming to blow your ass up? Over some chick you just met?" The words hissed out like water from a fire hose.

Bruno was taken aback. "Ah . . . ah, not exactly."

"Let go of him!" Lily chopped at his adopted brother's huge, unyielding fist, which pressed painfully against Bruno's Adam's apple.

Kev's fierce stare swung to Lily, taking in her furious face and fiery eyes. "This is the femme fatale?"

"Femme fatale, my ass!" she snapped. "Put him down, you jerk!"

Kev let go. Bruno ducked out of arm's reach, rubbing his larynx.

But Kev didn't attack again. "And then you don't call," he

said, more quietly. "What in the fuck is that about? Why didn't you call?"

Bruno glanced around. Everyone was listening for his excuse.

"Uh. Didn't want to worry you," he mumbled.

A harsh sound came out of Kev. "And when you got my text? Did you figure I'd just let it go, stop being worried? Aw, shucks, he didn't answer me, so I guess everything must be fine. Let's just go back to the beach. Is that what you thought?"

Bruno swallowed. "I wasn't really thinking," he admitted, shamefaced. "I was, ah . . . I was—"

"Too busy getting jerked around by your dick?" Kev suggested.

Lily shot up a few inches taller. "You asshole!"

"Kev!" A shocked female voice from behind made Kev jerk and glance over his shoulder. His lady, Edie, was staring at him, appalled.

Kev looked sheepish. Edie, a tall and willowy brunette with shadowy gray eyes and long dark hair, gaped at Kev as if she didn't recognize him. Everyone in the room stared. As if Kev had sprouted an extra head.

Kev flung his hands out and glared back. "What? Can't I get upset? Everybody else around here freaks out. Why not me?"

Bruno rubbed his aching neck. "He's not usually like this," he explained to Lily under his breath. "He's usually, you know, Mr. Zen. Supercalm. I'm the hyper one."

"So let me take a goddamn turn," Kev snarled.

Con spoke up from his perch at the end of the long bar. "Glad to see you still have it in you, bro."

Kev turned to his brother. "What the fuck does that mean?"

Connor took a meditative sip of his coffee. "A little emotion," he said, finally. "It's a good thing. Haven't seen a whole lot of that out of you. Like Bruno says. You're always . . . supercalm."

"And that's a problem?" Kev demanded.

"No way," Sean piped up, his voice as flat as Connor's. "No problem. Just a random observation."

Kev stared wildly from one brother to another. "What the fuck? What is this? What do you guys want from me?"

"*Niente. Non è niente.*" Zia Rosa bustled into the middle of the room and barreled into Kev's big body. She gave him a bear hug.

He hugged her back, fiercely. "*Ciao*, Zia."

"You two are just tired, that's all," Zia Rosa said. "And hungry. Sit down." She shooed them over to the far end of the long table, as far from Lily and Bruno as possible. "I got food, lotsa food. Ah, honey, lemme take a look at you." She grabbed Edie's chin, pinched her cheek. "You're fatter," she said approvingly. She stared into Edie's eyes, clucking her tongue. "You got that look, honey. The eyes, with those dark shadows? Eh? You losin' your breakfast?"

Edie shook her head, smiling. "No, Zia. I was just on a series of airplanes for the last thirty-six hours," she said. "My stomach's fine."

"Hmmph. We'll just see." Zia Rosa bustled off to procure food, clearly eager to test that hypothesis personally.

Bruno shepherded Lily back to her seat and sat her down, snagging a piece of toast to gnaw on, just to have something to do with his hands. Kev shot him a telling look from his end of the table. A look that said, *I'm not through with you yet.* Lily took a bite of her omelet, staring as Zia Rosa built two plates up to staggering proportions.

"So, the baby thing," she said. "It's just her schtick."

"One-trick pony," Bruno said. "Never fails."

She gave him a look that made his heart skip and hiccup. "She gets a spectacular reaction when she teases you. Who could resist?"

Bruno decided to shrug that off. "She's hell on wheels."

Her hand seized his. "It's just a Ranieri thing," she said. "That hell-on-wheels thing. Must be genetic."

They stared at each other. The energy between them felt like physical pressure. Lily tore her gaze away. "Your brother's no joke, either," she commented, her voice sharpening. "Wow, what a charmer."

"I swear to God, he's never like that," Bruno protested. "He must have taken up smoking crank. He's always been so mellow."

"Would you fix my locket?" A small hand grabbed his sleeve and tugged, and he looked down into Rachel's beseeching eyes. "It broke!"

Bruno turned his attention to Rachel's dilemma. It was simple to fit the two pieces of plastic back together and apply pressure until the joint hinge popped back into place. "Good as new." He handed it to her.

She draped the chain around her neck and turned, holding up the clasps. "Would you close it for me?" she asked, conscious of the honor she was doing him.

Bruno fitted the clasp together and got a blinding smile for his trouble. Rachel was beautiful, yet he had a heavy feeling in his gut. Something about the necklace, her slender neck . . . he couldn't put his finger on the feeling and wasn't sure if he wanted to. It wasn't good.

An old memory, heaving up out of the deeps. The bulk of it still hanging below the surface, like one of those deadly icebergs that brought down the *Titanic*. Aw, fuck it. He'd have the bellyache anyway, might as well dredge up the memory that went with it. At least then he'd have a scrap of data, not just nausea. Sort of. Memory was so damn malleable and tricky. It couldn't be trusted.

He sank into himself and followed the feeling back to its source. The pendant, the clasp, Rachel's neck. That day that Mamma gave him her necklace. There, that was it. That was the source of the ache.

It was the same day she'd put him on that Greyhound bus bound for Portland. It had been late at night, and they'd been riding in a taxi all over town. He remembered watching the meter creep up. Wondering why she was burning money, like they had any to spare. Mamma kept looking behind them, like they were being followed, but they weren't. No headlights on those wet streets. Just pools of streetlight.

At the bus station, she'd bought a ticket and hustled him to the gate before he knew what she'd planned, before he could put up a proper fight. She gave him the lecture, said her piece, about how she was leaving Rudy, that she'd get away, she swore to God, but he had to be good, she had to know he was safe first. She still had things to do.

What? he'd asked, blubbering so hard the snot ran down his face. *What the fuck do you still have to do here? Why not just come?*

Watch that language, punk, she scolded, herding him toward the entrance of the bus. Then she unclasped her necklace, the antique pendant that she never took off. She put it around his neck. It was warm from her body heat. *Keep this safe for me,* she said and hugged him from behind until he thought his ribs would crack. The bus driver said something snotty about hurrying up. Mamma mouthed off to him, but without her usual spark. Then she shoved him up the steps— *go, go, quick, quick!* into the sweetish, stale stink of the bus. Row after row of strangers' grotesque faces peering up, full of hostility, indifference.

The bus took off, swaying and lurching. He'd looked out at her face, staring up from outside. Stark and pale, dark eyes huge, receding into the distance. The last time he'd seen her in life.

He'd worn the necklace from that minute on, like a talisman. When Mamma died, he'd become terrified to let it get cold. He'd gotten the notion somehow that as long as the gold pendant stayed warm, he could imagine that it was her warmth. The last of her warmth.

Even though all the rest of it was in the hard ground.

Then Rudy and his goons came to the diner that morning, eighteen long years ago. Rudy had recognized the necklace and ripped it off his neck.

And that was that. Gone. That warmth had gone cold.

"Did you see my locket?" Rachel was crowing to Val, lifting up her dark curls, twirling and preening for her father. He held out his arms and she climbed up onto his lap, getting her due of kisses.

A drumroll on the edge of his consciousness became a crescendo of anxious urgency. Something he was supposed to do, see, understand, but what? It swelled, louder, until it filled him up. No room for his lungs to expand. Feelings pounding on the door of his higher brain functions from below, demanding to be translated into conscious thought.

He tried to relax, open up, fishing for it. Running over everything he'd seen, thought, remembered. Mamma. Rachel's necklace. Mamma's necklace, warm from her body. Rachel's delicate neck, like the stem of some heavy-headed flower, so beautiful it could break your heart.

Did you see my locket?

He closed his eyes, trying again, following vaporous trails of emotion, of thought while the drumroll got louder, the knocking more desperate. The scent of his mother's perfume, mixed with the tang of fear sweat. Her icy hands, fumbling in the dark, struggling with the clasp. Her hands had been trembling. She'd kissed the back of his neck.

Go, go, quick, quick.

"Zia," he said. "Remember Mamma's necklace?"

Zia Rosa turned from a tray of cupcakes that she was frosting. "Yeah, sure. The one Rudy took. Your great-grandmother's from the old country. A courting gift to your *bisnonna* from your *bisnonno*."

"That was a locket, right?" he asked. "One that opened?"

She frowned. "'Course. Magda kept a picture of you in

there. Same one I got in my wallet. A lock of your hair, too, remember?"

He shook his head. "I didn't know it could open at all," he said. "It never opened for me. Maybe it was soldered shut."

Lily touched his wrist, a worried line creasing her brow. She'd caught his vibe. It made her uneasy. "What is it?" she asked.

He seized her hand. "Tell me again, Lily. Exactly what your father said at the hospital when you saw him last."

Lily sighed. "Bruno, please. I've been over it a thousand times. He told me that you had to lock something, but he didn't say what, and I have no idea what he—"

"No." He cut her off. "No, just repeat his actual words. Word for word. No paraphrasing. Verbatim. Please, Lily."

And the drumroll crescendo was suddenly audible to her, too.

Her face paled. She swallowed, blinking as her eyes flickered to the side, narrowing in concentration. "He said . . . he has to lock it."

"He has the locket," Bruno repeated softly.

Her eyes went wide. She pressed her hands to her mouth. "Oh, God, Bruno. Oh, God. Magda had a locket? And she gave it to you?"

He nodded.

"Well? Where is it?" she burst out. "Who has it?"

He shook his head. "It's gone," he said.

She looked around, frantically, as if the locket should be lying around in plain view. "What do you mean, gone? You mean lost? Stolen?"

"Both, in a sense," he said.

Zia took over for him. "That filthy *figlio di puttana* Rudy, he took it," she informed Lily. "That day they came to the diner and attacked Bruno. Three big guys, against one twelve-year-old boy who just lost his mamma. *Teste di cazzo.*"

Lily turned to him, her eyes wide. "Good God. How did you—"

"Kev," Bruno said. "Kev beat the living shit out of all three of them. In about thirty seconds. Bam, pow, and it was over."

Lily glanced over at Kev. He gazed back, impassive. "What about Rudy, then?" she asked. "What happened to him?"

Kev got up, snagged two unoccupied chairs from the other end of the table, and hauled them over to Bruno and Lily's side. He took the frosting-smeared knife from Zia Rosa's hands and placed it on the bar. He positioned the chair behind her. "Sit, Zia," he said.

The others were starting to gather around, too. Kev pulled up the other chair, seated himself opposite them.

"What happened then was that we loaded the thugs into the back of Tony's old pickup and covered them with a tarp," Kev said. "Then we hosed blood into the gutter while Tony drove away with them."

"And with the locket," Lily repeated, as if desperately hoping to be contradicted.

No such luck. "And the locket," Bruno echoed. "Rudy put it in the pocket of his jeans. Tony didn't know. Kev had no clue. I was in shock."

"Were they, um, alive?" Lily asked, delicately.

"They were when we loaded them up," Kev said. "More or less."

"Wishing they weren't," Bruno commented. "Rudy had a fork sticking out of his crotch.

Every man in the room recoiled instinctively.

"I doubt they lived out the day," Kev said quietly. "Knowing Tony."

Zia snorted in disgust. "After attacking Bruno? Not a chance."

Bruno felt lightheaded. "Zia, do you have any idea where Tony took them? I knew better than to ask."

Zia Rosa shook her head. "You know how Tony was. If anyone got in trouble, he wanted to take the rap. Plus, I was a woman." She rolled her eyes. "He figured, three can keep a secret if two of them are dead. He took those guys out into the woods somewhere, put 'em down like dogs, and put 'em in a hole. And we ain't never gonna know where."

"He left around six A.M.," Kev said. "He got back late in the evening. We don't know which direction he went, or how far he drove."

Davy harrumphed. "That's a lot of woods."

They all pondered gloomily how much woods.

"He might have put them on his property," Bruno said. "That way, he'd have been more or less sure not to be seen or stumbled over."

"True," Kev said. "But that's still a hundred and forty acres of rough ground, lots of it steep mountain slope. A lot to dig up, without any assurance that they're actually there."

Bruno sagged. "Shit, shit, *shit*," he hissed. "One little clue, and bam, the door slams shut in my face. I wish I hadn't even thought of the goddamn locket. It's worse now than it was before."

"Not for me, it isn't," Lily said.

He looked up. Lily's eyes were glowing. "This way, I know I'm not crazy," she said. "And you all know I'm not lying, too. That's worth a whole lot to me, Bruno. You can't imagine how much."

He swallowed, bumping over the knot of old grief. "I was already convinced," he told her.

Her smile made his heart skip. "I know you were," she said. "Thank you. But even so, proof is nice to have. It makes me feel, I don't know. Less like it's all my fault somehow."

"I never thought that," he insisted.

Their hands caught, twined. Clung. Wonder unfurled inside him.

Rachel's curly head suddenly ducked under his arm and

popped up between them. She held up her plastic necklace. "You lost your locket? You could have my locket if you want," she offered.

The lump in Bruno's throat swelled so big, he was speechless. Something about Rachel's big, worried eyes behind her glasses in her innocent bit of a face, it just turned his screws that last brutal turn.

He grabbed the little girl, hugged her, and hid his hot face in her cloud of dark hair, struggling with all his strength not to totally lose it.

"Thank you, sweetheart," he said thickly. "You keep your locket. It looks better on you than it would on me. Turn around. I'll put it back on you." He clasped the trinket around Rachel's neck, dropped a kiss on top of her fuzzy head, and tried not to think about that last, tight hug before Mamma shoved him up onto the steps of the bus.

Zia Rosa was all fogged up, too. She gazed at the little girl and mopped beneath the lenses of her glasses, then seized a napkin from the holder and noisily blew her nose. *"Dolcettina mia, che carina,"* she burbled. "Goddamn Tony. He shoulda told me. He shoulda trusted me more. But he couldn't. He didn't trust nobody."

"It's not your fault, Zia," Kev said.

"It just ain't right. I know what I woulda done with them stinkin' *stronzi*. I'd have done like my *papà* used to say. Your *bisnonno*."

Bruno glanced in Rachel's direction. "Whatever *bisnonno* used to say, you censor it big-time, Zia," he warned. *Bisnonno* had been a pretty hardcore kind of dude, if family legend was to be believed.

But Zia was off and running. She switched languages, thank God, letting out a torrent of picturesque and uniquely nasty Calabrese dialect. Bruno and Kev, the only ones who could understand it, glanced at each other and tried not to smile.

First shadow of a smile that he'd seen Kev crack since he got here. Maybe the worst was over. Good old Zia, always providing the comic relief. Hell on wheels didn't begin to describe her.

When Zia wound down, red in the face, Lily poked his arm. "Translation, please," she said.

Bruno groaned. "No way." He gestured at Rachel. "It's foul."

"So paraphrase," she urged. "Give me the gist of it."

Val laughed and put his hand behind Rachel's shoulders. "Come, Rachel," he said gently. "Into the playroom with you."

When Val had herded the little girl safely out of the kitchen, Bruno concentrated to remember the sequence. "OK, so it started out with graphic descriptions of the various sexual aberrations of all the guys who came after me in the diner, most specifically their unhealthy fondness for barnyard animals. Then we moved on to these guys' kinky long-dead ancestors, and this bit about the unspeakably obscene things they did in the woods with Santa Anna and San Girolamo—don't ask me to explain, because I don't get it, either. And fountains of blood, teeth flying, dismembered corpses of vanquished enemies, yada, yada, and then the part about pissing on their disassembled bones until the day of the second ascension of *Cristo Santo*. And then—"

He stopped, his mouth hanging open. Everyone staring at him while that drumroll crescendoed again. His hairs prickled. He had to consciously remember to breathe.

"Zia," he said, as soon as he could control his voice. "That bit about pissing on the bones. Is that really something *Bisnonno* used to say? Or did you add that part in yourself?"

"Ah, nah, Papà always said that when someone got in his face," Zia assured him. "He was *un uomo cazzoso*. Everything bugged him."

Bruno looked at Kev. Kev was starting to smile. And nod.

"Did Tony ever say it?" Bruno persisted.

"Of course. Tony was *cazzoso*, too. Don't you remember?"

"Oh, yeah," Bruno said. "I do remember. And how."

Kev's face split into a huge grin. Bruno's, too. He shook with laughter. At least, he hoped it was laughter. Better not to check. But he covered his face, just in case. His shoulders were shaking.

"What?" Lily grabbed his shoulder. "Is something wrong?"

"No," Kev said. "Nothing's wrong. Everything's fine."

"Then what's going on? Why is he falling apart?" Lily yelled.

Bruno lifted his face, wiped his eyes. "I'm not. I just figured out where to dig, that's all."

22

"What part of 'no' do you not understand, Hobart?" King said into the phone, staring down at Zoe's inert form on the infirmary bed. The machines hooked up to her beeped and hummed in the quiet room.

"But . . . how do you expect . . ." Hobart's voice trailed off. He was intelligent enough to hear death in his creator's voice, but he continued to whine. "But you saw what these people can do! It's just Melanie and me! We need reinforcements if we're going to mount an attack on—"

"I don't have reinforcements to send you," King cut in, staring at the data generated by the machines attached to

Zoe. Her body was healing, but she'd indulged in two more doses of Melimitrex to make it to the rendezvous point. Zoe's tendency for self-indulgence should be no surprise to him at this point, but still. It was a wonder she wasn't dead from an overdose. She might be brain damaged. Time would tell.

The trauma had taken its toll. She had lost a startling amount of weight, and her face was gaunt and sunken. Broken capillaries marred her eyelids, and veins on her temples stood out, snakelike and discolored. King shuddered with distaste. Hobart was still babbling. King forced himself to listen. He had to close this tedious conversation.

". . . now, considering their resources! We're going to need at least eight to ten operatives to mount an attack on—"

"Who said anything about mounting an attack?" King said.

Hobart was lost. Incredible, that this specimen had escaped the cull. He wondered what criteria he had been using when he chose not to discard Hobart. Certainly creative thinking had not been on the forefront of his mind. Some other gift must make up for the lack, but it was not in evidence today. King would look into his specs before he eliminated him, to make sure. Housecleaning was in order.

"So far, we've attacked them frontally," he explained as if to a child. "The results have not been good. Alone or together, they've bested every direct assault we've leveled at them. What does this suggest?"

"That we have to increase the—"

"No," King said sharply. "No more frontal attacks. They have the McClouds behind them, and Tamara Steele, and Val Janos, just to start. Have you done any research on these people? Have you any idea of their backgrounds? What they are capable of?"

"Ah . . . yes, but Melanie and I—"

"Perhaps you and Melanie have not been paying attention. We cannot afford to engage an army. We're exposed, overextended. We have to control them. It's clear that he has bonded with Parr. He'll do anything to protect her now. Look at this." King tapped the keyboard, selected a portion of the video the satellite photo had taken.

It showed Bruno Ranieri basically dragging Lily Parr up a cliff by her wrist. Pulling her up onto a ledge. He crouched with her there, leaning in to cup her face. They spoke for a few moments. Then he kissed her, very passionately. She wrapped her arms around his neck.

"So?" King prompted. "Hobart? Did you learn anything?"

"But . . . but—"

"You and Melanie take Parr. And we control Ranieri with her."

"But Parr is in that Steele woman's fortress," Hobart whined. "The defense system is beyond state of the art. How can we possibly—"

"You and Melanie will go to Cray's Cove and set up base," King said. "Brute force is not working. Let us default to intelligence and guile. You two will listen, watch, and use the creativity and unconventional thought processing inculcated in you since babyhood. And we will see if any of that seeding ever took root, hmmm? I, for one, am curious."

"Um. Yes, sir." Hobart's voice was subdued.

"Watch that place like a cat watches a mouse hole," King said, giving in to the urge to micromanage. "Document every vehicle that comes and goes. Listen and watch. The device in Rosa Ranieri's purse needs constant monitoring. Sooner or later, they'll get careless, and you two will jump into action. You'd better hope it's sooner."

"We, ah, have a time issue?" Hobart asked.

King's jaw ached from clenching. The man had delivered the transcript of that conversation in Tam Steele's house the night before and had not made these connections himself. "Tony Ranieri's letter would inconvenience the Ranieri family," he explained. "The one that Rosa Ranieri holds. In her purse, we discovered. Which you held, Hobart. In your hands, in the baby supplies store. Entertaining, hmm?"

"But, sir, I had no idea—"

"Silence," he snapped. "Don't waste my time. Bruno Ranieri will focus his attack on his Ranieri cousins now, since he knows no other place to attack. If he leans on Michael, then I do have a problem. So yes, there is a time issue, Hobart. As you so euphemistically put it."

"But . . . then shouldn't we—"

"Silence," he snapped again. "You and Melanie take Parr. Bring her to me. No bodies, no noise, no police. And if you manage that small task, then maybe, just maybe, you will save your skins. We will see."

Hobart's shame and despair filled the silence. King decided to relent, just a little. Fear and shame were powerful motivators, but he was throwing a tantrum. Demoralizing the few functioning agents left to him was counterproductive. "Hobart," he said. "Wait. Don't hang up."

He pulled up Hobart's command codes out of his memory and judiciously chose a Level Five motivator sequence. It was a phrase of ancient epic poetry, written in medieval Georgian. It was designed to reinforce mood, stimulating endorphins. A fizzy rush to get a jump-start on the task at hand. More a lollipop than anything else.

Not that Hobart deserved a treat, but King was a practical man.

He recited the phrase, gave Hobart a moment to collect himself. "Now off with you," he said. "Get to it."

"Yes, sir." Hobart's voice was almost tearful.

King broke the connection and stared down at Zoe's wasted form, wondering if there was any point at all in rehabilitating her. He would never have considered such a thing before, after a failure of such proportions. She was played out. It might be dangerous to recycle her at this point. But he had just lost eight operatives, some in their prime, others entering their prime. It was no simple matter to assemble more, with his stable out in the world, busily engaged in various profitable enterprises. He didn't keep them around idle, kicking their heels.

He had to learn the lesson hidden in this terrible blow. It was his assumption of natural superiority that had brought him to this. He'd underestimated Bruno Ranieri. It was intriguing.

He turned away from Zoe's humming, blipping machines and pulled up the recorded satellite image of yesterday morning's debacle at the cabin, running the film forward until he got to the part he wanted.

Bruno Ranieri staring up at the sky. Giving him the finger.

Neil stared at the image for a long time, running it back and replaying the short sequence over and over. He wanted to hear the younger man's voice to analyze his speech patterns. Get inside his head. He dug his phone out and punched in Hobart's code again.

"Yes, sir?" Hobart sounded anxious.

"Reggie rigged passive surveillance at Ranieri's diner," King said. "Did you recover the footage of Parr and Ranieri's conversation?"

"Of course I did," Hobart said. "I'll send it immediately."

King hung up, swinging back to look at Ranieri's expressive face, his defiance. Admirable, really. Ranieri was shaping up to be a worthy foe. Not that King had felt any need for a foe, but there the man was.

He stared at the image for a minute or so, until a soft, musical *ping* from the speaker showed that the audio of the Parr/Ranieri diner conversation of three days ago had arrived. He was eager to listen to it, but he clicked "replay" once again, as if compelled.

He watched the younger man thrust his hand up again, middle finger extended. So small and ineffectual, yet so vital.

"Fight all you want," King said to the screen. "You're mine."

Lily shivered in the frigid garage. The only light was what spilled out of the door to the house. Bruno and the McCloud men were loading the SUV that Kev McCloud had rented at Sea-Tac Airport on his return from New Zealand. The men worked with a hard, grim focus that made her feel like extraneous fluff. Not strictly their fault, but it still sucked.

"I have a right to be there," she said again. "I can take turns with the shovel. I can use the geothermal thing. I can keep watch. I can pull the trigger of a gun. You saw me do it. Or, ah, heard me, at least."

The McCloud guys exchanged looks that clearly indicated how grateful they all were that dealing with her was not their problem.

Bruno looked at his watch. Ten P.M. Full dark. The plan was to ease out, no headlights, hoping to give the satellite eye the slip, driving with an infrared scope for a few miles before turning the headlights on and becoming another anonymous moving light on the highway. Then, back up to the cabin to Tony's famous pissing tree sometime before dawn. Two to dig. Three to guard. The best plan they had come up with.

Assuming they didn't drive into an ambush.

Lily hated it. Or more specifically, she hated the fact that the plan did not include her.

Bruno let out a savage sigh. "No," he said.

Anger boiled up inside her. "Hey. This is not your problem, Ranieri. It's *our* problem. What gives you the authority to say no to me?"

Kev, Davy, Connor, and Sean McCloud did the crazy-chick male-sign-language thing. By silent accord, they slunk away into the shadows.

Bruno's mouth was tight. "It's simple," he said. "Is it your car? No. Kev rented it. The thing seats five. The McClouds and me. You think I'm leaving behind one of them to bring you? Ain't gonna happen, Lily. You're not invited to this party. Tough shit. Get over it."

She struggled not to cry out of sheer frustration. "I want to be there when you find that thing," she said. "I *need* it."

"We might not find anything at all." Bruno hoisted some new, shiny shovels, price tags still attached, and tossed them into the back. A bag full of leather gloves flew in after them. "I'll tell you what you need. Stay safe. Take naps. Soak in a tub. Drink lots of fluids."

"Who gives a shit about naps and fluids? So far, I've only participated in the problem! I want to be in on the solution, too. You can't tell me no!"

"Can't I?" He loomed over her, his lips pressed flat. "I've got an extra ten inches and a hundred pounds on you. It doesn't give me authority, but it gives me an edge. I'll use it. No problem."

"You're doing it again," she said. "That macho bullshit power tripping. You bastard. How dare you."

He shrugged, unrepentant. "The one thing I've managed to do for you so far is get you to a place where you can rest. So you can goddamn well appreciate this small accomplishment of mine, OK? We have to dig up those bones, and those bastards are going to be watching. It will take hours, plenty of time for them to mobilize. And do you want me to fight like that again? Looking over my shoulder with my heart in my throat? It's dangerous for me, too, you realize that?"

She bit her lip. She was compounding her uselessness by acting stupid and unhinged. Lovely way to cement a budding relationship and endear herself to his extended family. No way a gun-toting, shovel-wielding six foot four behemoth should stay behind to make room for Lily Parr, who was totally losing her shit.

She was such a practical person. She didn't even know herself like this. Hands ice cold and shaking. Legs like jelly. So scared that he would drive away and never come back. She didn't want to be left in the world as it was. That enormous dead silence that would be the universe without Bruno in it. She'd go looking for the bad guys herself. She'd advertise for them. Put up a Web site. *Come get me. Hurry, please.*

Bruno looked pissed, as if she were trying to manipulate him with her tears. She wasn't, but the whiny, soggy bitch effect was the same.

Bruno gestured toward the stuff heaped on the floor. Geothermal sensors. An armory packed in black plastic cases too heavy for her to lift. "Which of this equipment do you feel comfortable using? You plan on taking turns with the shovel, with your strained tendons?"

"OK, I get it. Don't beat a dead horse." She mopped her nose. "What happened to your trademark charm?"

"It was a cheap trick," he informed her. "Some evolutionary thing related to primitive mating behavior. I'm in survival mode now, so kiss the charm good-bye. This is the real Bruno. Hello, nice to meet you."

"Oh, great," she muttered. "That's just peachy."

"Time to go," Kev McCloud called out.

The four men materialized and finished loading the equipment into the cargo space. They slid into their places in the SUV without looking her in the face. Lily crossed her arms over her chest. "Those bastards," she said. "Trying to get you out of a tight spot."

"Nice that they care," Bruno observed. "I could use the support."

"Yeah. And speaking of which. If you're going to get cozy with the McClouds, make it count. It's time you and Kev's brothers got your ya-yas out with each other."

His brows knit. "I told you. I've got no problem with them."

"That's a big fat stinking lie," she said. "But I wasn't re-ferring to that, actually. I was talking about the problem they have with you."

He looked blank. "Lily, we don't have time for cryptic bullshit."

She shrugged, shivering. "Nothing cryptic about it. You're jealous of them. They're jealous of you. Isn't that just a big joke? Hah, hah."

"Jealous? Of me? Horseshit. Why should they be?"

She shook her head. "I don't know why. But it's obvious. I'm shocked you haven't noticed it yourself. Probably you're just too self-absorbed right now. The new Bruno, sans charm and all that."

He shrugged a leather coat on over his bristling weapons load. "Is this some subtle form of female mind-fuck torture? To punish me?"

She shook her head. "It's not a male-female thing at all," she said. "It's a gender-neutral thing. Ignore it if you like."

He grunted his disgust. "I like," he said. "We'll save the group therapy for later. There's no time for this emotional crap right now."

She swiped tears from her eyes. "I imagine that refers to me, too?"

"Yeah, it sure does," he said. "Grow up, Lily."

It popped out before she could stop it. "Fuck you, Ranieri."

She regretted it like hell, but of course it was too late.

He'd been turning away, toward the SUV, but at that he turned back, considering her with narrowed eyes for a long moment.

Connor McCloud hit the horn, short but loud. Bruno ig-nored him and stalked over to Lily, grabbed her, and bent her over backward in one of those poster-worthy, soldier-going-off-to-war mega-galactic kisses.

Lily was too startled to resist. All too soon, he lifted his head, stared into her eyes. "I love you, too."

She was speechless. He gave her a crooked smile, like he didn't really expect an answer, and turned to the vehicle.

Blind panic surged. She lunged after him. "Bruno!"

Bruno caught her headlong rush, steadying her. "Yeah?"

Her mouth worked. She couldn't find words for feelings that were just too big, too wide for them. Standard phrases were too small, too flat. Feelings backed up inside her, building pressure in the bottleneck. All that burst out was, "Thanks for the, uh, translation."

The flash in his eyes made her heart thud. "I got it right?"

"Yeah." The word squeezed out, strangled by the burning lump in her throat. "Thanks for not going off, leaving me with that as the last thing I said. It would have sucked." *If you never came back.*

He rubbed his cheek against hers. "Took nerve, you know."

"You'll need nerve, hanging out with me."

And they got sucked into the heart of that apocalyptic kiss again. Her heart bumped like it wanted to jump out of her chest, and her soul ached to braid itself together with his, and the world went away—

Except that the world started honking the car horn and strobing the brights against the garage wall. Smart-asses.

Kev popped open his door. "Hey! Save it for later, Romeo."

Bruno cupped her face, stared into her eyes, breathing hard. His color was high. "Goddamnit," he muttered.

She pulled his face back down, kissed him hungrily. "You be careful out there. Or I'll kill you."

His grin flashed as he got in, and the vehicle was in motion before the door swung shut. Fleeing Bruno's hell-bitch girlfriend's irrational demands. Headlights cut out abruptly. The doors groaned slowly open. The SUV backed out. The doors ground shut again. And her, alone, like an idiot. Wondering if she should have paid more attention to those last moments, riveting every precious detail more deeply into her memory.

Tam stood by the door, closing the little control panel for the garage door. Edie, Kev's fiancée, was in the doorway, too.

"You OK, Lily?" Edie's voice was low and gentle.

Lily shook her head, pressed her hand to her mouth. She heard slippered footsteps padding, and Edie's arm slid around her. "Worried?"

Lily nodded.

"If it's any comfort to you, he's got four of the toughest guys you'll ever meet in that car with him. I'm talking rawhide. I pity the fool who messes with even one McCloud, let alone four of them."

Lily shot her a grateful, if watery smile. Edie applied gentle pressure with her arm, coaxing Lily toward the door. "I know it makes you feel useless," she said. "But you're not. You'll get your chance to have plenty more dangerous adventures before you're through, I bet."

"Hey, hanging out in Zia Rosa's clutches is a dangerous adventure in itself," Tam spoke up, her voice smoky with amusement. "Gird up your loins, girlfriend. That woman is going to take you to pieces."

They squeezed out into the corridor. Edie gave Tam a teasing look. "Seems like you and she get along better these days."

Tam rolled her eyes and indicated her swollen belly. "Of course. I'm engaged in repopulating the earth. So I'm now in the club of people who have the right to exist." She paused and swept her eyes over Edie's long, slender body. "You're not in that club yet, are you?"

Edie made a noncommittal sound. "Don't think so."

Tam turned her gaze on Lily. "How about you? Being careful?"

Lily didn't have a hope in hell of hiding the blush.

Tam smote her brow. "For God's sake. What are you *thinking?*"

"Leave her alone," Edie scolded. "It's a tough time for her. And it's not about thinking, Tam, it's about feeling."

"Feel all you want with your legs in the air and an implant in your arm!" She turned to Lily. "Do you want a morning-after pill?"

Lily faltered, stammering. "Ah . . ."

"Let me tell you something, Lily," Tam said. "I've been on the run for my life alone. I've been on the run for my life with my kid. Alone's better. Running for your life with a kid is hell on earth. Think about it."

Lily nodded, cowed.

Edie frowned at Tam. "Let's change the subject, please," she said. "Come on. Let's go up to the kitchen, make some tea. We can try another one of Zia's cupcakes. She made some with chocolate frosting."

Lily froze in her tracks. "I hate it," she burst out. "I'm here, sipping tea and nibbling cupcakes while Bruno's out there? What, should I maybe crochet a white lace doily while I'm at it?"

Tam and Edie exchanged glances.

Tam spoke, her voice dry. "Shot of bourbon, then?"

That hit her funny bone, hard. Lily laughed until her eyes filled with hot tears, and let them lead her inside.

23

It had started to rain. Hard, half frozen, dripping steadily into the neck of his jacket. His boots were drenched, his feet so cold he couldn't feel them. Bruno pried up another shovelful of rocks and dirt, and flung it up onto the heap of slop that had once been the pile of earth and was now threatening to ooze right back down into the hole from whence it had come. His shoulders burned; the blisters on his hands stung, gloves or no gloves. He wiped sweat off his face with his jacket sleeve, realizing too late that there was mud smeared all over it.

Davy worked alongside him, wrapped in his usual silence. Just monosyllabic grunts when speech was necessary, which, where Davy was concerned was rare. Amazing, that such a verbally challenged dude had managed to court and marry such a smart, pretty woman as Margot McCloud. And father children with her, too. The mind boggled.

All in all, after having worked for ten hours, since five o'clock that morning, with brief pauses for sandwiches, energy bars, and water, Bruno was starting to half hope that the mysterious attackers would put in an appearance. Anything at all would be a nice break from what he was doing, even a pitched gun battle. The hole was waist deep, which was as deep as it would go. They'd hit bedrock a while back and had started digging laterally. It was nine feet wide, almost as long, and still no sign of the pissed-upon bones. And it was filling with water. He'd have to dive for the skeletons soon. Search by Braille with a snorkel. Tony was probably spinning in his own grave. He imagined Tony's rough voice. *Four feet to the right, jerk-offs!*

"Give me the shovel. You go guard. I'll dig." It was Kev,

waterlogged and stoic. He hoisted the rifle, offering it to Bruno. "Go on."

Bruno drove the shovel into the soil, feeling the metal ring against stone. The shock vibrated through his body. He leaned on the shovel and checked his watch. "I've only been at it for forty minutes," he said. "You took a two-hour turn already. Come back in an hour and twenty."

"I asked Tam about your bruises," Kev said. "She said you looked like shit. Get the fuck out of that hole and take the gun."

Bruno met his adopted brother's eyes. "I'm fine. I'd rather dig."

The silence was charged. Then, amazingly, Davy spoke up.

"Well, now. Isn't that just touching as all hell." His gravelly voice dripped irony like a row of icicles.

Kev's gaze slashed over to his older brother. "What?"

Davy flung his shovelful of mud insultingly close to Kev's boots. Kev let himself be spattered to the knees without flinching. He stared down at his oldest brother, waiting for an answer.

Davy straightened, taking his time to shake out stiffened muscles. "It warms me to the cockles of my heart when you coddle him like that."

Bruno's jaw dropped, but Kev beat him to it. "Coddle?" Kev snarled. "What the fuck? The kid's been fighting for his life!"

"That's just what I mean," Davy said. "The kid. Poor little Bruno who never had a father."

"What?" Bruno burst out. "What does my father or lack thereof have to do with anything?"

But both men ignored him, too busy staring each other down.

"That's not coddling?" Davy asked. "Having a hissy fit when you got Sean's call? Having a tantrum in Tam's kitchen? Cutting short your trip to come rushing home for this smart-assed, ungrateful punk?"

Bruno sucked in air. "Who are you calling a punk?"

Still, both men acted like he wasn't there. Davy stared up out of the hole without even budging his piercing gaze from his brother's. It looked all the more weirdly bright from his mud-daubed face.

Sean slogged up over the rise, looking as happy to be there as all the rest of them. He frowned. "Aren't you supposed to be covering the back slope? We can't get sloppy. Those fuckers will slaughter us."

Kev jerked his chin in Davy's direction. "I'm waiting to hear what his problem is."

Sean took in Davy's expression. "Oh, shit. Now?"

"Now," Kev said.

Davy drove his shovel into the ground with the vibe of a vampire hunter planting a stake in the heart of the undead. "I've been trying to figure it out for the last few hours. I have a theory now."

"Let's hear it," Kev said.

Davy arched back, staring at the sky. "When Margot was pregnant with Jeannie, there was this album she played to calm her down when she had morning sickness."

"Yeah?" Bruno prodded. "And this tender domestic detail is relevant to this situation exactly how?"

"You shut up," Davy said to him. "I'm not talking to you."

"Oh," he muttered. "Sorry! I forgot. I'm just that insignificant, ungrateful, coddled punk."

Kev gave him a "shut up" arm wave. "Go on," he commanded.

Davy stripped off muddy gloves, wiped his face with the backs of his hands. "So she's not pregnant anymore," he went on. "But whenever she hears that music, she turns green. Even though it was her favorite."

Kev waited, a muscle twitching in his jaw. "Bummer. And? So?"

"So the last time I dug a grave in the woods, it was yours."

The words hung in the air, like some evil charm, turning them all to stone. They stood, unmoving, as the rain lashed down.

Connor limped out over the rise and gaped at them. "All here? Together? If those bastards corner us in this hole and mow us all down like assholes, we have no one to blame but ourselves."

No one countered his scold. Connor's eyes went narrow, wary.

"So what are you doing here?" Bruno asked.

Connor glanced at his watch. "Relieving him." He indicated Davy. "He's been at it two full hours. That was the plan, right? Taking turns?"

No one moved. "What the hell is going on?" Connor yelled.

"I'm still waiting for the theory," Kev said.

"I'm just contemplating the power of association," Davy said. "Digging a grave, in the woods, in the rain. It was raining then, too. In August. A freak storm. And you, burned to a crisp in a box. I'd just flown back from Iraq to dig your fucking grave."

"So?" Kev made an impatient gesture. "So what's your point?"

"No point. It's just that doing this particular job makes me want to vomit. And kill someone. Not necessarily in that order."

Kev's throat worked. The rain pissed ceaselessly down.

Bruno cleared his throat. "And, uh . . . the fact that he's now, um, alive? Doesn't that make things, you know . . . better?"

Sean let out a bitter laugh. "That's just it. It should have made things better. But it doesn't seem like things have changed that much."

Kev looked like he was braced for a blow. "Changed from what?"

"From when you were dead," Sean said.

Bruno bore that silence for about ten seconds. "Uh, I'll take that rifle and go do guard duty. You talk this private stuff out with your—"

"Shut up, or I'll rip off both your arms," Kev snarled.

Bruno winced. "Ah. Yeah. Right. Whatever."

"See? That's just what I'm talking about!" Sean pointed at Bruno. "You're alive to him! You rip his face off all the time!"

Bruno gaped at him. "And this is a good thing for you? A desirable thing? What are you, a goddamn masochist?"

Kev was too agitated to scold him about mouthing off again. "What the fuck do you guys want from me?" he bellowed.

"I don't know!" Sean roared back. "I just can't feel you! I can't reach you! It's been too long, I guess. All those years of forgetting about us. Out of sight, out of mind, right? But with you, it's out of mind, and therefore, out of everything! You no longer give a shit! Mr. Zen! Supercalm! Floating along, no worries! Fucking yay for you, man!"

Kev put the rifle down, walked over, and grabbed the front of his twin's jacket. "You *idiot*," he hissed. "You don't know what you're talking about."

"Then tell me, already!" Sean flung back. "I'd love to hear it!"

Kev shook Sean, a rattling shake that snapped his brother's head back. "I was brain damaged! Do you get that? Does that sink in to your thick skull? I didn't do it to hurt your tender little feelings, brother."

Sean's fist whipped up, whacked into the underside of Kev's jaw and sent him reeling back, slipping on one knee into the mud.

"Guess what," he said. "My feelings aren't little. Brother."

Then Kev was airborne, and they were off and at it.

Bruno watched with horrified fascination. Watching Kev in combat was always a spectacle, but those two men were so perfectly matched it was like watching Kev fight himself. One got in a foot jab to the thigh. The other whipped it around, torqueing the leg and sending them both toppling into the pit. The men landed with a muddy splat.

Bruno lunged toward them. Davy and Connor grabbed him.

"Let them have at it," Davy said. "They need it."

Bruno twisted back to stare at them. "How about you guys? Are you all going to need a turn to kick his ass? There's only one of him."

Connor and Davy did the is-this-coddled-baby-punk-for-real eye roll. "Shut up," Connor said again.

Bruno jerked his arms free, jabbed an elbow into Davy's ribs, got in a kick to Connor's bad knee. Both men jerked back, looking as startled as if some plastic mannequin had come unexpectedly to life and belted them one. Bruno drew the H&K, aimed it at them. "The next guy who tells me to shut up gets a bullet to the kneecap," he said. "Clear?"

Davy and Connor exchanged glances. They nodded.

Good. That was settled and about fucking time. Bruno walked to the edge of the pit and stared at the writhing, yelling knot of McCloud twins wallowing at the bottom of it. Dickheads. Maybe they did need this. Too bad. They could beat the crap out of each other in some other mud wallow, if mud wrestling was so therapeutic. They didn't need to do it on the bones of Mamma's assassin.

He pointed the H&K at the sky and fired. *Bam*.

They stopped writhing, staring up at him with identical, shocked looks as the gunshot echoed through the mountains.

"What the fuck?" one of them spat out. Kev, he presumed.

Bruno went for Kev's trademark steely glare. "You assholes cool it," he said. "This isn't the time or place to—oh, *fuck me . . .*"

The soggy ground gave way under his feet, collapsing, and he slipped and slithered right into the mud wallow, landing with a gloppy splash, his body sliding 'til it was half on top of the other men.

Aw, man. This shit always happened to him when he tried to act authoritative. He spat out mud and addressed Sean. At least, he hoped it was Sean. Who knew with identical mud-men. "Lily told me that you guys were jealous of me. I didn't believe her. She thought it was funny. Me, jealous of you guys. You guys, jealous of me. What a joke, huh?"

The mud-men looked at each other. One of them twisted around to stare at Davy and Connor, thereby identifying himself as Kev.

Davy and Con stared back, stone-faced. Not denying it, though.

"Jealous?" Kev's voice cracked. "Of Bruno? That is so fucked up!"

Sean struggled up to his feet. "It's true, I guess," he said. "I wanted so bad to find you, all those years. To have that connection again. And don't get me wrong, I was glad when we found you. Ecstatic, even. But you're just so . . . so damn polite." He sounded puzzled and exhausted. "I just wanted to get through the Plexiglas wall." He waved his hand towards Bruno. "You don't block him out. Just us."

"He's had you for his brother for about as long as we did," Connor said from behind them. "And it seemed to count for more."

Kev shook his head. He tried to climb out of the pit, but the edge collapsed under his knees and sent him slipping down again.

"I don't know how to explain it," he said, his voice halting.

"You don't have to." Davy looked embarrassed. "We shouldn't have done this to you. We know it's hard. It's OK. Forget it."

Kev ignored him. "The Zen thing. The calm thing. Back after what happened with Osterman, I couldn't talk, or sleep, or think. My brain wires were cut. I was trapped in a nightmare. I damped my feelings all down, or I would have gone nuts. I don't have a manual off switch for that. I can't just stop doing it on command."

"OK, fine," Connor said hastily, holding up his hands. "Please. It's OK. You don't have to harrow yourself all up for—"

"Shut up!" Kev barked. "You asked for it, you get it!"

"Uh. Yeah." Connor subsided, cowed.

"I did miss you guys!" Kev stared at each brother in turn. "I just couldn't get a grip on what I was missing. I was scared shitless but didn't know of what. I wanted to run, but I had nowhere to go. I was a mess. Chilling out . . ." He waved his arms. "It was a survival thing. I didn't mean to freeze you guys out. But calm was the way I had to be. It doesn't mean I don't care. It doesn't mean I wasn't glad to find you."

Sean pressed mud slime out of his long hair from between his fingers and flung the goop, grimacing. "What about him?" he asked, glancing at Bruno. "How'd he get to be exempt from the big freeze?"

Kev looked at Bruno and let out a snort. "You guys need to understand something about Bruno," he began.

Oh, shit and yikes. Bruno braced himself and waited.

"Bruno saved my ass," Kev announced. "I would never have learned to talk again without him. I would never have made it at all without him. So if you give a shit about me, you owe him. That's all."

Bruno was startled and moved. "Aw," he said to break the embarrassed silence that followed. "You're warming the cockles of this coddled, ungrateful punk's heart!"

Kev slanted him a speaking look. "Zip it, Bru."

"Maybe there's hope for you yet." Sean's habitual cheerfulness was rising back up. "Something tells me Edie's exempt from the big freeze, too. Maybe the glaciers are starting to shrink. Who knows?"

"Don't tell me you're jealous of her, too?" Kev looked hunted.

"Oh, shut the fuck up," Sean snapped. "I love you, man, OK? I missed you. Is that so hard to take? Does that scare you so damn bad?"

Kev looked away. "No," he said quietly. "It doesn't scare me. I missed you, too. All of you. It was a really long eighteen years."

Bruno looked at all four men in turn. Seconds passed. Nothing.

His disbelief grew. That was it? That was all? Oh, for the love of Christ. These guys were emotional retards, every last one of them.

"And now it's over," he prompted, loudly. "And that's great, right? Are we OK now? Everybody happy? Can we move on?"

Connor looked like he wanted to tell Bruno to shut up again, but he swallowed it back with some effort. "Amen to that," he said.

"Yeah," Davy agreed. Loquacious, as always.

"So we're done?" Kev looked at Sean. "Do I still need to rip off a limb to show you that I care? You really put me in the mood."

Sean's grin flashed white against the grime on his face. "I'm OK."

Kev turned his gaze on Con and Davy. "How about you guys? Knee to the groin, anybody? A couple of broken ribs? Anyone?"

Connor and Davy both looked like they were trying not to smile.

"No, thanks. We're good," Connor said politely.

"All right! Group hug!" Bruno held up dripping, muddy

arms. "C'mon, you guys! Hug 'em, Kev! Loosen up, everybody! Feel the love!"

A sound jerked out of Davy that might actually have been laughter as he looked at the foully mud-slimed Kev.

"Keep your distance, man," he warned. "You are disgusting."

"Aw, what's a little mud? You guys are so repressed," Bruno complained. "Those sticks, rammed up your butts. Hurts to watch!"

Connor turned to Kev. "How do you stand him?" he asked.

Kev propped his hands on his knees to spit out mud, laughing. "I have no idea. Dad would have knocked us all upside the head if he'd overheard this conversation."

"True," Sean said. "But Dad was no poster child for psychological and emotional health. Being schizo, and all."

"How about Tony?" Bruno offered. "The drill sergeant ex-mafioso, who shot guys in the head and plugged holes in the ground with them?"

"Our role models." Sean's voice was sentimental. "They made us the men we are today. Doesn't it just give you a warm, fuzzy feeling?"

Bruno's chest jerked with laughter. He braced his arm on the new lip of the hole where the mudslide had begun. He tried to drag his thighs up out of the sucking mud—

And stopped.

A human skull stuck out of the new muddy wall of the pit. It was held in place by plant rootlets and thick clods of earth. It looked at him sideways, grinning around a mouth full of dirt and stones.

As Bruno watched, it detached itself from the mud wall and rolled gently down the muddy slope, right into his hand.

He lifted it up, took a look. The jaw was no longer attached, but there was no mistaking that missing left eyetooth and the gold in the top molars. He'd seen those gold teeth a lot, when the guy had been screaming his beery breath into Bruno's face.

There was a hole in the forehead between the brow protrusions.

"Hey, Rudy," he said quietly.

"No way." Lily breathed the words out, horrified. "Your heart?"

Sveti, the waif-like girl who was hosted by Tam and Val to go to school in America, nodded from her perch on one of Tam's sofas. "Yes, my heart, my liver, my kidneys, and corneas, and other things." Her lilting voice had a faint Ukrainian accent. "They saved me just in time. Nick, Tam, the McClouds, and Alex, too. There was big fight. The heart transplant patient was in next room, waiting for her new heart."

Lily noticed the butter cookie in her hand. Heart shaped. She put it down on her napkin, her appetite gone. "So, ah, what happened to her? The heart transplant patient? Did they prosecute her?"

Sveti's dark lashes swept down over the violet shadows around her dark eyes. "No. She died. She was only fifteen. She couldn't wait anymore. She was gone by the time police came."

Lily's belly contracted. "That's awful."

"It wasn't her fault," Sveti said quietly. "She could barely speak. It was her parents who would have killed me to save her. And the people who took me, and Rachel and the others."

"Rachel?" Lily's eyes widened, and she looked at Tam. "You mean, your Rachel? Your little girl? She was . . ."

"Held captive by organ traffickers, yes." Tam's voice was hard. "Rachel was two, three. Bought from an orphanage like a pound of meat. An orphanage which has since closed, its operators nowhere to be found, or else they would be dead. I would see to it. Personally."

"Most of children were like me, though," Sveti added. "Children of people who had offended the Vor."

Lily shivered in spite of the warm sweater and the hot tea. "Are the people who did this all in jail?"

"Some are dead. Nick and Becca killed the Vor and some of his people. The others are in jail, and I hope they stay there forever."

"Me, too," Lily said, with feeling. "What about the parents of the girl who needed the heart?"

Sveti's mouth flattened. "They got off free. They pretended they did not know organ donor was still alive. They were very, very rich."

Lily considered that. "They'll pay," she said.

Sveti shrugged. "By having lost their daughter? They would have lost her anyway. But never mind. I try not to think about them. I work, I study, I plan future. I take exam tomorrow to test out of first year in university if I am lucky. I have better things to think about now."

Lily gazed at Sveti, who was staring out at the ocean. Two entire walls of the huge room were floor-to-ceiling windows looking out on miles of desolately beautiful shoreline in both directions and a sea of tossing conifers. Sveti stared at it without seeing it. The girl seemed both so young and so old. Slaving at two different jobs in Seattle to save money for school. Studying all night long. A shadow hung over her in spite of her youth and beauty. Lily knew all about shadows, and hard work.

She glanced around at the others. Liv was there, Sean's wife, stretched out on a chaise lounge, and Tam, sipping a mug of tea, a cross-legged pregnant Madonna holding court in the middle of one of the couches. Edie sprawled on the floor by a big, low wooden coffee table, her head propped on her elbow, doodling in a sketchbook. Her dark hair made a pool of swirling waves on the sand-colored carpet beneath her head.

The sun was low in the sky, and she'd heard stories from

each one of those women that would have curled her hair if it had not already been frizzed by coastal humidity. Evil geniuses wielding horrific mind-control devices, slavering mafiya vors, organ thieves, mysterious psychic powers, stolen babies, whee-haw. It was hard to take it all in.

She blew out a breath. "If you guys were trying to make me feel like my problems are trivial, you have almost, *almost* succeeded. The difference is that your horror stories are all behind you. I can't tell you how much I envy you all that small but important detail."

Tam nodded. "Can't blame you. But look at us. All in one piece. Living proof that you can get through your horror story, too."

A chill shuddered through her in spite of the fire on the hearth. Afternoon was winding down to evening. Still no word from Bruno. Just texts from Kev saying that the excavation was proceeding and no attacks yet. Bruno had no time to hold her hand while he dug up the skeletons of his mother's killer. Give the guy a flipping break already.

Val appeared in the doorway, holding Liv's squirming son, Eamon, in his arms. He cuddled the baby as he strode in, nuzzling the blond curls as he approached Liv's chaise lounge.

"He's showing off," Tam said. "The nonverbal message is, look what a real man I am in touch with my feminine side. Look and drool."

A dimple quivered in Val's lean cheek as he passed the baby to Liv. "He woke up from his nap and wanted that substance that only you can provide," he said.

Liv took him with a smile and opened her sweater. The baby fastened onto her breast with hungry suckling piglet sounds, gripping with fat little fists, eyes closed in a state of divine bliss.

Val turned to Tam. "Rachel woke from her nap, too," he said. "She's in the kitchen with Zia Rosa. Making biscuits."

Tam harrumphed. "That woman is going to kill us with food."

"Yes, but we will die happy and fat," Val said. "There are worse ways to go. She is preparing osso buco and roasted rosemary potatoes. And speaking of food, how long has it been since you ate lunch?"

Tam's eyes were golden slits. "An entirely appropriate interval."

"Eat a cookie," he commanded. "You need the calories. The obstetrician said so. Remember? Last Tuesday, at the ultrasound?"

"Don't fuss," she said.

He chose a pink-frosted star. "You are accustomed to starving yourself. Your perceptions about food are not reliable. Eat a cookie." He pressed a cookie into her hand and curled her fingers around it.

"I ate a perfectly adequate lunch," she said. "I said, don't fuss."

He crossed his arms, defiant. "Or what?"

"Or I'll break both your legs," she warned.

"Bah," he scoffed. "That is nothing. Bones knit together. You know that better than anyone. Eat a cookie for Irina."

A strange look flashed across Tam's face. "We talked about this," she said. "Please don't call her by name. Not yet. It's bad luck."

"It's all right," he said softly. "Our luck is good now."

"Don't push it," she said.

He considered that. "I will not push it if you eat the cookies."

Tam rolled her eyes, lips twitching. "So it's cookies, plural, now?"

"To buy my compliance, yes," he said. "Two."

"One," she countered. "I will not be bullied. Get out. This is a hen party. No one with a penis is invited. Except for Eamon. He can stay."

Val looked hurt. "You mean, you do not want to hear the tale of my valiant fight to save you and Rachel from the forces of evil?"

"Out." Tam leaned over her belly and gave his hip a shove.

"Two cookies," he repeated, backing out of the room.

Tam took a bite of the cookie after he left. "He's very nervous," she explained to Lily, patting her belly. "We lost a couple, before."

"I'm sorry," Lily said.

Tam acknowledged her words with a nod as she chewed. "To be honest, we can't quite believe we've gotten this far," she said. "I never thought I'd have kids. I wasn't the type. Then Rachel happened. And I had some organ damage from the poison in that incident that I told you about, so I thought probably nothing, in terms of babies. Which would have been fine. We have Rachel, and she counts for three. But voilà, here she is. Our little surprise." Her face tightened. "So far."

"How far along are you?" Lily asked.

"Twenty-eight weeks." Tam petted her belly, wincing. "Ouch. She's a wild thing today. But I like her that way."

"Twenty-eight weeks," Lily said. "That's almost home free, right?"

"Almost," Tam agreed. "Almost." She leaned to grab another cookie but couldn't reach them over the bulge of her belly. Edie sat up and passed a green-frosted four-leaf clover to her. "Here," she said. "For luck. I thought you didn't want two cookies. After all that carrying on."

"Oh, I'll probably eat four more. I just say no to him on principle," Tam confided. "If I give in to him at all, he becomes insufferable. Basic Val management." She lifted her cookie, as if toasting the women in the room. "To luck." She took a bite, frowning as she chewed, and directed her next words at Edie. "But wait. You're psychic. What are you, clairvoyant? How can you believe in luck if you can see the future?"

Edie shook her head. "Oh, no. I'm a big believer in luck."

"Maybe Edie should do a drawing for Lily," Liv suggested. "She could use some new fonts of information, don't you think?"

Lily fidgeted. Edie's tale had been as harrowing as any of the others, what with her and Kev's struggle against the mind-control freaks, but the psychic part was hard for her to swallow. She was pragmatic by nature. "Please don't take this personally," she said to Edie. "But I just don't know how useful that could be for me. I don't really believe in that psychic stuff. I'm very sorry."

Edie patted Lily's knee. "Don't be," she said. "I'm not hurt."

"You're not?"

Edie licked all the frosting off her fingers before she answered.

"Think of it this way," she said. "If you were watching a sunset, and you were with somebody who had been blind since birth, and this person said to you, 'I'm sorry, but I just don't really believe in pink, or orange, or scarlet, or purple, or violet,' would you take it personally?"

Lily pondered that. "I don't know. Are you saying that I'm blind?"

"Not at all," Edie said. "But if you're not tuned to that frequency, how could you be expected to believe that it exists? What's real for me is still real, whether other people believe in it or not. It used to be so painful when people didn't believe me. But not anymore."

"That's just because finally you're getting regularly laid," Tam pointed out, wisely. "Changes your attitude about so many things."

Edie snorted with laughter, spraying cookie crumbs.

Lily watched the women giggling, thinking about the

sunset. Imagining what it would be like to have never seen it. How these events might be changing her. If love might be able to change her, too. How it would feel to really let it unfold. What she might see, hear, or believe.

She didn't want to be so defensive, so suspicious and cynical. She was never going to get out of this maze if she insisted on blocking out the light. Sveti was watching her, her eyes so wise. A smile was forming on the younger girl's face, transforming it from wanly pretty to beautiful. Lily smiled back. The idea matured into a resolution.

She turned to Edie. "Will you do a reading on me?" she blurted, interrupting what they were saying. "Or, um, a drawing, I should say?"

Edie and Tam looked at her blankly. Edie collected herself. "Ah, of course. I'd be happy to. You have to promise me something, though."

Lily braced herself. "And that is?"

Edie looked like she was choosing her words. "Sometimes I see things people don't want to face. I can't control what comes out of my pencil. I'm just warning you. That you might not like . . . whatever it is."

Lily let out a sigh of relief. That was doable. "No problem," she said. "I've had practice lately dealing with dislikeable things. A bad psychic reading, hey, what's that compared to being shot at?"

"You have a point," Edie said, but she still looked uncertain.

"Don't worry," Lily assured her. "I won't blame you."

"OK, then." Edie rose gracefully to her feet. "I'll go get my big sketchbook. This one's too small. Cramps my style."

"So you, um, need the sketchbook?" Lily asked. "To see things?"

"Not exactly," Edie said. "Before our adventures, the episodes only occurred when I was drawing. Afterward, it was coming at me all the time." She smiled a secret smile.

"Kev helped me, though. We found ways to tamp it down. But I still find having a pencil helps me focus better." She gave Lily a wink. "Want to be my latest experiment?"

"I'm game," Lily said.

Tam looked at her with renewed respect as Edie left the room. "You're a braver woman than I," she said.

"You?" Lily let out a crack of laughter. "Who's braver than you? Get real. You're an ass-kicking bombshell commando. Please."

"But I've never let Edie draw for me," Tam said softly. "I don't want to see the monsters of my past. I prefer that they stay buried."

Lily shivered again. The sun had sunk behind the haze of clouds on the horizon and leached the room of color but for the firelight. "Anything," she said, her voice tight. "I'll look under any rock I can think of to help me beat this."

"Don't scare her," Sveti chided Tam. "I think it is good thing."

"Me, too," Liv said, snuggling her baby closer.

Tam nodded slowly, and a small smile softened her marble perfection. "I didn't mean to dissuade you. It was a compliment."

"Oh. Great. Well, thanks," Lily muttered.

The damage was done, though. She had full-fledged heebie-jeebies by the time Edie came back with charcoal and a large sketchbook. She flipped on a lamp and sat down on the floor a few feet in front of Lily, leafing through the pages until she found a blank one. She bent her leg to prop the sketchbook. "Sure about this?" she asked.

"Uh, yeah." Lily fidgeted. "Do I need to, um, do anything?"

"No," Edie said absently. "Just relax."

"Hah," Lily mouthed. "Right."

"Look out at the ocean," Liv suggested. "Think of something else."

Lily was so nervous, as if bracing for something painful. But the ocean gave her something to focus on. Vast, evocative, and calming.

No one said a word. Edie's charcoal scribbled, scratched, whirred. At one point, Lily gave in to curiosity and peeked at Edie's face.

She looked away, unnerved, although Edie had not seen her. The woman's eyes were lit by an iridescent glow. A trick of the light, shining on her silver-gray eyes. The pencil jerked and scribbled as if it had a life of its own. Lily composed herself with effort, looked back at the ocean.

Time passed. An agonizing amount. And finally, the pencil scratching slowed and stopped.

Lily looked. Edie was gazing at what she'd drawn, looking perplexed. Tam, Sveti, and Liv peered over her shoulder, fascinated.

"So?" Lily's voice was sharp. "What is it?"

Edie chewed on her lip, frowning for a moment. "I have no idea," she said. "I don't know what to make of it. Maybe you will."

Lily rose to her feet and realized, to her embarrassment, that her knees were too rubbery to bear her weight. She covered the defect by plopping onto her knees and then her butt next to Edie on the floor. Her teeth were chattering. "Let me see." She held out her hand.

Edie passed her the sketchbook. Lily took a deep breath. Looked.

Throbbing hot-cold darkness rose up and blotted out everything.

She was lying on her side. They were yelling her name from far away. Hands shaking her. Patting her face. Bit by bit, she came back. Edie and the rest were crouching over her, their faces anxious.

"I'm OK," she croaked, trying to push herself up. "Sorry."

"Rest," Tam said sharply. "Lie down. Just rest and breathe."

"Let me look at it again." Lily kept struggling.

Tam shoved her down. "No," she snapped. "I said to rest."

"And I said to let . . . me . . . *look!*" Lily sat upright, shoved the woman's hands away, and grabbed the sketchbook from Sveti's hands.

It set her heart thudding, but she didn't faint this time. Same image. Still there. She rubbed her eyes, still not trusting them.

A woman's face, in her sixties. Beautiful in a subtle way. Strong bones, well-cut mouth. Smiling. And her eyes. Oh, God, her eyes. They stared up out of the paper, straight at Lily. Soft with tenderness. With love. Lily covered her mouth with her hand as tears streamed down.

"Oh, my God," she whispered, rocking. "Oh, my God."

The other women waited patiently, and finally Tam's patience snapped. "For the love of God, Lily!" she burst out. "Who is it?"

"My mother," Lily whispered.

The others exchanged rapid, questioning looks. "Your mother. We never talked about your mother," Tam said, delicately. "Is she, ah . . ."

"Dead? Yes. Twenty-nine years ago, almost. The day I was born." Lily couldn't tear her eyes from the drawing. "She looks about the age she'd have been now. If she'd lived."

There was a dumbfounded silence.

"You're sure?" Liv asked.

Lily nodded. "There were pictures of her all over the house. My father was an amateur photographer. She was his favorite subject. I stared at those pictures for hours when I was a kid. But I never saw one where she looked like she was looking at me. Seeing me. Oh, God." She sniffed, almost angrily. "What is she doing here?" she burst out. "What does she have to do with anything? She never even knew me!"

Tears came down. Lily shoved the sketchbook away. She didn't want to risk splashing it with tears and smudging such a precious, astonishing thing. She buried her face in her hands. It roared through her, a flash flood of feeling, through a desert that had forgotten what flooding felt like. Grieving for a mother she'd never known seemed senseless, but there was no arguing with feelings that literally knocked her to the floor. The other women gathered around her in a protective cluster of warm bodies, stroking hands on her back, her hair.

"She did, too, know you," Tam said fiercely.

Lily peered up at her, sniffling. "Huh?"

"Your mother. She knew you perfectly well. And she still does." Tam grabbed Lily's hand and laid it on her belly just as the baby inside rolled and flopped. "You think I don't know this little girl? I know her, and she knows me. But the knowledge is on those other frequencies. The ones we think we can't tune into, but we can. You just did. You know your mother. Or why would you be crying?"

Lily laughed, soggily. "Oh, stress? Abandonment issues?"

"Stop being a smart-ass," Edie scolded and gave her a hug that set Lily off again. Then Sveti lunged in. The girl felt as delicate as a baby bird, but her grip was strong. "She wants you to know she's watching over you. That she loves you," Sveti whispered. "I am so happy for you."

Then it was Liv's turn, with Eamon squirming in between them, grabbing Lily's hair and trying to climb it, ouch. More hugs. More tears.

It was a long time before Lily could wipe her face and look at the drawing again. With wonder, fear. Something approaching holy awe.

For some reason, it made her heart lighter. Reminded her of a feeling she hadn't felt since she was young. Breathless wonder.

Tam tilted her chin up and smiled into her eyes. "I'm glad it turned out well for you," she said. She patted her belly. "Time to feed the fetus. Val said something about osso buco, right? And something tells me that you nonpregnant ladies could all use a glass of red wine."

Lily let out a watery giggle. "I can't think about food right now."

"You will when you smell it, trust me," Liv informed her.

Edie draped her arm over Lily's shoulders. They trooped out into the corridor, Lily clutching Edie's sketchbook. "I feel like I've just seen pink and purple for the first time," Lily told her. "Can I keep it?"

"Oh, God, yes," Edie said. "It's yours. Just let me spray some fixative on it so it won't smear. We'll get it framed for you, if you like."

"I would like," she said, tears welling. "I'll treasure it forever."

The other women exchanged delighted glances.

"Well, now," Liv said softly. "Listen to that. Excellent."

"To what?" Lily glanced around at them, bewildered.

"Talking about forever," Edie said. "That's a very good sign."

"Forever is a long time," Tam said, smiling. "Long enough for children, grandchildren, great-grandchildren."

"They'll pass that picture down through the generations," Liv said. "They'll tell the story of their ancestress, contacting her mother across the void between life and death, and invoking her protection."

Fanciful, but Lily liked the sound of it. The feeling inside her was so strange. It took a while to pin a name to it. She couldn't be sure.

But maybe it was hope.

24

The coffee was stone cold, and so was he. Bruno spat out the bitter liquid, wiped his mouth. He could hear it on the airwaves, the other men silently wondering how to break it to him about the point of diminishing returns. He took a bite of the peanut butter and chocolate–flavored energy bar, but the lump of soy protein and corn syrup just sat there in his mouth, dry and inert. He was too damn tired to chew.

He stared down at the unbeautiful fruits of their labors. Three skeletons, laid on a tarp, their bones more or less in order, since Kev of course knew the position of every bone in the human skeleton, of which there were hundreds. Kev also had some sixth sense that allowed him to distinguish a muddy, rodent-gnawed metatarsal from a twig or a rock. The fingers on the corpses' right hands, of course, were not there. Tony had chopped them off, sent them to the Ranieris. Clothes had long since rotted away. They'd searched the earth around each torso, combing through every pebble, every grain of sand. No locket.

He'd gone over so much dirt, particularly the dirt packed around Rudy's bones. First with the metal detector. Then sifting each individual handful. He'd gone over it and over it. His fingertips were sore.

The skeletons seemed so small. He remembered huge ogres. Now they were a fragile bundle of dirty sticks. Beaten with the rain.

Grim and sad. And ominous.

Bruno crouched and studied Rudy's mocking grin, or the top half of it, as if it could tell him something. The other men had been shot in the back of the head, execution style. Not Rudy. Tony had wanted to look the guy in the eyes as he pulled the trigger.

Kev appeared over the rise and approached the fallen tree upon which Bruno was sitting. He sat next to him. His silence said it all. The sun was down. The clouds were rolling in. Fog wreathed the trees. Night would fall soon. They'd been at it for fourteen hours. This was nuts.

He got that. But it made him so frustrated he wanted to kill.

"So," Kev began.

"Don't," Bruno snarled. "Don't start. I know."

Kev's eyebrow quirked. "What did you think I was going to say?"

Bruno dropped his head into his hands. "Don't want to hear it."

Kev sat there and didn't say it. "I just went up onto the bluff," he remarked after a while. "Called Edie."

"Yeah? So?"

"They were eating dinner," Kev said.

"Oh. Well. Bully for them."

"Osso buco," Kev said dreamily. "Rosemary potatoes, *insalata Calabrese*, with hothouse tomatoes and sweet red onion. Herbed asiago biscuits. And a nice, fruity *primitivo di Manduria* to wash it all down."

Bruno looked at the energy bar and spat the gluey, unchewed lump out. "You fucking sadist," he said. "What did I do to deserve that?"

"It was just for fun. Did I mention the chocolate cream pie?"

"You can't treat me like this," Bruno complained. "You said I saved your ass, right? Remember? You owe me."

Kev's grin flashed. "Don't let it go to your head."

"No worries. Nothing's more humbling than digging up corpses."

They let that happy thought hang in the air for a while. Kev spoke again. "Edie did a drawing." His voice was elaborately casual. "For Lily."

Bruno sat bolt upright. "One of her special ones? No shit?"

"Absolutely none," Kev said.

Bruno practically bounced with eagerness. After the zombie masters adventure, he was a big believer in Edie's supernatural abilities. "And? So? What did she see? What did she draw?"

Kev's mouth twitched. "Your mother-in-law."

Bruno gaped at him stupidly. "Eh?"

"You heard me," Kev said. "She drew a portrait of Lily's mom."

"But . . . but . . ." Bruno trailed off, baffled. "But the woman's been dead ever since Lily was—"

"Yeah, I know. Weird, isn't it? Edie was blown away. Lily, too. She couldn't stop crying, Edie said. It was super intense."

Bruno stared down at the skeletons. Steam backed up between his ears. He got up, paced to blow some of it off before his head exploded. "Super intense," he said. "Yay for dear old Mom. And completely and totally fucking useless, for all practical purposes. Why couldn't she have drawn a picture of the bastard who's doing this to us? Holding up his business card? With a Google map?"

Kev looked away to hide his smile, but Bruno sensed it from the shape of the crinkles at his temples. "Sorry," he said meekly. "The mysterious powers of my magic lady friend cannot be commanded."

"Great!" Bruno yelled it toward the sky. "Just great! The spirits from beyond rouse themselves to contact us, and what do I get? A picture of my late future mother-in-law! I need a fucking *break!*"

He punctuated the statement with a violent kick aimed at a chunk of rotten log that had been lying on some of the bones. They'd been forced to excavate it, hoist the thing out. It split into two pieces, rotten as a sponge, but the blow still sent a jarring *thwang-g-g-g* of pain shuddering up his leg. He shook the sore foot, feeling stupid.

Kev, being a genius and all, was smart enough to grasp that now was not the time for more bullshit. He picked up a metal detector and went back to his piece of dirt. God, how Bruno loved the guy for that.

Sean, too, soldiered grimly on. Raking the mud they had displaced so they could search it again. The men's movements were heavy with exhaustion. Davy and Con were out circling. Nobody said a word. He realized, with a heavy feeling in his guts, that he, Bruno Ranieri, had to be the one to call it quits. It was his life at stake, his locket, his dead mamma, his skeletal ogres, his girlfriend in danger. They were deferring to him. Nobody wanted to let him down.

The weight of the responsibility made him feel vaguely sick.

He checked his watch. Two minutes left of the ten-minute break he was allowing himself. He closed his eyes, saw mud-stained skeletons dancing, leering. An elusive glint of gold. He forced himself to think it through again. It could have fallen out of Rudy's pocket at any point in his rough journey here. It could have been dug up by an animal, carried off by a magpie or a squirrel who mistook it for a new kind of nut.

And after eighteen years, whatever could possibly be in it would be degraded beyond recognition. Anything on paper would be a blackened crust of mold. And what else could it be in such a small space?

This whole effort was probably a stupid waste of time.

Even so. He wanted it, damnit. He wanted to shine up Mamma's locket and put it on, so he could touch it. A tangible link to her. The thought of recovering it had taken hold in his mind. He couldn't let go.

He sank down on the log and stared at the bones. Unfair of him to get in a snit with Lily and Edie for taking the time out to have a tender extrasensory moment with her own mom. He shouldn't begrudge her that. At least he had some memories of Mamma in life.

Still. Jesus wept. A little practical help would have been so nice. If an entity was going to go to the trouble of crossing the great chasm between life and death, one would think it might try to multitask a little.

Whatever. Dead folks. Who the fuck knew what their agenda was, out there beyond the veil. Speculating about it made his head ache.

He rubbed his eyes, got grit in them. They started watering, and suddenly, oh, *shit*. He was hunched over, silently sobbing.

Oh, please. Those guys had already pegged him as a coddled baby punk. Sniveling when he didn't get the prize out of the cereal box. But he kept thinking about that hug from Mamma in the bus station at midnight. The locket, burning against his chest from her vital heat.

Mamma, where's the fucking locket, already?
Watch your language, you little punk.

He dashed tears away. First thing he saw was a beetle, trundling in the mud. He was brown, with a broad carapace and humongous waving pincers that meant business.

Tears turned to shaky laughter. Behold, the respectable country relative to the skanky urban cockroach. His appointed job to shred stuff and turn it into dirt. He wondered if this little dude's ancestors had provided that very personal service for Rudy and his thugs.

Mamma had loathed the cockroaches that had infested their tenement apartment. She'd waged a constant war with them, poison, traps. It was useless, but she never gave up. She didn't know how. That was Mamma for you. No off switch.

And it was time to move his ass, since the others were still moving theirs. Still, his eyes followed the bug as it bustled around the obstacles in its path. It climbed onto the rotten log that he had split, stopping at the top, at the sharp angle where the porous wood had been freshly broken. The wood was muddy on the outside, a reddish color inside.

What a fine-looking bug. Shiny and tough looking. He watched it, almost affectionately. He was punch-drunk, admiring insects. Fourteen hours of digging for bones did that to a guy. At least the bug was alive.

He was tempted to pick the little guy up, go ask Kev what kind of beetle he was, but that would be dumb and irrelevant, and they would be justified in slamming him hard. He'd had enough of that today.

He went over, crouched down to take a final look—and saw it.

Like a muddy piece of string, hanging out of a crack in the side of the log. He'd have taken it for dead grass, but a blade of grass would poke off in any old direction. This hung straight down in a plumb line.

Like a fine metal chain.

Bruno gently nudged the beetle off its perch so he could work his fingers into the spongy crevice. It scuttled and turned, looking up at him and waving its pincers madly.

"Sorry," Bruno muttered, wedging his cold, stiff fingers deeper, prying, prodding, flexing . . . and the rotten wood gave way, disintegrating in his hand. He held up the handful of wood pulp.

Mamma's locket was nestled in it.

He stared down at it, afraid to breathe. As if it might vanish into a puff of dust, but it was cold and hard and solid. Dirt was ground into the delicate relief work on the pendant, but otherwise it looked intact.

He looked down at the beetle, who was still watching him, gesticulating with pincers and front legs. All indignant.

His eyes were awash again. "Thanks, little buddy," he whispered.

He rose up, walked over to where Sean and Kev were working. He tried to call them, but his voice was thickened with emotion.

Kev glanced over. His eyes went wide as they zoomed in on Bruno's outstretched, clutching hand. "You found it," he said.

The other men crowded around him, peering at the object in his hand. Kev gripped his shoulder, his grimy face worried. "You OK?"

"I am now," Bruno croaked. "It was stuck in a crack in that rotten log. A bug showed me." That sounded so dumb. He didn't give a shit.

"May I?" Sean's hand hovered over his, awaiting permission.

Bruno nodded, let the other man pluck it from his palm.

Sean peered at it and tried opening it. "It's been sealed, but there are hinges," he said. "We could break it open with my blade."

They crouched around the black plastic tarp that held the skeletons. Bruno accepted Sean's blade, hesitating. He hated to break the precious thing, but his head would pop if he had to wait until tomorrow to open it. Mamma would understand. Hell, impatience had been one of her defining characteristics.

He slipped the tip of the blade in the seam between the tiny hinges, squinting in the dim light, until the point disappeared. He nudged it deeper, applied pressure, firmly . . . and *crack*, it snapped. Something thudded onto the plastic, a shapeless black wad. Bruno checked the inside. The two pieces were black with mold. Nothing else.

He slipped the delicate gold bits into his jeans pocket and leaned forward, prodding at the tiny wad with the tip of the knife. The back of it was some sort of fibrous, fuzzy material. The front was a layer of black gunk, which crumbled into flakes as he poked it. In between was something small, hard. Irregular. He scraped at it until the shape became clear. His throat tightened. He picked up the tiny thing, rubbing it between his fingers, scraping with his fingernails, until the black shreds came away. A tiny key, made of pure gold.

He knew this key. And his heart sank.

"What is that stuff?" Kev asked.

Bruno tapped the fuzzy stuff. "My baby hair," he said. "And this, that used to be my baby picture. And this . . ." He held up the key. "A key to a hidden compartment in my mother's jewelry box. Another courting gift from my *bisnonno* to my *bisnonna*, like the locket. There's a panel you slide aside, and behind it is a lock to a false bottom."

"And you have this jewelry box in your possession?" Sean asked hopefully. "It's a family heirloom, right? Does Zia Rosa have it?"

Bruno's shoulders sagged. "I don't have it. Zia doesn't, either."

Kev let out a long sigh. Sean got up, shook out the kinks in his knees. "Come on, Bruno. You don't know where it might be? No clue?"

"I knew where it was on March 28, 1993, at ten at night, when we left the apartment to go to the bus station," Bruno said. "It was on the bedside table in my room. Mom put it there so that Rudy wouldn't pawn her jewelry. Then we left. And I never saw it again. Or my mother." He shook his head. "Could be anywhere. It's been eighteen years."

It had started to rain again, as if to compound their misery.

Kev laid a hand on his shoulder. "No, not anywhere," he said. "It's in the possession of whoever might have had a right or an interest in collecting your mother's stuff from the apartment after she was killed. That's a select group. A short list, with your Grandma Pina on the top."

"Lovely prospect," Bruno said darkly. "If she doesn't kill me on sight. Or it was stolen by one of our neighbors and traded for crack. Or the super threw it into a Hefty bag, and it ended up in a landfill."

"So? You've got someplace to start. That's more than before."

True enough. At least he had the locket now. A little piece

of Mamma, glinting after twenty long years in the ground. A good-luck amulet. But damn, he wished he had more to show after those four guys had busted their asses all day long on his behalf.

Things moved fast after that. A reservoir of energy had been unearthed along with the locket. Davy and Connor were informed of the new development, and they decided to hell with guard duty, they'd just finish the job and get the hell out of there. It went faster with five working, but not fast enough, not with night coming on.

First, the bones had to go back into the ground. They rolled them into the tarp, and placed them back in the hole, then scraped as much of the dirt they had excavated as they could back into the pit. It was difficult, since they had spread it so much, and rain had liquefied more of it into slop. At the end, the hole was still a sad, sunken mud wallow.

So they collected boulders and laid those on top, as if to weigh down restless spirits. By then, night had fallen, and they were all wearing infrared goggles. When the cairn was knee level, they stopped.

"Satisfied?" Sean asked.

"Almost." Bruno looked at Kev. "You're forgetting something."

Kev let out a bark of laughter. "Oh, yeah. Of course."

Bruno and Kev unbuckled their pants. The rest followed. They hauled 'em out and had a ceremonial collective piss onto the tumbled boulders. Weird effect, with infrared. Hot pee. Cold mud.

It was a struggle, with numb, filthy hands, to get the goods back in order, pants buttoned, belts fastened, but they managed, at length.

"Nella faccia di chi ci vuole male," Bruno said quietly.

"Amen," Kev agreed.

Sean made an irritated sound. "The secret-language bull-shit makes us tetchy. Translation?"

"In the face of our enemies," Kev translated.

Davy nodded. "Yeah."

"Ditto, that," Connor said.

"Can we get the fuck out of here now?" was Sean's poetic offering.

Bruno gathered up shovels, hoisted them up onto his shoulder, while the other men loaded themselves up with the rest of the gear, and took the lead as they headed out over the long, treacherous rockfall.

"Thanks for the help, by the way," he called back. "Real generous of you all to exert yourself for this coddled, ungrateful punk."

Davy snorted with amusement, somewhere behind him. "Oh, for fuck's sake. You still got your panties in a wad about that?"

"Italians are good at holding grudges," Kev called from farther back. "Something in their genes. They get off on it."

"To be fair, you're a little long in the tooth to be a punk." It was Sean, right at his heels as they stumbled and slid across the rockfall.

"I'm gratified that you noticed that," Bruno said.

"Don't be," Sean said. "You know what an aging punk is?"

Bruno sternly choked off his laughter. "What, Sean? What is an aging punk?"

"An asshole," Sean informed him cheerfully.

Bruno considered different responses to that jibe, but he was so damn tired, he just went for the one that used the least amount of breath. "Fuck you, man."

Sean made wet smooching sounds. "Aww. I love you, too, honey."

Bruno stumbled, slipped. Dropped the damn shovels every which way, and slid down the slope for about three meters, arms flailing.

But when he'd drawn back from the brink of death, he was grinning.

* * *

"Not a chance in hell. Not a snowman's chance." Val made a furious gesture toward the group of women by the garage door.

"Snowball." Tam tapped his shoulder from behind, with a long, gleaning black fingernail. "The correct term is, 'snowball's chance in hell,' my love. Get them straight, or don't use idioms at all, please, OK?"

"Snowman, snowball, iceberg, I do not give a shit." Val folded his arms across his chest, radiating unquestionable authority. A skill all the men around this place tended to be scarily good at, Lily had noticed. Bruno being no exception.

"Val, I do not want to miss this exam," Sveti explained. "I have studied for four months for this test, and tomorrow morning is the only testing date. If I do well, I will pass out of freshman year and save, oh, forty thousand dollars that I do not have? Maybe more?"

"I will give you the forty thousand dollars!" Val snarled.

Sveti shook her head. "You are sweet, but you and Tam already give me enough," she said. "I am too much in your debt. Truly, I do not think bad guys will be interested in me and my exam."

"And since she has to go anyway, I might as well ride along. I need to get back to my bookstore," Liv said briskly. "My manager is short-staffed and coming down with the flu. So Edie's coming to help, and Margo and Erin are coming over with the kids tonight, so we can—"

"You are *stupid* to go out now!" Val glared toward the three women gathered at the entrance. Miles slouched in the garage doorway behind them, wearing his habitual long-suffering expression. Baby Eamon was playing enthusiastically with one of Miles's ears, cooing.

"Val, come on," Edie coaxed. "Nobody is after our blood. Sveti just has to take her test. She's worked so hard for this. Life goes on. You can't ground everybody. It's just not practical."

"I do not give a shit about practical. Why do you not call your man? See what opinion he has about this fucking trip to Seattle, hmm?"

Edie sighed. "That would be silly. He's always paranoid. It's just a McCloud thing. We have Miles with us. He's armed. He's tough."

All eyes swung to Miles. He stood up straighter, making an effort to look tougher.

"Why not just wait until the guys get back?" Aaro asked.

"Then I will miss my exam," Sveti said. "I cannot take it again until next year. Please, Val. It is important to me."

"Ah, *shit*," Val muttered. "I cannot even accompany you, not until the rest of the men get back! This is not fair to put me in this position!" He glared at Liv and Edie. "You know very well that Sean and Kev would throw screaming fits if they knew you were taking off without them."

"They can lecture us later," Edie said briskly. "Come on, let's go."

The women slunk out the door. Miles trailed behind, throwing an apologetic, what-can-ya-do-with-'em glance over his shoulder.

Val made an explosive sound of disgust, spun, and stalked away, muttering to himself. Tam hurried to follow him, leaving Lily to stare out, watching the garage door grind shut after the car left, blocking out the rare gleam of real outside air. Rainy and gray though it was today.

Clang. Shut in. In the darkness. As usual. Lily sighed. It was self-indulgent and ungrateful to feel pissy because she was left behind. The little girl who didn't get to go on the school trip, waaahh.

She was grateful for the first three genuinely safe nights in she couldn't even remember how long. She was starting to feel better. But that translated directly into the desire to move, fight back. She wondered when, if ever, she was going to get her life back. Such as it was. It was flawed, sure, but she wanted a chance to make it bloom. Why couldn't she have a chance, too, like everyone else? Restless anger prickled at her like thorns.

This was not the fault of the people around her, of course. They weren't her jailors. In fact, they were the only reason she was still breathing. *Be grateful, damnit.* She took to pacing again.

Fortunately, the house was huge and rambling, with lots of nooks, towers, and overhangs, beautiful details and incredible overlooks, even a walkway like a floating bridge over a sea of green to a different zone in the house. A leisurely stroll through the whole place, stopping to admire each vantage point, genuinely did kill some time.

She ached to have Bruno back. To hear his laughing voice, feel his kiss, his hard, tight embrace, his muscles shaking with emotion.

Not that she'd have him for long. Their brief conversation the night before, when he'd called her from the motel, had settled that issue. Nothing had changed for her, in spite of his having found the next piece of the puzzle. He'd just hare off to the East Coast to dig in his estranged grandmother's attic for some ancient jewelry box, while she stayed here, safely folded flat and hidden in a locked drawer. It was enough to drive an independent woman insane. She'd always had to fight for everything in life. Passivity was counter-intuitive for her.

At least progress had been made, even if she couldn't take credit for it. She'd cling to that. And trust Bruno. It was good practice.

It was getting dark by her third pass through the house. She stopped in the living room, puzzled, when she heard the sound. A voice, raised to a shout. Muffled, just barely audible. A woman's voice. Tam.

Lily ran through room after room, flinging open any door she saw that was closed. "Tam? Tam! Where are you?"

"The bathroom off Val's study." Tam's faint voice filtered through the walls to her right.

Lily blundered in that direction until she found a paneled, book-lined room. She flung open an interior door. Tam lay on the floor on her side, huddled around her swollen belly. Hugging it, as if someone wanted to take it from her. She looked up. Her lips were bluish.

"Call Val, quick," she said. "I'm spotting. Or actually, this is just plain old bleeding, I think, not spotting. Forgot to bring my cell in here with me. Such a goddamn fucking idiot. I'm afraid to get up. Hurry."

"Oh, God." Lily gasped. "Can I . . . should I—"

"Just . . . call . . . *Val!*" Tam's voice was soft, but Lily leaped to action, raced through the house, howling for Val. She ran into him outside the house gym. "Tam's bleeding," she gasped out. "Study bathroom. Hospital. Quick."

"*O cazzo.*" Val spun around. "Aaro!" he bellowed.

Aaro poked his head around the curve in the corridor. "Yeah?"

"We are all going to the hospital, for the baby," Val said. "Now!"

"Ah . . . can't I just stay with them here, while you and Tam—"

"No!" Val was backing down the corridor at a half run. "I cannot leave Lily and Rachel and Zia with one man only to guard! There is no one around here, for miles, and you would be trapped if they came at you with a full crew, like at the cabin! You would be fucked!"

Aaro raced after, with Lily on his heels. "The two of us together would be fucked, too," Aaro pointed out over the pounding of their feet.

"Only one-half as fucked. I do not have time to explain the defense systems. You!" Val stabbed a finger at Aaro. "Get Zia from the kitchen! And you!" He rounded on Lily. "Wake Rachel from her nap. *Run!*"

The tension in Val's voice propelled them like bullets from a gun.

Rachel was not psyched to be woken from her nap, but

Lily flung the child's squirming body over her shoulder. Even with panic to help her, it was a good thing the kid was so small. She snagged Rachel's sneakers and sprinted through the house, yanking the child's coat off the hook outside the garage door. Val was strapping a white-lipped Tam into the back of a black eight-seater van. Alex was at the wheel, engine growling. Zia Rosa sat in the front passenger seat, clutching her purse, staring back at Tam, lips moving as she babbled a litany of prayers.

Lily leaped in, tossing Rachel onto the seat. The vehicle surged forward before she slid the door shut. She got the whimpering Rachel strapped into her booster seat. The conversation came into focus.

". . . is too small for a hospital," Val was saying. "We will have to go to the hospital at Rosaline Creek. Take the Moss Ridge Highway north at Junction Thirteen. Twelve more miles north. Go fast."

Aaro obliged. Gravity slammed Lily back into her seat as the van's powerful motor roared. She strapped herself in.

Tam's eyes were closed. Her lovely face had that stiff, immobile look, like marble. As if she were bracing herself for something.

"Is she . . ." Lily stopped, swallowed. She didn't even have the nerve to finish framing the question.

Val would not meet her eyes. He stared at Tam, clutching her hand, his other hand resting on her belly. "We will see," he said.

"Mamma?" Rachel twisted around, too. "Are you sick?"

Tam managed a smile for her daughter. "I'm fine, baby."

Rachel studied her mother. Those big dark eyes were old beyond her years, much like Sveti's. "Is Irina fine?"

Tam flinched. "We'll see, honey. Can't talk now. Be still, OK?"

Rachel wrapped her arms around her knees and began to cry.

The van careened at ninety-five miles an hour down the

winding two-lane blacktop, squealing around the hairpin turns, swerving around the odd oncoming logging truck. Lily's eyes stung.

She wrapped an arm around Rachel's thin, trembling shoulders. Rachel grabbed her and hung on tightly.

25

"Drive faster! We have to get there before they do!"

"I know that, damn it!" Hobart cursed as the car fishtailed on the rain-slicked asphalt. "Calm down! This will be tricky, but it's our chance to show him what we can really do! To prove ourselves!"

But Melanie was too involved in her self-indulgent funk to respond to his pep talk. She clutched the headphones attached to the laptop to her ears, connecting her to the audio coming through Rosa Ranieri's phone.

"You know what happens if we fuck up, right?" she quavered.

"Melanie, this is not useful right now—"

"King will Level Ten us. And we will dig our own graves and slash our own fucking throats." Her voice was shrill. "Because he hates us, now." Her voice dissolved. "He just h-h-hates us."

Hobart glanced at her, dismayed. She'd been his podmate since babyhood, and he knew her weak points like his own. When she was stressed, she moped. She'd hidden her depressive tendencies from King in the testing cycles, but she couldn't hide them from her podmates.

The situation was critical. They'd barely slept in the three days they'd been ensconced at Cray's Cove. Steele's home was impregnable without an army to assail it, and there was no sneaking up on it by stealth, either. They had to wait for an opening, chewing their knuckles while the clock ticked, feeling King's disapproval like a cold fog curling all around them. They tried to get some sleep, spelling each other for half-hour naps from time to time, but they mostly relied on the pickup drugs.

The car that had left a couple hours before, full of Mc-Cloud wives, had been the first opening, but they'd been unable to take advantage of it, with King's imperative of stealth and guile. King should have sent them a dozen agents for backup. They could have stopped the car, killed the young man, taken the women and the baby hostage, and had a strong card to play. But no. They were being punished with an impossible task. But just maybe, that impossible task had now become possible.

The electrifying news they collected from Rosa Ranieri's cell gave them no time to prepare, to plan. Tam Steele was rushing to the hospital emergency room. Lily Parr was with them. It was never going to get any better than this—if they were brilliant, and quick as a snake.

If. He glanced over at Melanie's wet eyes and trembling mouth. Damn. That was a big if, with Mel in such bad shape. He wished he could call King and get him to give Melanie a Level Five pick-me-up like the one King had done for him. He'd taken care not to tell Mel about that. She was shaky enough already. "Take your patch, Mel," he ordered. "You need it. I already took mine, before we left the hotel."

"We'll slit our own throats," Mel moaned. "We may as well have gotten gassed with the other shredders, back on cull day. It would have been better to end it then. Instead of busting our asses, for years, for nothing. For him to just hate us. I can't stand it. I just can't—"

"Put on your fucking patch!" Hobart yelled. The car

screeched to a stop at the red light just in time. "Get yourself together!"

Mel fumbled for the Calitran-M. Hobart watched until he ascertained that the little red dot was affixed to her inner wrist.

"You're wrecked, Mel," he said. "We're changing the plan. I'll be the nurse. You be the drunk."

"Bad idea." Mel's voice no longer wobbled. "Rosa Ranieri talked to me for a half hour in the baby store. She liked me. She'll have a positive reaction when she sees a nurse she knows. Instant trust, in a box. Plus, you've done your face, and I haven't."

She was right. He didn't like it, but at least Mel was sharpening up. Hobart glanced at himself in the rearview. Not bad, for a rush job. He'd dyed his hair, reshaped his eyebrows, and shaved a new hairline days ago. He'd put a straggling dark wig and a ski cap over that for the first act of their improvised melodrama. With brown contact lenses, a jaw prosthesis, cheek padding and the goatee, Rosa Ranieri would never recognize him. She'd had eyes for only the babies and Mel anyhow.

So back to the original plan, such as it was. He stuck his hand into his pocket, fingered the glass-framed photograph he'd swiped from the desk in the office of the hotel manager, the tiny bottles of Jack Daniels he'd taken from the hotel minibar. They'd brainstormed madly in those last, fumbling seconds. Neither was satisfied with the plan, which was filled with uncontrollable variables. Too damn bad. They had counted minutes to execute it. They had to just go for it. Everything was at stake. Their lives, on the top of the list.

"You do know that if the nurse on duty in there is a man, we're fucked, right?" he said. "It'll be too late to switch roles. And if there are too many people on the nursing or the administrative staff? Or if someone sees us too soon? Or raises the alarm?"

She gave him a look. "We're fucked anyhow, Hobart," she said. "You know that. We have nothing to lose anymore."

He opened his mouth, but she shushed him. "Sssshhh, they're talking." She concentrated, pressing the headphones to her ears. "Val Janos is giving the driver directions to turn left up Trevitt Grade," she said. "We're still ahead. By about four minutes. There it is."

Water sprayed wide in a brown arc as Hobart accelerated through the puddle outside the hospital parking lot. He parked. He and Melanie looked at each other and linked hands, squeezing hard.

They leaped out of the car and headed toward the entrance.

Bruno tried calling Aaro for the fifth time. Still busy.

Everyone was on edge since Edie's phone call to Kev about Tam's emergency run to Rosaline Creek. Kev and Sean were the worst, being not just worried and tense, but angry, too.

"I cannot believe it," Sean repeated. "It's hypocritical. After the shit she gives me for taking risks? And off she goes, running back to Endicott Falls, today? Like, what the *fuck?*"

"To be fair," Bruno pointed out. "You ran off to shoot people and blow shit up. She went home to go back to work at her bookstore."

"What difference does the nature of the errand make, if there are killers out there?" The SUV swerved, hydroplaning on the oily asphalt.

Bruno cowered back into his seat. "Ah, yeah. Whatever, man. Just drive the car."

Kev sat next to him, likewise grim, since his lady, too, had committed the unspeakable crime of driving back to Seattle with Liv, Miles, and Sveti. Davy and Connor both looked complacent, their own lady wives being safely at home in Seattle with assorted offspring.

Bruno was nervous. It had been painful enough to leave Lily in Tam's fortress. Now she was a sitting duck in a hospital emergency room. The timing of this catastrophe was so bad. Meteors- flying-out-of-the-sky-to-hit-you-on-the-head bad. Bad with surgical precision.

"Aaro's with her," Davy said, reading his mind. "Aaro's no idiot."

Bruno declined to comment, not being personally convinced of that yet. Then Kev's cell phone buzzed. His brother stared at it, puzzled.

"I don't know this number," he said. "Never seen it before."

"Things are too strange not to answer it," Bruno said. "Pick it up."

Kev shrugged, clicked the button. "Yeah? . . . Yes, I am . . . ah. I see. How did you get this number? . . . Oh." He turned, gave Bruno a look that made his stomach turn to gelid slush. "Yeah, he is here," he said reluctantly, after a long, painful pause.

Kev passed him the phone. "For you," he said. "Detective Petrie."

Bruno winced and held it to his ear. "Hey, Petrie. What's up?"

"I can't believe you have the nerve to ask that, you son of a bitch."

Bruno was taken aback. "What? You're pissed because I didn't come in for questioning? I told you, man. I was running for my life. Still am. That's the only reason I blew you off. Don't take it personally."

"Blew me off? You think this is something personal? That I got my feelings hurt? That takes self-absorbed to a whole new level. You're wanted for triple homicide, Ranieri, and that's just for starters. I got the warrant signed two days ago.

It's in the Law Enforcement data system, the NCIC database. We are after your ass. Just so you know."

Bruno jerked upright. "It was self-defense. I told you."

"Was it self-defense to turn your phone off for five days, too?"

Bruno rubbed his eyes. "You've been trying to call me?"

Petrie made a derisive sound. "So where were you?"

Bruno paused. "I was out digging up skeletons from my past."

"Ah. How nice for you. Sounds like good exercise."

"Oh, it was," Bruno assured him.

"Got a whole closet full of those, do you?"

"Pretty much," Bruno admitted.

"No cell coverage out there in skeleton country?"

"Nope," Bruno said.

"Well, then, I've got a few more for your collection. I arranged for genetic testing for those bodies from the crime scene outside the diner. I also had the cadaver of Aaro's little friend tested, since he was so emphatic about her being involved, and the guy who shot himself on Wygant, the one I mistook for you. I got those samples fast-tracked, and compared to the sample of your DNA that we had in our database, as well as whatever bodily fluid of yours that the criminalists scraped off the crime scene—blood, vomit, what have you. And I got some preliminary results back today."

Bruno waited. "Well?" he prompted. "And?"

Petrie was silent. "You really don't know? You have no idea?"

The slush inside Bruno's belly hardened into ice. It was another one of those icebergs. Secrets, hanging huge below the surface of dark water. "Stop being coy. Were they in the system? Who are they?"

"No," Petrie said. "We didn't ID them. They're John and Jane Does. Why don't you help me ID them, Ranieri? Come on. Give it up."

"Me? Why me? What are you hinting at? Out with it!"

The car had gone silent.

"They're your brothers. And your sister," Petrie said.

Bruno sat there. Mouth wide. A sledgehammer had thwacked into his thorax.

"What?" he choked out. "How? Who?"

"The girl. The suicided guy, on Wygant Street, the one who looks like you. And one of the three dead guys on the street. There's this thing called the siblingship index. The stiffs share so much genetic material with you, the probability that they are your full brothers and sisters is overwhelming. Or double cousins. That is, if your mother's sibling had offspring with your father's sibling. The lab tech explained. It's the number of genetic markers that match up."

"My mother didn't have any siblings," Bruno said.

"Well, then. Back to scenario A. Full brothers and sisters, then."

"But I don't." Bruno felt lost. "I can't. Those people, the guys I fought—they were younger than me. Aaro's girlfriend was in her early twenties. My mother's been dead for eighteen years. I never knew who my father was. I was twelve when she died. She was nineteen when she had me. She didn't have any other children. I would have noticed."

"You think? That's fascinating. The jury will eat it up. The story of your deprived single-parent childhood, how it led to the savage murders of your unacknowledged, *unnoticed* brothers and sister. Your defense lawyer will have lots to work with. The insanity plea will be cake."

Bruno could think of nothing to say. His mouth worked.

"I hope I've given you something to think about. Thanks for keeping in touch, keeping me in the loop. You're a real prince, Ranieri."

"Petrie—"

"Just shut up, OK? I'm sick of your bullshit. Just shut *up*."

Petrie hung up. The rain pounded on the windshield. The wipers did their fast *squeaka-scrape, squeaka-scrape*. Bruno stared at the phone as if it were a poisonous snake that had just bitten him.

"What is it, Bru?" Kev prodded, his voice cautious.

"Petrie," Bruno said hoarsely. "The cop from Portland. There's a warrant out for my arrest. And he did genetic tests on those guys I, ah, fought, outside the diner. He says they're my . . ." His voice caught on the word. "My siblings."

Silence met his announcement. Every second of it burned like a lit fuse, crawling closer to that stick of dynamite that was himself.

"Jesus," Sean murmured. "I thought our problems were weird."

Kev twisted to stare at Bruno. "You know he'll have my signal triangulated, right? He'll pinpoint your location, if he hasn't already."

Bruno stared, still helpless.

"Why in God's name did Julio give my number to a cop?" Kev muttered. "What was he thinking?" He turned to Bruno. "We're barely a half hour from Cray's Cove. Petrie is going to know that, real soon. There's enough about all of us in the files for him to figure out where we're going. You can't go to Tam's. You have to go a different direction."

"They don't know about Rosaline Creek," Bruno argued.

"It's just a matter of time," Davy said. "Forget air travel. Get a car, get out of the state before the net falls."

"Find that jewelry box, or you'll be solving your mystery and conducting your love affair from inside a jail cell," Kev finished.

"Manhunt?" Bruno stared around at them. "I can't just disappear," he protested. "I can't do that to her! I have to see Lily!"

"No, you don't." Con's voice was hard. "If you give a shit about her, you don't. Man up. Do the hard thing. If nothing else, you'll draw them away from her. And if she's worth a damn at all, she'll understand. We'll look after her for you."

Bruno's whole body clamped like a fist around a scream

of frustration. "Don't give me your McCloud do-the-hard-thing macho bullshit," he snarled. "I have to talk to her."

He pulled up Aaro's number again. The line was busy. Still. Jesus wept. Aaro was a pathological loner, so socially challenged, he seemed practically autistic, and all of a sudden, he'd decided to be chatty.

Bruno slunk down still deeper into the seat and just repeated the call, at ten-second intervals. Obsessively.

"No, no. With the pinkies. Work them into the outside bits . . . yeah, like that, and then . . . turn the whole thing inside out. Excellent!"

Rachel held up the correctly inverted Cat's Cradle stretched out between her two hands, and beamed triumphantly. Lily grinned back, tickled that she'd remembered the sequence of knots she hadn't done since fifth grade. She used to do Jacob's Ladder, too, but that attempt had turned into a snarl of shoelace that had them both giggling.

They'd reached a small hospital on the outskirts of the next town in good time. Val had been out the door with Tam in his arms, loping toward the door of the Urgent Care entrance before Lily even got her seat belt unbuckled. By the time the rest of them had gotten Rachel's shoes and jacket onto her and trooped inside, Tam and Val had long since disappeared into the ER's inner sanctum.

And at that point, there was nothing left to do but find a row of benches, hunker down, and think of ways to keep Rachel occupied. They'd left in far too much of a hurry to think of toys, books, dolls, puzzles, or a fancy electronic device that would stream kids' TV. Zia Rosa was no help, sitting there with her eyes squeezed shut, muttering prayers. Aaro was even less help, surprise, surprise. He paced around their benches like a chained wolf, muttering savagely into his cell. ". . . of course not . . . if you ladies hadn't insisted on haring off to Seattle . . . oh, for Christ's sake . . . nobody's blaming anybody for anything! . . . Yeah, just get back here! We're sure as hell not going anywhere . . ."

The floor show had been for her to devise, so Lily picked a lace out of her shoe and started teaching Rachel to play Cat's Cradle.

Aaro was on the phone with Edie for the second time, trying to explain the fastest route to Rosaline Creek. It was clear from the tone of his voice that the stress level did not help their mutual comprehension one little bit. A nurse walked in, carrying a clipboard. She was a young, dark-haired woman in green scrubs, pretty in a fresh, scrubbed sort of way. She scanned the room with a thoughtful frown, and her eyes settled on them. "Are you the folks who came in with Tamara Steele?"

Aaro stopped pacing and snapped his phone shut. "Is she OK?"

The woman glanced down at her clipboard. "She's stabilized," she said, her voice careful. "We're doing all we can."

Rachel's hands dropped into her lap, still tangled with her shoelace Cat's Cradle. She burst into tears.

Lily pulled Rachel onto her lap. Tucked the curly black head under her chin so that waving fuzzy black fronds tickled her nose. "It'll be OK," she whispered to Rachel. Wanting so badly for it to be true.

But who better than she knew how untrue it could be? Rachel knew, too. All of them did, even Aaro. She didn't know Aaro's story, but she didn't need to. She knew he had one. She could feel it, vibing off him. All of them knew about stories with bad endings.

Just then, Zia Rosa concluded her cycle of prayers and opened her eyes. They widened as she saw the nurse. "*Ehi!*" she burst out. "But you are the nice lady from the baby store! How are you?"

The nurse looked blank for a moment, and then her face lit up. "Oh, wow! Yes, it's you! How nice to see you again! What a coincidence!"

"And how are little Hayden and little Phillip?" Zia's face lit with a sentimental smile. "I met her at the baby store in the mall," she explained to Lily. "With her twins. Boy and girl. Sweetest little *bimbi*, looked just like Bruno and Magda when they were little. My goodness, you didn't say you were a nurse, too! You must be a busy woman!"

The nurse laughed. "I am. The twins are great. They're with their dad, watching too much TV. We were visiting Jim's parents when we met you at the mall, but we actually live here, in Craigsville Heights."

Rachel slid off Lily's lap. "Are you going to save Irina?" she asked.

The nurse looked down at her. "Excuse me, honey? Who's Irina?"

"My little sister," Rachel explained. "She's inside Mamma."

"Ah." The woman stroked Rachel's curly head. "We will do our very best for Irina, sweetheart."

Zia Rosa peered at the laminated nametag that hung around the woman's neck. "Sylvia Jerrold, LPN. I thought your name was Kate."

"Ah." The lady chuckled. "My husband calls me that. My middle name is Katherine. Jim likes the name Kate better."

"Well, Nurse Sylvia Kate. Is there a chapel here at the hospital?"

The woman hesitated for a moment. "Ah . . . ah, yes, um . . ."

"I have to say a prayer to San Gerardo Maiella," Zia Rosa explained. "It works better in a consecrated church. Will you show us?"

"Can I go, too?" Rachel tugged at Zia's sleeve.

"No," Aaro snarled. "You stay here until I have backup. I can see all entrances and exits from here and keep an eye on the parking lot."

Zia Rosa drew herself up to her full height. "Tam needs an intercession from San Gerardo," she said haughtily. "My *nonna* prayed to him when her children were born, and they were all born healthy."

The nurse tucked the clipboard under her arm and gave Aaro a soothing smile. "The chapel is just down at the end of this corridor," she offered, tentatively. "You can see the door from here, if you poke your head out of the waiting room. It's, ah . . . it's really quite safe."

"No," Aaro ground the word out. "Don't make me sit on you, Zia."

The old lady's lips began to quiver.

"Oh, no." Lily wrapped her arm around Zia Rosa's shoulders. "Just pray to Saint Whoever right here, OK? I'm sure he'll understand."

"I am not falling for this manipulative shit," Aaro said stiffly. "Cry all you want, Zia. The saints can wait for my backup."

Rachel burst into tears, too. The nurse edged away. Lily didn't blame her. They must come across as a pack of raving lunatics.

"I'll, ah, just let you folks work these things out for yourselves," the woman said. "I'll let you know more about Ms. Steele as I have more information, so, ah, alrighty, then! Bye! Later!"

The woman scurried away. Aaro's phone rang. He yanked it out.

"Yeah?" he barked into it. "Of course we are." His eyes slid to her. "Bruno," he told her. "And yeah, I'll pass him over to you, but give me a second . . . uh-huh . . . Tam's fine, far as we know. A nurse came out, told us she was stable, whatever that means. Val's with her . . . yeah, Lily's here. What's got you all wound up?"

Trying to soothe Rachel and Zia Rosa while eavesdropping on Aaro's conversation was a challenge, but Lily tracked Aaro's every word.

"They're your *what?*" Aaro's voice rose. "That's insane!"

Lily tugged Aaro's sleeve. "What's insane?"

Aaro waggled his finger at her, universal sign language for "shut up and wait, you idiot." "All three of them? That's not possible, right? That's not even humanly possible! They must have got it wrong! Right?"

Then Lily saw the man. Or smelled him, actually, before she saw him. He reeked of whiskey, an odor that she viscerally hated, it having been Howard's drink of choice. She could smell it at fifty yards.

The guy weaved toward them, muttering. He was tall, with stringy dark hair dangling out of a gray ski cap and a puffy down coat. He clutched a photograph in a glass frame in both hands.

She saw him, but her attention was fragmented by Rachel's sobbing and by trying to gauge Aaro's reaction to whatever Bruno was saying.

Aaro tensed as the man approached. "Hold on," he barked into the phone. "Call you right back." He stepped out between Lily, Zia, and Rachel and the stumbling new arrival.

"Have you sh-sheen my Caroline?" the man asked, his voice slurred. He lurched closer, eyelids fluttering, eyes blurry.

Aaro held up his hand. "That's close enough, buddy."

"But have you sh-sheen my Caroline?" His reddened, imploring eyes fixed each of them in turn. "I'm looking for Caroline." He held up the photo. "This is her. She's my—"

"Keep back," Aaro warned. "I don't want to hurt you, man."

"But this is her picture. She's . . . oh!" The guy's shuffling foot caught on the rubberized floor mat. He pitched forward, stumbling. The picture flew from his hands. The frame shattered on the floor, an arc of glass shards. The guy lunged for it with a shout, scrabbling on the floor.

Rachel took advantage of Lily's slackened grasp and wrenched away. "I'm going in to Mamma!" She darted toward the door.

Aaro's hand shot out, grabbing Rachel's arm. Just then,

Lily realized that the man's hands, holding the shards of frame, were dripping with blood. The man realized it at the same moment.

He shrieked. His eyes rolled back in his head, and he stumbled, pitching forward like a falling tree. Right toward her.

Alex let go of Rachel and lunged to block him, too late.

The guy landed hard, sprawling across Lily's chest and lap, bouncing, sliding. Immensely heavy, limp and horrible. It was a chaotic blur, yelling and flopping, a nasty sting in her arm. The smell of liquor made her stomach lurch.

The weight lifted. She gasped for air, heart thudding wildly. The man was stretched out on the ground, Aaro crouched on top of him. Aaro's knee crushed the guy's chest, and his fingers were clamped around the guy's throat. The man twitched and writhed, grunting and gabbling, but he was immobilized.

"You OK, Lily?" Aaro asked, without taking his eyes off the man.

"Ah . . . ah . . ." Lily looked down at herself and dragged in a hiss of distaste. Oh, gross. He'd sliced her forearm with a piece of glass. The same arm that had gotten cut back in New York. This cut wasn't deep, though, just messy. It dripped down her fingertips. Her sweater and jeans were wrecked. "I'm OK. I got cut with a piece of glass. No big deal."

Aaro cursed in that language that he used only for cursing.

Zia Rosa gasped. *"O Madonna santissima!"* She dug into her purse, rummaged for tissues, and started mopping Lily's arm up, muttering madly in Italian as she dabbed and swabbed.

The nurse came running out. "Oh, no. Jamison, you idiot!"

The guy named Jamison made helpless choking sounds, flopping ineffectually. Aaro's iron grip did not waver.

"You can let go of him," the nurse told Aaro. "He's harm-less."

"Yeah? Tell that to my friend who's bleeding," Aaro said icily. "The guy's a goddamn menace."

"No, really," the nurse insisted. "He lives in a halfway house up the road. He has mental health issues, but he's not dangerous."

"Sad case, my ass. Call the cops. The judge can decide."

"Just let me clean him up and call his social worker," the nurse said briskly. "Then I'll stitch that right up for you. I'm so sorry about this. Jamison's a screwup, but harmless. I've known him for years."

Jamison began to snivel. "Caroline?" he choked out. "Caroline?"

Aaro looked pained. He lifted his strangling fist away, rose from his battle-ready crouch, taking his weight off the hitching, gasping man.

Jamison promptly rolled onto his side and curled into the fetal position, still clutching his bloody shards. He began weeping loudly. Blood was smeared on the floor beneath him, in gory, circular swirls.

Lily winced and looked away. It hurt to watch.

"Oh, dear," the nurse murmured. She tugged his arm. "Come on, Jamison. On your feet. I'll call Sandy for you." She looked at Lily. "I'll find someone to clean this up and be right back for you, OK?"

"Whatever," Lily said, distracted. "Don't sweat it. I've had worse."

They watched, transfixed, as the guy shambled from the room, clinging to the nurse's arm. Shoulders hitching.

Silence hung heavy in the air. Even Rachel had stopped crying, intimidated by the weirdness. Lily blew out a slow breath, squeezing the blood-soaked tissues over her arm. "That was strange," she said quietly.

Aaro stared at the door through which the nurse had

gone. "I'm sorry I let him get so close to you," he said. "This was my fault."

She rounded on him, appalled. "Your fault? Have you gone nuts?"

"He cut you." Aaro's voice was bleak. "He could have killed you. If he'd meant to. With me, standing there, three feet away!"

"Yeah, but he didn't! For God's sake, you guys are all alike! These insanely high standards!"

"Failure is unacceptable," Aaro said.

"Oh, shut up," Lily snapped. "Failure is also human, which you still are, more or less, last I checked. So get over it."

"Excuse me? Miss? You're up! Come on back!"

Lily looked up. The nurse beckoned her from the medical suite.

"Oh, don't worry about it," Lily assured her. "It's a scratch."

The nurse marched over with the air of a woman on a mission. "It's the least we can do." She grabbed Lily's arm, peeling up the wad of Kleenex. "Hmm," she murmured. She prodded it with a latex-gloved finger, making Lily flinch. "No, you come along with me. We'll fix this."

"Not alone," Aaro said. "Rachel, Zia, come on. We're all going."

The nurse pulled Lily to her feet and gave Aaro a quelling look. "No, you are not. Not while she's being treated. Hospital rules."

She took off, hustling Lily alongside her.

Aaro followed, grabbing Zia Rosa and Rachel by the hands and dragging them with him. "Too bad," he growled. "We're coming in, too."

"Are you her husband?" the nurse demanded.

"No, I'm her goddamn bodyguard!"

"Well, guard the door then," she snapped. "You're not bringing a loud, unruly crowd of people into an examining room while I'm stitching a wound, and with a small child, too! I wouldn't allow it even if it weren't against the rules, but it is, so wait outside if you're so anxious!"

"He's just nervous. We've had some strange adventures lately," Lily explained. She patted Aaro's shoulder. The guy thrummed with tension. "I'm sure this'll be quick. Tell Bruno I'll call him right back."

The nurse pulled Lily through the door, slammed it in Aaro's face, and turned the door lock. *Click.* Lily could hear Aaro, holding forth viciously in that language again. He was not going to be fun to deal with after this. There was a screen up, shielding the bed from the casual view of whoever was passing by the door. Lily took a step—

Whump, a wad of white gauze slammed down over her face. An arm jerked her back, pinning her arms.

Oh, *shit.* She struggled, squirmed against a tall male body, but the bare arm clamped over her torso was horribly strong, and there was some drug soaking the cloth. She tried not to inhale, but she was desperate for air. Taut, wiry muscles, clammy skin. His grip bruised her. Strength was draining out of her, a dark wave of chill and nausea surging up. The guy wore surgical scrubs. She twisted. Oh, God. It was Jamison. He'd taken off his ski cap. His long hair was a crisp brown haircut, and his goatee and mustache were gone, but he still stank of whiskey. He had a pleasant, unremarkable face.

He smiled at her, looking immensely pleased with himself.

Oh, God. She needed to breathe. She was going to yark, or faint. Or die. Probably in that order. She had to warn the nurse. She had to—

Sylvia Jerrolds stepped from behind the screen, clad in a tank top and underwear. She gave Lily that same friendly smile she'd used in the waiting room. But this time, Lily saw the death behind it.

The woman shoved discarded scrubs into a knapsack, tossed the laminated name tag she'd worn onto the floor, tugged a latex mask over her head. She worked fast. It was a good mask, the skin tone lifelike, turning her into a jowly old lady. Baggy, shapeless black wool pants, a round-shouldered wool coat, a gray wig.

"Hurry, Mel," the guy muttered.

The not-nurse put on a pair of pink-tinted, distorting glasses and smiled at Lily. "Off we go, sweetheart," she whispered.

Lily had to inhale. Darkness surged. The guy yanked her backward off her feet, into a chair. A wheelchair. With her last crumb of conscious awareness, she felt them twist her hair up, pull a wig onto her head. Glasses, on the bridge of her nose, a plastic oxygen mask settling onto her face. Cold. Ticklish. She could no longer move at all.

She saw Bruno's face in her mind. Felt a sting of aching regret. Something that was slipping away forever, but she couldn't grasp what it was, just that it was rare and lovely, and never again. She groped for it, but it was going, gone. She had no point of reference to cling to. The sadness, the ache of disconnected loss, the fear, it was all whipping up into a huge vortex, roaring in her ears like the souls of the damned.

It sucked her down deep into nowhere.

26

"If Bruno were here, he would never have let that *stronzo di merda* anywhere near Lily," Zia Rosa informed him. Aaro clenched everything he had. Teeth, hands, toes, ass.

"Thank you for that useful observation," he said, his voice rigidly even.

"He wouldn't have let that nurse lady bully him, either," Zia Rosa went on. "Bruno doesn't let anyone put their foot on his face."

"Yeah, Bruno's perfect. I suck. We've established that. Let's move on. Or better yet, just shut up."

"I'm going to see Mamma now." Rachel tossed her black curls.

He stared her down, eyes squinted in his best Dirty Harry stare. "No, you are not," he told her. "Stand there. Do not move a muscle."

Rachel sniffed and threaded Lily's shoelace around her fingers. Zip, snap, and yank. She showed him the knot form she'd made. "Look."

He looked. "Yeah?" he asked warily. "What's that?"

"My witch's broomstick," she announced. "Lily showed me."

He knew he was being set up. "You're a witch, now?"

"Yeah." She fluttered her long lashes. "I'm going to turn you into a frog. Or a pig. Or a bug. I haven't decided yet."

Aaro forced air out of his constricted lungs. "Do your worst," he said. Things couldn't get much worse. He did not look forward to telling Bruno about the day's events. The guy already thought he was pus.

"A centipede," Rachel mused. "Lots of creepy-crawly legs."

"Speaking of legs," Zia Rosa said truculently, fanning herself. "Get me a chair, Alex. I can't stand on these legs much longer. Standing in one place, they swell up! Like balloons! And my varicose veins, *madonna mia!* See? Look!" She leaned on the wall and stuck out one thick, swollen ankle for his inspection.

He averted his gaze hastily. "Suffer until Lily is out of there."

"Maybe I'll turn you into a big, slimy slug," Rachel suggested. "Or a spider. A big fat one, with hairy legs."

Aaro was suddenly afflicted by a pang of longing for his quiet, solitary house in the woods outside Sandy. Where he would have been right now, blessedly alone, if only he'd kept his various protruding body parts out of this god-awful mess. He banged on the door of the suite.

"How are you guys doing?" he shouted.

Not a peep. The nurse was punishing him with silence. Or to be fair, maybe they were concentrating on stitching up torn human flesh.

The door of one of the adjacent medical suites opened down the hall. An elderly lady backed out, muttering querulous instructions. A tall guy in scrubs followed, pushing a wheelchair that held another old lady, this one slumped low in the chair. Her head flopped to the side, slack. Gray hair was matted against the nape of her neck. A stroke patient, maybe. The trio moved slowly down the corridor away from them. The lady on her feet clutched the wheelchair for balance. An oxygen tank accompanied them, rattling along on a rolling trolley.

Prickles shivered over his flesh as he watched the little triad. A goose walking over his grave. Unacknowledged fear of death, age, infirmity. Who knew? He hated hospitals. They made him tense. But then, he didn't like introspection, either. There were enough threats coming at him from the outside to stress about. He didn't have the stomach to entertain the ones from the inside, too.

Besides. Threats from the outside were easier to kill.

Rachel started dancing from foot to foot. "I have to pee."

He stifled a groan. "Hold it," he told her.

"I can't! I'll pee my pants!"

A door flew open down the hall. A middle-aged black woman in a white coat came out, looking harried. She looked to the right, the left. "Sylvia?" she yelled. "Sylvia!"

She yanked out her beeper, punched numbers into it. "Angela? Goddamnit, where is everybody?"

"You looking for the nurse?" Aaro asked.

The woman gave him a sharp look. "Did you see her?"

"She went in there." He jerked a thumb toward the suite. "Our friend got a cut. The nurse is stitching it up."

The doctor's brow furrowed. "For God's sake. I'm already short-staffed, and now my nurse disappears on me!"

"I need to pee," Rachel moaned, dancing on her toes.

The doctor pointed down the hall. "Bathroom's there," she snapped and vanished back into the room.

Rachel gave him an imploring look. He strode down the hall to the bathroom, jerked open the door, ascertained that it was an empty one-header. He held the bathroom door open for them. "Go for it."

They went about their business. Aaro positioned himself between the two doors, and caught a whiff of . . . whiskey. Someone tippling on the job? Here? Not the bitch nurse. That chick was as sharp as a tack.

Maybe it was the ghost of Jamison, lingering in the air.

Still. He tried banging on the door again. "Hey! Lily?"

No answer. Maybe they'd gone into an adjacent room with an insulating door between them. Or maybe he'd just better stop being a chump asshole, listen to the hairy spiders and centipedes crawling on the back of his neck, and get a key for that goddamn door already.

He jogged up to the front, poked his head inside the enclosed space for administrative staff. "Hello? Anybody in here?"

No one answered. He stepped inside, saw the chubby legs in blue rayon slacks and sensible loafers sticking out under the reception desk.

Fuck. Fear stabbed, deep and fast. Oh no, no, oh Jesus, no . . .

He came at the medical suite door like a bullet, slamming

a flying kick into it with all his strength. The lock held. He tried the next door. Same thing. The next was unlocked. He thundered through the interconnected rooms to the one where the nurse had taken Lily.

The smell hit him first. Jamison's whiskey-soaked coat, lying discarded on the floor. A name tag with a fluorescent nylon strap beside it. A wad of gauze, no doubt soaked with some knock-out drug. A young woman in her underwear, crumpled on the floor. Not Lily. The nurse. A torrent of filth in Ukrainian was coming out of his mouth as he lunged to touch her carotid artery. She had a pulse, thank God.

The old ladies. The male nurse. Of course. What a fuck-ing *idiot*.

He burst out. Zia Rosa, Rachel, and the doctor stared at him, wide-eyed. As if he'd gone crazy.

"Your nurse was attacked. The receptionist, too," he yelled to them as he sprinted away. "They got Lily! Call the cops!"

He rounded the corner. The trio had been moving at a slug's pace, so maybe they were still . . . no. Not in the corridor, nor the waiting area, nor the drive-up. He thudded out into the parking lot as a black Mercedes sedan accelerated toward the exit. A clean-shaven Jamison in scrubs was driving. The crone in the hat sat in the passenger's seat.

No Lily. Unconscious in the backseat or in the trunk.

He ran faster, squinting for the license plate, but some-body had obscured it with spattered mud. He started to close the gap as they paused to merge with traffic. He drew his gun but hesitated to shoot on the run at a moving target with Lily in the back or the trunk.

The tire. He slowed, aimed . . . and the car slewed through a huge mud puddle. Icy water splattered into his face as he pulled the trigger. The shot zinged against the back of the car. It surged ahead unchecked. He wiped mud out of his eyes.

Jesus, no. Please don't let that bullet have perforated the trunk. Please don't let that bullet be lodged inside of Lily. Please.

He pounded after the Mercedes, shoving the nightmare thought away. They had a straight stretch now, no lights, no turns. The gap lengthened. He couldn't catch up, but he kept chasing, like a stubborn dog. Failure was unacceptable. Same old clusterfuck. Goddamn him for getting involved. He knew this would happen. It always did. He worked alone, he stayed alone, he kept it simple so he could avoid this scenario.

This clawing, frantic feeling he got when he let people down.

The front window came down. The fake nurse stuck out her hand, fluttered her fingers at him, a taunting little wave. *Buh-bye!*

They hung the curve and were gone.

"I'll kill the bastard." Bruno jittered on the car seat, fists clenched. Trying to breathe, trying not to vomit. "I'll rip his limbs off."

"It's not his fault." Kev's tone had the flatness of one who had repeated the same phrase many times. "He's not the one who needs killing."

"What the fuck was he thinking?" The words exploded out of him. "Letting the drunk guy within fifty feet of her? Letting someone drag her into a locked room? Was he on drugs?"

Connor spoke up, hesitant. "I can see it," he said. "They were good. The place was understaffed. Conditions were perfect. Taking out the receptionist and nurse while the doctor was busy with Tam. The woman established herself multiple times as the nurse, fabricated a legitimate job—Christ, they'd have fooled me. Give Aaro a break, man."

"No!" Bruno yelled. "I can't! I will not swallow this!"

"Nobody's asking you to, Bru," Kev said softly. "I'm sorry."

He stared out the window at the raindrops against the glass, jittering his leg while the next outburst built. "How the hell did they know?" he demanded. "About Tam's bleeding? That was random! Impossible to predict! How could they have known about the choice of Rosaline Creek? They could have gone to the Urgent Care in Craigsville, or Dawson Falls—they're all more or less the same distance! But those fuckers were in exactly the right place, lying in wait! *How?*"

Con rubbed eyes that were deeply shadowed with exhaustion. "They have tracers planted somewhere? A bug?"

"In Tam's house?" Kev let out a sharp laugh. "No way."

Con shrugged. "So? What else could it be?"

"I'm going to kill him," Bruno said again, though the words were empty, they did not release any of the tension. He rocked forward, folding over that stone hard lump.

"Bad as Aaro feels, he just might beat you to it," Davy murmured.

Bruno looked at him, and Davy glanced swiftly away. "Don't try to make me feel sorry for that incompetent fuck," he said harshly. "He'd better not. I want that satisfaction for myself. If nothing else."

Heavy silence. There was nothing anyone could say to this catastrophe. No comfort, no help possible.

They passed signs for an exit off the freeway, and Connor leaned forward. "Get off at the next exit," he said, looking at Bruno. "There'll be a car rental on the strip. Head east in this car. Just for God's sake don't get stopped in it. With the firepower packed in here, they'd take you for a domestic terrorist, and you have enough problems." He turned to Kev. "Assuming you didn't rent this car in your own name."

"Hell, no," Kev said. "With all the stuff going down? I knew we were going to need an invisible car."

"Wait a minute." Bruno looked around at the four men.

"How am I just supposed to drive away from this? I have to follow Lily!"

The others wouldn't meet his eyes.

"Follow her where, Bru?" Kev said. "You've got nothing else to do. Rosaline Creek is crawling with cops. They'll do their job without your help. And you're a wanted man. Remember? That little detail?"

"We'll follow every lead that we can from here," Davy offered.

"But what could they be doing to her? I can't . . . I don't have time to road-trip across the damn country! While they hold Lily captive!"

"You can't fly," Con said. "You'd never make it onto a commercial flight. Unless you have a good disguise and a fake passport. Do you?"

Kev's brothers looked at him hopefully. *"Vaffanculo,"* Bruno muttered, disgusted. "Of course not. I don't play paranoid games with myself like you McCloud boys. I can't just drive away from Lily!"

"You're not," Kev argued. "You're driving toward the only clue in the whole fucking world that we have. You're going where it all started. If you don't get a lead there, you're not going to find one anywhere."

"Thanks for the pep talk. You're warming my cockles again."

"You get more than encouragement," Kev said. "I'm going, too."

"Me, too," Sean said. "Wouldn't miss this freak show for anything."

"Right." Bruno stared at them. "Real smart for a guy on the lam to bring along six foot four, blond identical twins, one of whom has distinctive scars on his face. Might as well paint you both neon pink."

Kev and Sean glanced at each other. "If there are three of us, we can go faster," Kev said. "We can't go over the speed limit. If you get stopped, you're meat. You'll need someone to spell you."

"No, I don't. You think I'll sleep while those assholes have Lily? I'm never sleeping again. It's a piss-poor idea. You're not doing it."

"We'll be discreet," Sean said.

"Yeah? How? Wearing an old-lady mask? Rolling an oxygen tank?"

Sean pulled onto the exit ramp and entered a strip mall. The streetlights lit up hazy halos in the soggy gloom.

"There's a Hertz by that drugstore," Davy said. "Stop there."

"Don't speed," Connor lectured. "Keep your cell on you at all times. It's tagged, of course, so we'll be tracking you."

The men got out. Davy leaned forward, tapping Kev's window, which he rolled down. Gusts of chilly air dropped the temperature in the car. He gazed sternly at them. "Don't get killed," he commanded.

"Nope," Sean said cheerfully.

The two men turned and walked away together through the rain. Shoulder to shoulder in that classic, stoic McCloud way of theirs. Kev had the vibe, too. The macho cowboy, riding off into the sunset.

Bruno stared after them, wondering if he ought to stage another raving freak-out to get rid of these clowns. Problem was, part of him was relieved to have the company. It was the same part that felt guilty.

"You're kidding, right?" he said on principle. "I'm going alone."

"With exactly what pile of untraceable cash?" Kev asked. "You can't use your bank account or your credit cards, remember? I've got money socked away in accounts that aren't under my own name."

Bruno looked at Sean. "Your wife is going to kill you," he said.

Sean let out a mirthless chuckle. "She's the one who decided to go on a road trip with Eamon in the middle of this mess."

"That's how you'll justify this? She's going to kick your ass, man."

"Leave my wife out of this," Sean said. "Mouthy punk."

"I thought we'd established that I've moved beyond punkdom," Bruno retorted. "I've graduated to total asshole. Now I'm going for my advanced degree in raving shithead. So why don't you all just fuck off?"

Kev gave him a long look. "No. Give it up."

"Just let me do what I can do, all right? Nobody else has to die!"

"She's not dead," Kev said.

"You don't know that." Bruno's voice shook.

Kev's eyes did not waver. "She's not dead," he repeated. "If they wanted her dead, they could have plugged her with a sniper rifle and saved themselves all kinds of trouble. All that elaborate playacting? That means she's alive."

Bruno didn't dare reply. "You still shouldn't come with me."

"I have to," Kev said. "I can't let you go alone. Don't have it in me."

"And I just can't miss anything this bizarre," Sean added. "It's too entertaining. I can't resist. You couldn't pay me to stay away."

Bruno stared into Sean's eyes, straight through the guy's mask. "I'm in your debt already. You don't have to prove anything to me."

Sean's smile was crooked. "Don't tell me you still have that bug up your ass? After all we've been through?"

Bruno shook his head. "Not if you don't."

"Settled, then. Let's get going. We've got a job of work to do."

* * *

Petrie was starving, stiff, bored out of his mind. He'd freely chosen police work as a career, having had many options, and the only time he ever regretted doing so was during stakeouts.

But Rosa Ranieri would come out of that house eventually. He'd found a perfect side street with a view of Connor McCloud's front door, framed through the branches of a tree. No one had made him so far, and that was lucky, considering he was watching McClouds.

He wasn't worried about losing her. The GPS app on her smartphone nailed her to within a few yards. He'd called a friend of his who worked in the security office of her cell provider last week, promising to follow up on the paperwork asap, so he'd been watching her for days now. Thank God she reliably turned on her phone, unlike the other people in her family. Not that she ever answered his calls. Still pissed at him for the scare he'd given her. Didn't really blame her.

He'd put in hours yesterday in the DA's office arranging for a subpoena, so now it was legal and official, and everyone could breathe easy. And his ass was covered in terms of admissibility of evidence.

From Cray's Cove to Rosaline Creek and now back to Connor McCloud's house in Seattle. Rosa Ranieri got around. But suburban Seattle was a much better bet for arranging a chance meeting than Steele's cliffside fortress in Cray's Cove, so as soon as the woman returned there, he'd put things in motion, asked for some days off. Hadn't said anything to his supervisor about acting in furtherance of a case, though. Jake would have insisted on him hooking up with local detectives before moving an inch, and Petrie wanted to be able to jump in any direction, fast.

He'd get his ass kicked for this later, almost certainly. Wouldn't be the first time. He never had been great at following the rules. Just ask his dad.

It was a sunny day, Connor McCloud and his wife Erin

were out at their places of employment, and Margot Mc-
Cloud, Davy McCloud's wife, had left her two kids at her
sister-in-law's house as well. The older kids inside would be
agitating to be taken to the playground. He hoped that, anyway, having already spent half a day waiting for a chance to
have a word with Rosa Ranieri. The McClouds had circled
in. He didn't blame them.

Bruno Ranieri had dropped off the face of the earth. Lily
Parr as well. And bodies were piling up. Families, rather.
Petrie needed some answers. He was going to go crazy. This
whole thing made his flesh creep.

Movement at the front door. He whipped up the binocs.
Rosa Ranieri was the first out the door, her broad back first,
dressed in a crimson wool coat. She wrestled a baby carriage
onto the porch. The littlest daughter of Davy McCloud must
be in it. Two older children spilled out, a blond boy, about
five, a redheaded girl, about four.

Then he saw her. The dark-haired girl. She stepped out
with a toddler in her arms, in a black wool coat that showed
off shapely legs, little black half boots. She put the child
down on wobbly legs, helped Rosa maneuver the carriage
down the porch steps.

He peered through the binocs, zeroing in on her face.
Big, shadowy, wide-set eyes. High, sharp cheekbones. A
thick, swirly mane of dark hair hanging down. She scooped
the child up again, kissed her, smiling. She was a stunner. If
she were eight inches taller, she could supermodel. She was
tiny, though. Five-two, max. Maybe less.

This waif was no McCloud wife. None of whom were
anything to sneeze at in terms of feminine good looks, of
course. He'd spied all four of them, trooping in and out of
the house over the last two days, and had been duly impressed. But this one was too young.

Four little kids. One newborn, one toddling, and two bigger ones raising hell, that was too many for one old lady to
watch outdoors; he had nephews and nieces and could say

that with authority. So this chick was probably a local high school girl, paid to help Rosa babysit.

Which made him a slavering, oinking perv.

He got out of the car, irritated at himself. He started toward them, keeping an eye on the two women's progress as they herded the kids across the street. Once in the playground, the boy kicked a ball into the trees and ran after it. His redheaded sister or cousin followed, and the bombshell went running after, yelling for them to slow down.

Petrie took his time as he strolled into the park. The bombshell ran like a gazelle, hair flying like a banner, gleaming in the sunshine. Reddish highlights glinting in it. *Pay attention, dick for brains.* He focused his mind and headed toward the park bench Rosa Ranieri inhabited, jiggling the stroller with her foot, the toddler on her knee.

"Excuse me? Ms. Ranieri?" he called.

She glanced over. Instant, eye-slitted suspicion. She clutched the baby protectively to her bosom. The other hand dug into the huge purse that lay on the bench beside her. "Who wants to know?"

"I'm Detective Sam Petrie," he said. "Portland Police Bureau."

Her eyes opened wide, magnified behind her lenses. "You're that son of a bitch who practically gave me a heart attack last week? You have the nerve to come here? I should shoot your ass dead right now!"

He stared at her hand. "Tell me you're bluffing, Ms. Ranieri. You don't carry a loaded gun in your purse while you supervise toddlers."

She pulled her hand out. "Nah," she admitted. "*Bimbi* get into everything. What you doin' here? You're an asshole. You ain't welcome."

"I have something to show you," he told her. "May I sit down?"

"No!" she yelled. "What part of 'you're an asshole' and 'you ain't welcome' do you not understand, sweet cheeks?"

Sweet cheeks? He choked back a laugh, kept his face poker stiff. "I really need to ask you a couple of questions," he said.

"And I really need for you to piss off!"

"I swear. It's nothing that would harm your nephew."

She harrumphed. "Yeah? I'll be the judge of that."

"Of course you will," he said. "But how can you judge if you don't hear the questions? You could even warn Bruno of the direction my investigation is taking. I understand that. It would be aiding and abetting, of course, but a person's gotta do what a person's gotta do."

Her dark gaze was sharp. "Don't you get tricky with me."

"Nope," he said. "Just the facts. So may I sit down?"

"No," she snapped. "Don't get near the babies. Ask what you want, and then piss off."

He pulled the manila envelope out of his coat. "I imagine the McClouds have told you about the results of those genetic tests?"

She made a scoffing noise. "I figured you was gonna want to talk about that. Believe me, it ain't possible. I know it for a fact."

He waved the envelope. "I want you to look at these pictures. But they might not be easy to look at. The people in them are dead."

"I'm seventy-six, baby-face. I been looking at dead folk years since you was suckin' on your mamma's tit. How old are you?"

"Twenty-nine," he told her.

"Hah!" She cackled. "A baby! I helped lay out my cousin Torruccio when I was thirteen! He got plugged by bandits who was stealing his sheep. And when my Zio Rosario got thrown down a well, we didn't find him for six weeks, and when we finally pulled him out—"

"That's OK, you don't have to tell me," he said hastily. "I can imagine it just fine."

"He was messin' with somebody's wife," she said. "Pig."

They gazed at each other. He flapped the envelope against his hand, letting her curiosity build. "So," he said. "Can I show you these?"

She held out a plump, imperious hand. "Lemme see."

Petrie shook the pictures into his hand and handed them to her.

The first photo was of the stiff they'd found on Wygant Street, right after Ranieri's fight. Rosa Ranieri stared down. Frozen.

Petrie leaned forward and tapped it with his finger. "This is the guy that I mistook for Bruno. I'd seen Bruno's photo, the one that's displayed in the diner, that *Portland Monthly* magazine cover. I'm sincerely sorry about that mistake, but now that you see it, do you blame me?"

She made no reply. She looked at the second photo, Aaro's self-destructing barfly, and he heard her gulp. The pictures shook in her hand.

Then the third guy, the youngest one. The one whose neck Ranieri had admitted to snapping in the course of the brawl outside the diner. The resemblance to Bruno was less, but it was still there.

The other cadavers made no impression on her. She leafed through them without stopping and went back to the first three. The ones who shared genetic material with Bruno. Her silence told him what he needed to know. She was gray. Sweat had popped out on her brow. She breathed in shallow pants, patting her voluminous bosom.

"Ms. Ranieri?" He knelt down next to her. "You OK?"

"Madonna santissima," she whispered. "These people . . . it's not possible. These pictures are recent?"

"Taken a few days ago. They're awaiting identification in the Medical Examiner's office. They died within hours of each other. You've never seen them?"

She began to rock. He was getting nervous. The toddler squirmed in her arms and started to whimper. "I gotta go," she muttered.

"Go where?" he asked. "Back to Newark? Isn't that where your niece Magda lived when Bruno was a kid? Is that where he went?"

Her face sharpened, lips tightening. "No! You tricky son of a bitch, I ain't tellin' you nothin'!"

No problem, since she already had. "So you don't know them?"

Her eyes welled full of tears. "No," she said, her voice froggy. "I don't know these poor young people. Never seen 'em before in my life."

He studied her face as she said it. He'd listened to a lot of people lie. He was willing to bet that Rosa Ranieri wasn't lying about this. She would be a loud, blustering liar. Not a crying type of liar. That was a different type of woman. He raised his voice to be heard over the baby's fussing. "But you've seen people who looked like them?"

Her eyes flashed, defiant. "So what if I have? It happens, right? It's a coincidence. They say everyone has a double, right?"

"My next question," he said. "After having seen these, do you think there might be things you didn't know about Bruno's mother?"

She recoiled. "No! Magda was a good girl! And these people are too young! She would never have . . . it's not possible!"

"You mean, not possible that these are her children, too?"

Rosa Ranieri flapped her hand in denial, and the toddler started wailing in earnest. "She is *dead!* The only baby she ever had was Bruno, and she was a good mother! She died to save her son! She died a hero!"

"I don't doubt it, ma'am. But the DNA has been tested. The probability of these people and Bruno being full siblings is overwhelming. That's not random."

She began to blink. "Take the baby," she gasped, pushing the toddler toward him. "Call Sveti." The photos scattered at her feet.

"But I—but . . ." He held the yelling toddler out at arm's length, dismayed, as Rosa Ranieri toppled sideways on the park bench. "Oh, fuck," he muttered, looking around in desperation. The newborn in the baby carriage woke up and began its ear-piercing squall.

He spotted the bombshell, who was playing soccer with the two older kids, and bellowed at her. "Hey! Sveti! Help!"

The girl named Sveti spun around and sprinted toward him, shrieking at the kids to follow her. He tried to soothe the kid he held, jiggle the baby carriage, and keep Rosa from rolling off the park bench and onto the muddy ground by trapping her on it with his thigh.

"What did you do to her?" Sveti gasped, pounding toward him.

He registered her faint, attractive accent while he fished for a coherent reply. "Ah, nothing. I'm Detective Petrie, of the Portland Police Bureau, and I—"

"Give me that baby!" She snatched the screaming child out of his arms to his intense relief.

"I was just asking her a few questions about—"

"Eeeuuwww!" commented the boy, as he gathered up scattered photos that Rosa had let drop. "Are these people dead? They look dead!"

The little girl craned to look at the photos fanned out like baseball cards in the kid's grubby hand, and let out an ear-splitting shriek.

Sveti gasped and jerked the photos out of the boy's hand. "You show these to her?" She flapped them in his face, her voice quivering. "These horrible photo? You bastard! You are sick! You are sadist!"

"Ah . . . but I . . . but I had to . . . she said she could—"

"How could you? How dare you?" Her eyes blazed with fury. She was an avenging goddess, the kind that would tear off a guy's balls and use them for earrings. "Get away from her! Go!"

"But, uh, don't you need help with her? I could call a—"

"You have done enough! Go!" She lunged, batting at him with the photos crumpled in her fist. "And take obscene pictures with you!"

He grabbed the photos but resisted her shoving hand. "I can't move," he explained. "She'll roll off the bench if I move my leg."

Sveti dropped to her knees, gently put the toddler on the ground, and tried to push Rosa back up to a sitting position. With no luck at all, that being a whole lot of woman to lift. He hastened to help her.

The older woman's eyes fluttered open with a pitiful moan. They fastened on him, squinting in dislike. "You? Still?" she said. "Get lost."

"Yes, do get lost," Sveti urged. "Hurry. Go!"

He dug for a card. "Let me leave you this. In case you want to—"

Whack, Sveti batted his card away. "You take card and stick it right up into place you know very well!"

"You mean, up his ass?" the little boy piped up, helpfully.

"*Zitto!* No bad words!" Rosa Ranieri regained consciousness to hiss the reproof at the little boy, and promptly went slack again.

Petrie felt a bizarre urge to laugh. He backed away, resisting the urge to get one last hungry gawk in at the exotic foreign Fury. He had what he needed. Time to split.

Rosa Ranieri was the type who'd go nuts if she wasn't in on the action. It took one to know one. And when she acted, he'd know.

27

Lily fought consciousness as long as she could, but light pressed her eyelids, and pain throbbed redly in her skull with each heartbeat.

She took stock with her other senses before opening her eyes. Still air. Chill. Artificial light. The bitter smell of antibacterial cleansing foams. A churning stomach. A desperate need to pee. She cracked her eyes open a slit. Her head pounded like hammer blows. She rolled to her side, tried to sit up. Had to stop halfway through, squeeze her eyes shut, clench her belly against the churning flop of nausea.

She was in a small, windowless room, with metallic furnishings. A naked fluorescent bulb blazed down from the ceiling. She sat on a metal cot covered with a thin black plastic mattress pad. She wore a white cotton hospital gown, open in the back, bare butt hanging out. She shivered. Her jaw locked, twinging painfully with each shudder.

There was a different color of paint over a spot on the wall that had been walled over, where the window had once been. Her clothes lay on a shelf. She poked them. They'd been cleaned. Bloodstains on the sleeve. Brownish shadows on the nubbly wool. No shoes, though.

She herself seemed to have been cleaned, too. Her hair smelled like disinfectant. Ick. She shuddered to think of unfriendly hands touching her body while she was out cold.

There was a tray on the shelf. A plastic-wrapped ham sandwich, a banana, a bottle of water, a packaged square of brownie. A napkin, a wet wipe, and a paper packet of Excedrin. So they planned to treat her drug hangover before they tore her limb from limb. How thoughtful.

There was a camera mounted high in a corner of the room. No trouble taken to conceal it. It stared stonily down at her. She looked back, tempted to say something defiant to it, but she decided not to give them the satisfaction. She wasn't a circus animal to entertain them.

Bastards. Washing her clothes, giving her a brownie and headache medication? Twisted, sick bullshit. A proper dank, rat-infested, skeleton-strewn dungeon would be less offensive.

There was a small bathroom attached to the room. She stepped inside, took note of the camera there. So they wanted to watch her pee.

She took care of her business and dressed. Her arm was bandaged but still painful. The slash felt hot, and there were drops of old blood seeping through, and a halo of yellowish staining. Ugh. She peeked beneath. Huh. What do you know. Someone had stitched it.

Two possibilities. One, they'd decided to keep her alive just to torture her with fear and uncertainty. Two, she'd died and gone to hell. This was what she got for all that bad attitude, all that mouthing off.

There wasn't a lot of difference between the two scenarios, when all was said and done.

She stared at the tray of food. Hard to interpret whether her stomach was desperate for food or repelled by it. It hardly mattered. Calories might help. And whether it was torture or hellfire that awaited her, it was unlikely that they'd go to all this trouble just to poison her.

She perched cross-legged on the cot and devoured everything on the tray, including the Excedrin. She put the wrapping and the tray back on the shelf and sat down on the cot again, cross-legged.

She tried to keep her mind blank. There was nothing constructive she could think about. Thinking about Bruno hurt too much. He belonged to that other world, that fantasy universe that might have been able to exist, if she'd rolled the right dice. But she hadn't.

Tough shit. Here she was, here she'd stay. She stared at

the wall, keeping her eyes open, flooded with light, as if it could overexpose her brain like camera film, wash it pale and blank. No thoughts, no feelings.

Time passed. The throb in her head eased down. Her inflamed arm felt hot. Her belly grumbled for more food. She couldn't stop her teeth from chattering.

Dignity. Calm. Equanimity. This was probably it. She'd try not to snivel or whine. She'd had a good run. She'd bet money that she'd given them more trouble than they'd ever expected. It was the thing in her life so far that she was most proud of.

She thought of the drawing of her mother, and then of that sunset-tinged view of forever with Bruno, and her heart caught, twisted—

Not good. Chilly and detached. Blank was better.

She didn't have that long to wait. It was a half an hour or so before the door lock clicked and the door opened.

It was the fake nurse in jeans and a Columbia sweatshirt, dark hair pulled back into a high, bouncing ponytail. Fresh-faced, wholesome. A girl from the varsity volleyball team. The furthest thing from a scheming kidnapper/killer that Lily could imagine.

She forced old air out of her lungs. Oxygen, for the brain cells. She repeated her mantra. *Dignity. Calm. Equanimity.* She waited for the other woman to speak first, leaning on the impulse to babble, to beg.

The bitch looked delighted with herself. Her dark eyes sparkled. She held up a steaming paper cup. "We thought you'd like some coffee," she said. "Just how you like it. Dark roast, no sugar, real cream."

Saliva practically fountained from her salivary glands. "How do you know how I take my coffee?" Her voice was a fuzzy croak.

"We know everything. Here, take it. It'll make you feel better."

Lily stared at the rising steam, trying to gauge how many

notches of dignity, calm, and equanimity she might lose by accepting. She concluded that any loss of points would be offset by the advantage of caffeine. She had to choke back the urge to thank that scheming fiend, just for a lousy cup of coffee. She drank it without looking at the woman, who was probably primed for a barrage of questions.

But Lily had already decided that there was no point in asking. They would tell her what this was about, or not. The less noise she made, the better. When the cup was empty, she placed it on the tray with the wrappings and laced her fingers together.

The girl got impatient with the silence. "Come with me."

Lily ran that hypothetical action through the dignity-calm-equanimity algorithm, but the woman let out an irritated sound before the results could crunch. "Come with me, or I will physically compel you," she said. "I have black belts in eight martial arts disciplines."

"Tell me where I'm going," Lily said.

The woman's ponytail bounced as she tossed her head. "King wants to talk to you," she said. "What King wants, he gets." Her blue eyes dilated almost to black when she spoke the name.

"So King is the name of the guy doing this to me?"

"Come with me and find out," the woman said. "If you don't come willingly, you'll still find out, but it'll be more painful. As in dislocated joints, torn cartilage, snapped bones, missing teeth, broken nose, internal bleeding. Have I made myself clear?"

Data churned through the algorithm. Up Lily went, on her feet. The lure of information plus the avoidance of pain was a winning combination. The wooden floor was cold and smooth against her bare feet. Funny, how small and docile being barefoot made one feel. She supposed she should be glad they'd left her any clothes at all.

Pad, pad, pad. She tried to pretend her knees weren't knocking and her bowels churning. The food she'd eaten was threatening to make a surprise reappearance. Not good. Stress urping was not dignified.

She willed her spasming stomach to calm down, focusing on the squeaking athletic shoes of the ponytailed ninja bitch. The corridor was long and hardly lit at all. Light filtered in from each end. It looked like the corridor in an old apartment building or hotel.

They stopped and she was shoved into a doorway, into a large room, also white and windowless. A table against the far wall. A single chair, sitting under a horribly bright light. An interrogation room.

Two men. One was on his feet, the young one who had helped kidnap her from Rosaline Creek.

The other was an older man, one she'd never seen before. Even when he was seated, she could tell he was tall and well built. He was handsome, his perfectly styled hair discreetly graying at the temples. He had the patrician good looks of a powerful politician—or rather, an aging A-list actor who played powerful politicians. Real politicians didn't have time for this much grooming. This guy had gotten himself ironed a couple of times. His tan was too smooth, his jaw too taut. He smiled, activating deep, charming dimples. His teeth were unnaturally white.

"Ah, Lily. Finally you've joined us." His smile was jovial. "Please, sit down." He gestured toward the chair in the middle of the bleak room with the air of a kindly host seating her on a cozy sofa. "Hobart, are you ready with the videos? You look pale, my dear. Melanie, get Lily another coffee." He turned to her, brow creased in concern. "This time two sugars, I think. I know you don't take sugar, but indulge me— you look like your blood sugar is a little low. After all, you've been unconscious for close to three days. Sleeping beauty!"

Melanie shoved her down into the chair. "Indulge you?" Lily repeated. "Don't play bullshit games with me, you psychopath—ow!"

Her voice choked into a squeak as the woman he'd called Melanie twisted her arm up with a jerk that pulled her onto her feet, every nerve in the twisted arm screaming with agony—

"Melanie, that will do," the guy said in a tone of mild reproof.

Lily's butt reconnected hard with the chair. She wheezed with pain, feeling her shoulder. Surprised it was still attached at all.

"Melanie? The coffee?" the man reminded her.

The ferocious glow in Melanie's blank eyes damped down, like someone had thrown the off switch of a machine. She trotted to the corner, where a large coffee carafe sat. Crazed assassin, morphing instantly into perky waitress. It was chilling to watch.

"You have to excuse Melanie," the man said. "She's passionately loyal to me. All of my people are. They can't help themselves."

"Melanie?" she croaked. "And Hobart. So those are their names."

The man waved his hand dismissively. "In a manner of speaking. Their names are not registered on any official document. Their names are whatever is convenient to me. Their defining identity is that they ... are ... *mine*." His toothy smile spread wide, beaming.

Lily stared at the man. New depths of dismay yawned inside her.

"Oh, my God," she said. "This is worse than I thought. You are totally batshit, aren't you? All of you guys are."

Hobart lunged for her this time. She fell off the chair in her effort to scramble out of range.

"Back." King's command stopped the younger man as if he were a voice-activated robot. "Really," he chided his minions. "Don't take what Lily says so personally. She's been under terrible stress. And she is soon to be under a great deal more. A little empathy, people."

That speech went down Lily's craw like strychnine-laced Kool-Aid. She struggled up to her feet, sat carefully in the chair. Melanie handed her another cup. Lily sipped. Nauseatingly sweet. It made her cough.

It burst out, uncontrollable. "What did you mean by that? About that stress that I'm going to be under?" She hated herself for the weakness that prompted her to ask. More so when King chuckled.

"Hobart, are you filming this with the handheld as well as the fixed vidcam?" he asked, silkily. "I don't want to miss an instant."

The guy leaped to obey, and Lily took note of the two video cameras mounted on tripods, which watched her from diagonal corners of the room. Hobart himself held a third in his hand.

He began to circle her, constantly moving. It made her dizzy, the camera's eye constantly swirling around her, Hobart's blank gaze above.

"As to that," King said. "Well, you see, I've gambled a great deal of money and manpower on the hope that Bruno Ranieri actually does give a damn about you." His smiled widened, dimples deepening. "So, Lily. Think long and hard before you answer. Does he care?"

Weird, how such a boring, neutral suburban house with a well-trimmed yard and manicured hedges could somehow still be so ugly.

Bruno stared at the front of the house of Giuseppina Ranieri, his maternal grandmother. It was risky, and rude, to come at her with no advance phone warning, but he'd decided that it was riskier to call first. Give her time to organize herself and stonewall him just for spite. Grandma Pina was one of the most dislikeable people he'd ever met. Outside of the maniacs trying to kill him. One thing about psycho killers—they put the garden-variety assholes starkly into perspective.

"So? Shall we come along? Hold your hand? Is she that scary?"

It was Sean, jibing at him, but the jibes had lost their edge. The guy was just trying to rile him up, rev his engine so he could move.

It wasn't working, sadly. He was dog tired. Shit scared.

Get going. He'd faced bullets, knives, clubs, bombs, and fists. He could face down Grandma Pina.

"Be quick," Kev said. "We can't be late to the airport. Or we could pick up Zia Rosa and bring her back, and you can do the family reunion adventure with her. Would you rather have reinforcements?"

He recoiled at the thought. "No. You cannot imagine how much those two women hate each other. What was Zia thinking to fly out to Newark right now?"

" 'Thinking' isn't the appropriate word for what happens in Zia Rosa's head," Kev said. "Wish someone had stopped her, though."

"She called a cab and sneaked out," Sean reminded them. "Not their fault. Nobody knew they were supposed to duct tape her to a chair. Sveti said she was freaked after Petrie showed her the photos of your, ah . . ." He paused, delicately. "Alleged siblings. I can see how that would be nerve-wracking. Since they, uh . . . look like you and all."

Bruno shuddered. "I'll talk to Grandma Pina now, and get it over with. Then we pick up Zia. You two stay here. You'd scare her."

"And you won't?" Kev pointed out wryly.

Bruno glanced into the rearview mirror and looked away quickly. It was true. He looked like eight different kinds of shit. Vampire pale, eyes bloodshot, six-day stubble. Palpable desperation oozing out of his pores. And a dangerously long interval had passed since his last shower.

He marched up the walkway. Lily was in trouble. Personal hygiene could wait. But it was unfortunate to walk up to Grandma Pina's door looking like a desperado. She was not the type to see through to a guy's inner beauty.

He rang the bell, a hollow ding-dong. Several seconds passed and the door jerked open a couple of inches, blocked by the security chain.

Grandma Pina glared at him from the narrow slit. There was no recognition in her gaze. "What do you want?"

He knew better than to smile. "Hi, Grandma Pina. It's me, Bruno."

Her face froze, eyes widened for a moment before they squinched tight again. Her chin thrust forward. "I don't believe you!"

He shrugged. "It's me," he said again. "Why would anyone lie about being me?" *Or voluntarily claim you as a relative?*

Seeing her face gave him a queasy feeling. Pina Ranieri had been a beauty in her youth, when she'd been courted by and married to Rosa and Tony's oldest brother, Domenico. Her daughter had resembled her, but what he saw now was a chilling glimpse of how his mother would have aged if she'd taken a wrong turn in life early on and focused on nothing but how the world had let her down.

Not that Mamma had any chance to take a wrong turn. The world really had let her down, in the worst possible way. She'd reached the end of the line at the age of thirty-two. Which, coincidentally, was the milestone he would hit on his own next birthday. Huh. That fun fact hadn't occurred to him until now.

All thanks to Grandma Pina. He looked at the disappointment and anger etched on her face, furrowing her brow, pinching her nostrils, puckering her mouth. So like his mother's, and yet so horribly unlike her.

"You've grown," she said, still suspiciously.

"It happens," he said. "I was twelve last time you saw me. At Mamma's funeral." *Not that you saw me often. Never if I saw you first.*

"Don't you give me any of that back talk," she warned, as if she'd heard his smart-ass thoughts.

He squelched a snotty reply. "May I come in?"

"What do you want?" she demanded, again.

He bit his lip and tried again. "May I tell you about it inside?"

She slammed the door. The chain rattled. The door opened.

He walked past her into a house he barely remembered. Grandma Pina hadn't invited him and Mamma to come there often. Bruno's very existence was an irritation to her. A living reminder of her great disappointment in her daughter. Plus, he had tended to break things.

The living room was crowded with puffy furniture covered with shiny, impermeable plastic wrap. A glass coffee table was covered with little crystal doodads and ceramic flower sculptures. Pictures of kittens, flowers, sunsets, and seascapes hung on the walls. Spic-and-span. Dead and embalmed.

She gestured toward the couch with a martyred air.

"No, I'll stand," he said. "This won't take long. I just wanted to ask if you knew what happened to my mother's stuff after she died."

She looked affronted. "Well, after all these years, I never had any idea that you'd ever want any of that garbage! I don't know what you're insinuating, but I certainly never—"

"I wasn't insinuating anything," he hastened to say. "I just wondered if you had it, or knew who had disposed of it."

"Well, I went through it afterward. Packed up a few things that were mine to begin with, mind you, things that I wanted back! Most of it was trash. She didn't have a pot to piss in. Pathetic."

He unclenched his fists and kept his voice even. "I'm looking for one thing in particular. Did you remember an antique jewelry box? It came from Grandpa's side of the family. It was his mother's, from the old country. Mamma had it when I was a kid. About so big"—he indicated with his hands—"and covered with mother of pearl."

Grandma Pina's shoulders jerked in an angry shrug. "I don't remember it, but I suppose you can look through those boxes if you like. It's not much to look through."

His heart sank. The box was memorable. If Grandma Pina hadn't seen it, it probably wasn't there. But he had to be sure.

"Thank you," he said. "I'd appreciate that."

She led him through the ferociously clean house and a white, sterile kitchen decorated with framed cross-stitches of flowers, lambs, bunnies, and Bible verses. She flung open a door, flipped on a light, and hesitated, as if afraid to go down into a dark basement with him.

He sighed. "I'll go down alone, if you like," he offered. "Just tell me which boxes they are. Point them out from the top of the stairs."

Her lips tightened into a prissy arc. "No, I'll show you."

He followed her down. The room was lit by a single hanging bulb, and stuffed with boxes. She led him through a corridor between chest- and shoulder-high stacks of God knew what and into a dark corner.

There, on a raised wooden flat, was a pile of battered, dusty cardboard boxes. They were set apart from the others, a few feet of security distance around them, as if they were somehow contaminated.

She jerked her chin toward them. "Be my guest."

"Thanks," he murmured. His stomach fluttered nastily as he touched the packing tape on the topmost box. Grandma Pina just stood there, looking like a lemon was stuck in her esophagus.

"You could just leave me here to go through these, if you have things to do," he offered. "You don't have to stay."

She sniffed. "Hardly."

Oh, whatever. He tore off the tape.

Kitchen stuff. An espresso pot, cups, pots and pans. Ceramic salt and pepper shakers that he had played with as a kid. A shepherd and a shepherdess. The shepherd's crook and the flowers on the shepherdess's bonnet had been broken off. His fault. A pasta strainer. Plates. He rummaged to the bottom, making sure there was no place the box could be hiding.

Everything he touched made memories swirl up through his body. He tried to freeze them, hold them back, but the plastic plates, the juice glasses with Woody Woodpecker and Wile E. Coyote, the coffee cup Mamma had favored, all made his throat ache. The breakfasts with her. Cinnamon toast and cereal. Scrambled eggs. Teasing, laughter.

Next came her clothes. Just as bad. That sweater, that blouse, that nightgown. Light, pouring into a room in his mind that had lain undisturbed for eighteen years. He remembered every piece. He didn't know his own current wardrobe as well as he remembered hers.

He held her purple nightgown to his face and breathed in for the scent of her perfume, but it was long gone. Just mildew now.

"It was those trashy men she took up with." Grandma Pina blurted out the words as if they were under pressure, like she'd been waiting eighteen years for someone to bitch to. "They were the ruin of her. Starting with your father and downhill from there."

That sparked his curiosity. "Did you know him? Who was he?"

She harrumphed. "He was out of her life before you even started to show. So many things she gave up for you. All her prospects."

Bruno grabbed another box. Photo albums. He opened one. His baby pictures. Mamma holding a miniature Bruno, looking gorgeous and happy. He fogged right up. Closed the album, fast. Not now.

He felt around with his leaky eyes closed to make sure

nothing of jewelry box dimensions could be hidden there. Nothing.

"I told her." Grandma Pina's voice quavered with anger. "I can't remember how many times I told her that Rudy was dangerous trash, but she wouldn't listen. Stupid girl. She deserved what she got."

"We're not going to debate that," he said. "That subject is closed."

Something in his voice made her step back. "Don't threaten me."

"Don't bad-mouth my mamma. If you want to stay while I look through these boxes, fine. Just keep your mouth shut."

He looked away. Let her glare and twitch if she wanted.

He powered through the boxes, hope fading with each one. By the time he got to the last one, hope was gone. It was a catchall. Books, magazines, miscellany. Items he couldn't imagine why his grandmother had packed. Even a few of his old action figures. Rudy's little brass pipe, of all things, the one he'd used for smoking hash and crack. Envelopes, magazine subscriptions, utility bills, past-due notices. Stuff from collection agencies, threatening messages stamped in red. He felt the cardboard bottom. No jewelry box.

He couldn't start sobbing in front of Grandma Pina, but oh, God, he'd been hoping so hard for a break. "This is it?" The question was redundant, but it burst out of him anyway.

"Everything. Maybe your box got thrown away with the trash."

He tried not to flinch. "You would have packed it if you'd seen it," he said. "It was clear that it wasn't garbage."

"Then it was stolen by your no-good neighbors. Or Rudy. He probably pawned it for drugs."

"Maybe." He sat for a moment in a state of absolute despair. He wanted to sink down, become one with the chilly concrete. Just a dark grease spot. But desperation jerked him into action again. He leaned over that last box, rifling through it. There had to be something. Some clue, some opening. He yanked out the mail. Bills, credit card offers. Letters from the school guidance counselor about his bad attitude.

Then his eye snagged on a thick envelope, which was not addressed to Magdalena Ranieri but to Anthony Ranieri. He peered at it in the dim light. It was from the county coroner's office. "What's this?"

Grandma Pina squinted over her glasses. "Oh, that. The coroner's report of your mother's autopsy. Tony called them and requested one."

"He did?" His voice cracked a little. "Why?"

Pina flapped her hand. "Some silly notion of wanting a record of every mark they left on her. So he'd know what to do to the people who killed her. You know how he carried on. So violent. But then he and that mentally deficient sister of his ended up running off back to Portland with you before the report even came back. They had some absurd idea that you were in danger. Ridiculous, both of them."

Yeah." Bruno thought of Rudy and his switchblade. "Ridiculous."

"So, in the end, I had to deal with that." She pointed at the envelope with a martyred air. "When I was trying so hard to forget."

"I don't know," Bruno said, staring at the envelope. "Looks like you did OK. With the forgetting part, I mean."

She drew herself up. "I was devastated! My only child!"

"Yeah, yeah. So broken up, you never even opened it."

"How could I?" Tears trembled in her eyes. "How could I bear it?"

He could see where Mamma had gotten her flair for dramatics, but that was all she'd gotten, thank God. The flair, but not the content.

He ripped the envelope open, pulled out the sheaf of paper. He wasn't sure why. But it seemed disrespectful to Magda Ranieri that this official catalog of her death wounds should go ignored for eighteen years. No one had cared enough to open the envelope.

She had died from it. He could at least read it.

It was hard going. Seeing it all laid out in that dispassionate, scientific way did not distance him at all. He couldn't help but imagine the scene as it happened. See the blood. Hear the blows, the screams.

He couldn't help but imagine it happening right now, to Lily.

He was about to shove the thing back into its envelope just to save what was left of his sanity, when something caught his eyes.

. . . well-healed surgical incision over a resected left ovary . . .

Resected left ovary? Weird. He read it again. Yeah. One of her ovaries was gone. And "well-healed surgical incision" indicated that it had been gone before her death by torture and beating.

"Do you know anything about Mamma having an ovary removed?"

She looked affronted by the question. "Excuse me?"

He held up the report. "This says her left ovary was removed. Surgically. Why would they do that? Cysts, maybe, or a tumor?"

"I never knew a thing," she huffed. "Maybe she got a sex disease from one of her men. That kind of thing happens to women of her sort."

He should have known better than to ask her a reasonable question. She was like a backed-up sewer pipe. Spewing filth every time she opened her mouth.

The phone rang upstairs. Grandma Pina turned her head, clearly torn between the desire to answer and the danger of leaving an unsupervised lowlife thug loose in her basement.

"Go get your phone," he urged. "I'm almost done. I'll be good."

She sniffed again and scurried up the stairs. He was glad to see her go. His stress levels were high enough without her help.

He lifted the autopsy report and read on.

28

*D*oes *he care?*
The question echoed in Lily's head. Lily took a gulp of coffee. *Lie.*

"No, he doesn't care about me," she said. "It's just sex."

Her contrary nature made the words pop out. They were immediately followed by knee-melting fear that she'd just signed her own death warrant. The slow, bloody, screaming kind.

King just smiled. "Ah, Lily. That's not true."

She shook her head. "I've known him for, what, a week? I was only physically with him for half that time. For all I know, he was already screwing other women. He's a ladies' man. He'd boff anything female with a pulse. And he's attractive. Who could blame me?"

"Oh, no one, my dear. Was he good?" King asked brightly.

Lily paused, feeling for the trap. She wanted to spit on the floor and tell him to insert it straight up his nether orifice. But that did not jive with the not-caring persona. She gave them a bright, toothy smile.

"Very good," she said throatily. "Lots of stamina."

"Oh, really? A man can really give his all when he's in love, eh?"

She let out a cynical bark of laughter. "We had quite the mad affair. The guy talks a lot, but he never said 'I love you.' Not his style. He keeps things light. So don't try to control him with me."

King threw his head back as he laughed, showing off his excellent dentition. "That's good. I'm so glad you've been entertaining yourself."

"Oh, yeah, I was so entertained," Lily said. "The gunshots

and knives and explosions and all that, it really livened things up."

That set him off again. He chuckled until he wiped tears from his eyes. "Oh, that's funny," he murmured. "You are unique, Lily."

"I'm gratified that you're so amused. I live to please. I don't suppose you'd just tell me why you're doing this. I have no beef with you, other than that you've been trying to kill me. So what is your problem?"

King tilted back on two legs of his chair. "I'm afraid the simple answer will not satisfy you, my dear. Because it's really not fair to you."

He paused with that annoying half smile. She clenched her teeth against the urge to beg him to go on.

He finally gave in, probably to the hunger to hear his own voice. "It isn't anything that you did, Lily, or anything you know. It's more about who you are. Which is to say, Howard Parr's daughter."

She'd known that already. She'd known it from the beginning, but even so, she felt the pieces fall into place with an iron clang of finality.

"Why?" she whispered.

"It was about what Howard knew, my dear. Which was far too much for my comfort."

"About Magda, you mean? How you murdered her?"

He stared at her blankly and began to chuckle. "Well, now. You know even less than I thought. Howard never had a chance to confess, did he? Zoe stopped him just in time, bless her murderous heart."

"Zoe's the name of that nurse who slit his wrists?" Lily asked. "The one you sent after me to the cabin?"

He shrugged. "Insofar as—"

"Yes, I get that. Insofar as these wretched robot drones have any identity separate from you," she snapped. "I'm a quick learner, OK?"

His face froze. Her belly fluttered, terrified she'd gone

too far, speeded up the mortal agony part of the day's entertainment.

"Yes, you are a quick learner," he said. "But not quick enough. You never found out anything that could have hurt me."

"Then why me?" she burst out. "Why did you come after me?"

He shook his head sadly. "Once Howard pronounced the words 'Magda Ranieri' and mentioned her son, your fate was sealed," he said. "You had to be prevented from making contact with Bruno. Separately, the two of you had nothing that could threaten me. But together . . ." He shrugged. "Bruno was the fuse, you were the match. We didn't succeed in eliminating you before that contact took place. So all we could do after is to contain the mess, as best we can."

"But my father . . ." She shook her head. "How could he have . . . he was a doctor, a fertility specialist! He grew babies in test tubes! What could he have possibly known that would bother you?"

He shook his head. "That's none of your concern, now. Believe me, you have much more urgent things to worry about."

"Why didn't you just kill him, too?" she demanded.

He sighed. "I should have, in retrospect. Magda had to be eliminated because of the kind of person she was. In brief, just like her son. Can you imagine Bruno knuckling under, promising to be good? He would fight to the death, like Magda. She was indomitable." He looked dreamy, nostalgic. "An incredible genetic heritage. But I digress."

"Uh, yeah," she muttered. "You sure do."

"The simplest way to make sure your father never said anything would have been to kill him, of course," he went on. "But this may surprise you, Lily. I prefer to avoid killing, if possible. It's a logistical nightmare if the authorities get involved. Such a terrible drain of resources, and the risk of exposure, too. At the time, I thought it would be better to just terrify him into silence." He gave her a regretful smile. "It wasn't hard. Howie wasn't like Magda, you see."

That bastard. Her fists were clenched, her knuckles white. "So how did you do it?" she asked. "What did you threaten him with?"

He looked impatient with her dullness. "With you, of course."

She wouldn't have thought she could feel worse, but the day was full of surprises. "But I never even knew that you existed!"

"Of course not. That would have meant certain death for you both," he explained. "My people were discreet. We made sure that Howard was regularly reminded of what would happen to you if he went to the authorities with what he knew."

"Oh, Dad," she whispered. A sick ache of grief twisted at her guts.

"Every now and then, we would send him a fresh video," King said. "I have the originals. They were very effective. Terrifying. Artistic, even, in their own special way. Would you like to see them?"

"No," she said.

He burbled on as if he were doing her a big favor. "I'll have Hobart put a monitor in your cell. Some video entertainment, while we wait."

She tasted blood. She had bitten her lip. "That is so cruel."

"Cruel?" He looked offended. "I hesitated to orphan a ten-year-old girl who was already motherless! *That* would have been cruel! I was generous! He kept his life, didn't he? You kept your father!"

"Kept his life?" she repeated. "What life? I never had a father. You did murder him, you son of a bitch. You just took eighteen years to do it!"

He tutted. "Don't be overdramatic, Lily. You're being irrational. I'm disappointed in you."

"I'm glad that you are," she said. She stared at his hurt expression and the weird commando no-name creatures who hung on his every word. It clicked in her mind. His blind spot. He saw people as machines. He didn't perceive their hearts, souls. He didn't receive that wavelength. They were just dolls to him.

He was like a person who had never seen the colors of the sunset, but worse. He was missing a crucial piece, but in its place was insatiable hunger. Yawning greed and self-worship.

"Such hostility," he complained, miffed. "I'm surprised at you."

"I'm glad," she said. "I have to thank you, you son of a bitch. I've finally found out what my problem is, after a lifetime of wondering."

He blinked, expectantly. "And that is?"

"You," she said quietly. "I finally know who to hate. Not my dad. Not myself. Just you. Only you. What a gift you've given me. Finally."

His eyebrow twitched. "You're welcome," he murmured.

She ignored that. "I don't have to look any further for someone else to blame. The blame is all yours. You monster."

"Melanie, Hobart, back," he snapped as his minions leaped to attack her. The two subsided, clenching their fists.

King rubbed his hands together. "Well, then. Thank you, my dear. I think we have everything we need here. Hobart, let's get right to work."

"On what?"

"On our editing," he explained. "This footage of our debriefing interview needs to be edited for your precious Bruno's benefit!"

Icy fear pinched her. "You'll never get Bruno," she said. "He won't come looking for me. It's not like that. It's just bittersweet memories."

"That's a lie. He's coming. The power of love, or perhaps just sex, but power is power, hmm?" He patted her face, pleased with himself. "We know everything. We have a listening device on Rosa Ranieri's phone. She's the kind of woman who calls every hour, demanding a status report. He's coming for you. In the area already."

"What area is that?" She had no real hope that he'd answer.

"I suppose there's no harm in telling you," he said. "You're over an hour north of New York City, in a nineteenth-century railroad baron's country estate, perched on a cliff over the Hudson. Lovely place. Sadly, you will probably never see it. Someday I mean to remodel it, return it to its former glory, but I have other priorities right now. Melanie, my dear, upload the loop of her father's extortion videos. It'll entertain her while she waits. Lily, this just might give you some insight into your father's breakdown, his drug addiction. Perhaps it will give you some closure?"

His benevolent smile flicked off like a switch when the door opened and a woman came in. It took Lily a moment to recognize her, she was so changed. Wizened, jaundiced, like something had sucked all the juice out of her, revealing a frame made out of bent wire. Her cheeks were caved in, her burning eyes sunken in darkened sockets. But it was her. Miriam. Or Zoe. One of the nameless ones.

Their eyes locked. The woman's face contorted with rage. She launched herself at Lily with a raptor's keening shriek of rage.

Her body connected, flinging Lily and her chair to the floor. The coffee cup flew, lukewarm coffee spattered everywhere, and Lily gasped for breath as Zoe's thumbs bit down on either side of her voice box.

She clawed at Zoe's hands, but they were like steel. The woman's bloodshot eyes protruded from her wizened death's head of a face, lips drawn back over her teeth as her fingers dug, crushed . . . the world retreated . . . going dark, silent . . .

It came swinging back, brutally vivid, along with air sawing painfully into her damaged throat. They were lifting Zoe, kicking and flailing. Lily lay on the ground, clutching her throat, coughing.

"Zoe! Zoe!" King grabbed Zoe's shoulders, shook them, switched to a language Lily could not place. He shouted out a thundering phrase.

Zoe's legs buckled. She sagged, boneless, whimpering.

King offered Lily his hand. "So sorry about that," he said. "Zoe's been confused since that incident at the cabin. A sequencing problem, I think. She can't quite track the passage of time right now, poor thing, so she thinks she's still supposed to kill you."

"Aw. Really," she croaked out. She ignored his proffered hand, scooting back until she could use the wall for support. "How upsetting for her. Wow. My heart just bleeds."

He grinned in appreciation. "Ah, that's the ticket. The sarcastic comeback, no matter what. I can see why Bruno's so taken with you."

"But he's not," she repeated, grimly. "He's not. Dream on."

King turned back to Zoe, intoning another phrase in that incomprehensible language. She appeared to come to her senses, shaking off Melanie's and Hobart's grips with a petulant jerk of her shoulders.

"Zoe, my dear," King said. "You came to give us news?"

"Yes," she said. "Julian told us that Ranieri is inside his grandmother's house in Newark. The two McCloud men are waiting in the car outside. Julian's circling the place, awaiting instructions."

"Hmmm," King murmured. "They must be looking for this jewelry box. The one he found the key for. In the locket. Next to Rudy's skeleton. Hmm?" He gave Lily a smug, sly smile.

"How did you know that?" she whispered. "From Zia's phone?"

"We've been watching carefully. Hobart, call up a satellite view of the house and get a webcam ready. Melanie, get

me an untraceable line and call Pina Ranieri's home phone.
And Zoe, my bloodthirsty darling, do you have a knife
handy?"

A smile stretched her wizened features. "Of course." She
crouched, pulled one out of a sheath on her ankle. An evil-
looking thing, with notches and a curved five-inch blade.

"Excellent," he murmured. "Bruno is sure to remember
you from the cabin. Lily, sit down in your chair again, that's
a good girl. Hobart, get the webcam right in front of her, yes,
just so . . . and Zoe, get behind her. Put the blade up to her
face . . . yes, just like that, right under her chin. Excellent.
Oh, yes, that's just chilling."

The cold steel pushed against Lily's flesh, pressing every
time she swallowed over the bump in her aching throat.
"What is this?"

King dimpled, boyishly. "This, my dear, is showtime."

"It's for you!"

Bruno's gaze jerked up from the description of Mamma's
ruptured spleen and the internal hemorrhaging that it had
caused. "Huh?"

Grandma Pina was at the top of the stairs, holding the
cordless handset high like she wanted to chuck it at him.
"You gave my phone number to your lowlife friends?" she
scolded him. "How dare you?"

"No, ma'am," he said. "I never gave your number to anybody. I don't even know your number."

"That's a lie, or else how would this person know that
you're here?" She shook the thing accusingly.

His head went light. Oh, yeah. That's who might know.
The mystery hell-fiend, all-seeing, all-knowing. The one
with Lily in his jaws.

He shoved the coroner's report into his pocket. "I'll talk
to him."

"So what am I now, your secretary?" she shrilled.

He bounded up the stairs, plucked the phone from her hand. She continued to screech and scold, but he dialed her down to the far-off gabbling of barn fowl. "This is Bruno Ranieri. Who am I speaking with?"

"Hello, Bruno."

He waited for more. Man's voice. Standard American accent, no regional flavors. Bruno's hands clenched. "Who the fuck is this?"

The volume of Grandma Pina's agitated noise rose sharply in response to his word choice. He ignored her.

"You shouldn't be as worried about who I am as what I could do," the voice went on, soft and taunting.

Fear yawned afresh. That voice. Maybe he did recognize it. But he couldn't put his finger on where from. "Is that so? What could you do?"

"Do you have a videophone on you?"

He reached into his pocket, closed his shaking fingers around his smartphone. "Yes."

"Excellent. A picture is worth a thousand words. Pay attention." He rattled off the site, software, username. Bruno's thumb quivered as he tried to punch the info into the smartphone's tiny keyboard. He kept fucking it up. Each time he did, the trembling got worse.

Finally, he got the line open. The image appeared on the display screen. His heart jumped up into his throat to choke him.

Lily stared at the camera. Her face was strained. Glaring light washed her out to snowy paleness, her hair was a rat's nest halo, her eyes shadowed and haunted, but it was her. The bitch from the cabin was behind her, holding a knife to her throat. But Lily was still alive.

If this was live streaming, that is. "I want to talk to her," he said.

"Talk," the voice invited him. "Be my guest."

"Lily?" His voice cracked dangerously.

Her expression did not change, but her lips moved as she responded to him. "Hi, Bruno."

Her voice sounded wooden. Drugged, maybe. "Are you OK?"

Her throat bobbed. "I'm fine."

"So far, that is," amended the voice, which now emanated from two different sources, creating a slightly out-of-sync echo.

"What do you want from me?" Bruno burst out.

The guy chuckled again. "Ah, yes. I thought so. You'd do anything, wouldn't you? Zoe, put the knife up to her eye—"

"No! Please, no," he burst out. "Please, just don't. Just tell me what you want. You don't have to do this. Don't hurt her."

"Very well." The video image flickered, vanished. "Listen carefully. You will lay down that cell phone, and without saying a word, walk out the back door, holding the landline phone. Go between the garage and the garbage cans into the alley, where you will turn right and walk to the corner. A bronze BMW will pull over. Get into the backseat."

"But you—"

"Do not speak again, or I will have her cut," the voice warned. "Keep the line open. Do not try to give your grandmother any message to take to the men waiting outside. It's hard to tell which McClouds they are, since they look so much alike, but I happen to know from other sources that they are Kevin and Sean."

Pressure built inside him. He didn't dare speak.

"You're panting like a dog. Let's hope you're an obedient dog. Put down the phone. Don't be clever. If I see your grandmother approach the men, Zoe begins to cut. Understand? I give you leave to respond."

He coughed to clear his throat. "Understood."

"Are you holding a wireless receiver? You may answer."

"Yes," he croaked.

"Good. When the signal is out of range, drop the handset on the ground and walk on. Now . . . go."

He moved like a robot through the kitchen toward the back door, which led onto a patio, and from there, the garage and garbage cans that the voice had described. His grandmother hustled out after him. He could not follow the angry babble that came out of her mouth. His attention was locked on to the buzzing hiss of that silent open line.

Across the patio. Over a green, perfect lawn. The breezeway, between the shed and garbage cans. Grandma Pina was lunging to grab her telephone from him. He weaved drunkenly out of her range, out into the alley. She finally gave up and just yelled after him as he walked down that alley. The signal failed a few yards later, and he let the handset drop. He was passing by a dirty white van parked behind one of the neighboring houses, and he chose a route right past it and slowed to scrawl surreptitiously in the grime, in loose cursive:

Lily   had to   sorry

Twenty more yards took him to the avenue. The bronze BMW was waiting, its motor humming. Bruno opened the door. The driver didn't even turn his head as he slid inside and shut the door. The car took off, a surge of eager power that shoved him back against the leather seat.

The voice hadn't told him not to speak in the car, so he hazarded a question to the driver, just for the pure raving hell of it.

"Where are we going?" he said.

The guy turned his head and looked at Bruno. He smiled.

His face alone was the answer. Sweet Jesus. It sent thrills of dread through him. So much like himself. Younger, though. Like looking through a magic mirror back in time, except that the guy's hair was several shades lighter, and his eyes were blue. The difference was just enough to be jarring. How he'd look if he'd been dipped in bleach.

His rational mind fought it, reeling, but his cells recognized it. Alarm bells were clanging on every layer of his consciousness. He thought about the stiffs in the morgue, the ones who were related to him. Petrie hadn't been shitting him. It was true. But still impossible.

"Oh, Christ," he whispered. "You're one of them, right?"

The kid's full mouth, exactly like his own, stretched in another wide smile, activating the deep dimples. Exactly like his own.

"So are you," he said.

"It's been too long," Kev said, for the tenth time. "Too damn long."

"You think Grandma Pina's got him strung up by his thumbs in there?" Sean said. "I think Bruno can handle a hundred-and-ten-pound woman in her late seventies. You're just clock-watching, bro. It takes time to go through an old lady's attic, or basement, or whatever. It's a good sign that he's taking so long. Maybe he has half a chance."

Kev shook his head. Sean was trying to keep it light, but he was wasting his breath. "I don't care," he said. "I'm going in."

"He begged you not to, man," Sean warned.

"We can't wait. We have to intercept Zia Rosa before she descends on one of the most brutal Mafia bosses on the Eastern seaboard."

"She won't have a gun on her, right?" Sean said hopefully.

"Depends on if she checked luggage or not," Kev said.

"She totes a gun?" Sean looked shocked. "Holy shit!"

"Of course. She's a Ranieri. She's Tony's sister. She has her own guns, plus his whole collection," Kev said. "She's a walking armory."

Sean whistled, impressed, and checked his watch. "Hurry, Bruno. We gotta save the Mafia boss from your crazy aunt."

The front door burst open, and Giuseppina Ranieri herself shot out, as if the house had forcibly propelled her. She wore a coat, held a big purse.

"Oh, shit," Kev snarled. "He's gone!"

"Gone?" Sean looked around, confused. "Gone where?"

Kev waved his hand toward the old lady. "She would never leave him in her house unsupervised!" He burst out of the car and ran to intercept the woman. "Excuse me? Mrs. Ranieri?"

She spun around, wild-eyed, brandishing a can of pepper spray. "Stay away from me!" she screeched, spraying wildly.

Kev jittered and spun back out of range before he could get a faceful of the spray, and then lunged forward, nabbing the canister before she could plunge another one. "Just a quick word with you, ma'am," he said. "About Bruno—"

"So he was lying, then! He did tell his no good friends my number! And my address, too, eh? That lying little punk!"

Kev had no idea what to do with that. "No, ma'am. We're just his ride, that's all. We wondered where he'd gone. Is he still in the house?"

"I'll call the cops!" she howled. "I'll have you arrested!"

Sean hung way back, watching.

"Mrs. Ranieri, please, just tell me," Kev pleaded. "Did Bruno find the jewelry box? Is he still inside looking?"

"No!" she yelled. "There was no jewelry box! He just got that phone call, and out the back door he walks! As cool as you please, without so much as a word, or a good-bye, or even a thank-you! So *rude!*"

"The back door? He went out the . . . oh, *shit*." He and Sean exchanged horrified looks. "Oh, no, no, no."

He and Sean bolted as one for the narrow strip of lawn bordered by the neighbor's chain-link fence at the side of the house. The old lady followed them around back, shrieking and swinging her purse at them.

He tore through the back patio, the yard, through the breezeway, out into the alley. No sign of Bruno. He let the pepper spray canister drop to the ground, yanked out his cell, punched in the code for the phone Davy had given his little brother.

They heard the ring tone buzz from inside Pina Ranieri's kitchen.

He and Sean stared at each other in grim dismay.

"He left the phone?" Sean murmured, frowning. "Why did he leave the fucking phone?"

"Because they ordered him to! Goddamn it. *Goddamn it!*"

"Oh, and about that phone!" The breathless old lady caught up with them, her eyes bugging out. "He just walked away with my home phone! That phone cost me thirty-four dollars! I'll have him arrested!"

"Which way did he go, ma'am?" Sean asked.

She just stared at him, squint-eyed. Sean smiled at her. "Just tell us, and we'll try to recuperate your phone, OK?" he wheedled.

She sniffed suspiciously, jerked her thumb to the right.

They raced out, pounding down to the avenue. No Bruno. Cars zipped past in both directions on the busy street. He saw Sean pick up the phone out of a tuft of grass, hold it to his ear, give Kev a negative headshake. No line. Sean held the phone out to the sputtering old lady. "Your phone, ma'am," he said politely. "Safe and sound." He looked at Kev, his eyes full of dread. "Bro. Come here. Have a look at this."

Kev braced himself, and looked at the message on the van.

Lily   had to   sorry

"Oh, God. Bruno." Kev sagged forward, his forehead against the filthy vehicle. And he'd thought he'd gotten his shit together. That he had Edie and his family, that everything would be fine at last. That he'd earned a little happiness, a little peace. That it would finally be OK.

But no. The world was still able to tear new holes in him. It was so easy to just rip it all to pieces. Oh, Bruno.

Sean's hand closed on his shoulder. "Hey. Kev. I'm so sorry."

He couldn't answer. Just tried not to fall apart.

"Look," Sean said. "This sucks, but we have to sharpen up and disappear before that crazy old dame really does call the cops."

Kev gulped, stood up, wiped his face. "Yeah," he muttered.

"So let's go get your crazy Zia," Sean said. "And hope that she has some really brilliant new idea for us. Because I'm fresh out of ideas."

They caused screeching protest by their choice to run through Pina Ranieri's property again, but fuck it. The shrill sound was already fading, and it was the fastest way back to their car.

Not that they had a clue what they were hurrying for, anymore.

29

Lily stumbled as Zoe dragged her down the corridor. "No, really," she said. "You look like shit. What happened? Did you get the flu?"

"Shut up." Zoe jerked Lily off her feet. She thudded down to her knees on the cold, hard floor, with a gasp of startled pain.

"But it was only a week ago or so since I saw you, right?"

Lily persisted. Zoe looked wrecked. Stress would weaken her further, and if there was one thing Lily was good at, it was driving people nuts.

"You looked great up at the cabin," she went on. "Couldn't help but notice, even though you were trying to kill me. You looked pretty fine the day you killed my father, too. Killing seems to agree with you. But you look like crap now. You must have lost twenty-five pounds. You shriveled. What is up with that?"

"I said, *shut up!*" Zoe's voice was cracking around the edges as she jerked Lily upright, making her sore shoulder joint blaze.

"You ought to get that jaundice checked out," Lily barged on. "Liver function issues really trash your complexion."

"Shut . . . *up!*" *Whack.* Zoe whacked Lily across the face, slamming her into the wall, from whence she bounced down to the floor. Lily huddled there, her hand pressed against her throbbing face.

Zoe bent at the waist, hands braced on her thighs, and stared at Lily. She panted, jaw sagging. A muscle twitched prominently in her bony jaw. Everything showed in her face—veins, tendons, bones, all in sharp relief, like a skull that had been dipped in yellow wax.

Zoe squeezed her eyes shut, eyelids twitching. Veins pulsed visibly in her temples. She dug into the pocket of her cargo pants and yanked out a small envelope. She peeled the sleeve of her shirt back with her teeth. Small sheets of paper covered with red dots fluttered to the ground. A dot was already stuck to her wrist. As Lily watched, she peeled the last dot off one card and stuck it in the crook of her elbow.

She sagged back against the wall, breathing hard. Then she reached down, keeping narrowed eyes on Lily, and scooped up the rest of the fallen papers. She tucked them back into the envelope.

Her breathing was slower, veins no longer popping out on

her forehead. Her crisis was passing. So Zoe was some kind of a junkie. How very unsurprising.

"What the hell is that stuff?" Lily asked.

Zoe's purplish lips stretched in a sneer. "Mama's little helper."

"Would you give me one?" she blurted, for no reason she could fathom. "I could use some help."

Zoe let out a short, contemptuous laugh. "One dose of this stuff would kill you. You'd die of convulsions on the spot."

"But it doesn't hurt you?" she asked.

"I'm different," Zoe said loftily. "We're a different order of beings. You wouldn't understand how profoundly we've been changed."

"Deformed." The word popped out.

Oof, Zoe's boot connected with her belly and jackknifed her into a moaning vee. "Mind your manners," Zoe said. "Get up."

Lily struggled up. Zoe jerked her arm, twisting until Lily squeaked and writhed into a pretzel shape to ease the pain, but there was no escape. The pain jangled on through every nerve.

She shuffled, dragging her feet until Zoe yanked open Lily's door and flung her inside. Slam went the door. *Click, clunk* went the locks. Lily huddled, curled into a ball. She crawled to the wall, shook her hair down in a tangled veil, itchily aware of the camera's constant regard. She touched the bottom of her bare foot. Peeled off the grubby piece of paper stuck to it. Stared at it, behind the veil of her hair.

One of Zoe's drug patch papers. A full one. It held sixteen of the little red dots, four rows of four, and a protective sheet of plastic film on top. Lily held it concealed in the palm of her hand, palm down.

She had no clue what to do with it. At least she had a suicide tool, but that had never been an option in her mind.

She'd always been so angry at her father for trying it. But things looked so different now.

She started to cry. In shock, that she'd scored even that tiny victory. Terror, at the thought of daring to use it to defy them. Grief for her father, fear for Bruno. Too many reasons to count.

She curled up, clutching her prize, and gave into the storm.

It was an exercise in self-control. The agonizing, sweat-popping kind, never a talent upon which he had particularly prided himself. The driver of the bronze BMW, who'd confided that his name was Julian, had pulled over after ten blocks or so, offered him a bag to put over his head, and told him to lie down in the backseat.

Bruno stared at the bag dangling from the man's hand. Black, lined, drawstring at the border. He'd as soon lie down into his own grave. After a few seconds, Julian just shrugged, pulled out his cell phone, held it up to his ear.

Oh, no, no, no. Bruno promised to be good. He put on the bag and lay down on the seat. The new-car leather stink made him queasy. He was claustrophobic anyway, and not being able to see or breathe fresh air made him frantic. It would have been easier to bear if he'd been bound with rope, duct tape. But it was just fear that held him.

The car got on a highway. He tried to estimate the time, but anxiety skewed his perceptions. The best he could figure when the car got off the highway was more than one hour, less than two. Julian had tuned into Vivaldi's "Four Seasons," at high volume. The melody of the bouncy, shrill violins grated on his nerves like a car alarm.

After fifteen minutes, the car stopped, the window whirred down. Some muffled conversation, a shiver of cold air, and off they went again. The car moved at a sedate pace. It came to a stop. Doors, popping.

He was dragged out by more than one set of ungentle hands. Three people, from the sounds. Someone jerked his hands back, put the plastic cuffs on, yanked them tight. Sounds echoed, hollow and booming. Indoors, but the air was still. Very cold. A big garage?

They gripped him from either side, dragging him off his feet however hard he scrambled to keep his feet underneath him.

The first tract was a well-sprung wooden floor, and then he was shoved into a smallish elevator. A sliding cage slammed shut. It was so small, one of his captors had to stand right in front of him. He caught a whiff of perfume. One was a woman.

The thing made a surprising amount of jerking and grinding as it went up. Antique. He was in an old building. The elevator didn't go far. One floor.

The door dragged, clanged. They shoved him out and into another long corridor. Finally, a door opened, and he was shoved through it so hard he tumbled to his knees and then onto his face, without his arms to brace him. They dragged him through the room. His butt connected with a chair seat so hard it jarred his spine all the way up to his skull. They fastened his bound hands. Then his feet to each chair leg.

The hood was jerked off.

He sucked air into his starved lungs in wheezing gasps, blinking away tears from the influx of light.

He was in a large room. Several people were arrayed before him. Julian was there. The knife-wielding ghoul bitch from the videophone call. Another guy, too. Young, white, bland. All of them had a strange look in their eyes. Fascination. And focused, concentrated hatred.

Another guy stepped into the floodlight. Bruno struggled to bring him into focus. Big, tall, backlit by the powerful light. The man grasped Bruno's chin between his thumb and forefinger. His face swirled in Bruno's vision. That smug smile, those glinting eyes. Did he know this guy?

"Bruno," the man said. "Finally."

Bruno convulsed at the sound of his voice. The guy grabbed his chin and yanked his face up into that helpless, supplicating child-awaiting-punishment posture.

The question building inside him for the past three days burst out. "Where's Lily?" he yelled. "What have you done with her?"

The man gave his cheek a slap. "One thing at a time. Look at me."

His eyes streamed from the light. Tears ran down into his nose, a wet, ticklish flood, creeping down. He had no way to wipe his face.

It felt so fucking familiar. He wanted to scream, thrash. He got a grip on it and stared right back. "Yeah?" he said, belligerently.

"Do you know me?" the guy asked.

Yes. Yes. His gut knew, but his head still couldn't nail it; the how, the when, the who. "No. Who the fuck are you, and what do you want?"

Another stinging slap. *Whap.* "Don't play dumb," the guy said. "I know you're not stupid. Look again. And dig deep."

Terror swelled. He did know this man. The memory was locked in his body, in muscle and bone. He felt small, confused. Wanting his mother. So angry. Couldn't move. Struggling against restraints until the needle stung his arm and paralysis took him. And that face, so pleased with himself. That deep, horrible voice, setting his every hair on end—

"DeepWeave sequence 4.2.9 commencing," the guy said.

Bruno convulsed once again, violently. His body jerked as if electricity juddered through it. The heavy chair rattled, shook. "Oh, shit. No."

"Yes," the guy said. "Yes, it's coming to you now, right?"

Bruno wanted to deny it, but it was flooding back in sickening waves. "The dreams. You're that guy who talks in my dreams."

"Do I?" The man's eyes sparkled. "I'm delighted to know

that the programming went so deep, even in the experimental stages of my research. Remarkable, considering how short a time I had to seed it."

"Seed . . . what?" It took him a few tries to get his throat calm enough to choke the words out. "P-p-programming?"

The hand on his cheek petted him. He couldn't stop shaking his head no, even though memory was flooding back. "You're the guy Zia Rosa told me about. The one who kidnapped me from Mamma when I was seven. And then Tony leaned on Michael Ranieri to get me loose."

The man's face tightened. "I will always regret that," he said. "I should never have given in to pressure. At the time, the Ranieris were a vital source of my research funding. But this is no longer the case."

"But what the hell did you want with me?" he exploded.

"Oh, Bruno. You were my inspiration," the guy said, patting him on the shoulder. "You sparked a new line of research that has yielded fantastic results. You are my shining star, Bruno. My sine qua non."

"What in the flying fuck are you talking about?"

Smack, the guy whapped him again, on the temple. "Don't be vulgar," the guy lectured. "I don't like it."

"I don't care what you like," Bruno said.

The man pinched Bruno's cheek until his thumbnail sliced into flesh, stinging. "You will learn to care," he said. "It's time you learned."

Bruno sucked in a ragged breath at the pain. "Who are you?"

"Oh, Bruno." The man sounded peevish. "I tested your intelligence when you were a child. I don't know how much of that potential you've realized in adulthood—probably a fraction—but I know you're capable of answering that question unassisted." He released Bruno's cheek, his thumbnail smeared with blood. "If you need a name, call me King. Now put it together. What do you see?" He gestured at Julian. "Add that to what you learned from Petrie, about the genetic makeup of my lost operatives." He clucked his tongue. "Terrible waste. You can't imagine the time, training, and money I invested in those young people."

But Bruno was still fixated on Julian. "How old is that kid?"

King turned to the boy. "Tell him, Julian."

"I'll be seventeen in two weeks," the young man announced.

Mamma had been cold in her grave a year before this kid was born. Bruno shook his head again. It was data he was afraid to crunch. Conclusions he didn't want to face. But the mental process ground along without his conscious volition. He fidgeted against his bonds and felt the crackle of paper in his jacket pocket. The autopsy report.

It popped out at him, like a fun house goblin in the dark. "The ovary," he blurted. "You stole my mamma's eggs! You pervert!"

"Ah!" King began to clap. "Here's a glimpse of the Bruno I saw twenty-two years ago. All that potential. Like a nuclear furnace. It broke my heart to see how you turned out. All that potential down the sewer. All that was left of my pride and joy was a foul-mouthed punk with no aspirations that I could see other than seducing as many women as possible. No guidance, no discipline, no vision!"

Bruno listened to the guy's bitching, searching frantically for connections. "What the fuck?"

King cut himself off with a wave of his hand. "Excuse my rant," he said. "It's been a sore subject for me for decades, and I—"

"Oh, God." The realization burst painfully in his head, like popping flashbulbs. "Lily's dad. That's the connection! He was an IVF researcher, right? He made embryos for you. Out of Mamma's eggs!"

"Excellent, excellent!" The man beamed. "Yes, that's what Howard did for me. He harvested the ovum and made me dozens of viable embryos. I paid him very well for the service. He was brilliant, you know. He'd developed preservation techniques ahead of his time. Those embryos are still viable to this day. Amazing."

Bruno stared at Julian. This boy was his brother, his mother's son, with that blank stare. Born after she died, twisted and deformed. Never knowing Magda Ranieri's love or protection.

"You bastard. You cut open my mamma and stole her children," Bruno said. "How did you get away with that?"

"It was easy. At the time, your mother was too busy worrying about you to worry about her ovary. But she got worried at the end, when she figured out what I wanted to do with it. She even convinced Howard to be worried. She was so worried, she had to be, well, taken care of."

"You son of a bitch. I'll kill you for that," Bruno said.

The guy was unperturbed. He folded his arms and waited, lips twisted in a half smile. Tapping his foot.

"What?" Bruno exploded. "What do you want?"

"Go on," King said. "And the rest?"

"With what?" Bruno snarled. "Stealing her organs, kidnapping her potential children, that's not enough? Aside from murdering her?"

"You're not tracking," King scolded. "Don't tell me you skipped so many eighth-grade biology classes that you have no real grasp of the mechanics of human reproduction."

Bruno grunted. "Haven't gotten any complaints so far."

Smack. The slap rocked his head back. "Focus." King's voice cracked like a whip. "I do not appreciate crude sexual humor."

Bruno struggled to fathom what the guy wanted from him. Some trail of reasoning he was supposed to follow? About those embryos, but he couldn't . . . oh. Oh, shit. It started again. That drumroll. Another horrible truth he already knew but didn't want to know.

"You're talking about the sperm," Bruno said. "You're talking about . . . no. No fucking way. That's not possible."

King smiled, delighted, gave his head a pat. "It is."

"You?" Bruno's voice cracked. "You're not . . . not my . . ."

"Your father?" King's teeth gleamed, unnaturally white, as he finished the phrase for him. "Of course I am, Bruno. Who else?"

30

Zia Rosa didn't see Kev when she stepped out of the exit gate at Newark. She marched along, staring straight ahead, with the stiff, rocking gait she affected when her edema was flaring up.

He stepped out into her path. "Hey, Zia."

She stumbled back. "*O cazzo!* Kev! Whatchyou doin' here?"

"I could ask you the same question," he said grimly.

She sniffed. "I got business to take care of." Her voice lowered to a whisper. "Bruno ain't in here with you, is he? You gotta warn him that the cop from Portland is—"

"That's what I need to tell you," he said, cutting her off. He had to get this over with, quickly. "I have bad news. About Bruno."

Zia pressed her hand to her heart. "He didn't find the jewelry box?"

"No. Pina didn't have it. But there's more."

Zia Rosa's mouth started to shake. "No. Not my boy."

"They took him," Kev said, feeling helpless. "I'm so sorry. I tried, but they got him. And I don't know where he is now."

Zia Rosa sagged, toppling. He leaped to catch her, but he was positioned wrong. Fortunately, the man behind her lunged, grabbed her under the arms, and broke her fall. No mean feat, with a woman of Zia's majestic proportions. Between the two of them, they eased her to the ground. Kev looked up to thank the guy for his reflexes.

The other man spoke first. "Who took him?"

Kev's insides froze. He stared at the guy. No one he'd ever seen before. Tall, younger than Kev, messy dark hair, beard stubble. A tough, intelligent face. Sharp hazel eyes that knew too much about their private business met his over Zia's squashed helm of bouffant black curls. "Who the hell are you?" he asked.

"I'm Detective Sam Petrie," the man said. "Portland Police Bureau."

Oh, *shit*. His heart sank. "And what are you doing here?"

The man's gaze was very direct. "Looking for answers. And protecting your aunt, incidentally. She shouldn't be traveling alone."

"Oh?" Kev said, through gritted teeth. "Duh. Thanks so much for that blinding insight. How altruistic of you."

Zia Rosa's eyes popped open to shoot the guy a hostile glare. "Hah. Protecting me? In a pig's eye. *Opportunista*."

Petrie shrugged. "She spotted me on the plane. So I figured there was nothing to be lost by just talking to you, face to face, once we landed."

Kev grunted. "I doubt that the city of Portland is springing for your cross-continental air fare so that you can protect my aunt," he said. "What did you do? Tail her to the airport when she bolted?"

"Yes." Petrie hoisted Zia Rosa into a sitting position. "This isn't official. I'm here at my own expense. This case got me going. When I latch on to something like this, I don't know how to let go. So I followed her."

"That's a personality trait that might get you killed," Kev said.

"I know," Petrie said calmly. "Until then, I'll just do what I do."

They stared, sizing each other up. Petrie spoke again, his voice pitched just for Kev's ears. "I'm not out for your brother's blood. He told me he killed those men outside the diner in self-defense, and for what it's worth, I believe him. I want to know more, before I find any more bodies. If Bruno was straight with me, he has nothing to worry about. From the law, that is," he amended.

"What do you expect to accomplish here?" Kev demanded.

Petrie shrugged. "I don't know yet. I just want to know more," he said simply. "Your brother's in trouble, right? Maybe I can help. I'm another gun, at least."

Kev blinked at the guy, nonplussed. "You flew here armed? On such short notice?"

"Know a guy in the Portland Airport Police," Petrie said blandly. "Used to work with him. He took me around the gates, through the Airport Police office. I think I owe him my firstborn child now, though."

"That's your problem. Nobody asked you to," Kev growled.

"Fair enough," Petrie said, unruffled. And just waited.

Kev harrumphed. "Great," he said, sourly. "Zia Rosa wants to help. The cop wants to help. Everybody's in my face, wanting to help. This much help could kill me."

Petrie didn't drop his gaze. Kev looked at the guy and let his perceptions soften, broaden. It was a trick he was picking up from hanging out with Edie, like he could almost ride her brain waves when she was drawing. He'd always trusted his own instincts, but time spent with Edie had sharpened his perceptions still further. He felt around in that other dimension for the shape of the other man. His intentions, his vibe.

The feeling he got was . . . solid. Like a rock, but dynamic. The guy wasn't bullshitting him. He might be inconvenient, but not tricky. He wasn't here sniffing for glory. He was hungry for the truth.

Who knew? Maybe he really could help. At the very least, like he said, he was another gun. "That was a dirty trick, showing Zia those photographs," he said.

Zia Rosa batted away Petrie's supporting hands, her face martyred. "I was so shocked," she said. "I fainted."

Petrie shrugged. "I'm sorry."

People swirled around them, carts buzzing past, people dragging carry-on luggage trolleys, shoving strollers. Seconds ticked by.

"Who took him?" Petrie asked again.

"If I knew who, or where, I'd be there right now, blowing their asses to hell and gone," Kev said. "It's the same ones who've been trying to kill him for the past week. You heard that part of the story?"

"Might have heard that part better if he'd asked for formal assistance from the authorities," Petrie said calmly.

Kev looked at Zia Rosa. "We don't have time for fainting spells."

"'Course not!" Zia struggled to her feet. "Just tryin' to stonewall this bozo." She glared at Petrie and brushed herself off. "Get lost, babycakes. *Sparisci*. We got things to do."

Petrie stood, unmoved. Kev sighed at the thought of the conversation that would immediately follow his next statement.

"He's coming with us, Zia," he said.

"He's *what?*"

The yelling, the vituperation in Calabrese about his idiocy and Petrie's perfidy, etc., etc., lasted to the curb outside in the ground transportation area. There was no point in explaining to Zia about perceptions from other dimensions, or following one's instincts. That would be talking to a wall. Zia Rosa's opinion of cops was as dim as Tony's had been. Kev let the tirade flow through his head and past it.

Petrie marched alongside and had the good sense not to allow himself to look entertained.

Sean swooped in to pick them up. His reaction to Petrie's presence was not as loud as Zia's, but fully as strong. The look he gave his twin was more than enough. Kev looked away as Petrie got into the backseat next to him. "OK," he said to the car at large. "Ignore him if you want, treat him like a piece of furniture. Zia, where to?"

"Gaetano's house," she said promptly. "He retired to a place out in Rupert. He'll know who's doing this."

"Why him? Why don't we just go directly to Michael?" Sean asked.

"I don't know Michael from Adam," Zia Rosa said. "Gaetano's the one I got clout with. And Costantina, his wife. My man-stealing cousin. If Pina didn't pack up Nonna's jewelry box from Magda's apartment, that *puttanella* Costantina must have it. She always thought it shoulda been hers. Then she married the man that shoulda been mine. I bet when Magda died, Costantina went over and helped herself to it. It's time I had a talk with that dirty, thieving slut."

"That dirty, thieving slut is pushing eighty, Zia," Kev observed.

"So?" His aunt twisted in the seat and stared. "A slut is a slut. I ain't afraid of Gaetano. That bastard jilted me. He can't look me in the eye. *Lo mangio crudo.* I'll eat him raw, eh? For breakfast!"

Kev leaned and put his hand on Zia's shoulder. "Hey," he said. "Seriously, Zia. You wouldn't have actually wanted to marry that guy, would you? To be caught in Mafia turf wars for decades? Costantina Ranieri is not a lucky woman. Would you really want her life?"

Zia Rosa gave him a look that was completely real. No jokes, no theatrics, no hamming it up. A look that Kev had almost never seen on her face in the nineteen years he'd known her, aside from Tony's funeral.

She shrugged. "Boh," she said, her voice bitter. "The bitch has eleven grandchildren."

"No," Bruno repeated, for the tenth time. "You can't be."

"Yes, I can. You know that it's true. Look at me. See it?"

Bruno looked. The guy made his flesh creep, but he saw it. Those dimples. Like Bruno's own. And Julian's. The shape of the eyes, the teeth, though Julian's and King's had benefited from orthodontia that Bruno's had not. The guy's body, too. Tall, broad shouldered, lean hipped. The shape of his jaw, his hands. He'd seen it in the mirror. Bruno swallowed to calm his trembling throat. "So you were the pig who knocked my mother up and then ran out on her."

King looked affronted. "Not at all! I was in love with your mother. She was brilliant. But so uncompromising. We had discussions about philosophical positions that we did not share. She became angry, told me to leave. I took her at her word. She never told me about the child. I found out about you seven years later, Bruno. By chance!" He sounded aggrieved, as if he'd been wronged.

"She figured out that you were bugfuck and ran," Bruno said. "But by then she was pregnant. She tried to keep me a secret. But you checked up on her."

"Out of nostalgia, I suppose," the older man said. "I expected to find her married and fat, with six children, stirring Ragu, growing a mustache. But no. I discovered you." His eyes shone. "My own seed."

Bruno recoiled. "So this is all about your sick ego?"

"I had to see what you were made of! I'd already begun my training programs. I had four pods going already. Zoe was in training with three of her podmates. She's my oldest living alum, from my second generation. But I couldn't resist seeing what my own flesh and blood was capable of! With the cognitive enhancement drugs and my subliminal training techniques, I was sure that you could surpass—"

"Pods?" Bruno broke in. "What the fuck are pods?"

King looked irritated. "I grouped infant trainees into units of four," he explained. "Results are better when trainees are raised in a family-style setting."

"Infants?" Bruno looked around at the young people that were staring at him with fresh chill. "Oh, my God. You mean, you've been fucking with these people's heads since they were *babies?*"

"Cultivating them," King corrected. "I've been cultivating them, exactly as you were not cultivated. What you could have been, what you might have accomplished, if I'd had you since birth!"

Yeah, he'd be as crazy and twisted as these wretched robot fucks. He jerked his chin in their direction. "Are they all, ah . . . your—"

"My genetic offspring? Oh, certainly not." King chuckled. "That's just a pet project of mine that sprang to life when I discovered you. Only Julian is related to you, of the operatives gathered here."

Bruno shuddered, tried to drag his mind into focus. "So where did the other ones come from?"

"Various sources. I've tried many things over the years. Some I bought outright from pregnant girls—screened for their mother's intelligence level, their births never recorded. Some are children of catastrophe, like Zoe. A war, an earthquake, a tidal wave, and you have hundreds of thousands of displaced people, and presto, there are already child brokers on the scene, scooping up orphans for instant resale. I tried buying them from the sex traffickers, but that's problematic. So difficult to control prenatal care, nutrition. Many specimens were damaged. The cull rate was too high. My best results came after I found you. I decided to use Magda's genetic material, since our combined genes had already yielded an exceptional specimen."

But Bruno's mind had glommed on one scary phrase,

with a piercing stab of dread. "Cull rate? What's the cull rate?"

King looked annoyed. "Don't be dull, Bruno. It's just as it sounds. Not all of my attempts prove to be valid. Some just don't work out."

"So it's kill rate, then," Bruno said flatly. "Not cull rate."

"Not at all," King snapped. "It's very civilized. Gentle euthanasia, not killing. A painless injection or a bit of gas, and they drift away."

"Great," Bruno muttered. "So you're a mass murderer, too."

King made a frustrated sound. "Exactly like your mother. Fixating on irrelevant details. Deliberately missing the point, just to irritate me."

"How many were there?" Bruno asked. "Of Mamma's babies?"

"I had dozens of embryos to start with, but we trimmed down to sixteen of the best," King said. "Of those that were gestated, only six made it through the cullings over the years." He looked wistful. "Three of those operatives died this week. One at the diner, then Reggie died immediately afterward, as a result. Then Nadia, killed by your friend Aaro. Then there's my Julian. And the very last two. The little ones."

Bruno just stared at him. "Little ones," he repeated. "You mean . . . you mean . . . oh, Jesus, don't tell me you've made more of the—"

"Yes!" He beamed. "A boy and a girl. Twenty months old. Their test scores are off the charts. More promising than their predecessors, even you, Bruno, but don't be jealous! Hobart, hook up to the Pod Fourteen-Twenty-two webcam and show Bruno his little siblings. I can hardly wait to start programming, but DeepWeave prelim begins at twenty-four months. I've discovered that beginning earlier causes . . . well, let us just say the results have proven to be unfortunate. One simply must be patient."

Hobart clicked onto the pad. He held it in front of Bruno's face.

He saw a bright, colorful room, like any day care center, full of toys. Two children played there, dressed in identical blue smocks. The boy, racing around on a toy motorcycle, looked like his own baby picture. The girl, playing a xylophone, looked like his mother. His throat ached. His numbed hands clenched against his bonds. "She knew, right?" he asked. "Mamma found out about you messing with helpless kids. She knew you were growing her embryos in vitro. She was trying to stop you. That was what she was doing when she sent me away. That was the evidence she was gathering against you."

King looked wistful. "I gave her the option of joining me. Once I realized the potential in our genetic combination, I wanted to continue the classic, old-fashioned way." He leered. "She was lovely, after all."

"Don't go there, ever, unless you want me to vomit on you."

King's brows snapped together. "Magda was limited, though. Like you. I wanted to create supremely realized human beings, and she wanted to stop me. I did not see it coming, when she started gathering information on me through Rudy. I wouldn't have thought she'd have the stomach to get so close to such a brutal thug. But she managed it."

"I don't want to hear your comments," Bruno said.

"She was sneaky," King mused. "And he was stupid. Never even noticed her following him, documenting his activities. Not until the very end. At the time, Rudy was on loan to me from Michael Ranieri, helping with the disposal of culled trainees and other details of grunt work. It's been years since I've had to use those thick-necked criminals, thank God. I apologize for robbing you of your mother so young. I would not have done it if it hadn't been absolutely necessary. Such a blow."

"You can shove your apology up your ass," Bruno said.

King shook his head sadly. "Such potential."

Bruno had to look away. He couldn't let himself be taunted into a screaming freak-out. That served no purpose. All he could do for himself right now was gather more information. Even if he choked on it.

"One thing you haven't told me," he said. "One very important detail. What the fuck do you want with me?"

"Well, I'm afraid you do have to die," King said, with an apologetic air. "You're past saving, no chance of reprogramming at your advanced age, and even though you never did find your mother's evidence, you know too much to run around loose. I was so disappointed about that."

"About what?"

"That you didn't find the jewelry box. I wanted to recover it. It annoys me that there is information that could be inconvenient for me, floating around out there somewhere. That was one of the reasons I let you live so long. So you could solve that mystery for me, tie up that loose end." He sighed. "But I'll just have to let it go."

Bruno stared at the guy. King wore a noble, martyred look.

"But before I dispose of you, I want input for my next generation of DeepWeave programming," King went on. "The events of the past week have shown me the limits of my current programming. It's frustrating, but I must be humble, learn from my mistakes. And you will help me."

"Humble? You." Bruno grunted. "Right."

"Yes, Bruno. It baffles me that you, in spite of your disadvantages, in spite of your deprived upbringing, completely lacking in intellectual stimulation, you have come out ahead of my superbly trained operatives in every single encounter. Even your genetic siblings."

"What if I did? You got me now, right? Aren't you satisfied?"

"It's not that," King said. "Don't trivialize. My operatives are missing a crucial component that gives you some mysterious edge. When I understand what that component is, I'll synthesize it. It's just a matter of creating conditions, be they environmental, chemical, what have you. I'm an artist, you see, and I will not rest until my technique is perfect."

Bruno stared into the guy's eyes. Bottomless pools of madness. King was looking for a golden egg, and Bruno was the unlucky magic goose laid out on the slab. "I hate to break it to you, but I don't think it's something you can synthesize," he said. "You're talking about intangibles."

"Nonsense," King said. "An intangible is simply a thing that has not yet been adequately understood. I assume it has to do with human connection, relationships. I've already noted that operatives who bond with their podmates are more successful on every level. And I've created the conditions for passionate love. My operatives love me to distraction."

Bruno looked at the blank, slavish hunger in King's creatures' eyes. "That's not love," he said quietly.

"You think you know what love is?" King laughed. "That's funny. Love can be a strength or a weakness, depending on how the chips fall. Like Magda. She did superhuman things for you and for her unborn children. But you were her weakness, Bruno. I could have controlled her easily with you, if the Ranieris hadn't started throwing their weight around. And Lily is your weakness, isn't that right? Would you be here, facing certain death, if not for her?"

Blood drained out of his head, leaving him dizzy and faint. "Where is she?" he asked. "What have you done to her?"

King patted his cheek again. "I'm afraid you're in for a shock."

Part of him wanted to howl with laughter. As if anything could shock him now. The rest of him was frozen in fear for the one shock he could not face. "Wh-what?" he croaked.

The door opened. A young woman burst into the room. Her excited babble didn't penetrate. Then he saw the look on

King's face. It suddenly occurred to him that anything that could wipe that smile off that asshole's face was something he was interested in hearing.

". . . at the airport," she was saying. "They picked her up at the Newark airport, and they're headed to Gaetano Ranieri's house, right now! I checked the tags, and Michael Ranieri is there! Do you want me to warn him to get away?"

King stared into empty space for a moment. "No," he said.

The young woman exchanged startled glances with the guy who did the computer stuff.

"No?" she repeated.

"No. We're streamlining. My partnership with the Ranieris has ended, as of this moment. I no longer need them. Zoe, my bloodthirsty love—are you up to bringing a turf war to Gaetano Ranieri's door, while Rosa Ranieri and the McCloud brothers are there?"

Bruno's guts flopped. The woman's sunken eyes lit with joy. "You want all of them dead?"

"All," King purred. "Mow them down. I want carnage. Blood everywhere. But move fast. This is a fleeting opportunity. When you come back . . ." He gave her a seductive smile. "We will dine together."

Her face turned an unwholesome blotched red, eyelids twitching. "Yes. Yes, I'm on it." She scrambled for the door.

Melanie and Hobart turned to King as the door clicked shut behind her, their faces indignant and betrayed.

The young man burst out, "Sir, excuse me for arguing, but are you sure Zoe is right for this assignment? Alone? The McClouds are extremely competent, and I'm not sure that she's capable of—"

"Trust me, Hobart. I'm streamlining in more ways than one." He gave his minion a pat on the back. "Zoe's usefulness has come to an end. That's why I'm not sending backup. When she fulfils it . . ." He squeezed the young man's shoulder with a conspiratorial smile.

Hobart tentatively smiled back. "Ah, yes, I see. Of course."

"Of course." Then King leaned forward and murmured a phrase into Hobart's ear in a foreign language that Bruno could not catch.

Hobart seemed to grow three inches taller, his eyes dilated, and his cheeks flushed as Zoe's had done. He started to pant. Disgusting.

"Thank you," Hobart said, his voice choked with emotion.

Bruno's hands jerked against the cuffs. Every significant piece of his life was being destroyed. Kev, Zia Rosa, Lily. Even Sean McCloud.

King noticed him again. "Oh, you're upset? About your great-aunt, your adopted brother? Don't worry," he coaxed, patting Bruno's shoulder. "It's not like you'll be needing them anymore."

Bruno twisted to sink his teeth into the back of King's hand.

A hoarse shriek jerked out of King's throat. A fist came flying, connected with Bruno's face. His chair tipped, toppled. He careened in a slow arch, slammed to the ground, head cracking against cold tile. The world went wonky. A booted foot slammed into his thigh, then his gut . . . and the world swung and slid, pulling against his bonds as he slid this way and that. They were tilting the chair up, hoisting him into place.

King stood before him, whacking his face. Blood flew from the guy's fingertips. "Now where were we?" The mocking tone was gone. King was growling. "We were going to discuss your lady friend, right?"

Bruno cringed. He'd lost it. He'd mouthed off, and he was going to pay. Whatever this monster had in mind as punishment, it was going to be bad. He just hoped it wasn't Lily who paid. Let it be him. Not her.

"There are some things that I think you might not know about your lover, Bruno," King announced. "Most notably, the fact that she is one of my programmed operatives. One of the best, too."

That phrase had no effect on Bruno. It bounced right off his skull like a hard object, leaving him dazed, thick-headed, confused. Bewildered.

"Huh?" he said, stupidly.

"Hobart, set the video to play, please," King said. "Show him."

31

K ev killed the car engine with a jerk. "One more time, Zia, from the top. Keep the gun in your purse. Stick to the point. We talk about Bruno and the jewelry box. Only. Do not call Don Gaetano a pig. Do not call Costantina a whore. You got that straight?"

"But she is!" Zia protested.

"We don't have time for this!" he flared. "This is about saving Bruno, OK? You care about him, right? So you will be *good!*"

Zia did the big hurt-eyes thing, and Kev turned away, drumming his fingers on the dash in a staccato tattoo. His feet twitched, and there was a stone-hard core of fear in his guts.

Petrie and Sean were quiet, but he could tell that Sean was trying not to give in to nervous laughter, his standard coping device. If Sean got the giggles, Kev was shooting his ass up, no mercy.

He flung the door open. "Let's get this over with."

They marched through a big landscaped garden in front of the ostentatious house, around a marble fountain surrounded by rosebushes. The fountain was silent and dry but for the dots of rain on the marble rim. At least it was gray. Sunshine would be an insult.

Once on the porch, they rang the bell. An insultingly long amount of time passed, during which they were assessed by whoever was studying the security cameras. One was pointed right at them, mounted under the cornice of the porch roof. The door opened. A burly, dark middle-aged man peered out.

"May I help you?" he asked.

Kev opened his mouth. Zia blared. "I come to see Don Gaetano."

The man gazed at her blankly. "That would be my father," he said. "I'm sorry, but he's not well enough for visitors today."

"He's well enough to see me," Zia Rosa informed him.

"Oh?" The guy's eyes sharpened. "And you are?"

"I'm the woman he shoulda married," Zia announced. "The one who shoulda been your mamma. Tell him that, Michael."

The guy rocked back as if she'd hit him. The door slammed in their faces. Aw, shit. Great. "Zia," Kev ground out. "You promised."

"I didn't call no one a pig or a whore, did I?"

He didn't have time to answer before the door jerked open again. This time a much older man stood there, a guy in his eighties. Thickset like his son, but balding, with pitted skin and heavy jowls. He peered through horn-rimmed glasses with a scowl that knit his bushy brows.

"Rosa," he said. "It's you."

"*Ciao*, Gaetano." Her voice rang out. "Nice to see you looking so fit."

"You're looking well yourself, Rosa."

An elderly woman, small and stringy thin with a pouffy coif of hair dyed white blond and lots of bling, appeared behind him. "Who on earth is . . . oh. It's you. My God, Rosa. You got so big."

"*Ciao*, Tittina," Zia Rosa replied. "You shrunk."

"Nobody calls me Tittina anymore," the other woman said. "Not for the last sixty years. I never liked it. I'm called Connie now."

"Call yourself what you want," Zia said. "I know who you are."

"Zia," Kev hissed. He gave her arm a warning squeeze.

"You haven't introduced your friends, Rosa," Don Gaetano said.

Zia Rosa flapped her hand in their direction. "The two blond ones are my nephews," she said. "The other one is a friend."

"So." Michael gave them a smile. "What can we do for you folks?"

Zia Rosa ignored him. "I need to talk to you 'bout something important," she said to Gaetano. She paused. "You gonna invite us in?"

Don Gaetano stepped back with ill grace and gestured for them to enter. Zia Rosa stepped into the towering foyer, which had a three-story ceiling with vast solarium windows and skylights on the top. From an iron brace about fifteen feet up, a huge wrought iron chandelier hung, full of electric candles, all of which blazed in the day's gloom.

"*Ehi.*" Zia Rosa stared up at the chandelier. "That's Nonno's *candeliera*. The one from the *salone* in the country house, back home."

"It certainly is." Costantina's voice was triumphant. "Gaetano and I went to Brancaleone on vacation nine years ago. I brought it back."

"Who said you could have it?" Zia Rosa demanded.

Costantina bristled. "Who said I couldn't?"

"Zip it, goddamnit, Zia," Kev hissed. "Focus!"

"Come into the *salone*," Don Gaetano said, waving them into a lavish living room furnished in blazing white with touches of gold, bronze, and beige. Don Gaetano seated Zia Rosa at one end of a couch and looked at the rest of them. "Sit down, all of you," he said, dropping into the chair nearest Zia Rosa. "Connie, could you get us some coffee? And some of your delicious *pitta 'nchiusa?*"

Costantina flounced out of the room, muttering to herself. Petrie declined to sit, situating himself behind the couch. Sean stood beside him. Kev checked out Michael Ranieri, who had also stayed on his feet. He stood behind his father, rocking on his heels, hands clasped behind him. No doubt fondling the pistol under his shirt, Kev figured. A fair enough guess, since he himself was doing the same thing.

"This ain't a social call, Gaetano," Zia Rosa said.

"Oh, but you have to taste Connie's *pitta 'nchiusa*, Rosa," Don Gaetano said. "They're unbeatable. Just like Nonna used to make."

Zia Rosa let out a grunt. "Whatever." She opened her purse and dug around in it until she pulled out the crumpled envelope, the one that held Tony's letter. "We're here to talk about this."

Don Gaetano stared at it, grimly. "I heard about Tony's passing."

"Figured you would," Zia Rosa said.

"I thought the whole thing was finished," he said heavily.

"I told you." Costantina was in the entryway, laden with a tray. "I told you she'd screw you over first chance she got."

"Mamma, please," Michael snapped.

Zia Rosa gave Costantina a slit-eyed look, then turned her gaze back to Gaetano. "I thought it was over, too," she said. "I woulda never done anything with this letter, Gaetano. Not if you left us alone. But that bastard's got my boy again, hear me? Same son of a bitch as before. You leaned on him twenty years ago, and we got him back. I need you to lean on him again. 'Cause if they hurt him . . ." She slapped the letter against her hand. "This goes out. All the copies, like Tony said."

Connie marched over to the couch and set the tray down on the glass coffee table with a rattling thump. She poured a dollop of espresso from the pot into each of the seven cups. There was a heap of something that looked like tarts, with gleaming candied fruits and nuts in their centers.

She set the pot on the tray with an angry thud and straightened up. "Well?" she snapped at them all. "Come and get it before it gets cold. Don't tell me I made the damn coffee for nothing."

Kev sighed. The last thing he wanted to do with his gun hand was hold an espresso saucer with his pinkie in the air. He snagged a cup from the tray and downed the swallow of throat-scalding brew in one gulp, no sugar, nodded his thanks to the lady of the house, and took up his previous post, social duty fulfilled. No way were they going to make him eat one of the cookies. He had his limits.

Sean followed his example, and Petrie, too. Zia took her own sweet time, stirring in sugar lumps. She took one of the *pitta 'nchiusa*, looking at it from all sides, sniffing it before taking a cautious nibble.

Costantina watched intently as she chewed. "Nonna's recipe. Just like hers, isn't it? The trick is the wine you put in. Has to be a real good Calabrese red, or it don't work worth a damn."

Zia Rosa chewed, making no sign of having heard her cousin's words. She swallowed. Sipped her coffee.

"I don't need a cooking lesson from you, Tittina," she said.

"Let's get back to the subject, shall we?" Kev said, before the red-faced Costantina's head had a chance to explode. "The letter? The guy who took Bruno? Can you give me a name? That's all I want."

And he would get it before he left. If he had to take those two guys apart chunk by bloody chunk.

Don Gaetano cleared his throat. "Well," he said. "A lot of years have gone by. Things have changed. I don't think it'll be possible to—"

"I got this goddamn letter, Gaetano." Zia Rosa's voice began to shake. "I swear to God, I'll send it. And if you have me whacked, the lawyer sends it. And you will go down."

"I would never have you hurt, Rosa," Don Gaetano said gruffly. "But I'm an old man now. The letter don't really matter no more."

"Bullshit, it don't," Zia Rosa said. "I bet you'd rather spend your golden years in your fancy house, gobbling Tittina's *pitta 'nchiusa* than sitting around in cell block C eating red beans. You can't shit me."

"You don't understand what my father is trying to say," Michael broke in, his voice reasonable. "Times have changed. We just don't have the same kind of clout with this person that we had eighteen years ago."

"That's no problem," Kev said, his heart thudding. "Just give me his name and his address. I'll take care of the clout myself."

Michael and Gaetano gave him a stare. He returned it.

"The name, please," Kev said. "Give it to me. And we'll leave."

Zia Rosa put down her coffee cup with a clatter. "Tittina. Did you steal Nonna's jewelry box from Madga's apartment after she died?"

Oh, Christ, no. Kev cringed, inwardly. Zia's timing sucked.

Costantina thrust out her chin. "How dare you accuse me!"

"You did!" Rosa spat the words out. "It's true, eh? Eh?"

"I wouldn't call it stealing!" Costantina yelled. "I'd call it salvage! The no-good trash next door would have stolen it, or it would have ended up in the garbage! And it should have been mine to begin with!"

"Nonna gave it to me," Zia Rosa shot back. "Not you!"

"But I was older!" Costantina's face had gone purple.

"Yeah, and you was also a nasty lying little *troia* who couldn't keep her panties on!" Zia Rosa snarled.

"It ain't my fault nobody ever wanted to get into yours, *brutta zitellaccia!*" Costantina shrieked back.

Things degenerated from there. Kev cursed. He was about to grab Zia to drag her out the door—

And the room exploded in gunfire.

"Hobart? The video, please?" King prompted his servant.

Hobart went to the computer pad. He tapped it and held up the screen in front of Bruno's face.

"This is Lily's debrief," King said. "The whole thing would take hours. I selected a couple of highlights to illustrate my point."

The sound was tinny, but he would know Lily's soft voice anywhere, even distorted by the tweeter and rough with exhaustion.

". . . all I know, he was already screwing other women. He's a ladies' man. He'd boff anything female with a pulse. And he's attractive. Who could blame me?"

"Oh, no one, my dear." It was King's voice, coming from behind the camera. "Was he good?"

Lily froze for a moment. A smile curved her lips. Bruno had never seen that smile, or that strange, hard glitter in her eyes.

"Very good." Her voice went low to a sexy purr. "Lots of stamina."

The camera cut to a moving shot that swirled around her, taking in King and the woman, his other servant. "I was so entertained," Lily went on, with a light laugh. "We had quite the mad affair."

The camera flashed to King's reaction, laughing. "Oh, that's funny," he said. "You are unique, Lily."

She gave the camera that cold-as-glass smile again. It

chilled Bruno to the bone. "I'm gratified," she said. "I live to please."

"I know you do," King replied. "You've done very well, my dear. You've exceeded my expectations. I'm so pleased with you."

"I'm glad that you are," she said, her voice oddly wooden.

"In fact, after this is finished, I've decided to give you a very special privilege," King went on. "A great honor. I've chosen you for the qualities of bravery and cunning that you displayed in this assignment. I am starting a new crop of embryos for the pods, my dear. And I have chosen to use your eggs—with my sperm."

The camera cut to Lily's reaction. She looked dumbstruck. Tears glittered in her eyes. One of them flashed down her cheek.

"Why?" she asked, her voice quavering. "Why me?"

"Because you are so special, my pet," he crooned. "Do you have anything you want to say to me, my lovely Lily?"

She brushed the tears from her eyes. "I have to . . . to thank you," she said. "What a gift you've given me."

King's voice was soft. "I always reward loyalty and talent, Lily."

She sniffed. "I love you," she said. "Just you. Only you."

"And you belong to me, Lily? Just to me?"

She looked straight at the camera, her eyes blazing with raw emotion. "Yes," she said. The camera cut to her stark, graceful profile. "All yours," she added. The video flickered, disappeared.

Bruno couldn't breathe. He stared at the screen, eyes frozen wide. Hobart gave him a wide, unpleasant smile.

"Yes, Bruno, that's right," King said. "She's the chosen one. She reminds of Magda, you see." He chuckled. "Not a coincidence, hmm? She reminded you of Magda, too! That's why it worked so beautifully. I'll be so glad to have her in my bed again. She is delicious, isn't she? So affectionate, so uninhibited. But duty called." He rubbed his hands together. "Finally things can get back to normal."

Bruno's insides were a screaming hole. He fought the pressure. Hung on to himself. Who he was. What he knew. "That's a lie," he said, roughly. "You doctored that tape. You can't fuck with me."

King looked over Melanie's shoulder as she sprayed antibiotic ointment on his bitten hand and began to wind the gauze around it.

He shook his head with a sad smile. "I can, Bruno," he said. "You see, there are things you don't know about yourself. Things that I altered in you twenty-four years ago. Let's see if the preliminary command codes still work, after all this time." He grabbed Bruno's chin and spoke a harsh, guttural word that Bruno did not recognize and almost instantly could no longer remember.

King stared at him, expectantly.

What? Bruno wanted to snarl, but then he realized, horrified, that he could not speak. It was as if the nerves had been severed. He tried again. And again. Panic burst like fireworks inside him. He began to sweat. Cold chills racked his body. He fought his bonds, panting.

King was chuckling. "They still hold! That's wonderful. Listen to this, Bruno." He declaimed a longer phrase, also in that thick language. "Now, try to move," he urged. "Go on. Give it your best shot."

Fuck you, Bruno wanted to scream, to shake his head, to spit in the guy's face, but he couldn't. He was physically paralyzed now. He sagged in his bonds, his head lolling to the side.

"My programming and medications back in those days were relatively primitive but still effective. It was an intensive learning curve for you. You were strapped into the programming device in a hypnotic trance for ten to fourteen hours a day. Did you ever wonder why your physical reflexes are so quick? Why learning martial arts came so easily to you?" The chair was tilting from Bruno's weight, which was sagging to the side. King shoved him upright. "It was Deep-Weave combat tapes. Remember that fight at the diner? Did you surprise yourself that night?" He stared into Bruno's eyes and giggled. "Of course you did."

He waited for Bruno's response. "Oh, how funny—you're still locked! One moment. Let me think . . ." He blinked. "Wouldn't it be funny if I couldn't remember the code to free you? You'd stay like that forever. I could make you do anything at all, you know. Put a gun to your head, pull the trigger. Mutilate yourself. Stop breathing. The power of DeepWeave as I have conceived it is tremendous."

Bruno stared at him. Air sawed between his parted lips.

King slowly pronounced a phrase. A racking shudder went through Bruno's body. He tried to speak. A scratchy croak came out.

"Bruno, think back to your first encounter with Lily at the diner," King said. "Remember Lily saying the phrase 'you're my champion'?"

Bruno coughed as he heard the words echo in his memory. Lily's lilting voice. The image of her, bent over her coffee in that black wig, her lips vivid scarlet. That was his memory, private and precious, and he didn't want it to be fodder for this guy's crazed agenda. He didn't want it soiled and dishonored. But he had to know. "What if she did?"

"It was a command phrase, Bruno," King said. "Programmed into you years ago. I linked it to images of your mother. You were in a phase of development where you continually fantasized about rescuing your mother from monsters. And you dreamed about saving your mother from her attackers for years after her death, no? The perfect setup."

Bruno's jaw ached. He refused to answer. His only defiance.

"Knowing that phrase would trigger all those powerful childhood emotions, I arranged for those emotions to transfer onto Lily. And then, of course, you consummated your sexual relationship immediately."

Bruno clenched his teeth.

"The sex act that I commanded her to perform with you reinforced the programming. From then on . . ." He tousled Bruno's hair with his bandaged hand. "You were her slave. My poor boy."

"That's not true," he said. "You're lying." But even as the words left his mouth, he remembered those words she'd spoken in the diner. How they made him feel. She'd spoken them again, in the cabin, he suddenly thought. On that wild, incredible night. Soaring emotions, searing sex, right after she'd pronounced it . . . like a ceremonial vow.

All those feelings, all just because he had been programmed . . . ?

No. He shook his head. "It's a lie. Why mount those huge attacks? Why not have her drug me while fucking me? She had opportunities. There was no reason to risk your people like that, if Lily was—"

"That was a miscalculation," King said gravely. "I wanted you alive for the purposes of my research, and I wanted to perpetuate the fiction that Lily was an innocent victim under your protection for as long as possible. Had I known how difficult you'd be to subdue . . ." He shrugged. "By all means, I would have done as you suggested and had Lily take you out herself. Live and learn."

"No." Bruno just kept shaking his head, but King was laughing. He'd felt the impact of the barbs as they hit. He knew he'd won.

"I have some things to attend to right now, Bruno, but I see you are upset," King said. "If you like, I could pronounce a phrase that will put you into a deep sleep until I choose to wake you. What'll it be? Sweet oblivion? Or would you prefer to writhe in agony in a locked room, contemplating how you doomed yourself for the sake of a traitorous bitch like Lily Parr?"

The words exploded out of him. "Go fuck yourself."

King chortled. "Ah, Bruno. Why am I not surprised. Just like your mother. You don't know when to stop. Hobart, Julian, take him away."

They cut the bindings, fastened his legs to his hands. The hood swallowed him, drawstring pulled choke-tight. They dragged him somewhere. A door opened. He was flung onto a wooden floor. The door scraped shut. Locking mechanisms turned, clicked. He tried for oblivion himself, by sheer force of will, but his brain, flash-fried on stress hormones, didn't have that setting available.

Which left him with only writhing agony as an option.

32

Kev hit the floor. He saw Petrie lunge across Zia Rosa's lap. The picture window was shattered, glass everywhere. Coffee table, too.

Kev looked around for Sean across the carpet strewn with demitasse cups, spattered coffee, broken cookies, shattered glass.

And blood. Costantina sprawled next to the upended metal frame of the coffee table, mouth gaping. Her throat was a raw, bloody mess. Blood pooled behind her head. Her tangle of knotted gold jewelry was like a red wet noose around her neck.

Sean poked his head around the couch. Their eyes met. Zia was yelling. Kev could barely hear it. Deafened by gunfire. The yelling was a good sign. At least she was alive.

Petrie still lay across her lap, hand pressed to his side. His hand was red. Ah, *shit*. Not a good sign.

Kev pointed to himself, gestured toward the foyer. Pointed to Sean, then toward the shattered picture window. Sean nodded.

Kev writhed on his belly over the rug. Don Gaetano lay on his side, each breath a labored whimper. Flecks of blood spattered his lips and chin. He clutched his gut, his hand dripping. Shot in the belly, and it looked like he'd taken one in the thigh, too. Kev was sorry, but he kept on crawling into the foyer. Couldn't see out the windows this low, couldn't tell how many assailants there were, where they were shooting from. He slithered up the stairs to the first landing, peeked between the banister slats, through the high, towering windows.

He saw nobody on the lawn. He kept looking, waiting . . .

There! A spot of green, shifting and moving against the rosebushes in the fountain. Darting behind the door and coming this way. Kev clambered up onto the banister, poised himself. Leaped into empty space. He caught the huge wrought iron *candeliera*, hung on like a monkey. It swung through the air like a pendulum, creaking madly, the bolts sunk into the wall straining. He willed them to hold.

He careened in wide, lazy arcs, trying to drag himself up into a ball. In the other room, he could just barely see Sean crouched near the picture window. His brother peered past the drapes swaying in gusts of wind. He looked up, shook his head. Kev jerked his chin at the door.

Sean positioned himself, drew his weapon. The *candeliera*'s swinging was slowing, but it creaked and cast a moving shadow. Slower . . . slower. Swaying. Kev held his breath. The handle turned.

The barrel of an assault rifle preceded the guy into the room—no. Not a guy. They were slender, brown female hands that held the M4. An emaciated woman in combat gear, a drab green cap on her head.

She looked up to see what the shadow was. *Bam*, Sean squeezed off a shot. She stumbled back, and *rat-tat-tat-tat-tat*, pumped more rounds into the living room. Kev prayed she hadn't hit Sean, Zia, or Petrie, but he was airborne now, heading for the killer like a sack of cement—

Thud, he hit her. They slammed to the ground together.

Kev had his Beretta 8000 under the woman's jaw before she could recover. She was dazed and unresisting. Sean scrambled in on his belly.

"That's the one who came at us at the cabin," he said, yanking plastic ratcheted cuffs out of his pack. "I saw her through the scope. Are there more?"

"Don't know yet. Didn't see any."

Sean fastened the woman's hands behind her back. Then her feet.

"One more look," Kev said. "I take the door, you the window?"

Sean nodded. He crawled on his belly back to the living room while Kev edged closer to the gaping door. On his feet. Back to the wall.

He spun, Beretta at the ready . . .

No one there, just the wind, sighing, whipping the trees. He took a step out onto the porch. A nondescript white Volvo sedan idled on the street. No backup. She'd come alone? What the fuck?

Sean had come to the same conclusion in the living room. They met at the couch. Michael Ranieri was stretched out behind the couch, a hole in his forehead, blood fanned on the wall behind him. Don Gaetano was dead, too. His eyes stared up, blank.

They eased Petrie off of Zia Rosa, brushing the shards of glass off the white leather so they could slide the wounded man to lie full length on the couch cushions. Zia looked fine, underneath him. Wild-eyed, gulping for breath, but not hit. Petrie had taken the bullet for her. Amazingly, it hadn't gone right through him and into Zia. Maybe it had bounced off one of his ribs.

Kev ripped open Petrie's shirt and hissed with dismay. Big hole, leaking fast. Sucking sound at each labored breath. The bullet had punctured his lung. He was conscious, eyes open, teeth gritted. Sean was digging into his kit, yanking things out.

"I told you that habit of yours was dangerous," Kev said. "The curiosity thing."

Petrie flashed him an eloquent look.

"Zia, call the ambulance for him," he told her.

Zia grabbed her purse, smeared with Petrie's blood, and dug for her phone. She gabbled into it, giving shrill orders to the emergency dispatcher. He left her to it, and he and Sean worked over Petrie together.

The first flush of adrenaline was easing down, and under it was grief, fury, frustration. The only people who'd known the name and location of the fucker who held Bruno were all dead.

"Goddamnit," he exploded. "Just a name, before that bitch started shooting. Just a goddamn name, that was all I asked!"

"Calm down," Sean said quietly, his hands busy.

"Why? How can I? That's it!" he snarled. "The last thread I had to grab on to. I have no other trace! None! What the fuck do I do now?"

"You've got her," Sean said, jerking his chin over his shoulder, toward the bound woman lying in the foyer.

"The bitch is useless, Sean! These fucking nutcases self-destruct! She'll rip her own tongue out or explode in my face if I start to lean on her!"

"Having hysterics will not help," Sean said, taping the bandage into place. "We have her. We'll use her. We'll think of something, we'll improvise. Christ, I hope that ambulance hurries up. I've done everything that I can." He looked around. "Say, where's your crazy Zia?"

"Oh, fuck. No." Kev looked around the ravaged room. No Zia. "I'll go track her down."

He sprinted through the first floor. Formal dining room, enormous kitchen, breakfast nook. Teak-paneled personal office. Huge game room, with pool and Ping-Pong tables. Swimming pool behind the house. No Zia Rosa.

Back through the foyer. He leaped over the bound female shooter, who panted motionless on the floor, and sped up the curving staircase.

He found Zia in the master bedroom, which was white and gold and pink, full of baroque swirling like the frosting on a cake. A room fit for a Hollywood diva of the thirties. Zia sat on the end of the pillow-strewn white satin bed, clutching an inlaid jewelry box on her lap. She stared up at Kev, eyes wide and stricken behind her glasses. Tears streamed down, mixing with the blood spattered on her face.

Terrified hope jolted through him. "Oh, God, Zia. You found it?"

Zia Rosa looked lost. "We played together with this jewelry box when we were little, Tittina and me." Her voice was almost childlike. "We played with it. With our dolls."

Kev sank to his knees in front of her. He took the jewelry box from her and opened it. It was heaped with gold chains, rings, brooches.

He dumped them out onto the bed in a tangled, glittering pile, and shook the empty box. Something shifted inside. His heart thudded.

"There's something in here." He felt for the sliding panel. Sure enough, it slid open. But Bruno had the key.

"Nonna taught us to sew together," Zia went on. "How to make the blessed animal cookies, for *Natale*. We were best friends back then, Tittina and me. And now . . . *Dio. Poverina*."

He grabbed her hands. "I'm sorry. But we just can't do this now."

Zia Rosa ignored him. "That picture of Magda that I have

in my wallet? Just like Tittina, when she was little. Just like the little girl at the baby store. The one with that bitch nurse."

"Zia, we have to hurry—"

"I shoulda known about those two, but they were so nice, you know? Her husband, too! He even come running back to give me my phone after it fell in the baby's stroller! Aw, so sweet of him, I thought, to go to all that trouble, eh? Who'd have thought they was both killers? With those beautiful *bimbi?* Nobody woulda thought that!"

Kev went rigid as the picture shifted in his mind. New shapes, new possibilities, new scenarios. "Wait. Zia, those people at the baby store . . . they handled your phone? When you weren't watching?"

She blinked as she tried to remember. "I suppose they did. It dropped in the stroller. He found it and ran it back to me in the parking lot. Ouch! Kev! Don't squeeze so hard!"

He let go of her hands, his heart thudding. "Sorry, Zia. Where's your phone right now?"

"Downstairs, in my purse on the couch," she said. "Why? You need to call somebody? What's wrong with yours?"

"They loaded software on your phone, Zia. Or a tracking device, or God knows what." His voice shook with excitement. "That's how they've been following us, catching us. With your phone!"

She sucked in air. "*O Dio!* I'll flush the thing down the toilet!"

"No, no, no! It's all we've got to link us to Bruno! We'll use it!"

"How?" She flapped her hands. Her voice cracked. "How?"

"Who the fuck knows? I'll come up with something. Just listen to me. We're going downstairs. I'll take the jewelry box. I'm going to say, loudly, near your purse, that my phone's out of juice, and I'm going to borrow yours. You can call us using Petrie's phone."

"Where you going?" she demanded. "What will you do?"

"I don't know yet, but we're hauling ass out of here with the shooter, and you're staying with Petrie while he goes to the hospital."

She inhaled to argue. Kev clapped his hand over her mouth. "No, Zia," he said, his voice steely. "Not this time. Petrie took a bullet for you. You will hold his hand in the ambulance. It's the least you can do."

She stared at him. Gave him a nod. He could hardly believe he'd managed to convince her so easily.

A siren sounded far away in the distance. Good, for Petrie's sake. No time to smash the box open here.

"That's our cue," he said. "Come on. Move."

"Where is she?" King demanded. "What's taking so long?"

Hobart tapped the keyboard. "Just waiting for the database to—"

Whack! King slammed the side of the computer desk, making them all jump. "Do it faster!"

Hobart flubbed the string of characters he was entering. He blocked, deleted, entered it again. "Yes, sir."

King hung over the man's shoulder. Melanie and Julian stood by, eyes downcast, shutting down external signals, hoping not to be noticed. He swung around upon Melanie. "Have they said anything?"

Melanie's hands lifted to the earbuds in her ears. "Nothing new. No conversation. The McCloud who got wounded is just groaning."

"Good." King was glad the son of a bitch had taken a bullet. Let him ache and throb and bleed until he died. King wished him a nasty strain of antibiotic-resistant staph to gnaw at his suppurating wound for a few agonizing days before that happy event.

"I have it!" Hobart's voice was tight with excitement. "They're in a self-storage facility outside Newark!"

King peered down at the screen at the satellite shot of the McCloud brothers' vehicle. As he watched, the door opened and a man in a black knit cap got out. He went to the back of the SUV, opened it. Then opened the door of the unit. He returned to the car, seized a long, limp bundle. It did not move.

"Is she alive?" he demanded.

"Vitals all strong," Hobart said.

The man dragged Zoe into the unit and came back out, locking it. He got back into the vehicle. Melanie's hands flashed to the earbuds.

"Put the sound on the external speakers!" King snapped.

Hobart pushed buttons. Sound blared out, fuzzy and distorted.

". . . to the emergency room before I bleed to death, goddamnit!"

"Yeah, we'll go, OK? We had to stash her first. She'd be hard to explain parked outside the Urgent Care if she started to squeak. And I want a crack at her before we deliver her to the cops, so you can—"

"What the fuck do I care? I want to plug this hole!"

"Calm down. I'll take you to the Urgent Care, and then I'll come back and have a chat with monster chick. We're gonna get friendly."

"Tell me about it after," the wounded McCloud snarled. "I'm hemorrhaging!"

"That's not hemorrhaging. It was a ricochet, OK? Stop being such a pussy. I've gone out clubbing after worse than that."

"Yeah, and I want stitches and an IV antibiotic, so drive the fucking car . . . *now*."

No talk after that, just grumbling and the sound of the engine revving. The vehicle began to move. The screen showing the RF frequency bleeping from the chip embedded in

Zoe's clavicle remained stationary in the storage unit. The one in Zoe's cell phone and the one in Rosa Ranieri's cell, which her adopted nephew had conveniently taken, began to move. King watched the vehicle until it pulled into the covered area attached to the administrative office of the storage facility and was lost to sight. He calculated the timing. Came to a decision.

"Hobart, Julian," he said. "Go retrieve her."

Hobart's eyes widened. "But I thought—"

"Plans change. Her com device is with them. She's immobilized, probably unconscious, so she wouldn't be able to fulfill a Level Ten command even if I could deliver one. And I don't want her interrogated."

Melanie piped up, her voice anxious. "Sir, I could go with Hobart. I have more experience than Julian. He hasn't even completed his final training, and if the McClouds come back before we—"

"Your combat skills are not up to a McCloud. Julian's are superior to yours. Do not presume to question me again."

Melanie's face turned crimson. All three operatives were frozen, inert.

"For God's sake!" he roared. "Move!"

Hobart and Julian scuttled out of the room. In the silence that followed, King heard choked sobs.

His teeth clenched. His hands fisted. He carefully did not look at Melanie so as not to lose control completely.

How had a specimen so defective, so inferior, managed to get through his culls? He was tempted to initiate the sniveling cunt's mortal command sequences then and there. He forced himself to stop. He was down to a bare minimum of three functioning agents, one of whom was not even fully trained. He'd called back others from outside assignments, but it would be days before they came home.

He could get rid of Melanie when his ranks of attendants swelled to an acceptable number. Until then, distasteful though it was, he needed her. Which meant he had to hold his nose and manage her.

He softened his voice. "Melanie. Forgive my sharp tone. It's an act, for Hobart and Julian's benefit. Would you really want to leave me all alone here, with no one to back me up? As you so intelligently pointed out, Julian hasn't even completed his training program. Call me selfish, but if I'm going to have the support of only one sole operative, it has to be the best one." He gave her a conspiratorial smile. "And you can imagine why I can't say that in front of the others. Can't you?"

Melanie blinked away her tears. Her face illuminated. She stood up straighter, with a tremulous smile. "Of course, sir."

"Come here, Melanie," he said, keeping his voice soft.

Her face turned pink. She moved toward him, eyes shining. He smiled at her, trying in vain to remember her command sequences. He prided himself on knowing every operative's command codes by heart, but nothing was coming to him today. Too tired, too stressed. It irritated him. He grabbed his handheld organizer. Melanie waited, eyes wide and expectant, while he punched them up from his private database.

Ah, yes. Medieval Georgian. Melanie's whole pod had been command coded in that language. Why he hadn't been able to recall it was beyond him.

"Give me your hand, my dear," he purred. Her slender fingers were ice cold, though her face was pink, eyes exalted.

He recited a Level Eight reward sequence, and Melanie convulsed with a shriek, eyes rolling back. She sagged against him.

He caught her by the armpits and held her, cursing long and bitterly at the indignity of his situation. His creations were not supposed to fall apart on him when he needed them most. They were not supposed to lose consciousness when he gave them a reward sequence. They should not be so jealous, so competitive, so distastefully oversexed. It should not be so easy to destabilize them. This problem went beyond Zoe's breakdown. It was a general defect in DeepWeave that he had to address before he began with the new, fresh ones.

But first things first. He let Melanie drop to the floor. Took ten seconds to let his temper cool. He crouched and slapped her.

She moaned, opened her eyes. They were fogged with devotion.

"Get up, my dear." He kept his voice gentle, by brute force of will. "No time to wallow! We have work to do."

She scrambled ungracefully to her feet, still panting.

King clicked on the video interface until he found Parr's cell. The woman was sitting in the corner on the floor, positioned in such a way that he could not see her face, it being below and behind the camera's eye. Just jeans-clad legs and pale, bare feet. There was a dusting of scattered white dots around her on the floor. He peered at them, then at the movement of her fingers. She appeared to be picking at some piece of paper. Shredding it. "Did you send Howard's video archive to play on the monitor in Parr's room?" he asked Melanie.

"Oh, yes. She's probably seen the whole loop three times by now."

"I want to know what she thinks of it," he said. "Bring her to me."

"Lemme get this straight, mon." The dreadlocked Jamaican cabbie crossed his arms over his chest, releasing a pungent cloud of patchouli and weed. "You want me to drive your car to the Urgent Care alone. Groaning and cursing. Park in the ambulance zone, where they will tow your ass away. Take two cell phones into the emergency room and put them in the garbage can. And then walk back to get my cab."

"That's all," Kev said.

The man stared at the eight hundred-dollar bills fanned out in Kev's hand, clearly tempted. "That's fucking weird as hell, mon."

"Yeah, sure. But you have to go *now*," Kev said. "This thing's time sensitive. It times out in a minute. And so does the pay."

The man shook his head. His eyes were slitted with suspicion, but sharp. "What other kind of sensitive? I don' wanna go to jail, mon. I don' want no trouble with nobody."

"You won't be doing anything illegal," Sean told him. "You'll be helping save innocent people from criminals. I swear it, before God."

"Swear all you want, mon," the man said. "These bad guys, they gonna be mad, and I don' wanna talk to them 'bout it, after. I don' want to be caught on no security camera. I got me a woman, a baby girl."

Kev reached for his wallet again, peeled out four more hundreds. "This is for your woman." Another four. "This is for your baby girl." He pulled out two more. "These are for making your mind up, fast."

The guy shook his head again. "Fast is not good, mon."

Kev sighed through clenched teeth. "It is today."

The guy walked around Kev and Sean's vehicle. He opened the back hatch, looked in. Looked at the cases of equipment that Sean and Kev had unloaded. "What's in those cases?" he asked.

"Nothing you need to concern yourself about," Kev said. "They won't be in the car you'll be driving. And then abandoning. Forever."

"I will be on the cameras at the emergency room," the cabbie pointed out.

"Maybe so, but you won't have committed a crime," Kev

countered. "Just a traffic violation. In a car not registered to you."

The guy stared at the fan of bills in Kev's hand once again. His hand stretched out, even though his head was still shaking. The extra thousand had clinched the deal.

Kev looked at Sean. "Get the phones out of the trunk." He turned to the cabbie. "Listen up. As soon as he brings you those phones, do not say another word. Not one more word. Got it?"

"Ah! Bugged phones? This is so fucked up, mon. I don' like this," he said, but the money had already disappeared into his pockets.

"Me, neither," Kev said fervently. "Don't forget the cursing and groaning, like you have a painful wound."

"No problem. I groan real good. I drive all day, in this winter slop, and my arthritis kicks up. Auooow! Fuck, mon, that hurts . . . auooow!"

"Don't overdo it, for God's sake!" Kev said, alarmed. "Muffled groans, OK? Or they'll be able to tell it's not one of our voices. Got it?"

"Oh, yes, I got it, I got it," the guy assured him.

"Take them out of the bags before you go in. If someone sees you drop a handbag into the garbage, they'll think you're leaving a bomb."

The guy winced and opened his mouth, but Sean was there, finger to his lips, holding up the bag that held the phones. Kev clapped his hand over the guy's mouth and yanked the driver's side door open. Sean opened the back door and tossed the bag in.

The guy still looked miserably doubtful, but he climbed in. Kev slammed the door shut. Nodded farewell. The guy nodded back, started the engine with a roar. The SUV leaped and bumped out of the shelter, down the short concrete ramp, onto the street. It turned and was gone.

Sean walked over to stand beside Kev. They stared at the

place where the vehicle had left their field of vision. They couldn't step out of that shelter until the other piece of their hastily cobbled plan drove up.

"That was stressful," Sean commented. "I hope that guy doesn't get distracted and stop for munchies somewhere."

Kev shook his head. "He wasn't stoned. But he was scared."

"So am I," Sean said. "Do you think we're fucking him up?"

"I don't think so. There are no explosives in monster chick's phone. They must have gotten nervous about that after the cabin. And there's no way anyone could trace him back to the phones, even using fingerprints. He was wearing leather gloves. He's safe from the Butthead Brigade. Unless they recognize him personally, if he gets caught on some camera. And that's not likely."

"None of this shit has been likely," Sean said, darkly.

They stared glumly out at the rain-slicked street, and another vehicle appeared, turning onto the ramp. It was the aging but fit-looking Volkswagen panel van that Sean had spotted in a nearby used car lot.

The guy they'd met in the storage unit got out. He was a heavyset guy with slicked-back hair. "Here she is," he announced. "I got 'em down to thirty-six hundred and filled her with gas, like you said. She runs real good." He held out a handful of cash. "Here's your change."

"I appreciate the savings. Keep it as part of your commission."

The guy looked taken aback. He slid the wad of money into his pocket. "Uh, thanks. Why didn't you buy it yourself? You on the lam?"

"No. Long story, but nothing illegal. So, like I said. The van's in your name. We borrow it from you today. When we're done, we give it back to you, free and clear. I'll call your cell, we get you the van."

The guy shook his head, his mouth flat. "If you use it to commit a crime, I'm rolling over on you," he warned. "I will fuck you up."

"Fair enough," Kev said. "Say we stole it. I'm fine with that."

Kev and Sean began loading the plastic cases into the back of the van. The man stared at them. "Yeah. Sure. And, uh . . . now?"

"Now we go," Kev said. "And thanks for your help."

The man just stood there. "What did you put in the storage unit?"

Kev just looked at him.

"Yeah, never mind. Whatever." The guy walked away.

They climbed in. Sean started up the motor. It sounded pretty good. Kev opened up the laptop and opened the surveillance program, clicking open the view from the slap-on vidcam he'd attached with a single discreet gesture to the outside wall of the storage unit they had rented, using gray-brown putty and fuzz disguise, which made it almost invisible. They'd positioned repeaters to augment the signal at least to the street outside the storage unit.

"How far can we go and still get the signal?" he asked.

"Let's park around the first corner." Sean turned the van around and put it into park. "It's risky, though. They might just eyeball us when they come. Those two guys both think we're going to blow up the Chrysler Building, or something."

"I know," Kev said bleakly.

"You think they'll call the cops?"

Kev stared at the screen, watching as the guy they'd gotten the van from approached their newly rented storage unit and stared at it.

"They might," Kev said. "At least, the dreadlocked guy might. The other guy's still hoping to score a free car out of the deal. Best we can hope is that they'll wrestle with their consciences just long enough for us to snag a tail. Then they can do whatever they want, and welcome."

Sean shook his head. "It's so damn risky. Bringing strangers in."

"I know!" Kev exploded. "All I can do is try, right? I'm pulling this thing out of my ass as I go along! And I am wide open to suggestions!"

"Sure you are," Sean soothed. "I just hope the Butthead Brigade cares enough about monster chick to send someone to pick her up. At least she didn't blow up in our faces, like the cabin guy. Small mercies."

Kev reached down, rummaging for the inlaid jewelry box. He slid the back panel aside. "Give me your blade," he said.

Sean handed it over. Kev snapped off the entire back panel, splintering it as he wrenched it off. He slid the blade into the wooden seam of the drawer and pried. *Ker-ack*, the wooden frontpiece snapped in half. He fished out the loose piece, pried out fragments, wrenching loose tiny nails, until a dark slot opened up. He peered inside, heart beating so frantically it felt like it was banging his throat from underneath.

Something was in it. He tipped the box forward, tapped, knocked, shook. *Please, God. Let it be a lead.*

A clump of floppy disks slid out, scattering over his lap. The ancient kind that he remembered from college. Not even the rigid 3.5 plastic-jacketed ones. These were the ones that were genuinely floppy.

The two of them gazed at the ancient disks, disheartened.

"Fuck." Kev's voice shook. "Where are we going to find a machine that can read this prehistoric shit fast enough for it to matter?"

"Miles could," Sean said. "He's a specialist. He's got some real museum pieces in his dad's basement in Endicott Falls."

"Three thousand goddamn miles away!" Kev yelled.

"Hang on to your shit." Sean's voice was all steely calm. "Put them aside. We watch for the people who are coming for monster chick—"

"If they come at all! And if they don't?"

"We'll deal with that when the time comes." Sean studied him, narrow-eyed. "Those glaciers are melting faster than I thought. What happened to Zen Dude, floating over the rough edges of the world?"

"There is no Zen Dude," Kev snapped. "It was bullshit all along."

"That's a relief. Welcome back. Remember when it was me, flipping out, and you were trying to talk me down?"

"How could I forget?" Kev paused. "Unless somebody tortured me, inflicting brain damage that caused eighteen years of amnesia, that is."

"Yeah, there's that," Sean admitted.

Kev wiped moisture out of his eyes. "It's funny about Bruno. I think one of the reasons it was so easy for me to bond with him years ago is because he reminded me of you."

Sean looked alarmed. "Me? Bruno? That spastic bone-head? That smart-mouthed clown? Surely you jest."

"Nope."

Sean settled back into his seat and contemplated the rain-spotted windshield. "Uh. Yeah. I'm not quite sure what to make of that."

"Under the circumstances, I suggest you take it as a compliment."

"Weird compliment, if you ask me, but at least you're being real with me again. Thank God for small favors. I'll even thank Bruno."

If we ever get the chance. The thought hung there, unvoiced.

Kev gathered up the floppy disks and slid them back into the jewelry box. They propped the laptop against the dash and waited.

33

The camera followed her home from school, watching from a chillingly short distance as she hauled her knapsack up the stoop and into the house. She appeared to be about sixteen, judging from the haircut, the puppy fat. Then the camera cut to an odd, leaf-framed angle that she identified as being somewhere right outside her bedroom window, at just the right angle to peek in the gap of the venetian blinds.

She peeled her clothes off and headed naked into the shower.

The video cut abruptly to an indoor shot. The vidcam nudged the bathroom door open, staring at her blurred form behind the plastic curtain. She sang tunelessly as she sudsed up.

Cut to her room, staring at her clothes on the floor. Focusing in on her underwear, twisted into a ball. The latex-gloved hand grabbed them, looked at them with intense interest. Sniffed them.

Cut to some other space, without much light, the back of a van, maybe. The gloved hand yanking open its pants, training the camera on the flushed, erect penis that poked out of it. The gloved hand wrapped her pink panties around its penis and began to rub.

Lily dragged her gaze away. No need to watch this filth. The first two times through had been enough. But she kept thinking about Howard. How staring at that distilled hatred and cruelty must have made him feel. What it would do to a person, to a parent, to be ground down by terror and guilt, year after year. And she'd been so angry at him, too. He'd had his daughter's rage and disappointment to burden him on top of all the rest of it. Never a chance to explain, or to excuse himself. No wonder he'd fallen to pieces. She was halfway there herself.

She glanced up at the screen at the wrong moment and

caught the come shot and the camera's long look at the wet mess on her wadded panties. How absolutely disgusting. She had to clench her guts and concentrate to keep from tossing that miserable lunch they'd provided. She was going to need every last calorie. Not for a bid for freedom—she didn't aim so high or presume so much. Just for a chance to change the cards on the table. To see if she could shake loose of doom for a minute or two. Even that would be a victory.

She'd been glad to have something to do with her hands while she tried not to watch that video montage. She'd found a manufacturer's label on the mattress frame, peeled it off, and hunched in the corner, taking care to look defeated, terrified, and pathetic. In that position, she'd rolled the gummy adhesive off the back of the paper label into tiny, grayish globs of sticky rubber and attached them to the insides of the first joints of all her fingers. Sixteen little balls of goo.

When that was done, she hunched lower, shook her hair down over her face for that classic madwoman-in-the-attic look, working with the card full of red dots with extreme care. The drug would kill her, if Zoe spoke the truth. Lily had no reason to doubt her. Not about this.

It was hard. Her hands were clammy and stiff, and it was difficult to peel the spots off without touching the drugged adhesive side. She attached the protective paper side to the balls of rubber so that they clung, lightly, to her fingers, drug side out. No direct contact.

When that was done, she crossed her arms and dangled them off her knees in a loose, casual way that hopefully looked natural.

The door lock rattled. Terror exploded through her synapses, jagged and stuttering like paparazzi flashbulbs. This was it.

The door swung open. It was Melanie. She had a strange, bugged-out look in her eyes, a misty glow, as if she were high.

Lily's brain was in lock mode. Her stomach lurched, a speed elevator plummeting to hell.

"Get up," Melanie ordered.

Instinct took over. Lily hunched, hiding her face against her knees. A pitiful, huddled ball. Helpless. Destroyed. Poor me.

"I said to get up!" Melanie's voice cracked like a whip, but Lily just wailed incoherently and rocked, curling tighter.

The woman made an impatient sound. "Oh, for God's sake." Her sneakers squeaked as she strode over to Lily, grabbing a handful of hair at the nape of Lily's neck. She jerked it up, brutally hard. Lily let out a high-pitched yelp, flopped, kicked as Melanie lifted her—

And grabbed both of Melanie's wrists. Held on, hard. Squeezing.

Time froze, and in that eternal instant, Lily felt the woman's shocked realization through the hand that was wound into her hair. A split second of disbelief, and then a tremor, but her grip did not loosen. Lily pulled against it, gritting her teeth against the pain, to look up into Melanie's face.

Melanie's jaw sagged. Her hand in Lily's hair tightened into an unrelenting claw. Her eyes bugged. Her mouth began to work, her tongue to protrude. Her face turned purplish. Lily let go of the woman's arms, tried to unwind Melanie's fingers from her hair. Little red dots were stuck all over Melanie's wrists. She did not attempt to remove them.

She toppled. Lily's weight tugged her to the side. She thudded to the ground, jerking Lily down by the hair, and oh shit, that *hurt* . . .

Melanie began to twitch, convulse.

Lily struggled to loosen the woman's fingers from her hair, but it was a literal death grip. She pulled free with a muffled shriek, leaving a generous handful of hair still wound around Melanie's clenched fist.

Melanie was jittering, jerking. Foamy pink saliva came from her mouth, twin streams of blood from her nose. Her feet drummed the floor. Her eyes were frozen wide, spotted with red.

Lily struggled to her feet, staring at the woman for about ten blank, completely stupid seconds before her brain jolted into action. They were both wearing jeans. She could buy some time.

She dragged Melanie into the corner, propping her where she had been sitting. The woman had lost control of her bladder. Blood poured out of her ears. Jesus, how horrible.

The shoes. Melanie had shoes. Her fingers shook so hard, it was almost impossible to unknot the laces of Melanie's high-top sneakers and pry them off her feet. She fell back on to her ass as the second one came off and prayed that no one was watching as she tried to tug them onto her own feet. She left them unlaced, rummaged feverishly through Melanie's pockets. She found a cell phone, which she slid across the floor to the far side of the room. A bunch of keys, yes. A utilitarian knife attached, excellent. Too good to be true.

It took endless, fumbling minutes at the door to find the right key. She tumbled out into the corridor, looked up and down the deserted hallway. It was eerie. Dusty and mildewy, like a grandma's attic. No one in sight. No alarms. No voices. No footsteps. She darted toward a glow of light and came to a wide open space where the corridor became a balcony with a curving double staircase leading down to a great hall with a domed ceiling that towered two stories above her head.

And below, an enormous door, with greenery beyond it, glowing through the window glass. Freedom. She stared at it. She could run, like a rabbit. She might even break free.

But what about Bruno? She knew he was here. She'd heard King's orders. He could be behind any one of these doors. He'd come here freely, letting himself be captured to keep them from hurting her.

She started trying doors. She had no choice.

She couldn't leave this place until she found him.

* * *

"Holy shit." Sean's eyes were wide as they peered into the monitor. The object of his amazement was the guy who was now forcing the lock on their storage unit. "That's . . . no, that can't be—"

"No, it's not," Kev cut in. "It can't be, and it's not."

Sean shook his head, bewildered. "But he looks exactly like—"

"No," Kev said. "Look again. He's too young. Twenty, maybe. And too pale. His hair's ash blond. And he's not tall enough, and his shoulders don't have the bulk of Bruno's. And his eyes are set closer."

But Sean's head could not stop shaking. "This is so fucked up. So this is one of the lost siblings Petrie was going on about. But how about the other guy? He doesn't look like Bruno at all. But he could be the guy that Aaro and Zia described from the hospital."

Kev shrugged, indifferent. It was eerie, yeah, but he didn't care whose siblings they were or weren't. DNA be damned. They worked for the guy who was fucking with Bruno. That made them walking dead men.

Getting dead, of course, only happening after they performed the last and possibly only useful task ordained for them on this earth. Which was to lead Kev to wherever Bruno was. *Please.* If there was a God, he begged for this much grace. The rest he'd take care of himself.

"I still think we should have tagged her," Sean fretted. "We could have remote activated a dummy tag as soon as they got on the road."

"They're not stupid," Kev repeated. "They'd have found it. That's what they're doing right now. Searching her. Not just sweeping her, but physically searching her. That's why they're not already on the road."

Agonizing minutes passed. Kev stared at the screen, desperate to move. Air rushed back into his lungs when the young Bruno-esque dude poked his head out. He backed out, holding monster chick by the shoulders. Mr. Bland had her by the legs. She was still wrapped in the tarp, but less tightly now. They heaved her into the back of their vehicle without gentleness or ceremony. The Bruno look-alike slammed the door and headed for the wheel, like he was done with an unpleasant but necessary job of work.

"Huh," Sean murmured. "I am not feeling the love here."

"Maybe monster chick is tough to work with," Kev surmised.

"Ya think? But still someone ordered them to pick her up. Maybe they're short on staff. A lot of them got dead recently."

"Good," Kev said darkly. "Dead is good."

The vehicle was on the move. Sean fired up the van's engine and nudged it to the end of the street so they could see when the black SUV poked its nose out of the storage facility's main entrance.

It turned away from them, thank God. If it had turned right, the Butthead Brigade would have had a dead-on close-up view of Kev's and Sean's mugs behind the old van's windshield. Their first stroke of luck.

Sean hung back, let a car or two get in front of them on the busy street, and pulled out after them.

"Melanie? Melanie! Respond immediately!"

What in the hell? King tossed the com device down and swung around to click open the monitor that showed Lily Parr's room. Still those legs were stretched out, the bare feet looking pale and cold. The video played on; nothing had changed. Melanie had not yet arrived.

His blood pressure rose. Useless bitch. Unable to perform the simplest task. She'd been too fuddled by the intense orgasm he'd so unfortunately granted her. God knows, she didn't deserve it.

He had never felt so irritated, so exposed. Every last one

of his elite cadre of personal operatives was either dead or trying to cope with these irritants and tormenters. Leaving him alone to take care of all the myriad details of his enterprise—personally.

And they were extensive. Currently, he was monitoring the young ones in the programming room, who had been scheduled today for the eight-hour sessions of combat programming. He'd considered canceling it, but it had annoyed him to think of his smoothly running machine being disrupted by these hooligans. So he'd ordered Hobart and Melanie to retrieve the teens from the satellite dormitory facility and set them all up this morning, right on schedule, as if nothing were amiss.

So at this moment, ten of his trainees, aged thirteen to eighteen, were hooked up to the programming consoles, their senses and brain functions augmented by King's own brilliant drug cocktails, processing massive amounts of information at accelerated rates. With each of them, he came closer to his ultimate dream of plumbing the vast realms of untapped human potential. And using it for his own ends.

But he'd been forced to spend the last half hour checking their vitals, their brain waves. Eight of them were fine, but two of them, A-1423B, also known as Annika, and F-1684C, also known as Fallon, looked destined for the cull. The stressful DeepWeave and drug combination was provoking something like epileptic seizures.

Pity, but still. This crop's 80 percent success rate was statistically quite good. A steady improvement. In the beginning, back when he started with Zoe and her vintage, he'd enjoyed a 30 percent success rate. Indeed, if Zoe appeared to him now, with all her obvious flaws, he'd have culled her before she reached the age of eight.

Yes, his standards edged ever higher. That pleased him, this slow but steady march toward complete perfection. Utter control.

But it was a sensation he was not at liberty to enjoy today, with his staff scattered to the four winds, or dead, or falling to pieces. And he had the little ones to think of, too, the two children produced from the last of the viable embryos obtained from Magda. He'd had them brought over today with the notion of showing them to Bruno, for entertainment value as well as professional curiosity. He wondered, for instance, if that mechanism of noble self-sacrifice that had worked so well with Lily would work with the babies, too. If his son would feel an immediate bond with the children because of shared DNA. After all, look what mere sex had reduced him too, poor boy. Fascinating question. Brain candy.

Still. It had been self-indulgent to order the children delivered today. There was no one to attend to them when they woke from their drugged sleep. Hopefully that would not happen for hours yet. Their pod leader had been sent away, not being privy to the secrets of his enterprise. He'd decided years ago to outsource early child care for reasons of cost-effectiveness. Changing diapers and wiping mouths did not require millions of dollars of specialized training. The pod leaders were well paid to do exactly as he requested and to tell no tales—but they weren't welcome on the premises today.

Once the actual programming of the children began, he used only DeepWeave programmed staff, so as to avoid misunderstandings. Only a DeepWeave alum could understand the totality of his vision, or have the necessary loyalty and commitment.

He sighed and swung the chair over, clicking on the video monitor of the quiet, out-of-the-way room where the children lay in their drugged sleep. No movement.

He swung over to the opposite bank of computers and checked the tracer embedded in Zoe's clavicle, as well as the ones in Zoe's cell and Rosa Ranieri's. Zoe's signal was stationary, but the two cells were clustered together, on the move. He hit the key that brought the overlaid satellite photo onto the map and zoomed in. Yes, it appeared to be the same vehicle. So it was true. They'd left Zoe unconscious in the storage unit, and one of the McClouds was driving his wounded brother to the emergency room. They had not determined which brother was wounded, but it hardly mattered. McClouds were interchangeable.

He grabbed the earbuds, listened. Muffled cursing and groans were all he heard. No conversation. King sat there, drumming his fingers. He disliked leaving the nerve center of his operation unmanned, but Melanie had not presented herself. Anger simmered inside him. He pulled up Melanie's mortal commands from his personal database to have them fresh, at his fingertips. He'd ask her to swallow her own tongue. Choke to death at his feet. That would calm his nerves nicely.

He strode toward Parr's room, thinking about the groaning, whining McCloud with his bullet wound. Odd. The research he'd done on the McClouds would have suggested utter stoicism in the face of pain. But one never knew. Some of the toughest-seeming people were as soft as butter inside. And the opposite was also true. Take Lily Parr. Remarkable toughness. The riff about fertilizing her ovum for his next crop of research subjects had sprung into his mind out of nowhere while editing that video for Bruno, but the more he thought about it, the more the idea appealed.

Then again, he'd be gambling with the genes of her wretched failure of a father. Still and all. Chances were, her mother's attributes would predominate. Howard had been intelligent—that trait he shared with his daughter in full. But he'd had none of Lily's courage, her drive.

He mused about it tenderly as he inserted the key, imagining the results of the union of himself and Lily Parr. Their beauty, their fire. They might well surpass his and Magda's progeny, in terms of potential.

The door swung open.

He stood, frozen, while the information battering at the doors of his perception simply would not enter. He noticed the video still rolling. A seventeen-year-old Lily Parr, taking a shower. One of his favorites.

Then the doors of his realization burst inward all at once.

Melanie lay dead in the corner, mouth gaping. Her jaw, neck, and chest red with blood. Eyes bulging. *How . . . ?*

The red dots on her arms came into focus. Transdermal Melimitrex VIII. There was at least five times a fatal dose stuck onto her wrists. He'd taken them for drops of blood at first glance.

Death had released control of her bodily functions. He gagged delicately. The silence of the place seemed suddenly menacing.

King backed out of the room, staring to the left, the right. This was unprecedented. Himself, alone in this huge place, with no allies. Just ten drugged teenagers in the programming room, two drugged toddlers in the far wing—and two hostile elements on the loose.

He sidled down the corridor, punching Julian's code into his com.

"Sir?" Julian said. "We're on our—"

"Get back here!" he hissed savagely. "Parr killed Melanie and escaped! I'm alone, and I don't know where they are in the building!"

King hung up, peeking into the control room. Neither Ranieri nor Parr appeared to be in there, so he sped to the locked cupboard in the back, pulled out the revolver. Furious at himself for the arrogant choice of the Walther PPK as his emergency weapon. He'd liked the streamlined elegance of the small weapon. He'd considered it to have more a ceremonial value than anything else. Who could have dreamed of a situation in which he would need even six shots, let alone the seventeen of a semiautomatic? He'd molded an army to take care of those gritty details for him, and where were they all now?

Damn Ranieri. Damn Parr. He needed them dead.

A glance at the screen to track the tracers that identified Hobart's and Julian's positions showed them to be heading toward him at a gratifyingly fast clip, but still too far away for comfort.

He slunk to the door, peered out. Nothing but the creaks, pops, and moans of an aging mansion over a century old. A warren, full of places for concealment, possibilities for ambush.

He finally recognized the unpleasant sensation tugging at the underside of his intestines, like hanging icicles. It was fear. Banal, stupid, helpless fear of events that could not be controlled.

How dare they put him in this position. He, who had gone so far, accomplished so much. Anger steadied him.

They would pay for making him feel like this. They'd both pay.

Screaming.

Pain. Jagged, flashes of light, and every jolt, every sway hurt.

Zoe's eyes burned, her ears roared. A warm stream of blood was coming out of her nose. She was used to it. It was a common side effect of her special meds. But it tickled.

Zoe tried to reach up to scratch it. Her shoulders flared like hot coals. She was trussed, arms behind her back. The pain began to come into focus. Dark, smothering. A plastic tarp, stinking of mildew, over her mouth. She struggled, coughed, spat blood.

Someone ripped the plastic shroud off her face. It let in a cold, sweet rush of oxygen and a flood of blinding light.

"Coming around?" *Slap, slap*, the blows made her skull pulse with white-hot fireworks of agony. "Had a nice nap?"

She squinted to squeeze tears from her eyes, which felt swollen, full of fluid, like they were going to pop out of her head. Focused on the face.

Dislike registered before recognition did, but it clicked into place in a second. Hobart. That useless sack of shit who had been on her team in Seattle. The one who had fucked her up with incomplete supplies and inadequate intel. "What are you doing here?"

"Taking out the trash," Hobart said.

She struggled again. "Untie my hands."

Hobart just smiled. "No."

Alarm jangled through her nerves. "What do you mean, no? Undo my goddamn hands! When I tell King what you—"

"King is going to Level Ten you as soon as we get back to base," Hobart sneered. "You're done, bitch. You are so culled."

She jackknifed up so that she almost rammed her head into his face. He rocked back, evading her. "No!" she shrieked. "He trusted me! All alone! He sent me on a mission to—"

"It was a suicide mission. He was getting rid of you. Anyone with a brain that still functioned would have seen that. But you're trashed, Zoe. Strung out on Melimitrex. He was going to Level Ten you as soon as you mowed down the Mc-Clouds and the Ranieris, since it was such a simple task, no intelligence involved. But you couldn't even handle that much. Pathetic, you know? Really embarrassing, for one of us."

She shook her head, rejecting his words. "No! No, why would he send you to pick me up if he was going to—"

"Use what few synapses are still firing in your brain and figure it out." Hobart's voice dripped false pity. "He couldn't risk you ending up with the police, pulling an auto-destruct, like you antiquated older models were programmed to do. Like Nadia. We're too exposed."

"But . . . but he—"

"And you want to hear the really shocking part? We just found out that Lily Parr killed Melanie. And King is back at headquarters, all alone, with her and Ranieri on the loose, until we get back. Because of your incompetence, we're still miles away, Zoe. He's completely exposed, with two enemies on the loose. Think about that. Just think about it."

The horror of it transfixed her with guilt.

Hobart nodded, pleased with her remorse. "You'll see, when we get back. He'll fix you. And I hope I get to watch."

It ricocheted in Zoe's brain, echoes swelling, horribly loud. *Pop*, a pinpoint of agony bloomed in her eye. Too much pressure. Flashes of light. She saw Hobart's face through a veil of red. God, how she needed another patch. Her heart swelled, pounding like a trip-hammer.

Lies. It was all lies, the jealous, scheming, lying dickhead. "Undo my hands." Her voice shook now. "I need a patch."

Hobart laughed at her. "Fucking junkie trash. No reason to waste meds on you. You're being flushed, bitch. Down the tubes you go."

His face wavered, swam through that fog of red. His eyes began to glow, like red-hot coals. His mouth was open, laughing. He had fangs, like a predator, a panther. A demon. She couldn't get any air. Her lungs were locked. *A demon*. Both of them were demons. It all fell into place with a quiet *click*. How could she not have understood before?

Hobart and Julian were demons. They didn't love King, not like she did. They were only interested in power. They were malfunctions, abominations. They should have been culled at birth. They would stab him in the back if she did not stop them.

She was the only operative whose love was entirely pure. The only one who could protect him from the enemies who stalked him.

Hobart's demon face swam and wavered, and suddenly he yanked the smothering plastic back down over her face. She vibrated inside her dark plastic cocoon. Galvanized by her holy mission. She would save her King. She was the chosen one. Made for this, by his own hands. Molded, by his brilliant mind. He was her maker, her love, her God.

She was the one. The sureness of it steadied her, made her strong. He would see it in the end. She knew he would. He had to.

They belonged to each other. Forever.

34

So many rooms. Lily fumbled, inserting key after key, all unmarked, all perfectly similar. Room after room, some crowded with rotting furniture, some empty. The last three doors had not opened at all.

Click. Finally, one opened, and light flooded out. Lily peered in and realized why the three doors had not opened. They'd been boarded shut, since a block of rooms had been remodeled into one long room, pure and clean and starkly white. Crowded with blinking, gleaming medical equipment—and beds. The beds were not empty.

She scanned them. Sixteen beds, ten occupied. She tiptoed in with a sense of dread, swiftly ascertained that Bruno was not there.

These were young people. That boy couldn't be more than fourteen. The girl next to him looked even younger. What in the hell? They were strapped down. Leather restraints, webbing. Hands, feet, chests, heads. They wore goggles, earphones. They were covered with sensors, wires. They twitched and moaned.

She stood there, shivering. Bruno was not here. She had no business poking her nose into the filthy secret doings of these people. But something prodded her deeper into the room.

A couple of them seemed about twelve. She stopped at one who looked like she might be dying. A girl, Asian. Her body arched against her bonds, her head thrashed, her feet drummed. Her wrists were welted from her frantic struggling. The sounds coming out of her sounded like pleading, as if she were being beaten.

Bruno's dreams. Oh, God. That was what the girl was experiencing. It came to her like a splash of ice water. The experiments that had been done on Bruno. Happening, in real time, to these kids.

Lily was tempted to unhook the girl, but then what? Would she scream? Would she see Lily as another opponent and attack her?

No. She couldn't. The girl in the last bed, a blonde, was in the same condition as the Asian girl, thrashing and gurgling. The others just twitched and moaned, like dogs having running dreams.

Lily backed toward the door, murmuring a silent apology to them.

Bruno. Keep your mind on Bruno. No more distractions.

She peered out into the corridor, unnerved to find the coast still clear. What the hell were they all up to? She was too insignificant for them to bother with, maybe? Great. She darted to the next door. The next. The corridor made an L-curve, revealed another hall, just as long.

She worked her way doggedly down the hall. On the last door, the key clicked and turned and admitted her into a dim room, shrouded by heavy velvet drapes. A suite. She had to check connecting rooms. All this effort would be in vain if she missed Bruno out of sheer sloppiness.

The place felt deserted. The connecting room was a bathroom, with a door on either end. She peeked into the next room and saw two cribs in the light filtering through the narrow strip between the drapes.

She moved closer. Children were in them. Babies. They were very still. Pale. Oh, God. She crept closer, hung over the first crib, her hand clamped to her shaking mouth. *Please.* Don't let them be dead.

They appeared to be alive. She touched a cheek. Cool, not cold. Toddlers, not babies. She wasn't much of a judge, but she figured this one was about two. So was the other.

Two plastic travel bucket seats, with clips for fastening into a car, were perched by the wall. They had webbing restraints. No machines were hooked up to the babies, thank God. Then she saw the needles on the table. Sterile physiological solution, a clutter of powder-encrusted drug vials. A baby monitor. She spotted the vidcam. Someone could be watching. Sounding the alarm. Bells ringing, feet pounding.

She reached into a crib, held her hand in front of the child's nose, wishing she had a mirror. She could barely feel hot moisture, blooming with each exhalation. So slight, but they were alive.

It reminded her of the times she'd tried to find Howard's pulse, Howard's breath, amid a litter of hypodermics and other junkie trash. A sick, stomach-clenching memory.

Babies. God help her. She could afford to help these little ones even less than the teenagers. They were twenty-five to thirty pounds each, and fast asleep. If they did wake up, they'd scream the house down.

If she could find Bruno, maybe she could carry one, and he could carry the other. The authorities would have to help save the other kids. She closed the door quietly and continued with the doors. Empty . . . empty . . . empty.

Then a key caught, turned . . . and the door creaked as she shoved it open. She practically fell inside.

Bruno lay on the floor, tied hand and foot, his dark eyes open but strangely empty, as if he didn't recognize her. His face was white. Lip swollen and split, nostrils encrusted with blood. His eyes were hollow, shadowed.

But it was Bruno, and he was alive.

* * *

"Oh, thank God. Thank God." She ran to him, sobbing like an idiot, fumbling to separate the little knife on the key chain of her bunch of keys. She was babbling, incoherent. She sawed at the hard plastic cuffs that cut deeply into his empurpled wrists. Then the ankles.

He rolled up onto his side, sucking in air, a wheezing gasp of pain. She helped him sit up and hugged him, like she'd been dreaming of doing ever since she woke up in her cell. But he was stiff in her arms, like a block of wood. All his vibrant, buzzing vitality gone.

A horrified notion occurred to her. "Oh, God, are you injured? Your shoulders? Or your back? Did I hurt you when I cut the cuffs?"

He coughed, wincing. "Not injured," he said, his voice hoarse.

"Oh, thank God." She tightened her arms around him again. His lack of response was weird. He was so strange. Not himself at all.

And not happy to see her. Not one little bit.

Fear uncurled inside her, like dark whorls of smoke. "Are you, um, drugged?" she asked, almost hopefully.

"No," he said.

Well. That was uncharacteristically terse. She smoothed his hair back off his forehead. "My poor baby," she murmured. "They beat you." She touched the bruised cheekbone, his split lip with her fingertip.

He flinched away. "Don't!"

She was alarmed. "Bruno?" Her voice was small.

"Don't look at me like that," he said thickly. "Did he not tell you?"

"Tell me what?" she asked. "Who? King? He told me all kinds of things. Not many of them were worth knowing."

He made an impatient gesture. "Quit it with that. What I mean is, did he tell you that I know?"

"Know what?" She was baffled to tears.

"That the game's up," he replied. "No need to pretend anymore."

"Pretend what?" She was yelling. She tried to breathe. Think this through. He turned to look through the doorway, and she saw the blood encrusted in his hair. Understanding dawned with wrenching tenderness. She touched the egg-shaped knot on his skull.

"Oh, God," she whispered. "You have a head injury. Do you have a concussion? Are you nauseous? Let me look at your pupils."

He batted her hand away. She tried not to feel hurt. After all, he was in pain, injured, addled. "Bruno?" she asked. "What is this?"

His lips were flattened, as if something was hurting him. His face looked so different with that stark mask. Unrecognizable.

"Cut it out," he said. "I know. So don't do this."

Her practical side kicked in. Screw this. They could have this conversation later, after Bruno had gotten a shot of painkillers and a CT scan. "Well, hell. I don't know what you've found, but there's some stuff I found." She got to her feet, yanked his hand. "Let me show you."

Bruno got up, but the world swirled, swung, and he found himself draped over Lily's shoulder, and she was scrambling to keep her feet beneath herself.

He wrenched away, at the cost of bouncing into the wall. Touching her hurt him. Just looking at her hurt him. Those searching eyes. She was saying something. He couldn't understand. Sound cut in and out of his head. Something about kids, machines. Babies.

He couldn't take it in, any more than on her previous visits. She'd been here several times. An angel of mercy at first, and then she morphed, turned seductive and whorish, laughing at what a fool he'd been. Those visits had been interspersed with visits from Rudy, a bloody knife in his hands. And Mamma, wearing her death wounds.

Then his vision would clear, and he would see the room, the floorboards. Feel the bonds cutting into his body.

This new dream-Lily was using a new strategy. She looked more vulnerable, face white, hair tangled. Eyes full of love. She was going for realism this time. Drawing him in, making him want to protect her . . .

You're my champion.

And whammo, she'd put it to him. Straight to the tender parts.

He wanted her to go away. Either she was a bad dream, or she was a bad reality. But she was such a beautiful bad dream. She could tempt him to stay in the dream world forever. Except that he'd be crazy.

He was probably well into crazy already, though. He stared at Lily, wondering why she didn't dissolve into smoke, like the others. This dream-Lily was stubborn, like the real one he thought he'd known. She tugged his arm. Wanted him to follow her somewhere.

The memory floated up like a bubble, perfectly formed in every detail. The video footage King had shown him. *I love you. Just you. Only you.*

The phrase King had taunted him with: *You're my champion.*

He remembered how that phrase had functioned on him, when she'd said it to him in the diner. Like a switch flipping on, lighting him up like a torch. He'd have done anything for her. He would have died for her. Still would. He stared at her moving lips, her earnest eyes. Strange, that he was hip to the facts and still felt all the same feelings. He was still tempted to give in to the fiction, though it made no goddamn sense at all to perpetuate it, now that her boss had spilled the beans.

But she was a dream. Hey, dreams didn't have to make sense.

All he wanted was to go back to that fantasy world where

Lily was everything she'd said she was. Where he really had saved her, where she really did love him. Where Lily really did open the door, run to him, and cut his bonds. But any minute, he'd wake up, face flat to the floor.

You're my champion. She'd used that phrase to reel him in, bend him to her will. Twice. There was no other way King could have known about those exact words. No one had overheard those conversations. The first one in the diner, at four in the morning, at a secluded booth. Even less so the second time, at the cabin, in bed, just himself and Lily.

Those were the facts. He knew what he knew. Even if he hated it. Even if it killed him.

Lily dragged him down the corridor. He wondered if he should be resisting her, just on principle. But why bother? It was all a dream. He might as well go where she took him. See what trash his subconscious mind was littered with. He'd be back on that floor soon enough.

Her voice was shaking with emotion. So convincing. He trotted along behind her. His head hurt. Would a hallucination be so detailed? Cold hands? Pain? She stopped in front of a door, dragged out a bundle of keys. He almost laughed. What a discordant note in the fantasy. How did his dream Lily get a hold of those keys? A kung fu duel with one of King's operatives? One of the bad guys had a hole in his handbag?

He should have head-butted her the second she cut him loose and run like hell, dream or no dream. It was the dignified thing to do, on any plane of reality. She opened the door, and her words registered. ". . . like your video game dream. And it's killing some of them!"

The reference to his video game dream jolted him. He looked into the room. Saw the kids on the beds. Goggles, earphones, machines—

Memory thundered over him. He knew that room. Desperation. He thudded to his knees, braced himself against the door, retching.

Lily's hand, on his arm. ". . . so sorry! I didn't think. About your memories, of how it would affect you. God, I'm sorry, I didn't think—"

"Don't think." He wrenched free and staggered in, ignoring her anxious voice. Stared down at the first cot. A boy, black, gangly, stringy, and muscular. Hooked up just as Bruno had been for hours of torture.

He yanked the earphones off the boy, jerked the goggles off, tore off the sensors. There was an IV drip. He untapped it, plucked out the needle, left it dangling, dripping its poison out onto the floor. He jerked loose the restraints and smacked the boy's face. "Hey! You! Wake up!"

The boy's eyes fluttered open, dilated. He bolted upright with a scream. Bruno grabbed him while he thrashed and flailed. "It's OK, it's OK," he muttered. "You've got to get out of here, kid. Can you run?"

Out of the corner of his eye, he saw Lily doing the same to the girl in the next bed. He heaved the black kid off the table and shoved him in the direction of the door. The kid stumbled, tottered.

"Get out of the building!" he ordered. "Get out!"

The boy blinked at him, helplessly. "Move! Run!" Bruno roared. He backhanded the kid, hating himself for it. But it worked; the kid spun around, set off down the corridor.

Some of the others came to their senses more quickly. Some opened their eyes screaming and fighting. He paused at one cot where Lily stood, hands clamped over her mouth, tears running down her face. The girl lay still, spine contorted, her head at a strange angle. Lily had taken off the goggles, and the girl's large dark eyes were empty.

Bruno touched her carotid artery. No pulse.

He pushed past Lily without comment. Went on to the next bed.

It only took a few minutes to get the kids unfastened. The last girl was a goner, too. Eight out of ten. Six out the door.

He was shoving the last two forward when that deep voice made ice crystallize in his blood.

"Well, now. Look at this. You bad boy."

Bruno shoved the kids behind him. Lily dragged in a sharp gulp of air and flattened herself against the wall.

King stepped into the room, aiming a gun at Bruno's chest.

Too good to be true. Lily had known it since she got out of her cell. She hadn't been proposing a rescue mission when she showed Bruno this place, but she might have known how he'd react when he saw those kids. It was just the kind of person he was.

And now they were screwed.

King gave her a smile. "Thank you, my dear, for bringing him to me. Your powers are as great as you claimed. You convinced him to trust you again, in spite of everything!" He turned to Bruno, gesturing with the gun. "We had a bet, you see. She was sure you would fall prey to her powers of seduction. Whereas I bet on your intelligence and cynicism. Since you are my son. I lost, but I'll enjoy the penalty I must pay to her. Tonight." He winked, mischievously. "In private."

Lily looked from King to Bruno, back to King, bewildered. "I . . . what bet? But I . . . but he . . ." She turned to Bruno. "You're his *son?*"

Bruno's stiff, bleak face told the truth. And she started putting it together. *The game's up. No need to pretend anymore.*

He thought that she . . . oh, God, no. That she'd *betrayed* him?

King was still chatting at Bruno. "Thursdays is our day for Combat DeepWeave 43.5. It's much more sophisticated than the one I used on you, twenty-four years ago. They complement the program with intense physical training. Your brother Julian is their master on the practice floor. Very talented, like you. I suspect the martial arts training from that McCloud fellow you lived with complemented your DeepWeave combat programming like a key to a lock. Happy coincidence. Not that it will do you any good now." His mouth twisted. "Such a waste."

"Bruno, he's lying!" Lily blurted out. "You can't believe him, about me! It's not true, about me bringing you here on purpose—"

"Lily, stop." King's voice was testy. "You've proved your point. You need to learn when to quit." He turned back to Bruno. "I do hope you haven't permanently damaged my trainees, young man," he chided. "Ripping them out of the middle of a DeepWeave combat session, without any decompression, that's unprecedented! And dangerous!"

"You're a fine one to talk about dangerous." Bruno's eyes darted toward the two dead girls. "They deserved a chance."

"Oh? And did you think they would just run away from me?" He laughed, waving his gun in the air. "Fly away, little birds, be free!" he mocked. "No, they belong to me! They love me! Like you should have!"

"That's not love." Bruno gestured behind him at the bodies so still on their cots. "Those girls are dead," he said. "That's love?"

"No, that's natural selection." King's voice took on a lecturing tone. "They culled themselves, you see. DeepWeave is psychologically demanding, as you well know. Only the strongest survive."

"You sick fuck," Bruno said. "You really need to die."

"It's your day for that, son." King's voice was cheerful. "Thanks to your lady friend. She's a bit confused right now. It's been a stressful assignment for her. To say nothing of sexually stressful. The tales of your torrid affair make an old man blush."

"I never said anything about us! Don't listen!" she yelled, but Bruno would not even meet her eyes. It was a stab in the back she could never have imagined. "Bruno, you can't believe that I—"

"I said be still!" King thundered. "Get out of the way, Lily. I've had enough. This is a failed experiment, and it ends, now." He aimed.

Bam. The bullet hit a metal bed frame. Bruno dove, hit the floor, started to crawl. One of the kids screamed, clutching her arm.

King clucked his tongue. "Now look what you made me do!"

Bruno sprang up and upended one of the cots. *Bam*, the bullet punched through the mattress. Chunks of the latex foam flew. A window shattered. The girl who'd been hit was screaming, a thin, piercing sound. The other kid was yelling, too.

Bam, the bullet tore the wall next to Lily's head, gouging a hole. She dropped to the ground, crawling between metal posts, the clawed feet of metal IV stands, the rolling carts that held medical equipment.

Bam. She poked her head out. Bruno was swinging an IV rack at King, who darted back. The glass bottle of fluid smashed against the wall, liquid splashing, glass tinkling. *Bam*. Bruno upended another bed frame, pinning King against the wall. He darted out the door while the older man struggled to extricate himself. The bed frame teetered, fell on its side with a clang and a crunch. King took off after Bruno.

The room was silent now but for the keening of the girl with the grazed arm, which bled but not profusely. Cold wind whined through the broken window. The gun went off outside—again. And again. Lily flinched each time, hoping the shots hadn't found their mark.

She felt deafened. Numbed. Her legs shook and wobbled as she clambered her way over the snarl of wires, cables, overturned beds, and IV racks jutting out at crazy angles to get to the wounded girl and the boy with her, a freckled kid of about sixteen. Both of them huddled by the wall, looking confused and stoned out of their minds. Exactly why she'd hesitated to mess with them in the first place.

Slowly, relentlessly, her mind wrapped all the way around this stark new reality without snapping. Bruno had abandoned her.

To be perfectly fair, he was currently being pursued by a madman with a gun. But he believed that she'd set him up. That she'd betrayed him, his family and friends, and deliberately lured him to his death. A bubbly gurgling sound came out of her. The room swirled, wavered, and blurred. Snot, everywhere. So. She was on her own again. To the ends of the universe. So what the fuck else was new.

Onward. She proceeded with grim purpose, grabbing the arm of the first kid, shoving him in the direction of the door, kicking his leg to encourage him to move. Slowly, clumsily, she got the two young people out of the door, into the corridor. Onward. To the grand staircase, the main entrance. She nudged the young people into a stumbling lope. The huge sky-lit great hall ahead of them glowed, beckoning—

A big hand clamped onto her upper arm, twisting until a shriek of pain jerked out of her throat. Swinging her around, slamming her against the wall.

Crack. Oh, God . . . her head . . . oh, *ouch* . . .

"Where the fuck do you think you're going?" Hobart snarled.

Zoe struggled, kicking and thrashing. They'd left her trussed in the SUV and run when they heard gunshots. Running to show King how brave, how loyal they were. But she knew the truth. Pigs. Demons.

They thought she was finished, but she would destroy them and save King. She thought of the day they'd dined together. When he'd said the words that made the universe explode in song.

The memory strengthened her. She had so much love to give him. But first she had to show him her true worth and destroy his enemies.

She kicked free of the tarp and maneuvered herself backward until she found the door release. It opened, dumping her bound body onto the concrete floor. The contact hurt every ripped muscle fiber, every inflamed tendon. A chorus of agony. But pain was nothing to her.

She slithered through the huge garage, worming past several cans of gasoline piled against the wall to the workshop, the circular table saw. She pushed herself up against the edge of the blade, rubbing and scraping at the plastic cuff until it yielded.

The rush of circulation into her hands almost made her scream. She'd scraped her wrists raw. Blood dripped from her fingertips. But she was on a holy mission. Blood had to be spilled. To purify her, to show King her utter commitment to him. Body and soul.

She groped for a handsaw, and as soon as her slippery fingers closed around it, used it to release her ankles.

Her first act of freedom was to grope for the patches in the pocket of her pants. One of the cards was gone. She counted again. How . . . ?

Whatever. She'd figure it out later. She peeled off three, put them on. A large dose, but she had a very big job to do. Three of them would make her impervious to pain, to fear. To anything.

Two more gunshots in the distance jolted her into action. She grabbed two of the heavy cans of gasoline and ran into the house.

35

Zwangggh, the bullet slashed through the top of Bruno's ear, stinging. It plowed into the woodwork, sending splinters and chunks flying. Bruno kept going, blood trickling in front of his ear.

King had a revolver. Bruno had heard six shots. The guy would have to reload, unless he had another gun. He burst out into what had once been the great hall of the turn-of-the-century country mansion, and a towering vaulted ceiling with domes, cupolas, and innumerable windows opened up above him. It had been painted white and gold a long time ago, but now the paint was cracked, browned, and flaking.

Two symmetrical curving staircases led down to the first floor. He bolted for the nearest one. Julian was at the door, shoving the last of the teenagers out the main entrance. Julian swung around with a shout, pulling out his gun. Bruno lurched to the side—*bam*.

He slammed into the banister, bounced off, somersaulted, found his feet. Leaped off, straight at the younger guy. Their bodies slammed together. *Bam*. The gun discharged, bounced, and spun as Julian hit the floor, squashed beneath Bruno's weight, but the boy was only stunned for an instant. He punched, Bruno blocked. Julian snagged his wrist, twisted until the torque flipped Bruno over. He jabbed a finger under Julian's jaw. Julian twisted away. Strange to be so close to a face so like his own, but contorted with killing rage. He flinched back to evade a finger jab to the eye, and it gouged his cheekbone, snagged his eyelid. Blood, filling his eye. His body moved instinctively. Jab, block, kick and punch, chop and stab. Bruno had a slight advantage in height and bulk, but Julian was a decade younger, and Bruno was trashed

on every level. His combat buzz bore him up, but he gained
no ground.

They maneuvered for the gun. Julian lunged for it, jerked
back to let Bruno's flash kick swoosh by his face. He
dropped, trying to sweep Bruno's leg from under him. Bruno
danced back, rolled, flipped, dove—

Oof, the kid landed on top of him, but he got his arm
around Julian's head from below and jabbed the gun under
his chin.

And could not shoot. He simply could not pull the trigger.

Terror exploded inside him. Frantic gabbling voices, his
blocked survival instincts telling him not to be a fucking
idiot, *kill* him already—

No. He just couldn't. Not his brother. His mamma's son.

Julian was braced to die. Bruno slammed the younger
man's face to the floor and sat on him, keeping the gun
jabbed.

"Before you kill him, Bruno, consider this."

King's voice jerked Bruno's gaze up. King held Lily in
front of him at the top of the stairs, head jerked back, arms
twisted behind her.

The guy they'd called Hobart descended the stairs, holding a gun on Bruno. He was herding the last two teenagers in
front of him, shoving them on. The two young people gave
him and Julian a wide berth as they fled out the main door.

"Look what's around her neck," King said. "Remember
the fight at the cabin? The operatives' cell phones, wired to
their vital signs?"

"The ones that exploded when they croaked," Bruno said.

"Only my own personal operatives carried them. Those
who serve me directly. A small amount of explosives to destroy the mechanism after the information is erased. But
enough to kill at close range."

"Yeah, I know," Bruno said. "I was there."

"I learned from that experience," King mused. "Very

painful. Humbling, even. You see, before you, I considered
my own operatives invulnerable. But pride goeth before a
fall. Or an explosion, if you will." A strange, shrill giggle
burst out of him. "Today, I reactivated Julian's and Hobart's
old cell phones, with the explosives wired to their vital signs
again. On impulse." He indicated Lily's neck, where the
phones dangled on duct tape. "And here they are! If you
should kill either one of them, the explosion would blow her
head . . . well, if not off, then almost off. It would hang by a
thread. Picture it."

Bruno stared at the guy, his mind blank. What the *fuck?*

Lily stared down, unbending dignity radiating from her
body. Her face, her eyes, had that hard, glassy look he had
seen in the video. Now he sensed, in a rush, what that look
actually was.

It was endurance.

"Go down, Hobart," King ordered. "Have no fear. He's
neutralized." He studied Bruno's face, his gaze fixed on Lily.
"You may well ask, eh? Is she, or isn't she? Is she the Lily
you know and love? Or is she *my* Lily?" His voice dropped
to an oily croon. "My lovely, perfect, dirty Lily." He let go of
her neck, slid his hand down, grabbed her breast.

Lily jerked. "Don't touch me," she hissed.

King cackled. The sound bounced off the walls, blurring
like spooky canned laughter. "You know what's funny, Bruno?"

"I'm sure you'll tell me." He didn't take his eyes off Lily.

"Yes, I will. The funny thing is, this dilemma of yours . . .
it doesn't even matter! You're still bound, either way! Even if
she were holding a gun to your head, you wouldn't be able to
hurt her."

Bruno stared into Lily's eyes. "Lily?" he asked, quietly.

Her face was like marble. "If you have to ask, then there's
no point in answering you."

King guffawed. "Oh, so it's like that? Oh, Lily, that's
harsh. No mercy, eh? Let him dangle and twist, you heartless
bitch."

Lily did not respond in look or word. She just stood there, proud and cold. And pure. Like nothing could touch her.

And Julian vibrated underneath him, like a volcano about to explode. It was like standing on the pin of a grenade.

Had King been fucking with him all along? Hope made him almost giddy.

But hope was a luxury he could not afford. Hobart was moving cautiously down the stairs, his face wary in spite of King's assurances. King shoved Lily, forcing her ahead of him.

There was a pattering sound. A pungent smell. Gasoline.

They looked up. Zoe hung over the railing. If she'd been a death's head before, she was a full-out horror show now. Blood flooded from both ears, streaming down her neck. Her face was grayish, shiny. Veins pulsed in her forehead. Her bloodied teeth showed in a mad grin.

"I'll save you, sir!" she yelled in the unnaturally loud tones of a person wearing headphones. "Don't trust them! They'll betray you!"

"Zoe!" King howled. "Whatever you are doing, stop it!" He thundered out one of those phrases, but Zoe did not turn her head.

She sloshed more gasoline and lurched toward the staircase.

Julian's muscles constricted in a bid for freedom, and Bruno jabbed the gun under the guy's jaw more deeply, staring at Zoe. At the blood flowing from her ears. "She's deaf," he commented. "She can't hear your commands. You've got a rogue robot on your hands. And no off switch. Congratulations. Asshole."

"Shut up!" King pulled Lily back against himself. "Zoe!" He let loose with the gobbledygook again. Zoe ignored him. Gasoline pattered the dusty floor with shiny, oily drops. The fumes were sickening.

"Hobart!" King bellowed. "Stop her!"

Bam. Hobart tried to obey. Zoe shrieked as the bullet hit

her shoulder and spun her around. The gas can dropped, nozzle side down, glugging, cascading down the stairs. *Bam*, this time the thigh, but Zoe got up like a zombie ghoul and still came on, bleeding.

She hit the gas can with her foot. It bounced to the foot of the stairs, liquid still glugging out, spreading in a pool. Zoe tumbled to the foot of the stairs and lay still. Hobart walked over to her—

Her knife flashed up, stabbing into his hamstring. Hobart screamed. His gun went off, the bullet thudding into the stairs. He fell backward—and Zoe was on top, slamming her fist into his face.

A rapid movement caught his eye. Lily jerked to the side, and the movement caught King off guard, pulled him off balance. The two of them hit the aged, cracked wooden banister, which had born Bruno's weight when he fell against it but could not bear the combined mass of Lily and King together. It cracked, sagged. Gave way.

"No!" Bruno yelled as King and Lily toppled out into empty air.

They took flight. Part of her hoping maybe it was all over. She might break her neck, please God. But the fall wasn't far enough. They toppled in a sickening three-sixty flop, everything spinning—

Thud. The sudden stop stunned her. King was beneath her, his face empurpled, gasping for air. Horribly close. He'd landed on his back. Her on top. She'd knocked out his wind. She scrambled away and crab-walked through a puddle of gasoline, groping for the duct-tape necklace with the cell phones. Jerked them off, threw. One ended up in a pool of gas. The other fetched up against a tasseled velvet curtain.

Zoe and Hobart had paused in their combat to watch their idol fall, horrified. Lily looked frantically around for a weapon. A banister slat lay on the floor, a chunk of the handrail still attached, jagged and sharp. She seized it, hauled it back, loading a vicious swing at King.

Zoe and Hobart forgot each other and lunged to stop her.

Bruno jerked the pistol up. *Bam. Bam.* Hobart's head disintegrated. Julian exploded into action, flipping Bruno onto his back, slamming his gun hand to the ground.

The gun flew from Bruno's fingers, spinning across the floor. A pinkish arc of Hobart's blood and brain tissue had spattered across the room. *Boom.* One of the cell phones exploded. The sound hit him like a blow to the center of the chest. The puddle of gas burst into dancing flames with a *whump.* Flames licked, leaped, spread. Fast.

Bruno tried to regroup, but Julian drove him hard, and he could only catch what was happening in jagged flashes out of the corner of his eye, like stop-motion animation amid a desperate dance to avoid the blows crunching into his ribs, the boot heels flying toward his chin. Julian fought like a demon, but the stench of burning hair dragged a split second of attention Bruno could ill afford to see Zoe lurching to her feet—on fire. Hair, clothes, face. Her back was aflame, her hair a torch, her face blistering. She'd fallen into a puddle of gas.

She didn't seem to feel it. She just shambled toward King, arms outstretched. Smiling, as her skin crackled, melted. Come to mamma. Lily backed away from the flaming apparition. King staggered back, screaming desperately. Words Zoe's ruptured eardrums could not hear.

She came on. King's back hit the base of the curving wooden staircase. *Thwack*, Bruno's distraction earned him an elbow to the jaw that sent him spinning way too close to a pool of dancing flame. He twisted and skittered to keep from falling into it, which opened him up to a devastating *whap-bam* double punch to his kidneys. Down he went, *oof. Fuck.* Julian came at him, boots flying. Bruno jerked an arm to block a kick and saw Lily, swinging her strange, jagged-edged club—

Whack, right between Julian's shoulder blades. The kid stumbled forward with a startled grunt, turned—and witnessed King, clasped in Zoe's fiery embrace. Clothes aflame, mouth wide, issuing a rasping, inhuman sound. King fell, Zoe on top of him. Flames roared around them, closing until only their legs emerged, jerking. Shiny, blistered hands poked out of the blaze, groping for the bottom of the tasseled velvet curtains, which were also on fire.

Julian bolted toward his master. Dove in, heedless of the flames, trying to pry King loose. The blazing curtain gave way and billowed down onto the struggling knot of people, *tha-whump*. Crackling.

Bruno and Lily were alone in a roaring inferno. The heavy folds of burning cloth writhed, flopped. Bruno pushed himself up to a sitting position. Lily straightened and tossed the makeshift club to the ground.

Bruno got to his feet and gestured toward the door. "Let's go!"

Amazingly, she shook her head and backed toward the staircase that was not yet in flames. "No! The kids are still in there!"

Her voice sounded like it was coming through thousands of miles of phone wire. He shook his head. The movement made everything hurt.

"They got out!" he yelled. "Julian chased them onto the grounds!"

"Not them! The babies!" She headed back up the stairs.

Babies? What in the flying fuck . . . ?

Boom, the other cell phone exploded. Bruno barely heard it, he was so deafened by gunshots. A new pool of flames whooshed into existence, threatening to engulf the second staircase, where Lily had gone. The other was already a solid wall of flames.

The air was hot, the smoke thick and greasy. He heard

himself from faraway, screaming obscenities as he leaped the flames to the foot of the stairs, practically barbecuing his testicles in the process.

By the time he got to the top, the base of the stairs was engulfed. No going back down that way. It was brutally hot. He peered down the corridor after Lily. Flames crawled along the sprinkle of gasoline that Zoe must have laid down, licking hungrily at one side of the corridor wall. Fiery light lit the clouds of smoke into an eerie orange haze.

He spotted her at the end, a tiny figure, doubled over, hand to her mouth. She rounded the L-turn without looking back, and disappeared.

Not waiting for him. Not expecting help from anyone.

Aw, fuck. What else did he have to do? He bent down, pulled in all the oxygen he could without choking, and charged after her.

Lily crawled with her face to the ground. Stopped at the room she devoutly hoped was the one where she'd found those babies. She couldn't leave those little kids in those cribs while the house burned around them. Not if it killed her. Probably it would. She couldn't carry both babies or go back the way she came. The flames were rising. She had no air to breathe. She wasn't Tinker Bell. No wings. No fairy dust.

She leaned against the door, eyes tearing in the smoky air, fumbling with the bunch of keys. Zoe hadn't splashed her gasoline this far down, but the flames were advancing fast, even without accelerant.

Key after key. A figure burst through the haze. After one heart-stopping moment, she recognized Bruno. The graceful lines of his body, stretched out in a run, straight toward her.

Good. Another pair of arms. She'd squeeze every last drop of usefulness out of them. So, then. He was still a righteous, heroic dude, even if he had mistaken her for a rotten-hearted, back-stabbing whore.

He sagged against the wall, sliding down and coughing. "What the fuck are you doing, Lily?" he demanded.

"I didn't invite you, so I don't owe you a goddamn explanation." She shoved another key into the lock.

He watched, glancing toward the leaping flame. "How'd you get your hands on those keys?" he asked.

"How about you shut up and let me concentrate?"

He watched three more failed attempts before opening his trap again. "Um. Lily. Want me to do that for you?"

"One more word, and I'll rip out your throat and leave you to die."

"Ah." Bruno flopped onto the ground. "Yeah," he croaked. "Right."

She continued grimly plugging in keys in, with the sinking sensation that she'd missed the right one, when *click*—it gave, turned.

They practically fell inside. Bruno slammed the door behind them. They lay there, gasping the relatively untainted air. The room was dim, only a long slit of cobalt blue dusk sky showing between the drapes.

Bruno cleared his throat with a rasping gurgle. "So? What the hell?" he demanded, irrepressible. "What is this place?"

She ran through the bathroom. Bruno hurried after her. She threw open the drapes so that he could see the cribs in the dim light.

He stopped short. "Oh, shit," he whispered. "Oh, no."

Lily struggled with the window latch while Bruno leaned over one crib, prodding under a plump chin. "Are they even alive?" he asked.

"They were breathing when I came through before, and it's not too smoky in here yet. But they've been drugged. I don't know with what."

"Son of a bitch." Bruno sounded as scared as she felt.

Now what? He didn't say the words, but they were loud in the air as the smoke crept in under the door, fogging up the room.

Lily redoubled her efforts with the ancient brass window latch. Then Bruno was behind her, his big arms circling her, his warm hands closing around hers. She couldn't let herself like this feeling, not one bit. For a thousand reasons, imminent death by fire being on the top of the list. The latch creaked and opened. She elbowed him away, hard, and shoved the window open. She hung out of it, gulping cold, sweet air into her lungs. They stared out, assessing prospects for survival.

It didn't look good. No terraces, no balconies, no low-lying roofs or awnings from the first floor. Not even a ledge to creep along. Not a tree or a bush to break their fall. Just a sheer, thirty-foot drop, down to the rose garden. Hard mosaic tile and spiky pruned thornbushes.

Bruno cursed and yanked his head in. Lily turned to find him looking around the room. More smoke crept under the door. A hazy cloud drifted in through the communicating door, too. She went to the door to the corridor, laid her hand against it. "It's hot," she said.

"No shit," Bruno said. "So's the floor." He leaped up, grabbed two handfuls of the curtains, hung on them . . .

Rrrrrip, the fabric gave under his weight, ripping into tatters.

Undaunted, he groped around for the curtain cord. "The velvet's rotten," he said. "But I think this cord is silk. It still feels strong. There might be six yards of it or more." He gathered armfuls of the tattered fabric into his arms, rolling them around his forearms, and leaped.

This time, the arms that held the curtain rod snapped under his weight, and the rod, rings, and curtains tumbled down onto their heads, along with a choking cloud of dust.

They fought their way out from under it. "Drag one of those cribs over to the window," Bruno said. "They need air."

That sounded smart. Lily got to it. The little girl was so floppy when she lifted her. Bruno measured out the length of an alarmingly thin cord. She could barely see it, pale in the dimness.

"Will that hold a person?" she asked.

"I don't know. But it would hold one of them, if I could rig a way to lower them down. The curtains? Help me think of something."

"They have those baby seats over there for a car, with webbing restraints." Lily grabbed one out of the inky, foggy shadows.

Bruno glanced at it as he yanked out armfuls of cord. "Might work." He hung out the window, dangling the cord as far as it would go. "Shit. It's short. Over three meters short. Fuck, fuck, *fuck!*"

Lily peered at the shortfall. "And if you went down first?" she said. "And I lowered them to you? You could catch them."

He let out a coughing bark of laughter. "And leave you up here?"

"I'd come down after them," she argued.

"Yeah? Really? Hand over hand, on a curtain cord? You'd have to drop it anyway, to let the kids fall! I wouldn't be able to reach it to untie it. Unless I find something five feet tall to stand on. You go down first!"

"Bullshit," she snapped. "You're the only one with a hope in hell of catching one of those things if it fell on you from above your head!"

"I couldn't catch two at a time," he pointed out.

"Oh! Well, fine, then! News flash! Neither could I!" she yelled.

He shrugged. "I doubt the cord would bear my weight anyway."

"Then why are we fucking with it in the first place?" She was screaming now.

"Because there's nothing else to fuck with!" he yelled back. "There's not even a bed in here with a goddamn sheet! Nothing!"

She pressed her eyes until red dots swirled and danced. "The top hem of the curtains?" she offered. "The reinforced part, with the rings, the pleats? That might give us a little more length."

He pawed through armfuls of the dusty fabric until he found the top hem, jerking it to test its strength. "I need a knife."

"I have one," she told him. "A little one on the key chain I lifted off Melanie. I cut your cuffs with it."

She immediately wished she hadn't mentioned that. Bad associations. He took it from her and started hacking off the top strip.

"How'd you manage that?" he said. "Taking her keys, I mean."

"I had to kill her first," she said.

Bruno stopped for a second. "You did *what?*"

"Focus, Bruno!" she snarled.

"I am focusing! I'm multitasking!" He jerked at the curtain to test its resistance. "Seems like there's a lot I don't know about you."

"So I should think!" She couldn't hold back. "Since you thought I was that psycho's robot chippie! That's flattering, Bruno. That just does wonders for my self-esteem."

He hacked the curtain with renewed savagery. "Now you're the one who should focus."

"You can't blame me for taking offense," she said.

"Save the blame for when the kids are safe."

She blew out a furious, huffing breath. "Fair enough."

Bruno knotted cord around some of the rings sewn into the curtain hem and tossed the whole thing out the window to measure the shortfall. They gazed down, dismayed. Still over two yards short.

A vehicle rounded the corner of the house, bouncing and thudding. A white Volkswagen panel van.

Bruno grabbed the curtain and flung it out the window, flapping.

"That might be more of King's goons," she warned.

"So? So they shoot us," he said. "They're welcome to. Have at it. At this point, they'd be doing us a goddamn favor."

Ouch. Not what she wanted to hear. But he had a point.

The van jerked to a stop. Two people jumped out, waving. Lily squinted through the gloom. Not possible. She must be hallucinating.

"Oh, sweet Jesus, it's Kev and Sean! Kev!" he bellowed. *"Kev!"*

Kev waved his arms, yelled back.

"You got some rope?" Bruno yelled. "The floor's going to fall in!"

The two men leaped back into the van, accelerated over walkways and rosebushes until they were directly below the window. Kev got out, a coil of rope in his arms, stepped onto his brother's linked hands, and leaped up on top of the van. Tears streamed down Lily's face.

Kev grabbed the end of the curtain cord, gave it a reassuring tug, and threaded his coil of rope through it. He knotted it, tugged again.

"You go first," Bruno said, as he hauled up the rope.

"The babies first," Lily said.

"No. I'll work faster and better if I know that you're—" *"The babies first!"*

He crouched, fixing the rope to the steam radiator. "Then get one of the kids strapped into the goddamn seat, quick!"

Their furious activity was punctuated by grunts of effort, coughing, the odd Calabrese obscenity. Soon, the unconscious little girl toddler was strapped into her seat, secured with the five-point harness and the webbed restraints. Lily got the boy strapped in to his seat while Bruno snapped the carrier's handle into place and looped the rope around, jerking, knotting. The knots looked secure, but still they stared at each other, pale and sick when he poised the thing on the windowsill.

"This is so fucking terrifying," he said.

Lily coughed and gritted her teeth. "Go for it."

They watched the child's pale sleeping face slowly twist and twirl beneath them, getting smaller in the reddish glare as Bruno fed the rope out. Thank God the kid was still unconscious. The rope was more than long enough. Kev received the bucket seat, untied it. Bruno yanked the rope back up as Kev passed the baby to Sean.

The next one went faster. When the boy was safely down, Lily was able to breathe again, more or less. "You go next," she urged him. "Let me go last. Since this whole thing was my idea."

"Shut up," Bruno snarled. He jerked her arms up. Knotted a loop of the rope beneath her armpits.

She stepped off into empty air, elbows tight to her ribs, clutching the rope. Staring up at Bruno's anxious, soot-streaked face as he steadily lowered her down. She twisted and swayed, buffeted by blasts of heat coming out of the windows. The first floor looked like the pits of hell. Hands grabbed her from below. Yelling male voices. The world lurched, slid, twisted. Gravity sucked at her, buffeted her.

Then she was lying flat on her back on the hard stony tiles, ignored while Kev and Sean loped away to concentrate on Bruno.

She tried to get up, but her legs gave out, wobbling. She just propped herself up. The baby seats were near to her, the kids still asleep.

Crash, the second floor gave way. Heat and sparks blasted out, blowing her hair back. She screamed, stuffing her sooty fist into her mouth. Her heart stuttered. Her eyes watered so badly, she couldn't tell if Bruno was still . . . how could he be? There was no floor beneath him.

Then she saw his silhouette, backlit by red-tinged billows of smoke, dangling on the rope. He climbed swiftly down, hand over hand, and landed lightly on top of the van. He leaped off it to the ground.

She must have fainted for a while. Or just shut down. She remembered being carried. Blazing, flashing lights, voices. A blanket was tucked around her. People discussing her, prodding at her. She clawed her way back to wakefulness by brute effort. She couldn't afford to let herself go, like a fainting Victorian miss. She was alone. She had to keep it together, look out for herself. Nobody else would do it for her.

At some point, a hot paper cup of coffee was pushed into her hands. Someone wrapped her cold fingers around it.

She pulled her gaze into focus. She was sitting on a marble bench on the grounds somewhere in the midst of various emergency vehicles. Bruno crouched in front of her, his hands around hers. She looked away from him. The babies were gone. Whisked off to a hospital. The house was burning, great arcs of water from fire hoses pumping into it.

Bruno was waiting for her to look him in the eye. She looked at his hands. They were filthy, scratched, scraped, burned, knuckles bloodied. She shut her eyes again. Let him wait.

"Lily?" he said, finally. "Are you OK?"

"No," she said. No social lies left. It was all burned out of her.

"Please," he said, after an agonizing silence. "Look at me."

His soft tone sucked her in. She did, and wished she hadn't. She hated it. That soft look. It killed her. Because she couldn't trust it.

"Lily." His voice was rough with emotion. "About what happened in there, with King. I'm so sorry that I—"

"Don't." She jumped up. Hot coffee spattered all over Bruno's arms. "Any apology you could make would only make it worse."

She backed away, but he followed. "You have to understand," he pleaded. "This guy, he fucked with my head, Lily. When I was a little kid. He'd programmed me, somehow. And he knew details about us, things you'd said to me that only the two of us could have—"

"I don't want to know the gory details," she said. "I don't give a shit what he told you. He was a psycho. A monster. You knew that. And you believed him, instead of me. That's not something I can just put behind me. So . . ." Words failed her. She shook her head. "So nothing. Good luck with your life. Good-bye."

"No," he said fiercely. "I won't accept that."

"It's not up to you! Don't make me get ugly with you!"

He held his hands out, palms up. "But I—"

"Get one thing straight," she cut him off. "I appreciate that you saved my life, OK? I appreciate you saving the babies, too. Superheroic. Yay for you, you get big-ass points for that. Thank the McClouds, too, for their help. They have awesome timing. God bless them."

"Lily—"

"I even appreciate the fact that you didn't kill me on sight, being as how you thought I was one of King's drones." She hurried on, intent on getting it out before it turned to cascades of snot. "Very generous of you, under the circumstances. So thanks, OK? Thanks a million. And now, just please, please fuck off."

She turned her back and walked away, praying that he wouldn't follow, and realized that she was tiptoeing, listening for his footsteps behind her. Hoping that he would follow her.

He didn't, though.

Then the sniveling came, the tears. She clutched the blanket around herself and blundered on into the darkness.

Any direction would do, as long as it was away from him.

36

Six weeks later . . .

Aaro smelled Petrie before he spotted him sneaking a quiet smoke behind the conservatory while hiding from the wedding crowd. He looked good for a man who'd been shot in the chest six weeks before. His suit was flapping loose on him, but it stayed on.

Aaro sussed the suit with the expert eye of a person who'd grown up with gangsters. Versace, on a cop's budget. But he'd researched Petrie after what had happened at the cop shop with the girl. The guy came from money. He was wearing some of it today. Petrie caught sight of him, looked up. His face relaxed when he saw that it was Aaro.

"Got a death wish?" Aaro asked. "Sucking on those damn things with a hole in your lung?" He held out his hand. "Here. Give me one."

Petrie shook one out, gave him a light. They sucked their cancer sticks in companionable silence. Aaro pulled out his flask, took a gulp of single malt, passed it on. "Might as well slam your liver, too, while you're at it," he said. "So you're hiding, too? Why'd you come?"

Petrie sipped at the flask. "Had to. Zia Rosa knows where I live."

"Ah. There is that." Aaro blew out smoke. "The curse has taken hold. When they start inviting you to their weddings, you're meat."

Petrie's eyebrow twitched in unwilling curiosity. "Curse?"

"It comes from hanging out with the McClouds," Aaro said. "When I took up with them, my cars started blowing up. My house. These days, I sleep with a girl I meet at a bar, and pow, she explodes in front of me."

"You blame that on the McClouds?" Petrie's mouth twitched.

"Look at yourself. You get interested in them, and suddenly you're in intensive care, tubes up every orifice. I'm telling you. It's the curse."

Petrie let out a philosophical sigh. "Maybe so."

"Don't try to run," Aaro added, helpfully. "It's too late."

Movement caught his eye through the wall of the conservatory. A bright color that whipped his head all the way around to see if . . . yes, it was. Oh, holy shit. "That's Lily Parr," he said.

Petrie lunged to see and winced. "That's gonna be interesting," he said. "What's she doing?"

Aaro craned his neck to keep her in sight. She stood in the shadows of a rhododendron bush, looking pale and spooked. Her red-gold hair gleamed in the afternoon sunlight. "Lurking, like us," he said.

"Should we, uh . . ." Petrie hesitated.

"Tell Bruno? Hell, yeah." Aaro stubbed out his cigarette on the sole of his shoe. "I'll go find him."

Bruno burst out the door that led to the solarium, decked in a tux, a bag hanging over his shoulder. He held his newly adopted baby girl Lena under the armpits. He looked wild-eyed and hassled.

"There you are," Aaro started. "Good. Look, man, we just saw—"

"I need diaper wipes!" Bruno bellowed.

Aaro and Petrie exchanged panicked glances. "Huh?"

"Wipes!" Bruno repeated. "Lena's leaking! And the ceremony's about to start, and I've got the rings in my pocket! And I can't find Zia, or Liv, or Margot, or anybody with wipes!"

"Oh. Uh, well, shit," Aaro said, helplessly.

"Yeah!" Bruno yelled. "Like, literally! A lot of it! Cascades of it!"

Sveti wafted out, looking stunning in a dress that swirled and fluttered. She waved a package. "I found wipes! Erin had some."

"Thank God," Bruno muttered.

In the distance, the string quartet started a wedding processional. Bruno jerked. "Oh, Christ," he moaned. "Not now. Not yet."

"Go, go," Sveti urged, grabbing the toddler and bag from him. "I'll change Lena for you and take her to Zia. You hurry."

"Wait!" Aaro shouted after the man as he loped away.

Bruno stopped in the doorway. "What?"

"Just thought you should know. We saw Lily Parr outside."

Bruno looked like he'd turned to stone. His mouth moved. No sound emerged. "Where?" he finally croaked.

"That way. In the rhododendrons outside. She's hiding."

"Bruno!" Sveti shouted as he lunged blindly in the Lily-seeking direction. "The ceremony! The rings! You have to go! For Kev!"

Bruno swung on his heel, confused and agonized. He fixed Aaro with a burning stare. "You. Find her for me. Do not let her get away."

Don't fuck up again, being the subtext of that directive.

Aaro nodded. "Got it."

Bruno's stiff arm dropped, but he still could not seem to move.

Aaro touched his shoulder. "Bruno," he said quietly. "Breathe."

Bruno bolted, leaving them with Sveti holding the wriggling baby girl, and a very uncomfortable silence. Sveti was the first to break it.

"Well?" she said crisply. "I could use some help."

Aaro and Petrie exchanged terrified glances. "Uh, what kind of help?" Aaro asked, nervously.

Sveti's eyes narrowed. "This table where I must change her is cold, hard glass, see? So unless one of you gentleman has a blanket or towel . . . ?" Her eyes fell to their suit coats. Oh, man. Harsh.

Petrie slipped of his Versace, spread it out on the table with a martyred air. Sveti sniffed and gave him a horrified stare. "You *smoke?*"

"Uh . . ." Petrie's eyes shifted. "I, uh, just quit."

Sveti harrumphed. She lay the wriggling baby girl on his coat and started the smelly process. "One of you get out wipes for me."

The men looked at each other over the back of the girl's slender bowed neck, exposed under gleaming, elegantly twisted-up hair, and the graceful, sweeping curve of her pale, mostly exposed back.

"*Now*, please!" The razor edge in her voice made both men jump.

Aaro took three steps closer to this smelly biological event than he had ever wished to, and popped open the package of wipes.

Sveti glared at both men in turn. "I know why you two are out here, hiding, eh? Sucking on cigarettes and liquor."

"You do?" Aaro passed her a handful of wipes.

She swiped the poopy, wiggling bottom with practiced ease. "Yes. I do." She directed her blazing stare upon Aaro. "You are sorry for yourself because they took Lily from you at the hospital, eh? I am sick of your attitude!" she scolded. "Remember when Novak took Rachel? His men took her right out of my arms! There was nothing I could do. I wanted to die, you know? I wanted to disappear!"

Aaro stuffed more wipes into her hand.

"Oh, yes, I know you think because you are big man, lots of muscle, big gun, that it should be different for you, but it is not different! It is same! Get out diaper, quick! Lena will get cold."

"Yeah." Aaro fished out a diaper. Baffled, but meek.

"And you!" Sveti turned her burning glance on Petrie. "You should be ashamed. Dirty opportunist. Attacking Zia with pictures of corpses!"

Petrie sighed. "You're still hung up on that?"

"I am disgusted by that!" she shot back.

Petrie's face had gotten some color, Aaro noticed. But a guy would have to be two days dead not to have his blood pressure affected by Sveti in a low-cut evening gown, spitting nails at him.

"Doesn't taking a bullet for her cancel that out?" Petrie asked.

Sveti snapped Lena's onesie closed and started wrestling the little girl's white tights back onto her chubby thighs. "No. Any fool can catch a bullet. You just have to be in its way. Why should a bullet excuse you for being an asshole?" She lifted Lena into her arms, slung the bag over her shoulder. "You can take your jacket back," she conceded.

Petrie picked it up, sniffed at it. Shrugged it gingerly back on.

Sveti glared at Aaro. "You, go find Lily, like he told you. And *you*." She hefted the heavy, stinky diaper and plopped it into Petrie's hands. "You get rid of this." She stalked off toward the music. Lena's bright dark button eyes regarded them with wonderment over Sveti's shoulder.

They stared after her, their minds wiped blank by that surreal encounter. Aaro recovered first. "Wow," he said. "Ouch. She hates your scrawny cop ass, man. She hates it bad."

"Looks that way," Petrie agreed.

Aaro unstoppered his flask and passed it to the other

man, who took a grateful sip, his eyes still fixed on the last place Sveti had been.

"Just as well," Aaro offered, by way of comfort. "She's too young."

Petrie's gaze swung around. "How young?" he asked.

"Oh, nineteen, twenty, I think. Put her out of your mind."

"Right." Petrie took another swig, passed the flask back. "Right."

Aaro slid it into his pocket. "I'm going to go stalk Lily Parr now. Go watch the ceremony, man." Petrie looked like he was rooted to the ground. Aaro joggled the guy's shoulder, remembering the healing bullet wound too late when he saw Petrie flinch "Hey," he said. "Breathe."

A ghost of a smile flashed across Petrie's face as he held up the noxious diaper. "With this thing in my hands?"

Lily focused intently on the string ensemble in the back of the conservatory playing the wedding processional with great verve.

It was hard not to stare. The musicians were very easy on the eyes. Six drop-dead gorgeous chicks in plunging sequined evening gowns. And they played their instruments beautifully, too. Go figure.

Lily could not believe she'd talked herself into this. Yes, she needed to express her gratitude to the clan; yes, she did need to wish Edie and Kev the best; yes, she owed Tam congratulations for her baby.

And yes, she needed to speak to Bruno.

She'd thought, why not do it all in one fell swoop and move on from there? Liberated and lightened, with new clarity of mind. Right.

Wrong. It wasn't going to be like that. She was in deep shit.

She'd tried to be unobtrusive. She'd swept her hair up into a fuzzy roll. Worn smoky charcoal gray, but the beaded gown was pretty. She'd painted her face carefully to mask her pallor. Rented her own car for a sure getaway. This Parrish mansion, one of many, was located outside the city. She'd hung back in the bushes, in the cold, until the processional began so that everyone else would be already seated inside the old-fashioned glass conservatory where the ceremony was being held.

She'd lurked by the door. She had no intention of going to the reception afterward. As if. But in spite of all her efforts, Sveti had spotted her. And of course, the girl jumped up, waving, and ran down the center aisle like a pink-tinted gazelle, dress fluttering behind her like fairy wings, her face lit with one of those incandescent smiles, so that everyone had to rubberneck to see who she was running toward.

And Lily was so very busted.

Sveti hugged her and dragged her up the aisle to where all the other McCloud women and kids were sitting. She was forced to field big smiles of welcome and a ripple of fierce whispering. Liv was there, and Zia Rosa, too, all jubilant smiles and winks. There were a number of women she hadn't met yet, holding babies and toddlers, exchanging speculative glances. The McCloud men were all up front, standing up behind Kev, along with Bruno. She tried not to look, but her gaze was sucked to him. And Bruno stared straight at her. Shockingly gorgeous in his black tux. Thinner. Sharper. His dark eyes burned.

The eye contact stopped her breath. Her face went hot. Everyone watched her blush. Well, not everyone. Some people were probably watching the bride and groom. Kev looked so happy. Edie was the most beautiful bride Lily had ever seen. She wore a draped chiffon thing, with bias-cut ruffly edges that perfectly suited her tall, graceful form. Her long hair flowed loose, accented by vaporous bits of lily of the valley.

The couple gazed at each other, hands linked. True lovers who'd passed through all trial and danger, and had finally come home to each other. They shone together. They were literally bathed in light.

It made her heart burn and ache. Jealousy was unseemly in the face of such perfect happiness, but she wasn't an angel or a saint. Good thing tears were appropriate at weddings. Tough to tell the difference between heartfelt good wishes and plain old rancorous envy.

Tam stood up with the bride, along with a pretty girl who had to be Edie's younger sister, from the looks of her. Tam was looking trim and elegant, in spite of having given birth to her daughter, Irina, only two weeks before. News of that event had filtered back to Lily, in spite of the shields she'd put around herself. Tam studied Lily, her expression hard to read. It looked like approval. Showed how much Tam knew.

Everyone seemed to think a happy ending was guaranteed. But she'd gone over it a thousand times. She'd been so sure. Positive she and Bruno were linked, heart and soul, 'til the end of time. And when she realized he didn't trust her, that he didn't believe her, well.

She just wouldn't be able to survive that a second time. And if it happened once, why not again, when she least expected it? In spite of her discovery. She was still reeling from it. Riding a hormonal roller coaster.

Lily broke eye contact with some difficulty, Tam being Tam. She scanned the crowd until she found Val a couple of rows behind her. A tiny baby swathed in hot pink chenille was draped on his shoulder over a burp rag that protected his elegant black suit. Rachel was beside him.

Val gave her a nod, a smile. Rachel bounced and waved. Lily's throat tightened, looking at the tiny baby. She was so glad for them. At least some stories had happy endings. And not just this one. There were two rambunctious black-haired toddlers crawling all over Zia Rosa's and Sveti's laps. The very kids she and Bruno had pulled out of King's burning house. So Bruno had gotten custody of his little siblings.

Something good had come of all this evil. There was that to cling to.

She dragged a Kleenex out of her purse. Bruno stepped up behind his brother to give him the rings. Their gazes crossed. No getting away. They stared at each other while Kev and Edie exchanged their vows.

Lily didn't hear a thing. She was trapped in an airless, invisible prison. All she saw was Bruno's face. All she heard was her heart, thudding. Emotions rose up, swelling out of control. Threatening to burst out in some inappropriate, badly timed way, a sobbing fit, a fainting spell, a freak-out. She'd worn low heels in case she ended up running. And waterproof mascara. The gummy stuff weighed her lashes down like they'd been painted with tar.

Then Kev and Edie joined in a clinging kiss so joyful and inevitable the room broke into cheers, howls, applause. Everyone rose to their feet, yelling and whooping. So happy that these two fine people had found such joy together. Something snapped. The sobbing part was coming on.

Oh, shit. Not now. She jerked loose of Sveti's hand and ran toward the back of the conservatory, out into the garden, pointing herself blindly toward the parking area—

A hand seized her arm, bringing her up short with a jerk.

She gasped, wet eyes wild, staring into the face of Alex Aaro. She sagged, trying to catch her breath as her heart tripped and stuttered.

"Oh, God," she quavered. "Oh, God, you scared me to death."

"Sorry," Aaro said. He sounded both apologetic and sullen.

She stared, pointedly, at her trapped wrist. "I will accept your apology if you let go of me."

"Uh, no," he said.

She was alarmed. "What do you mean, no?"

"I just mean no," he repeated. "You can't leave yet."

She yanked at her arm. "How dare you?" Her voice began to rise in pitch. "How dare you push me around? Let go of me, goddamnit!"

He easily managed her flailing and struggling. "I'm sorry."

"Why?" she shrieked. "I have had enough of this shit!"

"Yes, you have, absolutely," he said. "And I will let you go, I promise, as soon as Bruno gets out here."

Her stomach went into freefall. She began to shake her head. "You can't do that to me. You just can't."

"I'm sorry," he said, helplessly. "I have to. I promised. I'm sorry."

"You'll be sorrier when I start screaming!"

He shook his head. "No, Lily. Every person here, every last damn person, will back me up. Go ahead and scream. You'll see."

"Then I'll just tear your face off, if no one will help me," she snarled. "Say good-bye to your eyes right now!"

"I don't care," he said, grimly stoic. "I would rather die badly, right here and now, than let you disappear on him a second time."

She realized how her abduction in the hospital must have felt from his viewpoint. The crowd was spilling out into the garden, curious people looking their way as the string ensemble started to play again.

"You don't understand," she said, haltingly. "Things are different now. Between us."

"I don't care," Aaro said. "That's for you guys to thrash out."

"That's exactly it!" she wailed, jerking at her trapped arm. "I can't deal with any thrashing right now!"

"Lily."

Bruno's voice wiped her mind clean. She forgot Aaro existed. The manacle on her arm disappeared. Along with all the available oxygen.

Close up, she could see the damage he'd sustained in their

adventure. Shiny pink marks on his cheekbone, the thickened eyelid. A notch in his ear. Burn scars on his hands. But it was the pain in his eyes that made her feel like a fist was squeezing her heart.

Bruno released her eyes, flicked his gaze to Aaro. "Thank you."

"Anytime, man." Aaro slunk away.

She watched him go. "Anytime, my ass," she muttered, sourly. "Does he take hostages for you on a regular basis?"

"No," Bruno said quietly. "Just you, Lily. You're special."

"Not really," she said. "I've been enjoying my non-special status lately. My life is so normal now. Quiet."

His jaw contracted. "I see," he said. "Congratulations."

They stared at each other. Now was the time to deliver her bombshell. The timing was terrible, but how could she see him again, on another occasion? Torture herself, over and over, with these feelings?

But it was absurd to pile another burden onto a man who had just single-handedly shouldered the responsibility for two toddlers.

Bruno, I'm pregnant. Uh, OK. So? What could he do about it?

This was not the moment. She'd miscalculated. She called on her minimal knowledge of wedding choreography for a distraction. "Um, aren't you supposed to be in a receiving line, or something?"

"I bailed to come after you. Skipped out on the exit march, too. Like a rhino on stampede. Ronnie had to go out on Sean's arm. Edie's aunt is going to tear me to shreds and stomp on the pieces."

"Oh. Well, then. That's bad. You better get going," she urged. "Can't have any of that. Tearing and stomping, I mean."

"It doesn't matter," he said. "I'm used to it. Being stomped on."

She shrank away, sensing a trap. "Um. I think that's my cue to—"

"Are you staying for the reception?" His scarred hand clamped her wrist. Her wrist went nuts at the contact. A ripple effect that shot bright sparks all through her system.

"I don't think that would be a good idea," she quavered.

"I have to talk to you," he said. "Please. Come with me."

She grabbed a wrought iron gate and hung on. "To where?"

"To the receiving line. I can't risk letting you out of my sight."

"No problem!" Liv McCloud popped up, Eamon in her arms, and leaned to give Lily a kiss. "Glad to see you, Lily. You're wanted urgently in the receiving line, Bruno. Hurry. Edie's aunt is twitching and frothing. Don't worry, Eamon and I will babysit Lily for you."

"I don't need to be babysat!" Lily snapped, testily.

"Of course not." Liv took her arm. "Let's go pay our respects to the bride and groom, shall we?"

It was a unique form of hell to have everyone hugging her, exchanging grins and winks, thumbs-up, when she was just going to let them down again, once they knew the truth. The receiving line itself was the worst. She was passed from one McCloud to the next, getting fierce hugs and significant glances from each one. Bruno grabbed her when she got to him and held her tight, in a hard, breathless clinch. The raw, burning look in his eyes just undid her.

Edie gave her a hug when Bruno finally released her. "Thanks for coming."

Lily laughed, soggily. "I had to, right? To get the portrait of my mom. Holding it for ransom like that, that was a very dirty trick."

"Whatever works, right? I kept my side of the bargain. It's in the car, all ready for you," Edie assured her. Her arms tightened around Lily again. "He needs you, you know?" she whispered.

Lily's heart was squeezed. She extricated herself, greeted Edie's sister, a dewy creature named Ronnie. Then Tam gripped her arm.

"Congratulations for Irina," Lily offered. "I saw her during the ceremony. She's beautiful. I'm so glad things turned out well."

"Me, too," Tam said. She leaned forward, breathing the words into Lily's ear. "Far be it from me to criticize a sister for giving a man a hard time," she murmured. "Just be sure you don't make yourself pay too high a price for it. Satisfaction's hollow when you're all alone at night."

Lily jerked herself loose. "It's not that simple!"

"Right. Nothing ever is." She shoved Lily right into Zia Rosa's waiting arms. "Good luck."

Zia's smothering embrace was sharply perfumed with jungle gardenia. Zia cupped her hands, pinched her cheeks. "*Ehi*, you're pale! *Sciupata!* Not eating?" Her eyes slitted. "How's the tummy?"

"Just fine, just fine," Lily assured her hastily. "The best."

"You seen our little Tonio, and Lena? Ain't they cute?" She jerked Lily's chin around. "See? Look! Miles has Tonio, and Sveti's got Lena."

Lily looked. The kids really were beautiful. Tonio giggled madly, head and shoulders flung back over Miles's arm as Miles yanked up the kid's crisp white blouse and snuffled his belly. Lena was on her butt on the floor in her white dress, trying to take off her little white Mary Janes, while Sveti crouched next to her, imploring her to reconsider.

"They are beautiful," Lily said with utter sincerity.

"Ah, but they need a mamma, hmm?" Zia Rosa murmured sentimentally. She pinched Lily's cheek again.

A strong arm slid around her waist, pulling. "Zia, that'll do."

Lily didn't know whether to be grateful or panicked when Bruno swept her away from them all, maneuvering her into the ballroom all decked out for dining and dancing. A band was setting up, and the glamorous string ensemble she'd no-ticed at the ceremony was tuning up, too. "What's with the musicians?" she asked him.

"The Venus Ensemble?" he asked. "What about them?"

"Six gorgeous girls in low-cut sequined gowns, and they play really well, too? It just seems like a statistical abnor-mality to me."

Bruno grinned. "Nah. Remember what happened to Kev and Edie? The mind control, and all that crazy shit?"

"Sure I remember," she said.

"Those were the girls that got imported to do the crown-ing jobs. Trafficked from Moldavia, Belarus, the Ukraine, with all the usual tricks. Promises of jobs, green cards. Since the best crown interfaces were with female artists, the traf-fickers recruited girls from conservatories. And obviously, they favored the pretty ones."

"That's so creepy." Lily looked at the group of beauties busily tuning their instruments, chilled at the thought.

"It is, but it turned out OK. After Kev saved them, they got green cards and formed this string ensemble, and now they're raking in the dough. Posh weddings, receptions, con-certs. They're famous, and hot, and they kick ass. Their agent can't handle all the offers." He waved. A dark-haired violin-ist smiled back. "But this gig they're playing for free."

The first violinist lifted her instrument to her chin. The others looked at her for a moment of expectant silence.

A nod, and they launched into Vivaldi's "Four Seasons."

Bruno gasped as the music slammed into him like an eighteen-wheeler. He hung on to reality by a thread. The music dragged him back to that hour in Julian's car, lying in the backseat with a smothering black mask over his head, wondering what was happening to Lily.

His blood pressure dipped, his stomach flopped. He gasped for breath. Everything swirled and spun.

". . . the matter? Bruno? Are you OK? Bruno!"

He was against a column, Lily's shoulder bracing him. He dragged her anxious face into focus.

"Are you OK?" she asked. "Should I call someone? Are you sick?"

"Just get me away from this fucking music. Please. *Fast.*"

He kept his arm around her as she steered him away from the music. It almost disappeared when she pushed through a door into a dark, quiet corridor. She opened the first door she found, which proved to be some sort of library. She positioned him in front of a wingback chair. He thudded into it, still gasping for breath.

Lily put her hands on her hips. "So. What's this all about?" she asked. "You don't like baroque violin suites?"

"Nah, they're OK." He swallowed, his mouth trembling. "That particular piece was playing on the car radio while Julian was driving me to King's headquarters. It's just . . . it's a bad memory."

"Ah. I see." She squeezed his shoulder. "Wait here. Be right back."

"Lily! Don't—" *Don't go.* He was saying it to empty air.

He lurched to his feet, but his knees wobbled, and he flopped back down again, despair opening inside him like a sinkhole.

He'd scared her off. Too needy. She didn't want any part of his cracked-up, stressed-out bullshit, and he didn't blame her.

He could chase her through the ballroom, bleating for her love, but how pathetic, how useless, how undignified would that be? How painful for everyone to watch. All he could do now was try not to lose his shit at Kev's wedding. That would be selfish and childish.

"Hey." The door opened. His heart sprang up into the air.

Lily held a steaming cup in her hand. "I saw them setting up the coffee station. Thought you could use a shot of caffeine."

His eyes drank her in and overflowed. He covered them with his hand. "Thanks," he said thickly.

Her shoes clicked toward him. She held the cup out. He drained it in a couple deep swallows. It helped. He grabbed her hand. "Don't go."

"Um." She stared down to where her wrist was swallowed by his hand. She was looking at his scars. He wasn't sure at what point in their adventure he'd gotten them. That whole last day was a blur of pain and fire, with a few highlights pointing out like spikes.

Like the part where he'd let King convince him that Lily was one of the guy's operatives.

She wasn't pulling away, though.

"So you've got the kids," she said. "You've adopted them?"

"I'm in the process. They've been with me for a few weeks now."

"Are they, um . . . OK?" she asked, delicately.

He shrugged. "They seem to be OK. They're great kids. Holy terrors, particularly Tonio. Zia Rosa tells me he's exactly like me."

"How did you find out their names?"

"We didn't. We named them, Zia and I. For Tony and Mamma. Antonio and Magdalena. They didn't have names. Evidently King didn't assign names until the third year, when the programming began."

She shivered. "How awful."

"It's better," he said. "It was appropriate to name them for Tony and Mamma. Tonio's a big boss. He runs the show, or thinks he does. And Lena's a diva, pulling all of Tonio's strings. They're awesome."

"And you?" She tugged his hand gently. "How is it for you?"

He smiled and shook his head. "It's good," he said. "Difficult. Crazy. I don't sleep much, but I never really did. I love those kids. And I'm glad to be doing something hard and important. I'm lucky I have something to give a shit about." He paused. "Under the circumstances."

A tremor went through her. "So," she said, with forced brightness. "What do they call you, then? Bruno? Uncle Bruno? Zio Bruno?"

"No," he said. "They call me Daddy."

She blinked. "They don't need a brother or an uncle," he went on. "They need a father. I never had one, but they're damn well going to."

"Ah." There was an awkward silence. "Well. It's amazing. And so lucky that you got them before King started, um, messing with them."

"Wouldn't have mattered if he had messed with them. King messed with me, and my mamma still thought I was worth saving."

"Of course you were," she soothed. "I wasn't questioning that."

Her eyes were big, wary. He was making her nervous. *Cool it.*

"What happened to those other kids we found?" she asked timidly. "The teenagers who were in the white room? Are they OK?"

He shook his head. "They're struggling," he said. "The fewer years of programming they've gone through, the better off they are. There were thirty younger ones, and they're hanging in there. But don't you know all this? I figured Liv or Edie would keep you up to date."

Since you refused to take my calls or respond to my e-mails.

"I've been incommunicado," she said. "Trying to figure out what to do with myself. Everything is different, now that Howard's gone. I don't have to write term papers for pay anymore, thank God. After what happened, I couldn't stomach any more of that. Whatever I do from now on, it has to be real. Even if I make only a quarter of the money."

"I hear you," Bruno said, with feeling. "So you're going to write papers for yourself, then?"

"I was considering it. I think I'd like academia. Maybe teaching English, or writing, at the high school or college level. We'll see."

"You'd be good. Your students will love you and fear you."

"We'll see," she hedged. "Who knows."

"I know," he said. "Believe me. I know."

She flapped her hand at him. "And the adult operatives? Did they ever find the ones who were running around loose?"

Bruno shook his head. "The older kids identified some of them for us, but they'd committed suicide by the time we tracked them down. Probably all of the operatives out in the field did, when they heard about King dying. There's no way to know for sure."

She winced. "That's terrible."

"Yeah. They were monsters, but they never had a choice."

Her lips tightened. She waited for a moment before asking the next soft question. "How about your biological brothers and sisters?"

"We found them," Bruno said quietly. "At least, I assume we have. We can't be sure until they do genetic testing, and that'll take time. King told me there were sixteen embryos brought to term, and that Tonio and Lena were the last ones, besides Julian, after all the cullings. If there had been more alive, he would have taunted me with their existence, rather than lying about it. And there were mass graves on the property. Some of the older kids talked about the cullings. They found the graves using infrared aerial photography."

She winced. "Oh, God, Bruno. I'm so sorry. How awful."

"Some were more recent. Some were older, corresponding to the info my mother left on those disks that she hid in the jewelry box."

"I'm so sorry," she whispered again. "It's so horrible for you."

"Yeah, it messes with my head that there were sixteen of

my mother's children alive, and now they're all murdered. Some by me."

"Bullshit!" she burst out. "You never murdered any of those people! They were trying to rip you to pieces! And me, too!"

He was taken aback. "What, defending me now? I thought you hated my guts."

"Don't be ridiculous." Lily jerked her hand away. "I just know a self-pitying, masturbatory load of shit when I hear one!" She wound her arms across her chest, which did awesome things to her lush cleavage.

He dragged his eyes from her tits. "That's intense."

"Oh, you have no idea," she told him.

He contemplated the hot buzz in the air between them. The glow of heat. Of hope. It took a long time to work up the nerve to risk it.

"Then you still have feelings for me," he ventured, quietly.

Lily's face contracted. She took a step back. "I'm sorry," she said, her voice choked. "It was a mistake to come here."

He headed her off at the door. "No. Please, Lily. Let me talk."

"It's not going to work." Her voice shook. "It doesn't matter what my feelings are. It doesn't matter."

He reached behind to the knob and clicked the lock shut. Maneuvered her back into the room, setting her into the chair.

"There's no point in going over this." The words burst out of her. "You didn't trust me when things got bad. And in my experience, things get bad a lot. If we don't have trust, we don't have anything."

He sank down in front of her. "I know. But listen to me."

"I can't face that again. I couldn't survive another—"

"Listen!" he broke in. "I'm begging, Lily. On my knees. For you to just listen to me for a second. OK?"

She nodded, swiping angrily at the tears rolling down her face.

"It does matter what your feelings are," he said. "And this is why. Remember that first conversation we had in the diner? I offered to kick asses for you? And you said, 'you are my champion.'"

"Yes." She wouldn't meet his eyes.

"King told me that phrase triggered my programming," he said. "Later on, Seth and Con and Davy went through the diner, and they found remote-activated sound gulpers attached to every table. He had a record of our conversation, Lily. That's where he got that phrase."

"So?" She opened her eyes, glassy and glittering.

"So? My error was in assuming that it was impossible that we could have been overheard in the diner. If we weren't, then there was no other way he could have known that phrase."

She shrugged. "I fail to see how it changes anything. You were wrong. Why does it matter what the reason for your wrongness was?"

His scarred knuckles turned white. "What matters is how I felt about it," he said. "It blew my mind. That I could know for a fact that you were one of his, and still love you. Still be willing to die for you."

Her mouth quivered. She looked almost scared.

"I thought, at the time, it was because he'd programmed me. But it wasn't that, Lily. It was my heart that knew the truth, all along."

She shook her head, eyes squeezing shut. "That's not fair."

"I don't give a shit about fair. King messed with my head that day. But he never touched my heart. My heart never faltered, Lily. I don't have to make excuses for it. I don't have to apologize for it. I loved you all along. Only you. I always will."

Lily rubbed at her eyes with the backs of her hands. "I don't know if I can do it again."

"Do what?" He grabbed her hands, kissed her wet, salty knuckles.

"Trust you," she said. "It's not like I have manual controls. It's an 'open sesame' kind of thing. It's magic."

Hope leaped up, hot and eager. "That's no problem," he said. "I like magic. I go for challenges. I'll make you trust me again. Let me give it my best shot. You can give me regular updates on my progress, say, every fifteen years or so? Sound good?"

She dissolved in giggles, sniffles. "You are so full of shit."

"Not about loving you." He cupped the back of her head, pulling her into the kiss he'd been dying for ever since he jumped out the window of that inferno.

And she didn't pull back.

It bloomed, hot and wild and beautiful, warping them into that magic place, out of time, out of this world. He'd known they could make it back here, to this wild, secret verdant place where their souls were joined. That in this place, he would be able to show her how deep the roots of their love penetrated. To the ends of the earth, and beyond.

He offered himself to her, and joy exploded in him as she did the same. Her heart had never faltered, either, beneath it all where the real truth lay, like a secret pearl.

They twined together, trying to get inside each other.

Her dress was down to her waist and her bra undone before he knew what he was doing. He was cupping, suckling, licking, and worshiping her sweet, kissable tits with frantic tenderness while his other hand was busy under her skirt. Stroking and petting those velvet hot inches of soft bare skin above the gartered hose.

He lifted his head to admire her, glowing against the black lace underwear, thighs wide. His heart was going to crack open. She was so beautiful.

He plucked the panties aside and stroked the tight, furled folds of her pussy, glowing, gleaming with lube. Cherishing her, hungry and breathless and reverent as he kissed her mouth, fingers and tongue delving, dipping into both sweet-hot wells of sensation at once.

He could have made her come right off, but he danced around it. This was too important to rush for a quick thrill. This moment would seal their bargain for all time. He could wait and wait. Every sweet stroke a message, a poem. A song of love and longing.

After a whole lot of that, she was lifting herself against his hand, her pussy clenching around his fingers. Pawing the front of his pants.

"Damn it, Bruno," she panted, crabbily. "Give it to me!"

"But I wanted to make you come before I—"

"*Now!*" she snarled.

Oh, well. That worked for him. He helped her with the pants and whipped it out. He was hard as cast iron, hot as a brand. He hoped he'd last long enough to bring her off. Please, God. At least that long.

She grabbed his forearms, her nails digging into the coat of his tux. Their eyes locked, jaws clenched at the terrifying significance of every gasp, every sigh. He fitted himself against her. They moved, seeking the angle . . . found it . . . and oh, God. The heat. The wetness.

The long, tight, blissful slide to oneness.

They paused. He was terrified to let her move, afraid he'd explode, that it would be over too soon. Then Lily touched his face and brought her fingertips, wet with his tears, to her mouth.

His fear vanished, drowned in a swell of emotion. Her legs wound around his, and they surged and moved. Her bright gaze was the thread that held him to the world as he knew it. He never wanted it to end, but it wasn't up to him. It was life itself, swelling up huge and glowing.

Until it burst its bounds and carried them away.

Some time later, he felt Lily's hand in his hair, gently stroking the scar. She smoothed the mark on his cheekbone with her thumb.

"There's something you've never said to me," he prompted. Not giving a shit if he came across as needy or grasping. "I said it to you, but you never said it back. At least, not directly."

Her lips curved. "Well. You know me. I'm a cast-iron broad."

"Right," he murmured. "So hard, you'll run into a burning building to save two little kids who aren't even yours."

She waved her hand dismissively. "You did, too."

He shrugged. "They were my brother and sister. And you were in there, too. I couldn't live without you."

Tears welled in her eyes. "I figured you were too good to be true," she admitted. "And when it all fell apart, suddenly you were. Part of me wasn't surprised. I never quite believed it could be real."

"It is too good to be true," he said. "It's fucking amazing, Lily. But it's true, too. And you know what? I'm still waiting for you to say it. Spit it out. First time's the hardest. Go on."

She gave him a tremulous smile. "Um, Bruno. There's something I need to talk to you about first. It's—"

"I know," he broke in, staving her off. "I know what you're going to say, and I knew this was coming. It's because of Tonio and Lena, right?"

She bit her lip. "Ah, actually—"

"It's true," he admitted. "My place is a madhouse. My bathroom stinks of the diaper pail, my sink is full of bottles, I'm drowning in laundry, I've got Zia Rosa smeared all over my life. It's not like before."

"Um, I knew that," she said. "Actually, I was going to say—"

"It's not like I can whisk you off to Paris on a whim, like

before." His voice was tight. "It was my decision to take Tonio and Lena. I made it alone, and I'd understand if you didn't want to—"

"Bruno, I'm pregnant," she said.

He stared at her. He gasped for breath. "Pregnant?"

"Six weeks. We played with fire, remember? More than once."

Lily cupped his chin, pushed it until his jaw clacked shut. She waited for his reaction, soft lips pressed flat. Bracing herself.

The sun was rising inside his chest. "You, ah . . . you want to . . ."

"To have this baby?" she finished. "Yes. I do. I plan to."

"Ah," he said, helplessly. "I, uh, see."

"I was going to give you the same spiel you just gave me. That I'd understand, if Tonio and Lena are enough for you to deal with. I made this decision alone, and I don't hold you responsible if you don't want—"

"Oh, no," he burst in. "Oh, no, Lily. You got it wrong. I want it. I want it so bad." He hid his face against her belly and lost it.

It took a long time for it all to work its way through him. His feelings ran so deep. They were entwined with everything else. Mamma, Tony. The lost brothers and sisters.

And now, suddenly, his future, too.

She curled herself down around his head, kissing his hair, stroking his shoulders. He pressed his face against her belly, tears soaking into her dress. He was amazed, humbled, at the idea of new life, flickering into being inside her. Making them one. Oh, yeah.

He loved it. A little brother or sister for Tonio and Lena.

He snorted back tears, lifting his head. "Oh, shit," he said, appalled. "I think I trashed your dress."

She laughed silently and dug a tissue out of the purse that lay on the carpet by her feet. "I don't care," she said. "So. Your life is all diapers and bottles. By a funny coincidence, mine will be, too, in a few months. So I guess it makes sense to just—"

"Marry me?" he blurted. "Immediately?"

She froze, midword, mouth still open. "Ah . . . ah . . ."

"I was raised a bastard," he said. "I want my kid to have my name. I feel very strongly about it. I hope that's not too antique for you."

She shook her head, eyes wide. Speechless.

"Good," he said, with feral satisfaction. "Mine. All mine."

"Oh, stop it."

"Let's go tell everybody," he urged. "Right now."

"Um, no," she said, primly. "Not yet. I need to clean up first."

There was a bathroom attached to the little library, oh joy and rapture. He stood outside the door while Lily put herself back together.

So happy, he was terrified of it. It was too good. It couldn't be real.

He didn't take his eyes off the door, and even that wasn't enough to soothe his nerves. Like she might vanish into the mirror, dissolve into smoke, slip out a ventilator shaft.

But a few minutes later, the door opened, and there she was, dress straightened, makeup refreshed, lips crimsoned. She'd taken the pins from her hair. It rippled and swirled. The fuzz above her crown backlit by the light was illuminated like an angel's halo. She made his eyes ache.

"My God, you're beautiful," he said.

Her lashes swept down, the lips curved up. "Thank you," she said demurely. "So are you, incidentally."

"I'm so happy, I think I'm going to faint," he warned.

"No problem," she assured him. "I'll just get one of those ice buckets and dump it over your head. Since it seems to be our God-given job to provide entertainment for this event."

His chest shook. "You know, the second we step out there, they're all going to know," he said.

"Of course," she said, steadily. "I am so ready. And by the way?"

"Yeah?" he said.

"I love you, Bruno." Her smile made his eyes water. He felt his chest puff out. His feet floated up off the floor.

They went into the corridor, pausing at the door to the ballroom. They could hear music. The swing band was playing the first dance. The tune was "Stand By Me." How fucking perfect was that?

He offered her his arm, gallantly. "May I have this dance?"

She went up on her tiptoes, branding him with a lipstick mark.

They shoved the door open, letting in noise and color, the racket and the chatter. The music and the laughter and the chaos.

They stepped out together, into the light.

If you enjoyed *Blood and Fire*, you won't want to miss *One Wrong Move*, Shannon McKenna's next thrilling romantic suspense novel featuring Bruno Ranieri's comrade Alex Aaro. . . .

SECRETS NEVER DIE

Alex Aaro has spent most of his life on the run from his Ukrainian mafia family. But when he learns that crazy Aunt Tonya, the only relative who ever gave a damn about him, is dying, he risks returning home to say goodbye. He's prepared for anything except the call from his friend, Bruno Ranieri, that sends him on a wild and dangerous ride with a mysterious woman with a deadly secret and a white hot passion that binds them together.

Social worker Nina Moro knows her life is forfeit if she makes a wrong move and the ruthless syndicate hunting the terrified Ukranian prostitute she is hiding discovers her involvement. And so Nina avoids the inscrutable interpreter who suddenly appears on her doorstep. Until that six-foot-four rock hard slab of lean muscle is the only thing between her and certain death. Now Nina and Alex are in a race against time, death, and their desire for one another . . .

Turn the page for a special preview!

A Kensington trade paperback on sale in October 2012.

Rudd had to speed this up before his head exploded. He fumbled for the point of contact with Stillman's mind. It was easier to find this time, and when he had it, he locked eyes with Anabel, who was sipping a glass of soda water at a nearby table. He smiled at her as if only just noticing her, and gestured her over.

Stillman turned to look at her, and did a double take. He wiped his mouth, dabbing at shiny, purplish, discolored lips. His close-set eyes glinted like a predator as he looked Anabel over.

Time for the big guns—which was to say, Anabel's tits and snatch. She used them like a terrorist used a fertilizer bomb. No mercy. No prisoners. No survivors.

Anabel's face brightened with an incandescent smile. She waved a finger flutter that said *oh, goodie! What a coincidence!* She jumped to her feet and headed toward them, weaving gracefully between the tables. Beaming. Glowing. Shining. For the love of God, she'd dosed herself up, the naughty slut, and after he'd expressly ordered her to wait. His teeth ground. Her psi-max enhanced glamour had taken hold. Rudd winced, as heads turned all over the club. *Don't*

*overdo it, you vain whorish bitch. It's just Stillman. You don't
have to fuck the whole room.*

Too late. Slim, curvy blond Anabel was pretty enough to
turn heads even without a psi-max fueled push, but there
was nothing she liked better than starting to sparkle, watching men pant, trip over their feet and forget their own
names—or that they were arm in arm with their own wives.
Anabel had been known to cause car accidents when she was
sparkling at the peak of her dose. And that was on top of
telepathy, her primary talent. Not many manifested more
than one.

She stopped at the table, and bent gracefully to give Rudd
a peck on the cheek. "Hi, Uncle Harold!"

He beamed at the self-indulgent slut, the picture of avun-
cular benevolence. "Anabel, my dear! This is Senator Ben
Stillman. This is Anabel Marshall, the daughter of an old
family friend," he explained to a transfixed Stillman. "She's
working on my campaign. She's a pearl without price, so
don't even think of trying to steal her!"

The two men chuckled. Anabel blushed prettily. Stillman
eyed her high, jutting bosom, showcased in the tight black
ribbed turtleneck. Anabel preened and posed and sparkled,
extravagantly.

And in that unguarded, thoughtless moment, Rudd gave
the final, judicious little tipping shove . . .

. . . and Stillman's decision clicked into place, covered by
Anabel's tinkling laugh, her chatty bubbling. Stillman's support was his. *Yes.*

Now? Her query pinged against his mind, along with a
montage of powerful mental images. Her naked body entwined with the senator's, hips jerking in various different
acrobatic sexual positions.

He smiled at her, rather stirred. "My dear, would you be
kind enough to entertain Senator Stillman for a few minutes

while I go see what Roy needs? I'll take him up to the suite for a bit of privacy, but we shouldn't be more than ten minutes or so in there."

Understood. Ani beamed at him. "My pleasure," she cooed.